Davidia and THE KNOWLEDGE TREE

Ken Spargo

Published in Australia by Sid Harta Publishers Pty Ltd,
ABN: 46 119 415 842
23 Stirling Crescent, Glen Waverley, Victoria 3150 Australia
Telephone: +61 3 9560 9920, Facsimile: +61 3 9545 1742
E-mail: author@sidharta.com.au

First published in Australia 2020
This edition published 2020
Copyright © Ken Spargo 2020
Cover design, typesetting: WorkingType (www.workingtype.com.au)

Spargo, Ken
Davidia and the Knowledge Tree
ISBN: 978-1-925707-12-0
pp336

About the Author

Ken lives in Melbourne, Australia.

His first venture into writing began on a sewerage farm whilst engaged in an aquaculture project in 2002. On a boring Friday afternoon, his imagination got the better of him and he decided to fill in his time by writing a nonsense short story called *The Frog who Hopped on One Leg*. Within a year he had written a series of short stories and a year later began his first novel *Stumped*.

Imagination supplies an endless supply of ideas used to create and craft his crime and fantasy fiction novels, his preferred genres.

He loves to travel with many places he has visited providing inspiration for his novels. He has travelled extensively throughout Europe, Asia and other parts of the world and actually lived and worked in Austria, Europe, New Zealand and Papua New Guinea. Caravanning locally is also of great interest.

Ken's primary occupation is an accountant currently running his own business.

Sport has been a major influence in Ken's life. His two crime fiction novels have both been influenced by his involvement with sport (cricket and golf).

Ken's inspiration for writing the Davidia series of novels has been his daughter, Sophie. He has assisted in raising two children.

All novels have been written with a sense of humour which is a refreshing feeling and allows the seriousness of life to relax. 'We all need escapism at times.'

Other titles in the Davidia series:
Davidia and the Prince of Triplock
Davidia and the Six Sisters
Davidia and Grandma's Memories
Davidia and the Foreboding Dinner
Davidia and Aunty's Curse
Davidia and Senora College

*To Jill, for managing to stay focused during
our time together and ensuring my fantasy is not real life
but an enjoyable time to share.*

CONTENTS

1. The School Library 3

2. The Discovery 16

3. Outdoors/Indoors................................. 29

4. Science 44

5. Mathematics 78

6. Geography................................. 110

7. History 146

8. Conika 184

9. Single L................................. 216

10. Double L................................244

11. Hill Time 274

12. The Final Puzzle 296

13. Home................................. 326

PROLOGUE

The darkness inside the Hole in the Hill hid a strange secret. Roland the Rotter was conducting a cleansing of the intelligent members of his population as they provided a threat to his obsession of controlling the world's written language.

A family of three intelligent twigs were being interrogated about how much they knew of the written language. Roland the Rotter wanted to ensure that his population remained ignorant and would carry out his every command without question.

'You will never escape,' he said to the three quivering twigs.

There were the two fully-grown mature twigs accompanied by a young sapling. They had all originated from the same rootstock as Roland. That rootstock had now been destroyed to avoid any intelligent suckers emerging from it. Roland and the three twigs were distantly related.

'You can't selfishly control all of the world's written language,' said the senior twig. 'Written language is available for everyone.'

'No, it's not. It is all mine. Either you give up your quest to educate your fellow twiggers, or be destroyed into the compost pit.'

Roland's path had been determined.

'We must oppose you.'

'For that you will be destroyed.'

Roland was a chameleon and before he could expose his secret control force, the two senior twigs chanted the most unusual short poem, called The Poem of Ickle:

'*Ickle wockle weeny fing,*
Ickle wockle weeny fing,
It cannot sing, it cannot sing,
Cut its flamen head off.'

A large dust storm was immediately created. A hidden tunnel suddenly opened up in the Hole in the Hill and they were spirited safely through it into the atmosphere.

'Never return,' he yelled.

He felt safe for now, but was he?

1   THE SCHOOL LIBRARY

'You nasty b….,' whispered a jealous female, who was intent on being Miss Popularity at school; however, her mantle as premier *femme poseur* was under threat by the intelligence of another. Her remarks were meant as a threat.

Her audible sounds of "endearment" were heard by a group of fellow students on study assignments in the library. Sniggers were heard behind cuffed hands trying to stifle their amusement. The librarian glanced over her *pince-nez*, turned her head slowly like a pig on a spit and haughtily tossed her loose tresses like an A-grade model, often the subject of intense male focus. The crowd had resettled and pretended to study, waiting for the next witty remark or a stretch of the language to form an abusive sentence.

'Did you forget to shave this morning?' was the response from the first abused.

It was a reference to a lack of body maintenance that morning, which showed fine, wisp-like stubble barely discernible to the naked eye on the recipient's legs. It didn't matter that they were almost invisible. It was the placement of the thought that conjured up the emotional lack of confidence. Language can be used as a torment to others when properly invoked and swallowed like a gullible phrase.

Davidia and Slirander were quietly minding their own business at the next table when the interruptions kept on flowing.

'Leave my man alone or I'll damage your intelligence with a well-placed kick.'

The reference got lost in the translation; however, the groin seemed to be the subject of the comment.

'Girls, keep it down. Other students aren't interested in your male battles. Ensure that tripe is kept for the school ground and preferably off premises. Remember that this is the place of shush,' whispered the head librarian.

Her stern look held authority.

Davidia and Slirander tried to ignore the disagreement between the female rivals. They quietly thumbed their way through research textbooks trying to grasp the meaning of the written word. It was everywhere in each book that they opened. Pages upon pages of black alphabetic shapes all arranged in an understandable sequence called language. Some of the words were too large or written in such a way as not to be understood. Knowledge of their meaning hadn't yet filtered through. They were two young sixteen-year-olds climbing the learning curve of knowledge, which was a time-consuming process.

The period was almost over when Davidia needed to borrow a history book to refresh the thoughts that her teacher had discussed earlier. The head librarian pointed her in the direction towards the back of the room. She stopped and gawked at the massive volumes of books waiting for users to flick through their pages. She thought that it was a wonderful source of information, imagining all sorts of adventures held within. It seemed like an eternity as she stood there toying with the fantasies in her mind. Unbeknown to her, someone else had been in the same area prior to her arrival, but she had paid no attention to whoever that was.

The school library had been a learning institution for years. Past old boys and girls of the school had donated finely bound volumes of the latest literary works. The school fund was raised to add to its considerable collection. The books were housed on wooden shelves and placed at every metre — a column would dissect the shelf and act as a divider between topics and authors and give strength to ensure the shelves didn't collapse under all that weight. Knowledge could be a heavy burden. The school was undeniably proud of its written storehouse. A gap had been deliberately left where a borrowed book was out for what Davidia thought was a visit. As she turned away from the shelves, she stubbed her petite school shoe with the soft leather upper on a solid, hardback book.

'Yeow! That hurt,' she whimpered.

Her toe throbbed. She bent over to retrieve the harmful obstacle. It was the exact history book that she was looking for. How did it become floor fodder to be unintentionally abused by an unwary foot? There was no one nearby to blame for its problem. She returned to join Slirander, who by now had enough refreshing and adding groups of new words to her memory.

'What book is that?' she asked. 'It's so huge. Maybe it's written in a huge font with large words?'

'I found it on the floor. Someone hadn't returned it properly. I stubbed my foot on it.'

'Is that the book you wanted?'

'It sure is. It's an old master called *The History of Words*. Mr Smeckle said I should use it to assist in understanding language.'

Davidia placed the book on the table. It was so heavy she momentarily felt that her arms had stretched. She turned each page slowly and carefully so as not to damage them. Each page was an eager participant to express newly discovered knowledge.

'Slirander, these pages feel damp in the top right-hand corner. Go on, touch them.'

She timidly felt the damp section.

'They're certainly damp. How would they get that way?'

'Look, each page has been dampened with an identical finger-print, the size of a person's middle index figure. How odd? I'll put it back and tomorrow I'll borrow it again when it has dried out. It will be easier to turn over the pages.'

The school bell rang to signify an end to the day's school activity.

'Why don't you have a sleepover at my house tomorrow night. It's Friday? Ask your parents,' said Slirander, as she waved goodbye.

'See you tomorrow.'

*

The following day, period five, the first after the luncheon break, was spent at the library. Davidia and Slirander sat together as always and *The History of Words* was retrieved once more. There were no other misplaced books on the floor, so sore feet didn't occur again. The book was thumped onto the table.

'That was easy. It feels much lighter than yesterday when I could hardly lift it. You try and lift it,' said Davidia to Slirander.

'I'm not very strong,' she replied. 'I don't work out at a gymnasium or do weights or push-ups and that type of thing. I'm more of a heavy thinker.'

'Look, one hand.'

Davidia was showing off when it accidentally slipped from her grasp and headed with the full force of gravity toward the floor. Slirander dived like a dolphin and caught it. She rolled over in a ball and as quick as lightning stood up with the book securely held. Davidia was stunned.

'How did you move so fast?' asked Davidia amazed at her agility.

'Did I?' replied Slirander, trying to deflect any attention to her speed skills. She had a secret and she wanted it kept that way. 'It's not so heavy after all.'

The book was carefully placed on the table. They didn't want to jiggle it about in case a spell fell out and they would be cursed. Davidia opened the first page and squealed in surprise.

'What is it?' asked Slirander, sensing deeply that the squeal wasn't a pleasurable one.

'Look. Where have all the words gone? Someone has stolen them,' she babbled.

'Rubbish. No one can steal the written word. That's preposterous. Let me see.'

Slirander stared in amazement at the blank spaces that filled the book. Only the written word had disappeared. All illustrations, maps, graphs and any other additions to the quality and character of the book weren't touched.

'How would they be taken? I haven't seen anyone eat the alphabet recently.'

'Could they be erased with a special eraser?'

'That would take too long and, besides, the pages would be damaged.'

Davidia ran a slender-fingered hand over each page hoping her hand detector would suck up the truth from the pages. Unfortunately, evidence of misappropriation couldn't be located. The book was much lighter and the written language had been lessened by the word losses.

'Where would they have gone? No one can walk out with them, could they? They may have been written in lemon ink and only show up under light.'

They held the book up to a small reading lamp. Even it was unhelpful.

'Ask the librarian if she has noticed anything at all,' said Slirander, hoping Davidia would be distracted for a few moments.

Davidia approached the librarian, a female around the mid-thirties, with her hair so tightly bound in a bun it was difficult to tell if she was bald or not. Each day her hair was done differently to represent a character in one of the library books. Today was the strict schoolteacher who pleasured herself by scaring the bejesus out of the students with a husky, authoritative tone. She couldn't actually speak loudly in the palace of silence, but her Adam's apple rippled slightly as she husked her vocal cords.

'Excuse me, Miss Placed, one of the library books has lost all of its words,' said Davidia, quietly, trying not to disturb the other students and to stop them from thinking she was an idiot at not being able to find any words in a book.

'Pardon! What lost words? I'm afraid words can't get lost in a book. Their meaning may be lost on you, but you can't lose the actual words. You aren't on any medication, are you? It wouldn't surprise me the way youth behave today.'

Before a lecture developed, Slirander was seen motioning to her.

'Thank you, miss. I think my friend has found them.'

Miss Placed's shoulders slumped in resignation, believing that Davidia was sorely mistaken. If children can't read the written word right in front of them, how will literature continue?

'Have you found them?' asked Davidia.

'No, but I selected another book next to it and look at this.'

The second book also had the same disturbing fingerprints on each page and it too was a sea of blank pages as if ink had never been imprinted on them. The girls shook their heads in disbelief. What was happening? They pinched each other and the ensuing pain assured them that they weren't dreaming.

'We'll have to tell someone besides Miss Placed, the librarian. What about Mr Smeckle? He'll understand, won't he?'

'We can try, but don't expect his cheery characteristic to translate into common sense. He's slightly theatrical. The last time we spoke, he mentioned the letters IQ. His take on it was an icky, sticky substance on a toffee apple and not a yardstick for measuring intelligence.'

'May we borrow these two books, please, Miss Placed?' asked Davidia, as she held aloft the two volumes of lost alphabetical language.

'Please return them quicker than that student Schnook.'

Slirander's ears suddenly throbbed. Was it due to the guttural verbal performance Miss Placed was role-playing or the harshness of enunciation of the word Schnook? No. She grabbed an ear lobe to stop it swinging. Her long hair hid her hearing antennae. No one had ever noticed her ears. Did anyone wonder why?

'Are you okay, Slirander?' asked Davidia, quite disturbed at her friend's peculiar behaviour.

'Sorry. You said Schnook. Why mention him?'

'He's been borrowing books every day for the past few weeks. He must be the most committed student in school.'

'Could you please check whether he has borrowed either of these two books?'

Miss Placed read her register and affirmed that they were borrowed only yesterday.

'Are you sure?'

'See for yourself.'

The register listed most of the books in the library. It didn't make any sense. No one could read all that literature even if they had learnt to speed read. There was a rotten smell and it wasn't self-emanating.

'Let's check a few of the other books that he's borrowed,' said Slirander, with her ears still throbbing.

They both worked their way through part of the list. Every book reviewed had lost its written language.

'This is incredible. There aren't any words to read. How will we learn?' said Davidia, truly perplexed by the strange events. 'He wouldn't have swallowed them, would he?'

Slirander was equally flummoxed. Just then they heard the swishing of turning pages.

'Shush.'

The girls crept between the aisles and removed a strategically placed book to allow a clear view of a busy finger-licking student. There was Schnook, busily licking his fingers as if he had a fast food delight and page-flicking at a rapid rate. The pages pushed the air aside in urgency as they were raised, then flopped onto one another until each page had been dampened with a dose of spittle. No sooner had he finished with one book; his busy tongue kept flashing out like a lizard in preparation for the next one. He was so absorbed in his task that he didn't hear the girls approach. Slirander touched him gently on a shoulder. His tongue was exposed when he was touched and the shock forced him to bite down so hard, he almost severed it. Blood flowed onto the open pages and the open book virtually disintegrated into a mass of wet pulp.

'You rotten little sod,' yelled Slirander. 'It's you.'

Schnook turned around red-faced, limp-tongued and, suddenly, one eye almost popped out of his head at them. He looked so odd that Davidia jumped in fright. A nasty, sneering smile spread across his face like floodwater. He grabbed his tongue and tried to escape by avoiding the girls. Slirander was so fast it was difficult to see her move. Schnook tried to speak, but with his damaged tongue, his muffled words weren't quite understood.

'Yayayaya wwwoonn''ttt fffiiinnnddd ttthhheee wooorrrddss. Ttthhheeeyyyrrr'''ee llllooosssttt fffooorrreeevvveeerrr.'

'Do you know him?' asked Davidia.

'He's the sneaky kid who has been stealing books from the other students. I saw him the other day. It really looked like he was going to eat them, when I noticed that he licked his finger before turning each page. I thought his modus operandi was similar to what you discovered with that book, *The History of Words*. Now we have seen him do it, it's definitely him. I'd recognise that fingerprint anywhere.'

'What are we going to do?'

Slirander turned toward Schnook. His odd-shaped eye had subsided, his tongue had ceased leaking and his face was screwed into an unpleasant shape. He was a most unattractive looking student. He did his school uniform no credit. It was bloodied and crumpled. Someone could have stabbed his face with porcupine needles, it seemed to be in so much agony. It was either that or he had a very bad acupuncturist. His vocabulary was now distinct again.

'I'm telling my dad what you did to my tongue.'

'Let me see your fingers,' said Slirander, ignoring the threat.

'What for?' he hesitatingly replied.

Slirander turned them around slowly, noting the whiteness of their tips. They were constantly moist from the continuous licking.

'Have you been trained to lick your fingers like this? Do you know why you lick each page of any book?'

'My dad says that's what I should do at school.'

'Aren't you here to learn?'

'Learn what?'

'The written word, language expression, knowledge, history and so on.'

'Nah, but I know a good licking.'

'You Rotter,' said Slirander, deliberately.

Schnook's face became contorted with rage. His odd-shaped eye threatened to leap out of his head. His tongue lolled around like a dog ready to lick its private parts and his body tensed like a spring.

'Why did you call him a Rotter?' asked Davidia, not quite understanding its meaning.

'Watch,' replied Slirander.

Schnook's body wiggled with anger. He feigned headaches. His arms flapped like a flailing windmill. His legs wobbled and he had an ugly face to compliment a most unsavoury looking person. The action thriller of bad behaviour lasted all of one minute.

'You'll hear from my dad,' threatened Schnook, as he left the library without a book for the first time in days.

Miss Placed couldn't believe the bad disruptive manners in the palace of silence, where learning in quiet surrounds was its mantra. The other students were bemused. Bad behaviour was becoming almost commonplace. No one except Slirander took Schnook's behaviour seriously. Davidia felt he was just plain stupid. If all boys acted like he did, having a boyfriend might not be the bonus the other girls thought it was. Even Miss Popularity would draw the line at such stupidity. Mr Smeckle was next on their list. They entered his office after lightly knocking. He was practising his thespian talents when they entered.

'Girls, it's almost home time and I do have a busy schedule. What is it?' he said, exasperated at losing the theme of one of his acting moves.

'Sir, we believe that someone is stealing the written language from the library books.'

He stared at them as a moron does when appearing intelligent. He shook his head so hard that anything loose would have rattled. It probably did, but no one heard it.

'What absolute nonsense! Nobody can steal the written word unless they take the book that it is written in. You obviously have the book, so how can it be stolen. I suggest you both see the school psychiatrist or get a new set of glasses.'

'Please look, sir. If you say the words are there, we'll do as you suggest. If not, what's the explanation?'

'Oh, alright. Give it here.'

He snatched the book like a recalcitrant child wanting its own selfish way. He opened the pages and the stunned mullet wasn't actually a hairstyle.

'Oh, my god! There's nothing here. Where did they go? You haven't substituted these, have you? It's not a prank you're playing on me? It's not April Fool's day today, is it? Who put you up to this?'

Mr Smeckle was suffering from word phobia. If he can't see it to read, his world was lost like many affected readers.

'Sir, they have gone elsewhere. Something has turned the alphabet into nothing. If we lose the written word, then education will suffer. How will we be able to read a street sign if it didn't exist? No road map could guide us anywhere. It would be terrible. Motorists could drive down a street, get booked, then not fined, because no one could name the street where the offence took place. That's only the beginning.'

'I see the predicament. How many books has this happened to?'

'We borrowed these two, but in the library many other books have lost their words. It's some form of alphabetical virus, but definitely not caused by misspelling. We think we know who did it, but not how the virus operates,' said Davidia.

'We'll expel whoever is responsible.'

'I think they have already expelled the language, sir, we're too late.'

'Have you any ideas?' said Mr Smeckle, wondering whether he should express his arms or legs for his next acting movement.

'Rotters, sir,' said Slirander.

'Rotters? What are Rotters? I know teachers sometimes joke

about having little disruptive rotters with bad behaviour in class, but that's only an expression.'

'Rotters, sir,' was all Slirander would say.

'Goodnight, then,' he said. 'I have to rehearse for the starring role in an imaginary play.'

'Not quite the full biscuit, is he?' said Davidia, who knew Mr Smeckle's eccentricities quite well.

'Goodnight, sir. Use your arms more. They make you look taller.'

'Quite, quite.'

The girls headed home.

'Come for a sleepover tomorrow night. Tonight, I have some reading to do,' said Slirander. She took the two borrowed library books with her.

Davidia waved goodbye to her friend. A cool breeze blew by sending a shiver through her school uniform. She wondered what Slirander was going to read in the books with no words.

Davidia had once accidentally found her brother Dan's special stash of photogenic books hidden in his cupboard under pairs of old trainers. Her natural curiosity triggered an interest. She opened a few of them and they were full of pictures, not suitable for a school library, with no written words also. She thought that the books were of quite a different value.

*

'Mum, have you ever heard of words being deliberately stolen from a book?' asked Davidia, hoping for some adult assurance that it doesn't happen.

Maybe someone had stolen the original works and replaced them by fakes. At least that would explain it. Explanations are often problem-solvers and when given appropriately as a proper answer and cause for an event that had happened, they are usually accepted with the good grace they are given, because it makes common sense.

'Not to my knowledge. Why do you ask?'

'At school today, I borrowed a book and there were no written words inside it. They had vanished without a trace. Slirander and I wondered whether there was a mystery attached to it. It has never happened at school before. There was this boy finger-licking every page. I thought he was odd.'

'I'm sure that there is a logical explanation for it. After all, you are attending a highly respected school with some of the top teaching brains in the country. If they can't provide you the answer, then there must be more to it than it seems. What do you think you should do?'

'Have a sleepover at Slirander's tomorrow night. She has taken two library books home to read. Odd, isn't it, how she said she was going to read them, but there was no writing. Maybe her imagination is working on a treadmill. Can I stay overnight?'

'Enjoy your night with your friend. I like her.'

That night in two separate households, two young female minds were gnashing through their thoughts trying to unravel the mystery of the missing words. They both had interrupted sleep.

'You Rotters,' Slirander mumbled often during the night, as she twisted and turned.

Soon, all was silent, just like the library.

2 THE DISCOVERY

'Your parents are dressed in hessian bags,' remarked Davidia, as she was led to the room in which she would stay overnight at Slirander's house.

'Are they?' replied Slirander, completely oblivious of her parents' normal attire.

'You aren't poor, are you?' asked Davidia.

Her experience of hessian bags to date was limited to grain and farm food storage.

'They're just different. Here's where you will sleep.'

Davidia scanned the room. The double bed was carved from tree branches hewn by hand. Large bolts and nuts held it together. She thought that this was a kid's cubbyhouse. The bed was soft and inviting. A singly strung light bulb dangled from the ceiling like loose fishing nylon. It swayed with the slightest wind movement. Shadows danced off the walls revealing that the walls were once found in wooden cottages from the Wild West. Character oozed everywhere from the timbered construction. Central heating was absent. Davidia would have to be careful in case she splintered any part of her anatomy.

'What do you think?' asked Slirander, beaming like a beaver that had displayed its best building talents.

'Unusual, but I like it.'

The two friends giggled in delight. The sleepover was their first together and whatever panned out, it would be exciting.

'This is cooler than school. Have you invited anyone else to stay here before?'

'You're my first friend to be invited. The other kids think I'm a bit odd and stay away from me. You don't think I'm odd, do you?' asked Slirander, feeling out her friend's valued opinion.

'Like no. I'm rapt to be here, living in the forest.'

'We are on the edge of the forest, not in it,' corrected Slirander, who had a penchant for accuracy. What difference it made, if any, to Davidia passed her by.

'Girls, dinner is ready,' called Slirander's mum, in a high-pitched voice sounding like grating metal.

'Yes, mum. Come on, meet my parents.'

The two lithe girls ran down the stairs like startled ante-lopes. The kitchen table stretched the length of the room. It was wooden, heavily laden with fresh bread, fruits and steaming bowls of stew, or was it pie?

'There aren't any animals in there, are there?' asked Davidia.

She swore she saw her food bowl jump. It may have been the excitement of the occasion.

Slirander's mum was a lean, one-point-five meters tall. Her hessian dress was made from two bags, due to her height. The stitching looked perfect. On closer inspection they didn't appear to be the rubbish bags that Davidia had thought they were. Fine joins abounded. It was very professionally pieced together. Sli-rander's dad was a short, little man with an oversized pair of glasses precariously balanced on the end of his nose. A sud-den sneeze would see them clutter to the floor. He only wore one hessian bag. A miniskirt on a male wasn't Davidia's idea of current fashion. Both parents were literary buffs who enjoyed reading immensely. The written word was a daily staple mental ingredient. Their minds as well as their bodies required feeding. Both were university lecturers who caused great consternation by attending their lectures in hessian-made clothes. They had a wardrobe of dresses — well, dad didn't — tops, long pants and all made from this ghastly fabric. It was difficult to sew intelligence into a dress code, but there they were; the odd couple. They possessed a special power rarely used and it wasn't their intelligence. Davidia absorbed information like a sponge. Her surrounds were odd, the parents were odd and perhaps the food was too.

Davidia watched the parents intently. She noticed that the mum had an odd-shaped ear and the dad did too. There was a piece missing from each of them. Maybe it was a disease that they had suffered, or a feral cat had bitten them off. She felt both of her ears just to ensure that they were there. They were. What a relief!

'Not quite. The food is fresh from the garden. We farm wild minnor. It's a small, tasty, meaty animal, originally farmed by our forebears. We continue the tradition. It tastes like beef. There is only a very small portion in each bowl. We make a meat sauce to flavour the vegetables underneath. Everything we eat here is home-grown. Slirander can show you around tomorrow. Enjoy.'

Davidia tentatively placed the spoon to her lips. Her small tongue with the aching taste buds ventured out between her lips like a snake feeling the air with its incessant flickering. Zing, they met. The taste convulsion was overwhelming. Her tongue ran riot around the inside of her mouth as it tried to dispense the brown sauce down her gullet. It was a slippery substance. The family looked on, all smiles, as Davidia grappled with a new food source. During the meal, Davidia had noticed nearby the two library books that she had borrowed with the missing written words. A page lay exposed. She wondered why. There's no point in reading a book with nothing written in it. Even she wasn't that stupid. The logical explanation would hopefully be found after dinner.

'What do you want to be when you grow up?' asked the dad, smiling widely as if he had asked the unanswerable question.

'An adult. Isn't that what we all become?' replied Davidia, exercising some of her smart-ass impertinence.

The reply almost undid his hessian stitching with surprise as he nearly rolled off his seat.

'I meant occupation. We are both university lecturers and Slirander will be one day too. What about you?'

'I'm not sure. I do like writing, maybe an author.'

'What a delightful occupation. You need to read a lot for depth and research of language if you want to succeed.'

'Is that why you have that book over there, with nothing written on the page? I couldn't learn much from that, could I?'

The dad suddenly realised that the exposed page was easily seen.

'Mmm. That book is peculiar. There isn't any written language within it, but you already know that, don't you?'

'We borrowed it from the library. We saw a boy lick his fingers and place them on each page. He did it to many other books too. Do you know what it means?'

'Rotters.'

'What are they?'

The mum coughed subtly to divert the conversation elsewhere.

'Supper is ready,' she said.

A huge pile of ice-cream appeared like a vision from a mist and landed on the table. There was happy ice-cream spooning for a few minutes. It was nearing lights out. Davidia was still curious about that book.

'Can you please explain what Rotters are?' she asked again. 'I've never heard of them. Slirander said the same thing yesterday.'

'Maybe I should show you this,' said Slirander.

'Are you sure, darling?' said her mum.

'She's my friend and the only person not to think me odd.'

'Go ahead then.'

Slirander hooked her fingers in her hair and slowly pulled it back to reveal her odd-shaped ear. She had the same missing piece as her parents. Was it by genetic transference that they all had it? Davidia gulped in an extra lungful of oxygen. She exhaled it with spots of spittle from surprise.

'Be careful. That's how the Rotters achieve their evil deeds.'

'Sorry, I choked. You have the same ear as your parents. No other kids at school have it. Is it contagious?'

'I showed it to you so you will understand that we are an odd family and each of us possesses this particular oddity. There are many other oddities around, but they are difficult to find. No one knows of our condition except the Rotters. My parents are protectors of the written language and that is why they are university lecturers. They keep an eye and most of their ears alert to detect any loss of language. The Rotters are the cause of language loss,' explained Slirander, as she covered her particular oddity.

'Davidia. I'll tell you a story that you must never repeat to anyone, not even to your family,' said the dad.

'But that's unfair. Why tell me?'

'You discovered the books with the missing words. That means you now have a special ability to solve the problem, but first you must learn about the Rotters and how dangerous they are. Never trust them. You will only do it once, then its curtains for you. A one role act.'

'I'm only a girl, what can I do?'

'Never underestimate the power of youth and an inventive imagination. Swear on that half-baked pie, that you'll honour the Rotter secret.'

'If I knew what it was, I'd say, yes. Okay then. I'm in.'

The dad took the half-baked pie, which was now considerably cooler than when it was presented as a meal and smeared it on

Davidia's hands. The greasy feel she expected was absent. It felt more like the soft hand lotion that mum kept in her special personal cupboard in the bathroom. Even the slight meaty-tinged odour was inoffensive. In fact, it appealed to her.

'When can I wash my hands? They've turned brown. Can I eat the tiny meaty lumps?'

No one else spoke. Silence shrouded the room. It wasn't a strange séance was it? Davidia noticed the dad's ear twitching. She thought that it might have an ear mite building its home in it. Both mum and Slirander twitched also. She thought that this was oh, so weird, like it's a plague or something. After a few minutes, the dad took both her hands in his and chanted a nonsensical spell—

> *'Ickle wockle weeny fing,*
> *Ickle wockle weeny fing,*
> *It cannot sing, it cannot sing,*
> *Cut its flamen head off.'*

Perhaps it was a reference to an animal. Davidia was clueless as to its meaning.

. Suddenly, her hands fell by her side weighing as much as a five-kilo dumbbell each. Only the table stopped her from toppling over. As quickly as it had begun, the initiation of the half-baked pie was over. There wasn't much use in eating the leftovers. Her body returned to normal.

'Do you feel any different?' asked Slirander.

'In what way?'

'In any way.'

'All I have is a pair of dirty hands, that's all.'

'Well done, Davidia. You have just passed the purity and honesty test as a person trustworthy to learn about the Rotters,' said the dad. His hessian clothing was decidedly crinkled. 'Come, sit.'

Davidia wasn't sure what it was she was about to hear. Odd

ears, odd family, now an odd story. She thought it couldn't get any weirder, could it?

The dad began 'Once …'

'Daddy, wake up,' yelled Slirander, as she prodded her dad.

He hadn't told this story for such a long time, his body's emotions always suffered badly during the telling.

'… from times past, in a small isolated community hidden well away from prying eyes, a colony of Ignorants flourished. They survived in a mountainous region protected by a high mountain range. It was rumoured that a strange kingdom existed, but myths abounded, so the truth became an unsubstantiated assumption. I'm telling you, they were very real. The world, as it was known, was in a learning revolution. Languages were being developed and somehow this small, isolated, backward kingdom of bad enunciation was missed and left out of the good education guide that was sweeping the world. The land was known as Rotland, with its leader called Roland the Rotter. He was so incensed at being ignored in the learning process, he vowed as an act of revenge to destroy the known written languages. He was a nasty piece of badly programmed adulthood. It took him a while before he had found that spittle infected with an unsavoury virus that he had discovered, had the power to destroy the written language. His followers were fed a special diet including this, a before unknown, destructive virus. He kept it secret, so no one knows what it is.'

'There wasn't any in my food tonight, was there?' asked Davidia, not wanting to constantly lick her fingers. Fast food enjoyment had its limits.

'You're safe for tonight,' answered the dad, smiling. 'Their knowledge and thirst for language left them embittered because they never appreciated a good expression after that event. Roland organised special classes to teach his followers the art of spittling.

This was the degrading art of spitting which wasted so much useful mucus it was labelled inefficient. A finger-lick was far more effective: less saliva was used, notice wasn't drawn to the spitters as they cacked their way through a gob full of waste, and it felt good to have permanently clean fingertips. Finger-licking classes became the rage. Members had to be speedy and possess a continuous flow of saliva in the most stressful of conditions, for example, being discovered or running short of time; and be confident, believing that they should remain ignorant of language. No one ever licked another's fingers, it could have dire consequences, depending on where have they been? That's a quandary. The team of spittlers had lost the art of word relationships: using a good phrase or witty expression, speaking a complex sentence, and writing a poem, short story or novel. It was terrible. Knowing any languages was detrimental to being destructive spittlers because they would question why they are destroying something that they would love to learn from. Roland himself kept the only written language books in his own secret office, which we assume is hidden inside a mountain cave, but no one knows where.'

'Does he control these people? It sounds absurd that finger-licking is taught in a class. We lick them all the time after eating fatty fried foods, fairy floss, melted chocolate and so on. By having classes to teach finger-licking, he doesn't sound very bright,' said Davidia, not believing her ears.

'He was very intelligent. The virus he fed his followers had side-effects, which could manifest into a real oddity. Every Rotter possesses an oddity. It may be the angry eye, the nasal twitch, the double tongue, a six-fingered hand, two left feet or missing ear parts. There is an indeterminate range of effects. You must always be alert for any signs that signal a Rotter.'

'Does this Roland travel the world destroying languages?'

'Yes; however, his oddity is so unusual, no one knows what it is. It hasn't been discovered. Be careful wherever you go because if you meet Roland, something unsavoury could happen.'

'Do you think we'll meet him?'

'I'm sure of it.'

'But you have an odd ear,' said an interested Davidia.

'That's enough for tonight. Girls, it is bedtime,' said the mum, who knew exactly when to interrupt a conversation to avoid learning a truth or at least the beginning of understanding something that is quite raw in knowledge at present. 'Slirander, show Davidia the bathroom.'

'Yes, mum.'

The two girls dashed upstairs into their own world. The bathroom had only the essentials, in keeping with the rest of the house. Davidia washed off the half-baked pie solution. The chunky bits disappeared down the sink as drain clot; however, it was strange that her hands had become a dark, tanned colour and she couldn't wash it off. She looked like a tan-and-white minstrel, only with the hands and arms though.

'My hands are brown. I've never had such a good hand tan before,' she said admiring their new colour. 'You don't have brown hands, why me?'

'It's complicated. In the morning all will be revealed.'

Davidia didn't understand that her oddity was the tanned hands and she was blissfully unaware of what it meant.

'Your dad tells a strange story. Is there any truth in it? It seemed unbelievable.'

'Just enjoy a relaxing night. Tomorrow, I'll show you something.'

That night, Davidia constantly tossed and turned like manure being spread around with a garden fork, or perhaps as a card in the game of snap being belted with a loud thump. Occasionally, she expressed butt wind from the awkward positions her tossing placed her in. The bed clothing was a cape of contest as it became contorted and stressed with wrinkles of movement. Her mind was in Ferrari mode having left the Datsun thoughts for the slow lane. What a strange story! Finally, her mental activity subsided to allow some rest. Did she really have an odd something now and if she could choose one, what would she have wished it to be?

*

The sun arose at its normal time sending rays of warmth to its worldly kingdom. The forest came alive with chirping birds exercising their wings and searching for that fantastic entrée meal of the day; grubs. The day had a perfect feeling to it. Was that about to change? Slirander's home slowly warmed up as the sun belted the wooden walls with heat. Aromas permeated the rooms. The kitchen was in full swing.

Davidia bounced out of her bed in excitement, treating it as a trampoline. She hurriedly dressed. Her hands were still a dark tan. The day couldn't begin fast enough for her. She ran down the stairs barely touching the steps.

'Good morning, Slirander,' she excitedly blurted out.

'Hi,' was the animated response.

'Where are we off to today?' she said, beaming.

Her infectious smile usually softened any tensions.

Slirander's face had a serious look of concern. Footprints of disagreement had exploded everywhere. Her face sagged as if someone was tugging at it from underneath. Davidia twigged that it wasn't her best set of emotional looks.

'There has been some terrible news. Our school rang mum and dad early this morning. Apparently, there was a break-in overnight, but only in the library. That Rotter-infested little sod, Schnook, was caught in a reading frenzy. Books littered the floor like a literature carpet with him finger-licking his way through every page. The police were too late and didn't understand what he was up to. It was discovered that the library has no written language left. It's gone; poof, like a puff of smoke. We have to retrieve it.'

'If it's gone, where did it go? It has to have gone somewhere, if we are to find it.'

'Wherever it went, you and I must find it because no one else has witnessed Rotters carrying out their evil task. They do it so secretly. Whoever exposes the perpetrator of the lost language is empowered to solve it. We both saw Schnook licking his fingers, so we must restore the balance.'

'What do we do? You mean he's a real Rotter, a language destroyer. How do you know he's a Rotter?'

'Remember when his eye misbehaved as he bit his tongue. That was his giveaway. He possesses the odd, angry eye. Many others do too. Anger makes it obvious, but we can't upset everyone we meet to prove they are Rotters, can we? What a great start to spoil our weekend. It's never someone else's problem, is it?' whined Slirander, disappointed that her weekend was disrupted by such a simple thing as losing the library's written language.

'It's mine, too,' said Davidia, proudly puffing out her developing chest. 'What do we do first?'

'Have breakfast.'

'Good morning, girls,' said the mum. She was wearing her weekend hessian huggers, which were trousers with cut-out holes in both knees. Youth didn't have a mortgage on fashion. Sometimes, a set of well-made, torn rags doubled as good fashion, ask any sixteen-year-old. 'Did you sleep well, Davidia?'

'Yes, but I had an odd dream. I dreamt about the no-language-page books. I was in a cave of some sort with water squirting everywhere. I didn't understand it.'

'It's working, then,' said the dad, who was dressed in odd coloured trouser legs.

Its message was confusion. He, too, was unconventionally colour co-ordinated.

'Slirander, dad and I have to research a rumour that students are allowing bad language to rule their better language expressions. The university needs us today to solve the cause of this bad expression. We will be away for the day. Please be careful. I have an uneasy feeling, but cannot explain it. I'm sure you will find enough amusement around the property.'

The door shut. The girls were alone.

*

'My fellow Rotters, the success of destruction of the written language clearly rests on your shoulders. You are now a highly skilled trained working force, able to lick your way through any literature, in a soft or hard-back, in any language, parchment, paper or book ever printed. I'm so proud of your destructive abilities. The finger licker winner of the group goes to Fnoops. Your speed, dedication and continual saliva flow are extraordinary. You are probably the most ignorant licker of all, but that is the quality we strive to develop. The less you know, the more you try to succeed. Well done,' said Roland, the lead Rotter.

'Fanks, Mr Roland. If I can't read a word then it has no use. Is that right?' said Fnoops, who was a phrase short of a sentence. The crowd erupted in support.

'I'm so proud of your lack of knowledge, ability to understand any language and the way you try so hard to be destructive.'

'We have had a good teacher. Down with words, down with words,' he began to chant.

The crowd swayed enthusiastically. They had no idea of

language as Roland had deliberately kept them ignorant. Words were a danger to his controlled, freakish world. He couldn't dare risk anyone in Rotland learning to read, as that would undermine him and would question the ethics of what they were doing. He collected all the books in his kingdom and had them hidden for only his eyes to read. He was well-read, knowledgeable and loved a good turn of phrase. Pity he didn't convey any of that to his monosyllabic followers. He was peeved-off by two well-educated Rotters who often contested the validity of ignorance. They were eventually banned, but their oddity went with them. The banned Rotters lost their capacity of ignorance and, whatever their oddity, it remained with them forever. He knew that the cure to reverse his destruction had been compromised. The two banned individuals took with them the secret formulae. However, it was useless unless a Rotter was discovered in the act of finger-licking destruction. Nearly all oddities would never be triggered as the Rotters were so well-trained in the subtlety of action. A secret is only a secret if no one ever finds out what it is. Roland felt secure that none of his followers would ever be exposed. Ignorance is bliss, but not knowing any alternative, a Rotter always felt secure.

3 INDOORS/OUTDOORS

'Let's go outside,' said Davidia, hoping that Slirander's parents' departure would allow them to enjoy the feel of the forest nearby. The morning hummed peacefully. The air was still, feeling afraid to move.

'Not everything is as it seems, Davidia,' said Slirander, posing a warning comment.

Davidia was more interested in simpler dialogue than subtle comments.

As they walked out of the back door, there in the distance stood a massive tree with a magnificent canopy. It stood tall with its many branches pointing somewhere, but each branch ended with flower fingertips. Its trunk was thicker than the largest individual elephant leg. It was wrinkled and allowed ease of access for climbing. Each leaf was the size of a huge umbrella. Davidia thought that they would be great for hiding under if there was a rainstorm. It seemed out of place, a misfit of vegetation. It commanded viewing and favourable comment.

'What sort of tree is that?' asked Davidia, pointing one of her tanned hands.

'It's a Moonatric tree,' replied Slirander.

'A what tree?'

'A Moonatric tree. They're quite rare.'

'I don't remember seeing it there yesterday when I arrived.'

'We didn't go into the yard then.'

'It's so massive. No one would miss seeing it.'

'True. It's a special tree. I can only say it's beautiful. As a child it was a friend to me. Many hours were spent in its foliage. It's amazing what a tree can teach you.'

'It's just a big tree. What could it teach you?'

'When the time comes, it will reveal its identity.'

Davidia wondered whether Slirander had been sniffing an illegal herb or spent too much time in social isolation on her computer to conjure up such comments.

As they neared the tree, its branches began waving. Davidia thought it was the wind, but Slirander knew better. It grew in a dense black, prized, muddy soil, so rich in compost, that any tree or astute gardener would love to use it for growing and fertiliser. The grass beneath it grew in neat squares like a quilt. No lawn mower or angry whipper snipper had ever severed any of its shoots. It also looked oddly misplaced in its location. The girls stood on the grass. They removed their shoes and stood in bare feet to feel its softness. Suddenly, the grass began to grow up Slirander's legs. Davidia screamed in panic.

'Your legs are turning green. That grass is alive.'

'Don't worry, we're friends. It's a welcome greeting.'

No sooner had Slirander finished speaking than the grass had retreated. Her legs were still there as they were before. The freshness of the environment matched her skin. It too was a growing and developing new life.

'That is so totally weird. It didn't harm you, did it?' asked Davidia, unsure of what she had just seen.

'It's the normal greeting. When I was a child, this Moonatric tree was a constant companion. It has always been a part of my life. It protects my family. My parents and I have sat under it many times, being taught many things.'

'How can a tree teach? It doesn't speak, turn up to school and it's not a schoolteacher in fancy dress, is it? It has no mouth and who says it can move? They stay put in the soil. They can only

30

move if they are dug up. I've seen gardeners working and know how they do it.'

'Patience. Things can be and mean different things at different times. It takes a little imagination, faith and an open mind. At our age we're supposed to learn all the time at an accelerated rate. The Moonatric tree is a very wise growth. It has qualities that will show in time. Let's sit down for a while. Soon, I want to take a walk in the forest. The shadows move in mysterious ways and there's a special place and friend that we must meet.'

The girls sat down. Davidia felt the cool grass embrace her buttocks and soothe her shapely, thin legs. Looking toward the house, it appeared that it was becoming smaller. Were they drifting? Was someone stealing it, or was she dreaming?

'Slirander, this grass is floating.'

'Not for long though.'

'Will I fall off?'

'We are completely safe.'

Davidia wasn't sure. Her odd-eared friend with the odd family, house, Moonatric tree and climbing grass were all a shamble of thoughts at present. School wasn't this exciting except for that Schnook episode a day or two ago. They were high above the forest canopy. Trees appeared to be bonsai in size. The tree canopy looked so solid they could almost walk on it. A large, dark cloud drifted by.

'Are you interfering with the atmosphere?' it whispered.

Two large eyes mischievously lolled about. They could have been two big chocolate drops.

'We're travellers,' Davidia whispered back.

Suddenly, a huge downdraft began to suck them earthward. The bonsai trees were now plainer to see. They were no longer bonsai in size. The small, flying, grass doormat was taking a beating by gravity as it was pushed down, down, down. The girls screamed in fear, but there was no one to hear them. The forest canopy parted like a huge mouth. Davidia shut her eyes tightly, not believing that she would see her family ever again. Why me? I'm so young. Slirander was relaxed. Had she done this before? As soon as it had begun, it was over. The grass had quietly settled on the forest floor. Once again it grew up Slirander's legs, then retreated and melted into the earth.

'That was quick-absorbing compost,' said Davidia.

Her day was becoming highly unusual, or was it odd?

'It's this way,' she said.

'What's this way?' asked Davidia. She was shaken. Her hair was knotted. 'Is that a bruise?' she yelled.

Slirander brushed off a few flecks of disturbed bark from her arm. No damage done.

'We must meet that special friend in a special place that I told you about.'

The forest was damp, dank and greyness filtered through the trees, giving the feeling that shadows were following them. A few minutes later, Slirander stopped. She tugged at her odd ear and spat violently on the ground. A tormented slug avoided the mucus missile. It didn't want another headache. Minute dust particles danced in the air having been misplaced by a wet, gooey and inedible substance. Davidia was astonished. Did she have hay fever, bad sinuses, a cold, blocked nasal passages, or an excess of saliva? Whatever the reason, she had never seen such a huge mucus globule. Suddenly, Davidia saw a team of waving leaves advance toward them. She couldn't believe her eyes. Six huge umbrella-sized leaves appeared. They didn't have legs, but somehow they walked.

'Rotters,' screamed Slirander in high C pitch. The leaves trembled. They fell to the ground forming a circle of wrinkled foliage around the mucus globule.

'Don't stand on them,' said Slirander.

She motioned to Davidia to stand in the centre of the leaves, ensuring nothing stuck to her shoes. Cautiously, she did so. They both held hands.

Ickle wockle weeny fing,
Ickle wockle weeny fing,
It cannot sing, it cannot sing,
Cut its flamen head off.

Davidia remembered that it was the same stupid chant that Slirander's dad had used and the reason she now had brown hands. An open mind was certainly needed to understand her current predicament. The huge leaves arose in pristine condition and formed a tent-like covering over them. A minute passed. They could have been girl guides out camping.

'Rotters,' Slirander yelled in high C pitch again. It echoed around them.

When the sound had ceased reverberating, the leaves quietly disappeared, leaving them standing in an underground cave.

'Where are we?' asked a frightened Davidia.

'With friends,' was all Slirander would say. 'It's this way.'

The walls of the tunnel cave were completely wrinkled just like the Moonatric's tree trunk. There was nothing symmetrical about them. They had to bob their heads, twist and turn to avoid being jabbed, poked or pricked by protruding branches and woody growths which seemed to have no semblance of where to grow. Anywhere was the answer.

'This place isn't diseased, is it?' asked Davidia. 'It feels as if we are walking along a school corridor with all those admiring boys staring at us. Creepy. How come we can see in the dark down here?' It was growing weirder by the moment.

'This is a disease-free zone, I assure you. This used to be my cubby house as a child. I spent many adventurous days in here playing hide-and-seek.'

'But there's no one down here to play with.'

'There is, but not yet revealed to you. Up ahead it opens into an open space. My friend is there.'

Soon they stood in a huge cave. A large well was centrally located, being the focus point. Its depth was indeterminable. Light filtered through the misty haze, mimicking shards of glass. They reflected off the cave floor dispersing fractured light rays at all angles. Davidia looked around. There was nothing but wrinkled rock walls, neatly carved as if someone cared about how they were cut and shaped. She somehow felt safe.

'You played here when you were smaller?'

'Yes, and occasionally I come here to study. It's ever so peaceful. Besides, I get help from being here.'

Davidia thought she'd let that comment pass to the keeper. Rocks assisting with homework was a trite hard to swallow. What had she let herself in for by having a sleepover with her odd friend? She had never met anyone like Slirander before and began to wonder whether she was the full penny. Her family were a little off the planet. Davidia went to sit on the edge of the well wall. It moved. She froze.

'Did you see that? It moved.'

'That was Font.'

'Who?'

'Font. The Font of Knowledge. It's a friend. Come and meet it.'

Slirander sat on the edge of the well wall. It remained solid to her touch. The cool rocks sent goose bumps shivering down both her legs.

'It's alright. New friends are a puzzle for it. You can sit down and experience its wisdom. It doesn't take an instant like to anything new. Rarely is anything allowed entrance to where we are at this moment.'

'What exactly is this place?'

'We are in the root system of the Moonatric tree. This place is a haven from anything harmful as well as a learning centre.'

'You're kidding me, aren't you? Learning centre? I don't see any here.'

Davidia was becoming more confused by the minute. She could feel Slirander blending into the environment. Maybe she was an imitation rock that a life force once gave life to. A slow, rumbling sound was faintly heard. With her ears straining for identification and direction, Davidia was highly tensed.

'Listen, there's something alive down there,' she said nervously, pointing a delicately shaking hand down a rooted tunnel.

Small dust particles were disturbed into movement by the vibrations. Each needed a resettling spot and Davidia was suddenly very popular. She was new. The room swirled with activity. Clear vision quickly diminished as the disruption to their serenity continued.

'Where are you?' called Slirander, wondering if her friend had fallen into the well.

'Over here,' wherever that was.

In the dark, turgid atmosphere, the Font of Knowledge had emerged from its hidden home deep down in the well. It had now awoken to entertain its visitors. The dense, dust-filled room began to clear. Davidia saw a twirling spout of the purest water. She could see clear through it. There was Slirander on the other side. Nothing got wet. That was amazing. The well entrance had closed over into a flat floor of patchwork stone. *There must be a stonemason somewhere,* thought Davidia. It was perfect. In the middle of all this cacophony of sound, dust management and turmoil, appeared a small bowl delicately balancing that mucus globule that Slirander had spat out earlier. It shimmered like a brilliant diamond in the most exquisite display case. Rays of light danced merrily alongside it. It seemed like it was all family.

The bowl also contained a small amount of the purest water, which surrounded the globule. All became quiet. Davidia was mesmerised by the beauty of that small bowl. It would be a great accompaniment to her jewelled musical box.

'Welcome, Slirander,' said a whispering voice. 'Who's the non-believer?'

'Font, this is my friend, Davidia.'

'She's got tanned hands. Is that the best your dad could do? Why not give her an odd nose or a pair of non-matching eyebrows? His flair must have got lost in those old clothes he wears. Oh, well, if its tanned hands then, at least that passes the test. She has an odd something.'

'Who are you talking to?' asked Davidia.

She had never been in a psychiatric ward before and began to wonder if she was in one now. There was no visible anything she could see that spoke.

'Font. It's right in front of you.'

'You mean that small bowl.'

'That's Font.'

'Sorry for the surprise, but I do love a good acting role. Welcome to my humble home. I suppose you are curious as to why you are here.'

'I thought we were going on an adventure.'

'You are, but maybe not one you thought you were going on.'

'Why are we here then?'

'Ah, the mystical inquisitiveness of youthful brains. Slirander and you have an important task to save the world from losing all its written language. You both unintentionally discovered a right little Rotter destroying the words of our past. Because you are living witnesses to that destruction, you must right this enormous wrong. Language is a beautiful communication tool and without good expression, stories, history, mathematics and its inclusion in classics and every subject known, we risk losing it all forever and return to a moribund, monotone, lesser IQ society. Sameness and ignorance would abound. Then, only one individual would control all of what is left; Roland the Rotter. He has stored languages in his secret location. It must be discovered and destroyed. He has infected literature with the Destrusto Virus. It's a language-based virus, which, when mixed with saliva, ruins any written letter in any language when placed on paper, which acts as a transmitter. He has perfected it. He feeds an infected letter to his followers and immediately they become a carrier. He has a mobile finger-licking force of language destroyers. You were so fortunate to locate a Rotter in action; now an antidote can be prepared. Had you not discovered that Rotter, then the written language, as we know it, would all have completely disappeared.'

'Wow! How do you know all this?' asked Davidia, who was now paying close attention.

'I once lived in Rotland and so did Slirander and her family. They possess a genetic resistance to infected letters. Roland could never subjugate them into becoming morons. Their intelligence protected them. They somehow escaped and took me with them. I was a language teacher and through an unexplainable phenomenon, became the Font of Knowledge. I had to become a real font to remain safe, so here I am. I have been deliberately hidden in this form in case all language is lost. If that catastrophe ever occurred in the future, then I could at least restore any lost language if that opportunity ever arose. However, an ideal situation would have to exist. Besides, I haven't discovered any Rotters like you two have.'

'That's amazing,' said a stunned Davidia. 'What are we supposed to do?'

'See that shining globule, it is the basis of the antidote.'

'You mean that mouthful of ghastly spit?'

'Slirander has a special gift.'

'Even I couldn't do one that large in the middle of winter. I'm surprised it has stayed in one drop.'

'Slirander, could you pick me up and place me near that protruding tree root?'

She did as instructed. A few discoloured water droplets playfully hung onto the end of the tree root. Davidia swore she heard them sing as they plunged into the font. The drops were gobbled up. Maybe it was that *ickle wockle weeny fing* again.

'Slirander, kindly place me near that wrinkled rock wall.'

It resembled the skin of the Chinese Shar-pei dog breed. A single cockroach approached Font and clambered over the globule. It left behind a distasteful liquid colouring, which was quickly absorbed.

'There is one final task. I now need to be placed over there, near that white pebble. Thank you.'

Font and the white pebble seemed to tremor slightly in each other's presence. Suddenly, as if it was breeding a litter, six small white vials emerged from the white pebble. All were completely intact. Each had their own individual atomiser. Inside each container was the mixture that Font had secretly mixed together from the unusual ingredients. The six vials stood like miniature porcelain soldiers, which would perfectly adorn any mantelpiece as prized ornaments. Instead, they held the secret reversal formula to language loss. It was a huge responsibility that the two sixteen-year-olds had been entrusted with.

'My mother's perfume looks exactly like that,' said Davidia, anxious to spray one of them.

'Girls, you each have three vials. Secrete them in your clothing and never disclose to anyone or anything that you possess them. These six vials contain the antidote to reverse all language loss. Each one gives off a light, misty spray, which must only be directed at literature. Use sparingly. Inside are the soldiers of the Pebble of Purpose. They are a precocious lot, full of fight and purity. Treat them carefully and they will fulfil their destiny.'

'Is that it? We must spray this on books that have lost their words. It doesn't sound that difficult.'

'Davidia, we must be careful. If given any opportunity, the Rotters will destroy your good diction and you too could be lost in their world of bad grammar and poor expression,' said Slirander.

'The saving of all written language depends upon your success. Remember girls, do not be discovered when you spray any literature because the Rotters can make the antidote impotent before it can take effect by touching it with their saliva. It takes thirty seconds for it to be fully effective and irreversible. Secrecy is the key. If you meet any Rotters, pretend to be ignorant, speak in poorly formed sentences, say stupid phrases, act like a moron, whatever that means, and be aware that you mustn't appear to be too bright. It's a linguistic camouflage for your own protection and safety,' explained Font, who felt that her two youthful friends had enough gumption to pull it off.

At school, the girls acted with a self-confidence that belied their years. It fooled the boys into thinking they were eighteen-year-olds. If they could do that, then it was a shoe-in to save the world's languages. Hope, an eternally optimistic word, was riding high today.

'When do we start? Where do we go?' asked an excited Davidia. 'I love spraying perfume.' Her mind began to wander.

'Davidia, this is important,' said a stern Slirander. 'This is not a video game. We may not come back and if we become damaged, we may not be able to be repaired.'

'Who stood on your toes?'

'Girls, it's time to leave.'

The cave suddenly became full of swirling activity. The girls grabbed the vials. In an instant, the cave had returned to the well. The floor had disappeared. The light shards became distorted. The wrinkled walls moved like an ebbing tide. The whole area was in total confusion. Slirander and Davidia hid their heads in their hands to avoid the dust stinging their faces. Whoosh! A clear wind wiped away all the activity. The girls opened their eyes and found themselves at the base of the Moonatric tree once again. The quilted grass ran up Slirander's legs, then quickly receded.

'What are we doing here?' said Davidia.

'Finding the key to the Tree of Knowledge.'

'What's the Tree of Knowledge?'

'The Moonatric tree. It's here for a reason. Are your vials safe and secure?'

'Yes.'

'It is here somewhere.'

'What is?'

'The key.'

'What does it look like?'

'I have no idea, but we must find it.'

Davidia loved a game of hide-and-seek. The harder the task, the more she tried. She decided that the quilted grass needed a hug, or was it that she needed the comfort hug? She lay flat on its surface hoping it would climb all over her. It didn't. She was disappointed. As she was about to stand up, a growth appeared underneath her. Was it time lapse photography she saw of a growing mushroom? It was about half the size of her foot. She bent over to pick it up. As she did so, a twin grew beside it. This was some strange ground.

'Slirander, there's two lumps under the grass. They won't let me pick them up to see what they are.'

Slirander came over and gave the grass a pretend kick. It

immediately released the secrets hidden under the two lumps. It avoided any pain, real or otherwise. She picked them up.

'What are they?' asked Davidia. Had she won a prize? Was one of them hers?

'They are special pocket dictionaries. The Moonatric tree suggests that they will be invaluable on our journey. Open it and see what it says.'

Davidia attempted to do as suggested. There was no way the book would open.

'It won't open,' she whinged. 'What a stupid bloody book.'

'Do this,' suggested Slirander.

She took her book and rubbed it on her odd ear. It immediately opened.

'I don't have an odd ear.'

'But you do have oddly tanned hands.'

'Yeah, you're right.' Davidia rubbed the back of one hand on the book and it also immediately opened. 'Wow!' was all she could utter.

'Nothing else can open these dictionaries. They have now been impregnated with your personal signature, which is the back of your hand, mine is my ear. No Rotter, intelligent or dumb, can break that code. The words contained inside are totally safe.'

No sooner had she finished speaking, when both dictionaries flashed all their pages before them. The read images were stored in their minds. The books closed and adhered themselves to the inside of their jackets. Was magic afoot? Is it really happening? Davidia hoped she wasn't dreaming.

'I feel more intelligent than I did before,' said a smiling Davidia. Reading was so much fun.

'We still have to find that elusive key.'

'How will we know what it is?' asked Davidia. 'And why do we need one?'

'I'm not sure, but mum and dad said I needed one when I wanted to fully understand this tree. I've never found it. Perhaps it can help us locate the Rotters. The Moonatric tree has an unusual power and by its pet name, the Tree of Knowledge, it must be important.'

It was late afternoon. The air was moistening. The light was escaping and fading. A cool breeze wandered by, unsure whether it was to be a zephyr or an active blower.

'Brrr, brrr,' said Davidia, rubbing the goose bumps on her arms.

The little skin piles arose seeking comfort.

A creaking, groaning sound like a crashing tree immediately surrounded them. They turned around and watched in awe as a huge leaf began to rotate. The wrinkled tree trunk wobbled like jelly. Slirander lay prostrate on the ground. The quilted grass blades covered her with a protective coating.

'It's not going to fall off, is it?' said a worried Slirander.

'Don't be afraid,' said the quilted grass. 'The tree is talking to you. Davidia has found the key to its secret. It's not brrr, brrr, but burr, burr. Its hearing isn't fully tuned in to speaking people. At its last location, a few of the local birds decided to peck its bark and slightly damaged the areas it uses to receive sound. Wait until it is still. It will invite you in.'

'How do you know that?'

'We have grown at its base for eons. There is something it will show you.'

Slirander waited. Near the base of each leaf was a bulbous tree burr with a gnarled exterior. These were treasured deformities that furniture makers prized to make unusual furniture pieces. No one had dared tangle with the Moonatric trees oddities.

Finally, it was still. Davidia stood with mouth agape for catching flies, Slirander lay on the quilted grass snuggled in a grass doona and the wrinkled tree had decreased in height for ease of climbing.

That elusive key had been found. What was its use and how will the Tree of Knowledge assist them, if it could? The girls had no idea how to locate the Rotters and how would they go about restoring lost languages.

School had never been this difficult.

4 SCIENCE

'Who woke me up?' grumbled a disgruntled voice.

'I did,' replied Davidia.

'What is it you want? Which century am I in?'

'We're not sure and it's the current one.'

'I haven't been awoken like this for a very long time. It must be important for my leaves to turn. They ache something chronic. It's not often they get to twist me.'

'Hello, Moonah,' said Slirander, quite pleased that her old friend was awake again.

The huge tree bent over for closer inspection. Its eyesight, which was well-concealed in its many twisted wrinkles, began to focus. It recognised the small girl at its roots.

'It has been a while, hasn't it? Do you want to climb me? I've grown since you last did. Why are you here? Where am I this time?'

Slirander explained that it had travelled with her family and had been in its new location for the years she had been at school.

'I suppose you learn things there.'

'We do,' piped up Davidia. A talking tree, now that was odd.

'Who are you? I haven't met you before, have I?'

'This is the first time.'

'I can't stay awake for much longer. Standing still in the one spot for so long gives me root cramp. If I sleep, I can't feel it.'

'Moonah,' said Slirander, twiddling with her odd ear, 'we have been visiting Font who told us that we must save the loss of the written language from the Rotters. We don't know where to begin.'

'Don't you dare use that name in my presence.' The Moonatric tree shook violently. Nothing fell off. 'They are the reason that no one reads about me anymore. I have gradually been removed from all reference books of ancient growths. It's criminal that such ignorance exists. I knew there was something wrong. I felt it in my ancient roots. You must listen carefully. Never trust a Rotter or anything that you might think is one of them. The reason I am awake means that my services are required. Treat them with suspicion. Once I open the gate of entrance to where you might get sent, you may never return. Be true to your language and use it intelligently. It is your only safeguard. Once my secret is shown to you, it will be deleted from your conscious mind, but remain hidden within your subconscious. To re-engage with it needs you to trigger it by a random phrase, word or comment that only either of you two can utter. There is no reliability on what that would be. With your depth of language, I'm sure the appropriate response will be found. Now climb onto my trunk and walk along that waving branch.'

'You mean that yellow coloured branch. It looks like a huge beach umbrella.'

'Stand in the centre of it.'

'It's so slippery. Did you wash before you woke up?' asked Davidia. 'It feels like soap slime.'

'You are entering the world of Science. Be careful of the experiments.'

'What has this to do with Rotters and language?'

'I told you never to mention that name.'

The yellow Moonatric tree leaf shook vigorously. The girls lost their footing and plunged deep into the leaf. They slid down a thin filament path with no idea of their destination. For an instant, they felt they were flying. After a brief journey, they landed in a strange city both had never seen before. They landed safely standing upright.

'Isn't that a university?' said Davidia, hoping one day that she would be old and smart enough to attend one.

'It has the name on its façade, so it must be,' replied Slirander.

The building's name was The University of Scientific Discovery. It was built with a lean and so were all the other buildings. Angled construction certainly ensured that the city retained an odd status. In all directions, people performed their monotone tasks of walking in the street, crossing roads, and sitting in parks, but with only one noticeable difference. Everyone walked, sat or moved at an angle. There wasn't one straight standing upright-bodied individual anywhere. Both girls felt that they were the oddity. For a few moments, they watched the puzzling world of angles and how it all operated.

'Your parents should be ashamed of you,' said a bent-over individual. 'Have you no pride. Your angle is atrocious. No one here has grown like you have.'

'Does everyone here grow at an angle?' asked Davidia. 'We don't.'

'You should get it fixed. You will be a laughing stock, the butt of jokes and stared at until you do.'

'But we can't change our shape. Do we need to?'

'To fit in, changing is essential. In that university is a scientist, a Professor Doonow, who can assist you to physically conform. He's done it to many others who have travelled through the city.'

'Do we need an introduction?'

'No. Turn up and he will be pleased to meet you.'

'I suppose we should thank you.'

'That would be a change.' The individual wandered off.

'Should we just walk in?' asked Davidia.

'Let's give it a try.'

As they made their way toward the building, an angled bike rider flew past and threw a pile of papers held together by a thin, wire band onto the ground. It was the newspaper delivery to the newsagent nearby. The front page had a few photographs of sporting idols all in angular poses. The shopkeeper picked up his bundle of future millionaire sales and placed them on display; however, there were no written words on the day's edition front cover. Davidia noticed that they were missing. She went over and selected a magazine to read. On each page, she noticed that there were no written letters of any description.

'Excuse me, sir, what type of magazine is this?' she asked.

The shopkeeper looked up in surprise. Were they being invaded by aliens, had someone grown an oddity child, or, worse still, could they read? Whatever his thoughts, they were angular in result.

'It's a science magazine with the latest updates of development in experiments in the city,' he replied.

'Where is the written language? There are no letters in it.'

'Are you sure? They were there in the previous edition. It doesn't matter anyway. No one understands science and won't miss any explanations.'

'Doesn't the loss of the letters concern you?'

'I can't read anyway, neither can most others, so it makes no difference.'

'How many books and magazines do you sell?'

'None, but my shop is always busy.'

'How do you make a living?'

'I do. That's all I need to know.'

Davidia wondered if there was a planet peanut because she thought she had encountered one of their followers. She was appalled by the lack of attitude to the loss of the written language. She thought that everyone should be entitled to learn to read and have letters available to at least have an opportunity.

Slirander had also been observing human behaviour and noticed that each magazine picked up by an individual was quickly flicked through and returned to the rack. She thought that they surely couldn't have read it in that short period of time. Her curiosity flourished into action. She had to satisfy her own curiosity. She began flicking through the magazines and, to her surprise, there wasn't one written letter to be found anywhere. Did this mean that the Rotters had already invaded the written language with the Destrusto Virus? If so, where was its source? Slirander sat down and pondered how it could be here. Did the Moonatric tree know something they didn't? Did it send them here because it knew where to start looking for the Rotters? What a clever tree.

'Davidia,' called Slirander, 'there are no written letters in any of the magazines in the shop. I fear they are here ahead of us.'

'You mean the Rotters?'

'Yes, them.'

'Sir, have you ever heard of the Rotters?' asked Davidia, not shy of asking probing or upsetting questions. She waited for an adverse reaction to the question.

'Sorry. I can't help you. Are they a sporting team?' he asked.

'He's not one of them,' said Slirander. 'Let's try the university. It's a seat of learning and must have an extensive written research program. I wonder if it's safe.'

'Which is the university building? Didn't it have a name on the outside? I can't see it,' said Davidia.

There wasn't a building in sight with any name on it. It didn't matter from which angle one looked, there were no names anywhere.

'I think that largest building over there is the university. Besides, a lot of angled people are entering it. Why would they go there if there wasn't anything to learn? Do you get the feeling we are being stared at and gossiped about?' said Davidia, feeling uncomfortable at being only one of two upright bodies.

'That could be the place the Rotters are hiding in. It's a place of learning, knowledge, historic research, filled with extensive literature and an ideal place to begin viral activity. The books in there reach far and wide. If they infect a letter and they are handed out to the students, imagine the damage it could cause. They travel everywhere. An infected letter of the alphabet could invade every home and cause untold damage.'

Davidia faced outwards for a city view and suddenly turned around without looking and bumped into an obtuse angled student. Books and papers flew everywhere. Fortunately, there was no breeze to blow them away. She insisted on helping retrieve them all. Without warning, a rather large letter S fell out of a book onto the ground. It had nowhere to hide.

'What's the letter S doing in your bag? It should be in a book resting with all other printed matter. Where did you get such a finely shaped letter?'

The angled student gave an unusual angled gaze. She smiled on a slope. The shock of seeing someone straight had momentarily frightened her.

'It is a gift from Professor Doonow. After each class, which are now mainly oral, he hands one out to each student. It's a gift of appreciation for the studies we do,' replied the angler.

'Is it only the letter S that he gives out?'

'It's a special letter representing the science academy. He bites each letter as he hands them out. See, his teeth marks are indented there.'

Slirander took a closer look at the indentation. One tooth prong was deeper than the other. Maybe he had odd teeth.

'You said oral lessons. Don't you read them anymore?' asked Slirander.

'There aren't any written books available. The research library keeps losing them, so there is less to study from.'

'Has this been going on for very long?'

'It began early this week. The professor said it would take most of the week, but he'll have the issue resolved by then.'

'When is that?'

'Tomorrow.'

'I appreciate your help.'

The student gathered her memento S, little realising the dangers it held. There would be no more written studies and the ever-expanding spread into the community of the infected letters would decimate the written language everywhere. Once a book became infected, it sent out the virus by the readers' fingers and if pages were left open, letters could book hop and activate their destructive forces. Time became important to meet Professor Doonow and solve the case of the infected S.

The university was no different than any other except that it was angularly built. Davidia and Slirander both had to be careful where they walked in case they banged their heads on any shapes that angled precariously for them. It was difficult to miss every object and they occasionally bumped into them, some pointed and painful, others just in their way. Finding their way to Professor Doonow's classroom, they travelled through a labyrinth of corridors. No architect had ever heard of a rectangle, square or right angle. All shapes were distorted into angles. They wondered why the city and people were built and born this way. Was it one giant experiment they were in? Would everything eventually fall over? They didn't have time to solve the angle problem, but the letter concerned them more. Maybe the professor was a Rotter in disguise. They were the sneakiest of adversaries.

'Excuse me, can you direct us to Professor Doonow's classroom? I hear he's biting letters. Would he give one to us, even though we aren't students?'

The student stared at them. Her words of response weren't

written down and the request by upright non-students floored her. She turned to her friend and they both laughed nervously.

'Professor Doonow is such a gentle and caring individual, he believes that everyone should have a memento letter S to remind them of their university years. He is the only professor to give his students any form of reward or praise. The other day he said that his students were a group of ignorant, right little Bs. He shared that letter with us. We were so proud that he used both the S and B letters where our group was concerned.'

Davidia smiled. There was no point in enlightenment of what he really meant. Their capacity for word absorption was as plausible as walking backwards a hundred kilometres on one leg unaided.

'Do you have one of his letters?' asked Davidia.

'We sure do. We have twin Ss because we are sisters. This is mine. You can look, but don't touch.'

Its surface was also indented with the same bite mark that they had seen earlier.

'Thanks. Which way is it to his classroom?'

The girls pointed with their angular fingers, which Slirander had interpreted as meaning that corridor.

'Thank you and happy reading.'

The girls giggled and waved goodbye.

'What did you mean by happy reading? They'll only end up with a book full of pictures.'

'Precisely,' said Davidia.

'Make way for the freaks,' a student yelled.

'You can't bend properly, so who'd go out with you,' another chimed in.

'Watch out for the pushovers.'

They ignored the good-bantered humour, or was it bullying humour? Either way, the comments flew about waist height. A huge room with an angled letter L hanging loosely by a resistent screw came into view. It was the science library. They peered in the window. Students were busily flicking through pages of scientific knowledge. Nothing appeared out of the ordinary. Davidia felt a minor bump on one of her shoes, followed by a tiny metal clang. She looked down and there was a dazed S not knowing whether it was upside down or not.

'Are you okay?' asked Davidia, unaware if it could speak.

It lay flat on its back, exhausted. At least Davidia knew that many excellent words began with the letter S. Should this one be saved? It could be infected. She leaned over and carefully picked it up.

'Be careful,' it squeaked.

Davidia jumped.

'You can speak.'

'All letters can speak. Just because we are printed or pasted on a page, we can mentally speak and some of us can physically speak, like me.'

'Have you been bitten?'

'Certainly not. There are no impurities on my shape.'

'Why are you here?'

'I'm trying to find a location where I can be part of a story. There's a library around here somewhere. That's the ideal place for me to be in a book to begin many magnificent sentences or just participate as a support letter in any word that needs my assistance. Do you know where it is?'

'Where did you come from? You haven't been bitten. We were told that all letter Ss, such as yourself, are given away as presents in the science faculty. You don't seem to have any peculiar indentations.'

'I escaped. Just down the corridor is a press that prints us *en masse*. I was accidentally dropped and slipped down a crack in the floor. No one noticed me missing. Thank goodness I'm a slimline letter as I would never have been able to crawl back up that thin crack if I was a chubby W or an unbalanced Y. I'm a language letter that requires use. Now, where is that library again?'

'Would you like to earn the chance of being read?' asked Slirander, who thought that their untarnished new friend might be just the opening to enter any book and reverse the disappearance process.

'Oh, yes. I haven't had any expert eye pass over me in a written context. Perhaps I should be shown in upper case and not lower case. There's more prestige in being big bold and noticed. I'd enjoy that.'

'You must promise me one thing.'

'Anything.'

'Remain perfectly quiet.'

'You mean like a silent H in some words.'

'Something like that.'

'I'm your letter. Which book do I start in?'

'Davidia and I will select the most prestigious and important work for you to commence your reading career. You must also be prepared to travel.'

'A travel book? How exciting.'

The letter S was tired. Davidia placed it in her inside pocket. The plan at some future stage would be to spray it with the antidote and let it loose at the appropriate time.

'Slirander, what will we do with it? We can't take it as a souvenir, can we?'

'It will become very useful. We must look in the library. There seems to be too many students in there all reading at the same time.'

'Do you think a Rotter may be amongst them?'

'Probably more than one. Look how frenzied they are at

turning over the pages. We must try and experiment first to prove that the antidote works. We must find a book that has lost its written words.'

They entered the library and were basically ignored by all those present; however, a couple who side glanced noticed their presence. Language had consumed the students. Had it been real food, it would have been an angle-fest. The angled seats were bad for good posture. One had to balance the edge of their buttocks on what little flattish seat there was and then place the feet solidly on the floor and push back just to maintain a seated position. Their legs would cramp, and their bum would become numb after a long sitting session. The girls would have to work fast and efficiently to deter back pain and numbness. The rows of books seemed perfectly in place. They were all properly categorised in subject matter and beautifully bound. It was the premier scientific library research facility. Observations alone didn't reveal clearly that there was skulduggery occurring. Slirander ran her fingers along the books' bindings as one does a stick along a corrugated iron fence; however, the big difference was the silence in a library as against the annoying rattle of tin. A slim finger suddenly stopped at a book still clearly labelled. The hand grapple grasped the book and jerked it out from its shelf refuge. She put her hands on the front and back covers and paused for a moment.

'It's not a hamburger book, is it?' asked Davidia, as it reminded her of when her parents cooked them for dinner. They held the beef patty between both hands and flattened it for cooking preparation. She had never eaten a book before.

'Shhhhhh,' said a nearby student.

'Davidia, this book is losing its language. I can feel it becoming lighter.'

'Are you guessing?'

'Let's say it's playing into my hands. Go sit over near that window and we'll open it.'

The window was above an open courtyard where a fresh breeze wrestled with their hair. They both had long, unkempt tresses, which the boys at school teased them, saying they would make a good skipping rope and so on. This time the breeze only toyed with them. Slirander silently opened the book. Not one word jumped out to escape. There were no words left to read. Only the outside binding had letters left. The loss of words always began from the inside first because no one could identify the destructive event until the binder had lost its identifying title. It was the last gasp to retaining language.

Nearby, a sinister pair of angled eyes watched the strangers with the strange body structure. It stopped licking its fingers for a moment. Study could wait. Slirander and Davidia were whispering quietly to each other. No one could hear them. The interested student was intrigued, or was it? Was there a reason for the interest? Were they up to no good? Maybe the student was?

'The Rotters have licked their way through this book. Feel how light it is,' said Slirander. 'There is no other explanation.' Davidia picked it up.

'It's as light as a paperback. It shouldn't be. It's bound in a heavy cover and full of so many pages.'

'Now is the time to prove that the antidote works.'

Davidia took the letter S from her pocket and placed it on the table. A nearby student noticed the S. It was identical to the one it had been presented with, inclusive of bite marks. Why would these strangers have one? They didn't look like students. It moved over to the girls and took them by surprise.

'What are you doing with a study appreciation letter?' it snarled.

An angry angle defied good looks. Slirander sat controlled and comfortable. Davidia jumped in excitement, passing a small amount of wind to waft with the gentle breeze blowing through the window. It was an inoffensive moment.

'It's my new bookmark,' said Slirander. 'I borrowed it from another student. It's a practice run before I receive my own.'

'Which student?'

'There was one passing me in the corridor, and we got chatting.'

'Has it been stamped with the teeth of approval?'

'Not yet. It was a new one that was on its way to the professor to be approved. He's got a nice bite. I liked its shape, so my curiosity took advantage of how it would work as a bookmark. Do you have one?'

'Yes, it's on my table.'

'Would you like to swap your indented one with a new fresh one? It hasn't been damaged. All your friends would be jealous of you. You would have the only bookmark without teeth marks. Your peer group would be impressed.'

The student thought for a moment. The language was being lost, the students weren't learning anything from research and the letter S was a bribe for performance good or bad. The student who hadn't passed with good scores suddenly felt that the undamaged S might increase her status within her peer group and overcome her lower educational ability.

'Is this book I'm looking at, about Rotters?' asked Slirander.

'Why do you ask?'

'I'm trying to find some friends, that's all.'

'I have no idea, but you can have my letter S.'

'It didn't react,' said a relieved Davidia.

Slirander took out a vial under the cover of her hand and gently sprayed the letter S with a minute drop of antidote. Inside the antidote, the Pebble of Purpose's soldiers were awoken.

'This is it, lads. Time to prove how literate we are. The world is our learning curve.'

They anxiously waited for the drift to land them on their first letter S.

'Look at that. What a beautifully shaped letter. No wonder it's a pleasure to read and restore damaged languages. Team, we must succeed.'

'Why did you spray my letter?' asked the student.

Slirander gave her a friendly look.

'It's from my special perfume spray. I only ever allow my new friends to have a whiff.'

It smelt like an exclusive, exotic jungle plant — no one ever explained which one it was — where the special ingredients were extracted from a mysterious continent and relied on a professional sales campaign to allude to its perfections. The student took a sniff and was completely mesmerised by the spin Slirander had given her. It was another convert to purchasing all things sweet smelling. The price tag being incidental.

The exchange of Ss took place. The angular student loped off and sat down again, satisfied that it had been given a new and very special gift. A smile gradually grew across its face. It had been absent for a long while. Now it had a reason to smile; a pristine S. Davidia and Slirander turned their attention to their new infected S. The bite marks made them wonder about Professor Doonow. Why did he bite each S? University lecturers can be quite unconventional, but to chew on solid inedible material and then distribute it to the class with a spot of your saliva, represented peculiarity. Maybe he was a Rotter of interest? They looked over and saw that the student had placed the sprayed pristine letter S in her book as a bookmark. The potential for language restoration had begun.

'We'll check the title later,' said Slirander, and see if it has worked.

Davidia had noted that the title was Shellfish. Their new letter S friend would blend perfectly into the title.

The infected letter S they now had in their care was studied closely. The teeth marks were prominent. Had it been bitten with disregard to the intelligence of his students and why would a bright professor want to waste language, the very thing he used to teach his students with?

'It doesn't look well, does it?' said Davidia, wondering how it would look as a centrepiece on a new necklace she could design.

'It probably is the Destrusto Virus causing it to deteriorate badly. The paint is flaking, and the edges are warping. It seems that once it is infected with the virus, it appears that it self-destructs and all that the students have achieved is to let loose the loss of language in exchange for a piece of waste material. I'll spray it and see what happens.'

Each time the spray was used, a new set of soldiers performed the language saving tasks, somewhat like a paramedic saving lives each time they attended a call.

'Lads, time to restore some damaged material,' said the soldier leader, as they approached their target. 'This will need our best patch-up job.'

They landed on the S surface. It was a non-speaking S. They scrubbed its surface, straightened out its warped edges and gave it a good coat of special paint excreted from their mist glands. Soon the letter S was as good as new. The bite marks could not be removed.

'One more bookmark ready.'

It took less than thirty seconds. There was no external interference to prohibit the work done, so there was a good chance of success. Slirander replaced the book on the shelf. Now all she had to do was wait to see what reaction occurred.

Once the antidote had completed its task in a book, its

restorative soldiers book hopped and spread their restoration process to any literature they found. They multiplied by working hard. The more they worked, the larger they increased, so they could cover vast libraries, newspapers, magazines and any matter with letters on them. They only ceased operating after a full language restoration had been achieved.

*

Professor Doonow had been at the university for many years and was an esteemed tutor. He was so respected that every student when asked to prepare something for their science class, eagerly complied. His classes were full of humour, learning, and successful science experiments even though some may have been over the edge and a place of achievement. At the end of the final semester for those who graduated, and that was everybody, he gave out a memento to his students as a reminder of their achievements. He had undertaken a recent trip to the mountainous regions of Rotland on the recommendation of his dullest student to experience the beauty of the region. Being inexperienced in travel matters and listing at a very bad angle, he encountered a helpful local who befriended him with the promise of straightening him up. It was a female, so the professor was very nervous about the relationship. He was only used to handling science experiments, not real-life ones. The female was exceptionally nice. They exchanged pleasantries. When the female heard of his science background and where he lectured, she began to salivate. Trails of dribble fell from her jaws onto the ground. It made a small pond that a frog could enjoy. She quickly apologised for her over-reaction and excused herself for a few moments. Her son, a snivelling, young, dull nerd was hovering behind a cloth curtain.

'You get here,' she said. 'Go to the Hole in the Hill and tell it we've got an opportunity here.'

'What's an opportunity?'

'Do as you are told, otherwise you'll have to learn something.'

'Not that.'

It seemed that to learn something was worse than death. It wasn't, though. In a flash he was gone. The threat of learning was enough to send shivers down any Rotland inhabitant's spine. Roland the Rotter had successfully kept his subjects ignorant so that they could be trained like seals to deliver his Destrusto Virus without knowledge or question. The young boy made it to the Hole in the Hill. No one had ever entered it before, and no one knew why. It was another oddity to live with and not understand. He yelled the message of opportunity, deep down into it. There was no echo or reply. It acted like a non-reversible sucking vacuum cleaner. The young boy felt that he had lost something when he yelled, but he didn't know what. He returned home.

'Are you hungry, professor?' asked the female.

'I could eat the eye (I) out of a pie,' he replied.

'It's not necessary to trick me with clever words and we don't eat body parts here. We're simple folk.'

The professor began to wonder whether it was a good idea visiting Rotland. A knock was heard at the front door.

'Special delivery,' someone yelled.

'What is it?' the female enquired.

'Alphabet soup with the compliments from the Hole in the Hill.'

'That's a nice gesture.'

The soup was placed on the table. It was full of Ss only. The rest of the alphabet wasn't invited. It did look delicious. Steam filled the professor's nostrils with aromas that reminded him of his science experiments. He was delirious with pleasure.

'What a thoughtful meal.'

He ate so heartily that he didn't notice the female, or her nerd son, eat anything. When he had finished, he felt that his body wanted to do something beginning with the letter S. He had a wide choice of activities to select from, but remembered that a toilet began with the letter T not an S. For a moment there he had a blank. The word "sit" begins with an S also and sure enough, that's what he did. He had a sit with a capital S and a silent H, which wasn't included in the word.

'Did I eat the whole meal? Isn't there anything left for you?' he said, concerned that he had greedily eaten everything.

'The meal was meant only for you.'

'I must thank whoever provided such a feast.'

'That's not possible. Enjoy a good night's sleep.'

How odd. Free alphabet soup made with only one letter. That night the professor had a restless sleep. His body had been infected with the Destrusto Virus and he would be an unsuspecting carrier of the deadly language virus that no one would suspect him. Roland had chosen an ideal purveyor of his evil plan. By next morning, the professor had a personality change and noticed that he had one tooth longer than the other. Had a dentist snuck in during the night? The bed he slept in was flat, not angular, and it played havoc with his all his angles. Nothing was easy. He left Rotland in a hurry.

*

'These corridors go on forever,' said Davidia, tiring of dodging angled furniture, angled students, irregular roof lines, and so on. It seemed endless. She didn't want to walk at a forty-five-degree angle. She wouldn't be able to walk properly and perhaps she would constantly fall over.

'It must be nearby,' replied Slirander, keeping a close eye, not an odd eye, on other students. She wondered who amongst them was a finger-licking Rotter.

'I think we are being followed, Slirander. Each time I turn to look behind me, a small group parts like a bad smell into the classrooms. Then, when they appear around the architrave to see what we're doing, it unsettles me like a dose of stomach rumbles. This place is odd. I wonder what it is that they really want.'

'They're probably jealous that we walk upright, and they might want to find out how we do it. They'll probably try to copy us. Ignore them. They aren't as bright as that S Professor Doonow gives out,' replied Slirander, who knew a thing or two about good posture.

'Yeah, where is the professor's classroom? That could be it up there, where that queue is forming,' exclaimed Davidia.

A line of female angles had formed and kept on moving lightly from one foot to another in an agitated manner. Their facial expressions registered some form of pain, or it might be anxiety. There were no signs above the door to identify what classroom it was. It was assumed to be Professor Doonow's. The girls approached.

'Is the professor in?' asked Davidia.

'In where?' replied a grimacing student.

'In that classroom.'

A few of the girls managed a smile and a shake of the head.

'That's the toilet. There aren't any professors in there and if there were, they should be arrested.'

Davidia and Slirander walked away a little red-faced.

'How was I to know it was the loo?'

'At least we know where to go if we need to.'

'Those dipsters are still following us.'

'Let's see what they want,' said Slirander, who enjoyed a game of cat-and-mouse, especially as she was always the cat.

They stopped and waited for the small group to catch up. The girls stood eyeball to angle. Slirander felt uneasy. Shaking hands amongst young girls wasn't the normal greeting, but she wanted to test something.

'Hi. Nice to meet you. My name's Slirander and this is my friend, Davidia.' They waited for a response. 'We're looking for Professor Doonow. Could you tell us where his classroom is?' A few suspicious blank looks greeted that question.

'It's the next room on your right, the science classroom,' replied a helpful student.

'Thank you.'

Slirander, had noticed the white fingertips of two of the students who had tell-tale dribble hanging from the corner of their mouths. They weren't prime candidates for a passionate kiss. They were more in need of a wet wipe swipe. Their fingertips were grainy from being wet for too long. Slirander, unsighted, placed her fingers into her mouth for a saliva handshake. She proffered her hand to both the students of interest.

'Slirander, they've both got six fingers. Are they twins? Imagine what they could scratch with those,' Davidia quietly remarked.

The students were taken aback at a hand forcibly shoved at them. Slirander wasn't withdrawing hers until touch was achieved. Reluctantly, they shook hands as a gesture of a friendly greeting, not knowing what else to do with it.

'Hope to meet again,' said Slirander, and quickly walked off.

'What was that all about?'

'Take a look.'

Both girls were shaking their hands in pain. Their fingertips were burning.

'They won't be finger-licking any more books in a hurry.'

'Are they Rotters?'

'Yes.'

'How do you know?'

'Instinct. Now for the professor.'

Davidia was amazed by her odd friend. She seemed to know much more than her years gave rise to.

Professor Doonow's classroom was the next entrance. Above the doorway, hanging on a piece of sagging string, was a collection of Ss, pretending to be a list of letters. None of them had been indented with stamped tooth marks. They peered inside. There were only a few stray students mingling around hoping for some intellectual inspiration. All that Professor Doonow was doing was pandering to his students' under-achievements by rewarding them with an S, the key they thought that would lead them to science success. Slirander didn't know if the professor was infected with the Destrusto Virus or whether he was aware of the literary havoc he was promoting. He could be a cunning Rotter pretending to be a professor. Remember, no one knew what Roland the Rotter looked like. He could be anybody. They walked in.

'Hello, professor,' said a confident Slirander, hand outstretched in a cordial greeting.

Davidia stood quietly next to her. Her attention focused on two dribbly students who she was sure weren't eating; lunchtime was well past.

The professor gawked in shock at seeing an upright body. It had been a long time since he had to bend one over. He wondered if she was to be his next experiment. A small saliva smile from a squashed angle would only appeal to a slug, because that's what looked like was escaping from his mouth.

'Excussse me,' he drawled. 'Where did you ssspring from? Rrrr'sss you lost?'

'No, sir, we're science students ourselves from a different college and wondered what your academy does here,' explained Slirander.

Davidia kept watching the slinking angled pair who hovered over a pile of books. No book wanted a dog-eared pet, but a lot of them seemed to have achieved it. The corners were peeled back. She felt in her pocket for her spray, held it firmly and approached the two angular readers. They studied the stranger. She wasn't the right shape. Davidia leant over and, without forewarning them, let a squirt escape at the same time she pretended to sneeze. The small offensive airborne particles were thought to be germ-infested mucus droplets, which if they landed on them could cause some form of injury.

'What a bitch to spit like that,' they said, as they ran hastily from the classroom.

'Mission accomplished,' she said, smiling.

The antidote spray began its work immediately.

'This is one tough bugger of a cover,' said the leader, as they strained to get an opening. 'This must be in a foreign language. It's so resistant; perhaps it's in French. They are as stubborn as.' The soldiers began to take over the reading material. The books revealed that letter tampering had occurred. 'I never did understand why they're are so difficult, but trying to restore their language takes hard work. We'll probably get no thanks and let's hope we speak French too.'

Davidia turned her attention to Slirander and the professor who were still at the meet and greet stage.

'We ssstudy ssscience. The sssemester isss finissshed thisss year. Do you want to C my latessst experiment?'

'You seem to struggle a little with some parts of the language, sir,' said Slirander, quite astonished at his poor diction in such a prestigious position.

'It'sss my Ss. Bending over all daysss isss not easssy. Sssome thingsss mussst give. Can I asssisssstsss with sssomething?'

Standing in front of a class all day tutoring was a difficult task. It was probably time for the professor to seek an alternative interest. He smiled at Slirander who noted his distorted teeth with a sharp pointed exaggerated elongated molar. The rest of the set were interspersed with odd shapes. None were identical. His dentist would be confused if he had to treat him.

'I want a special bookmark and some of the students explained that you gave them out as a memento of their studies. I wondered whether you could give me one, please?' said Slirander, suffering from a bout of good manners.

Is it always better to be nice than nice to be better?

The wily, old professor suddenly lost his smile. Its replacement was an evil flash of odd eye, which almost detached itself from its socket. One eyeball almost hit Slirander's forehead as if it was playing a tennis forehand. She jumped back in shock at the ferocity of his response. It quickly recoiled into its unpleasant dispatcher. His mouth curled into a nasty snarl. What had she triggered? Maybe he was hiding behind a character façade and had now only revealed his true self.

'No one asks for an S. It is I, Professor Doonow, who decides who gets my precious gift. The impertinence, to ask for something that you aren't entitled to,' he ranted.

Davidia noted that there wasn't one error in his expression or use of bad diction. Slirander gathered herself. She had seen another Rotter, but couldn't let on that she knew.

'I'm sorry professor, I wasn't aware of their meaning to you. I hope I haven't offended you. Are your Ss offended also? That whole basketful on the floor ready for gift giving seemed to move as you got angry. Is there any connection? I haven't seen that happen before.'

'They moved because I stamped my foot on the floor. Reverberation made them jump. You certainly are inquisitive for a young girl.'

'That's because where I come from, we can ask questions and learn from all sorts of various books, just like your students do at this university. I saw many of them in the library studying hard from any book they could find.'

'They are knowledge feeders. Can't get enough of a good thing, can they? If there's one thing I can be proud of my students for, is that they know what to do with every word they read. Can you do that?'

The professor had set Slirander a challenge of sorts. She knew that this piece of Rotland was bad for the school. It was obvious that he had been sent, knowing or unknowingly to destroy the world of science. His behaviour screamed Rotter.

Davidia was quietly mulling in the background. The professor could only see her in the dull whiteboard reflection full of scientific scribble. It blurred any good visual to observe what she was up to. She paid close attention to her friend and the oddball professor. The basket full of Ss were up next for the distribution network of destruction. She wondered what would happen if she sprayed them with the antidote first before the professor sank his molar into them? Once again, she pretended to sneeze as she sprayed the antidote over them.

'Wipe your nose,' said the professor, on hearing the sound of many SSSSSs which a sneeze produces. It was his favourite letter.

'Thank you,' replied Davidia.

The thirty seconds for the antidote to be at risk, passed slowly. There were no obvious signs that it had worked because all the spray had been absorbed by the letters. This time, the soldiers of the Pebble of Purpose knew that they had to remain silent because they had been placed in a position of restoration prior to any destruction occurring. They had to lay in wait until the destruction was triggered, then their restoration work could begin.

The professor was tiring of Slirander and her intelligent comments. Maybe one of his students could grasp what that was; however, he believed that science had no place in the world, but only in Rotland where every page was a blank. Ah! That's mental bliss at not having to learn a damn thing. It was nirvana for a Rotter's brain.

Davidia signalled to Slirander that it was time to leave. She walked over to her friend.

'I sprayed that basket full of Ss with the antidote,' she whispered. 'I wanted to see what would happen.'

Slirander knew that it would have an adverse reaction on the professor once he bit into them.

'Excuse us, professor, but we have to visit a sick aunt,' she fibbed, as they back-pedalled out of the classroom.

The professor was glad to see them go. He had more students to reward. The basketful of Ss were placed on his desk. A new batch of dopes stepped up for their achievement award. The professor bit harder than usual with a rising anger level. This was to ensure a good supply of bad spittle, a non-erasable indentation and an extra effort at destroying language. His face contorted in surprise.

'These are the tastiest Ss I've ever had to bite. I must compliment my batch maker,' he said.

He continued biting each S as a source of pride. He became so enamoured with his own success, nothing gave him the Ss. The basket was emptied in record time.

'Missile coming in,' said the leader. 'Let's stick it up the purveyors of bad diction and letter loss. Are you ready lads? Let's give this our greatest scrub-up.'

As each new S went with a student, the restoration process was assured. They were now assisting in saving the written language of science, not its demise.

The professor began to feel ill. His supply of spittle had dried up. A foul taste circled in his mouth with no hope of escape. A mental terror was unleashed. His bent stance tilted closer to the floor. His body was fighting a chemical imbalance. The antidote had unleashed a potent erasure process, where the special pebble soldiers task force searched the professor's body for the badness that Rotland had infected him with. Deep in the incubation chamber of his stomach, swirled the mass of infections that crawled up his throat into his mouth and then were delivered by a salivary bite. The source had been discovered.

'Down there, boys, blast it out.'

The soldiers created an internal whirlpool of bile, infectious matter, and wind for an eruption, and stirred it so speedily, it wasn't long before the professor regurgitated all over his desk. His body ached at its own destruction.

'Let's ride this animal like a rodeo, cowboy lads. I love my job.'

Each soldier sat on infectious matter and rejoiced in the explosion of cack that the professor spat out. It was a challenge to be attached until the final burst. The disease-ridden infection, once exposed to the atmosphere, shrivelled up to become ineffective dried waste.

'Arghh! What a putrid mess,' exclaimed the professor, 'someone will pay dearly for this.'

Both his angry eyes exploded out of his head in unison. The two maniacal winkers thrashed around in confusion at the epicentre of an angry fit. They desperately wanted to pinpoint the responsible party and sighted both Slirander and Davidia watching from outside the classroom.

'It was you two,' he screamed.

All his angles raged with revenge. He gave the strangest of echoing calls at the top of his voice range. Throughout the school, the army of infected Ss — those that hadn't been converted to restoration — slipped out of every book and ran toward the originator of the fearsome shriek. Suddenly, the awards became an army of joint destruction. Each Rotter in the university also ran toward the shriek. As they did so, each one scooped up a volatile S and raised it as a weapon of harm. The Harmy Army was prepared to inflict extra damage other than the loss of language letters. Davidia and Slirander were now in a direct line of real danger. If they were hurt by an S, in the words of the wise old Moonatric tree, 'you may not come back', flashed inside their foreheads.

'This way,' yelled Davidia. 'To the library. They are all attending the science classroom and we must hide amongst the books.'

'Why there?' asked Slirander running at full tilt.

'It's a feeling I have.'

They ran along separate corridors to the Rotters and their Ss. No one saw them slip into the library.

'There isn't a book big enough for us to hide in,' said Slirander.

'We aren't hiding in any of the books. That office over there is ideal for camouflage. We need an escape plan.'

'What! We are stuck inside a yellow, scientific leaf, somewhere on the planet, and with no idea how to get out. We could be stuck here forever in the world of leaning angles. How long do you think we could remain standing upright?'

Davidia had remembered a video game where contestants tackled each other with word games. Maybe a clever phrase, a witty comment, a humourous joke, large words the Rotters didn't understand, or a something out of nowhere comment might be the answer. The Moonatric tree did say they had to use their intelligence and that they'd think of an answer to save themselves; however, no one gave them any advice as to what that was.

A huge, noisy, hostile, yelling crowd seemed to be heading their way. The sound was like a long lisp, similar to that above the science classroom door. The chant was 'S, S give them an S.' Any longer and they wouldn't remember what it was. Moments before the library door burst open with more people in attendance than before, Slirander snatched off the shelf the book on shellfish, the first restoration that had taken place with the antidote. She quickly flicked through the pages. It was in perfect condition. The Font of Knowledge and the Pebble of Purpose had successfully formulated the right formula. Now she knew that it worked, all language could be saved. Her confidence soared. What phrase did she know that could send fear through any letter?

Professor Doonow stood at the head of the insanity Harmy Army, with his two extended eyeballs on wildly waving elastic strings. All Ss were raised in the strike position. It looked like a sea of monosyllabic letters. The group lowered their chant to the sound of hissing tyres. 'SSSSSSSSSSSSSSSSSSSSS.'

'Thisss isssn't hide-and-ssseek,' drawled the professor. 'You cannot essscape your fate.'

'And what would that be?' Davidia called out.

'To remain ignorant. Angledon is your new home. Now come out and dissscusss thisss sssensssibly. I might need you for an experiment. I promissse you won't be harmed.'

The professor had reverted to his sinister character, which was the real him. Slirander didn't want to be dumbed down. The professor would obviously try and inflict the Rotter intellectual dictionary on her, which would mean losing most of her language capabilities. That wasn't going to happen. A blank page needed to live through language and not be vacant like the Rotter intellect.

Davidia was always clowning around at school and often played made-up games for the amusement of others. Silly things were said in the moment of frivolity. Was now the time to act stupidly? There was nothing to lose. She whispered something to Slirander who nodded and smiled. She reached into her pocket, took out the antidote and sprayed some into her hand. She rolled it into a ball and whispered to the soldiers what was at stake.

'We love reconnaissance and a surprise attack,' said the leader. 'Leave it to us.'

Slirander wasn't the right age to be a lawn bowler, but her action of rolling out the antidote ball along the floor toward the professor and his rotten group, was the perfection that most bowlers dreamed of. The antidote ball rolled into the midst of the congregated group.

'What is it?' said a confused Rotter.

The professor who tilted so closely to the floor, tried to sight what it was. His two mad eyeballs that were erratically trying to sight everything, banged into the floor. His vision was momentarily blurred. He was the only one capable of recognising any danger; and that moment was lost.

'It'sss a fluff ball. Theysss mussstt be trying sssome new game on usss,' he said, in response. 'My eyesss don't half hurt. I've got eyeball ache.'

As his anger level began to subside, both eyes retracted into his forehead. It didn't improve his appearance.

The Rotters lowered their Ss as there was nothing to strike at just yet. It felt like the danger they feared had diminished. After all, it was only two teenage girls who had threatened them, but they didn't know in what capacity. Davidia and Slirander had agreed that the signal for the antidote puffball to gently explode would be a preconceived two silly words that Slirander had already whispered into the puffball prior to rolling it out. The leader and his attack force of language restoration breeders were itching for a fight. They were well-primed for a skirmish. It was their time, this time in force.

'I'll get as many Ss before they realise they have been attacked,' said the leader. 'Are you ready, lads, to fight and retain the written language?'

A silent puffball cheer erupted.

Slirander yelled out at the top of her voice, 'Gooley Goo.'

Suddenly, the puffball burst its circumferences and sent an invisible mist of soldiers into the air. Their only target was the many letter Ss. In no time the team was dispersed, and each attached to its designated letter S. The soldiers had an internal task force of letter breeders, which ensured a continuous supply of workers until the job was completed.

The professor and his group were stunned by the stupidity of the word. Perhaps the world is better off without written words if that is all that is on offer via education. He was disappointed with the comment.

'Time to come out,' he sneered.

Davidia and Slirander had accomplished their Save the Science world languages because the strength of the antidote soldiers they would leave behind were sufficient for the task. The problem now was how they could save themselves? They had no idea how to return from the insane landscape of angles; however, they fronted the problem head-on. They walked from their hiding place and stood tall in front of the group who had all crammed into the library for a closer look. Their leader, Professor Doonow, began to salivate at the prospect of victory and future experiments. His dribbling was the signal to all in the group to drop a drop or two as well. The floor soon became an unhealthy slippery mess. The drops seeped to close the girls in. They were disgusted by their dribbly bad manners. Maybe the words Gooley Goo, which seemed so stupid a few moments earlier, weren't so stupid after all. The concerned looks on their faces delighted the professor. He knew it wouldn't be long before the drops on the floor had their feet encased. Doom was a lovely word for evil doers to enjoy. The scene for capture was set.

'Slirander, how do we escape from here?' asked Davidia, fearing that her reading days might be over.

'Think of a phrase, comment, anything that might be the key to get us out of here.'

'I don't think that they would listen to me. They have awfully bad manners, don't they?'

Slirander began to cite large words and a few witty phrases that she had acquired at school, and threw them at her audience. They stood stunned that someone knew so many different words; however, not one had any effect on them at all. The window of freedom was being squeezed like an orange.

'What about that stupid phrase your dad used on me when he gave me the brown hands? It was so stupid, it was unbelievable,' said Davidia.

'My dad doesn't say stupid phrases. He's a professor,' defended Slirander.

'Well, how do you think I got these brown hands? I didn't paint them myself.'

The professor couldn't believe the silly bickering of the two girls in their moment of danger.

'If the phrase was so stupid, you say it,' said Slirander.

'I can't remember all the words.'

The mess on the floor was seeping closer. Their window of time as future readers was gradually being closed. The phrase would only have the required strength if Slirander said it; however, neither girl knew that. Davidia had a good feeling about her friend who she thought was odd and that this phrase was right up her alley of utterances.

'Why should I say them?' asked Slirander.

'Because you sometimes like to hear the sound of your own voice.'

'I do not.

Ickle wockle weeny fing,'

she yelled in anger. 'There, I said it. Happy now?'

The professor and his group all sighed in anguish in a chorus of sighs. The seeping mess stopped moving. The girls were astonished. It was as if time stood still.

'I told you it was the most stupid of phrases that I've ever heard and look what it has done. It has stopped that dribble dead in its tracks. They all seem to be a bit nervous, don't they?' said Davidia, sensing a reprieve from doom. 'Say it again and see what happens.'

'*Ickle wockle weeny fing,*'

she repeated.

Another gasping sigh filled the room. The professor began to act erratically. He began to scratch his angled feet and joined his fingers together like the joining of two gloved hands. The floor mess had retreated and now encased his feet.

In a moment of desperation, he shouted to the Rotters, 'Throw your Ss.'

A choreographic impulse saw each Rotter throw their deadly Ss at the girls. They swished menacingly through the air with every shape, intent on harm.

Slirander saw the danger and screamed out the final two lines of stupid phrases from the one verse of allegorical poetry,

'It cannot sing, it cannot sing,

Cut its flamen head off.'

A silence filled the library. All Ss melted into harmless puffball mist trails and fell to the floor. A strange feeling crept into the room unnoticed. Was it invited? Who sent it? Was it real? It was so eerie that each book on the bookshelf held tightly onto all their written letters. A secret signal of preservation had been sent to them. Apparently, that silly phrased verse was a potent restoration force of some kind. Maybe the Font of Knowledge had secretly empowered that phrase with healing powers? Whatever the reason, it had a startling effect.

'See, I knew you knew the words,' said Davidia. 'Now what?'

A long, wrinkled tree root suddenly appeared through the library roof. Slirander recognised it as her friend Moonah's.

'Grab hold of it,' she said to Davidia. 'This might be the way home.'

The tree root shrunk into the heavens with the two girls clinging tightly. Below, the city of angles, Angledon, began to reshape into more conventional square and rectangular constructions. The population, which needed straightening out, also began to alter. The language of science had been saved and the miraculous transformation of evil had disappeared. Whoever said that a stupid phrase doesn't make sense?

The girls were returned safely seated on the yellow leaf of science. The shellfish book that Slirander had taken from the library would now be retained in her father's library. It would be a lesson to all.

*

'I feel sick,' said Roland the Rotter, having heard that his S soup didn't succeed and that there was now a powerful force to contend with in his quest for language destruction and ignorance. His Hole in the Hill home had suffered a blow to his literary ego. He thought that his next messenger would be better prepared. Mmmm. 'That might be my next subject letter,' he mused.

'Whoever is upsetting me will regret any contact by their actions. Nothing will thwart my attempt at universal ignorance. I have warned the world. No longer will alphabet soup exist.'

*

'Where are we?' asked Davidia.

A floating cloud passed by.

'You aren't interfering with the weather again, are you?' it said.

'We aren't meteorologists.'

'Back home, well, almost,' replied Slirander.

The girls were safely in the foliage of the Moonatric tree, but there was nothing else around it that they could see. It was as if a large blanket had been thrown over the tree and enclosed them within.

'There's no ground, no home and a whole lot of nothing. What's happening?'

'Apparently, we can't return home until all language loss has been solved.'

'You mean there's more. My parents only let me stay for a sleepover, not a month's holiday.'

'I'm tired, let's rest.'

Soon, the floating Moonatric tree with two young girls was silent.

5 MATHEMATICS

'The yellow science leaf has turned green,' said Davidia, refreshed from her nap.

'It's closed. We can't go back there,' said Slirander. 'Now what? Your family certainly has some peculiarities. You must have some secret powers that I don't understand.'

Slirander smiled. It's true that there was something odd about her family, but whatever it was she wasn't letting on what the full truth was. They were now in the middle of a grey nothingness. Strangely, though, neither of them felt cold. An invisible protective film enveloped them and kept them away from any harmful elements. The Moonatric tree provided all that was necessary to keep them safe. It was a mysterious growth that, one day, Davidia would fully understand.

'Brrr, brrr, it's a little cool,' said Davidia, rubbing her arms as they began to grow goose bump humps.

A slow grating sound was heard emanating from the wrinkled Moonatric tree.

'Not again. My arthritic branches don't need this rushed exercise. You can't stay on that leaf,' said Moonah, 'it will soon fall off. Try the nearest leaf.'

As they made their way to the next leaf, it slowly turned over to reveal a bright red surface which glowed proudly. They stood in the centre of it for safety.

'I'm not an exercise tree for young tree climbers. This is my second leaf you have awoken. It doesn't get any easier each time I turn one over. Years of growth haven't improved my flexibility. What is it this time?'

'We're not sure. A dreadful thing almost happened to us in a science laboratory and, fortunately, we ended up back here.'

'Oh, that! Yes, I did assist. Try not to get into too much trouble. I suppose you are enjoying your ride here. You mustn't stay long. There is work to do.'

'We're not employed, we're schoolgirls,' said Davidia, who wasn't quite at the stage where her parents would agree with her to work part-time in a fast food outlet.

'Yes, yes,' chuckled the Moonatric tree.

Its branches began to sway with laughter. The red leaf shook also. Suddenly and before they knew it, the girls were swallowed into the red leaf and once again they hung onto a thin tree filament that guided them safely to the ground. Thump.

'Where are we this time?' asked Davidia.

'That Moonatric tree is probably delighting in getting us lost,' replied Slirander.

'It looks like we have landed in the middle of a mathematical puzzle. I wonder if there is a doorway that leads outside.'

'You won't find it,' said a voice.

'Why not, and who are you?'

'I'm a difficult equation to solve.'

'Do we have to solve you first before we can leave here? What is it that we are actually in?'

'I'm not solvable and, besides, there's no need to solve me. A hidden door will allow you to leave. You are inside a doodle puzzle.'

'I've never heard of it,' said Davidia.

They were soon surrounded by a curious mixture of letters, numbers, shapes, unusual squiggles and formulas all waiting a turn to be useful. The girls watched in amazement as tricky mathematical manoeuvres were performed in front of them.

They didn't understand the difficulty of what they were doing. It just looked complex.

'What exactly are you doing?' asked Slirander, whose grasp of mathematics was in the novice stage.

School mathematics hadn't reached the complex stage whereby she would recognise and understand some of the arrangements of letters and numbers.

'We are practising problem solving in case the real world wants to make use of us in a new format.'

'Is that an algebraic problem?' she said pointing at a few x and y's trying to mix it with a few small numbers.

'Good. That's easy,' said the difficult equation. 'Call me E. Why are you here?'

'To solve a puzzle also. Are all currently existing formulas in this particular doodle puzzle? There must be others as well. What happens to you once your formula is required?'

'There is a whole valley of doodle puzzles. This one is the premier problem solver, so we go first. The smartest letters and numbers work here.'

'How often are you needed to provide solutions?'

'Funny you should say that,' said E, 'we seem to be losing more of us more quickly everyday than before. There are so many new variations in here it's hard to get a good formula mix anymore. We've been invaded by misbehaving numbers that haven't got any clues of where they should fit in a good equation anymore. We don't know who tutors the new supplies. The supply of poor grade lettering worsens the situation. It appears as if they deliberately visit, then after they settle into a proper functioning solution they fade away resulting in industry malfunctions and lots of damage. So, we are under mathematical stress levels never encountered before,' explained E, who was solely a capital letter performer.

'How are you accessed?' asked Slirander, formulating her own idea of escape.

'Electronically. A brute of a letter, Big B, visits each day. It carries a computer encapsulation machine. It reads out a list of preselected formulas that industry needs. Immediately, the groups in here band together into the correct formula and it is then transferred to the computer screen and taken away, never to be seen again.'

'You haven't been taken yet,' said Davidia, listening intently.

'I have been careful so far. I'm not one to mix with the sub-standard letters or numbers. I'm quality rocket material. There hasn't been any demand for me yet.'

Davidia needed to get out of the doodle puzzle and wondered whether any Rotters were in there with them. If so, could they trace their source?

'Have you met any Rotters recently?' asked Slirander.

'Never heard of them. What are they?' said E.

In the background, quite a substantial number of letters winced in pain and began to fade.

'Slirander, grab one before it fades,' yelled Davidia.

'Leave me alone,' cried a small p, which began losing its shape.

'I'll twist you into an odd shaped b, if you don't cooperate,' threatened Slirander.

'I can't help you. Besides, I'm only a part of a small formula. Look for an M,' said the small p, as it disappeared into nothing.

'Isn't that odd that a letter would fade away like that? There must be an outside influence. They are probably trained to react to the word Rotter, because nothing else was said or done to affect them,' said Davidia, slowly recognising the serious evil being portrayed around them. It all seemed related to that one word, Rotter.

'E, you mentioned a secret door as the only means of leaving this particular doodle puzzle. Does anything else use it?' asked Slirander.

'Occasionally, when a formula malfunctions badly, a restorer accesses it to correct and re-programme some of us into a coherent working item,' said E.

'Will you assist us to escape from this particular puzzle? We promise that a rocket formula, where you will be the major equation contender, will be your reward. Is it a deal?' Slirander was a good negotiator.

'How can I trust that you will keep your word?'

'We're girls.'

'Is that what you are?' said E, not understanding what a girl was, but Slirander did promise. At least that was computed correctly. 'Agreed?'

'How is the escape thing done?'

'Leave it to me. Hey, you with the flat top,' E was talking to a capital T. 'What formula are you due to appear in next?'

The capital T had a straight head problem and resented being called flat top. Any formula with his inclusion was treated as a premier formula. If E could dent his flat top, or, better still, delay him from appearing in a next formula, the Big B would send a restorer to correct any T malfunction. It was a long shot, but when cooped up all the time in a doodle puzzle, affirmative action for escape had to be taken.

'Mind your own business. My work is too important to discuss matters with a lower-case e.'

'I'm a capital letter, just like you,' replied a resentful E.

T was preparing for inclusion in an advanced formula. E wasn't invited to participate. As T was postulating with his equation partners about where his position in the formula would be, E slipped by and tripped up T. He landed on one end of his top and dented that extension point. The formula was ruined.

'Malfunction, malfunction,' screamed the doodle puzzle computer. In a trite, a restorer had opened the secret door wondering what in the hell had gone wrong with such a premium formula. When he had located the damaged section, he tried to restore it. It was more difficult than expected. The secret door had been left open long enough for Slirander and Davidia to sneak through unnoticed. They gave E the V sign, but that was another complex formula of meaning to understand.

The girls ran out into a strange world. All buildings were constructed in the shapes of letters and numbers.

'There's a row of fours with fives balancing on top,' Davidia pointed out.

'That street a few blocks away is full of Js with Ls built above them,' said Slirander. 'This is so unusual. A city built in letters and numbers. I wonder where we are.'

A group of 7s ran past being chased by a group of 3s. A few lower-case letters played with a few straggly numbers and they seemed to enjoy mixing together practising solutions for when they grow older. Both girls were mesmerised by the amazing world they had entered. There was an absence of shops. What if they wanted to purchase something? Perhaps the right number might assist.

They approached a group of young numbers playing hopscotch. Each number in a square lay down on the ground as others jumped on them in sequence. It was an early numbers training exercise. Davidia got excited and joined in. The numbers became incensed as she was too heavy. *What letters was she made of, because numbers are usually light?*

'Stop!' yelled the 8. 'Who invited you to play?'

'We play hopscotch all the time at school. It's so much fun.'

'Not when a heavy letter lands on us, it isn't. What letter are you?'

'I'm a D and my friend is an S,' said Davidia, realising that these numbers were too young for complexity in an explanation of exactly who and what they were. 'I didn't mean to upset you.'

'These are my friends from 7 down to 1. Zero has lost interest and joined the letters because he almost looks like one of them. You are strange looking letters.'

'Can you tell us where we are?'

'Mathematica. The land of equations and formulas. Problem one day, solution the next. We love it here. Every day is a challenge.'

'The street seems to be full of playful numbers. Where are the playful letters like f for fun, h for happy and their groups of friends? It seems very quiet.'

Number 8 suddenly bent over so low he looked like an o. His two loops had become one. The other numbers stopped jumping also. Playtime had ceased.

'There used to be a lot more letters around here, but lately very few come to play with us anymore. Those that do are so tired and by the time they get here they fade away. All of us had lettered friends, but now we play with mainly our own kind, numbers. The letter neighbourhood used to be much larger, but it's getting smaller every day. We don't understand why? The other day an angry equation walked by. It was so upset that the letter required for a complete solution faded away in the same manner and the equation was useless.'

'Is there a central place of mathematical learning anywhere?' asked Slirander.

Her feeling of happy numbers told her they weren't that happy.

The source. One must find the source of the infection before a cure is found. Letters should be much stronger than the feeble faders they had been told about. A letter projects clarity of explanation. Why they fade is a mystery? Number 8 directed them to the letters' area.

'All of the great equations emanate from there. I hope you meet them. They are fantastic solution solvers.'

'What about the doodle puzzle letters? Are they as good as they believe they are?'

'They're just average; however, don't tell them. An upset formula is not a good mix,' said 8.

The girls walked down an arbour street under a series of numbers — six and nine — which formed a canopy. Many windows above them were filled with a mixture of numbers, hoping the girls had a solution to the disappearance of their lettered friends. They looked on, believing that the letters D and S would fade as well.

'Another game of hopscotch, anyone?' asked Davidia.

The numbers all quickly scattered.

*

The girls wandered along streets of numbered buildings. It was like a giant mathematical jigsaw. Number upon number upon number. It was endless.

'That faded p mentioned M. Look for an M. It must be a sign of some sort. I wonder if it means McDonalds is here. It has a huge, brightly-coloured M,' said Slirander.

'Maybe we can have something to eat if it exists here,' replied Davidia.

McDonalds wasn't one of her favourite foods; however, it seemed very popular at home. Maybe it was because of the way it was spelt? The world was filled with oddities.

'Stop!' Slirander yelled to Davidia, 'we're being followed. Don't look, but I've noticed a huge number 9 darting in and out of building doorways. It sometimes converts to a 6 for concealment. I wonder what it is up to. When we turn the next corner, hide in a doorway and we'll surprise it.'

Davidia nodded. In the next street they did exactly that. The 9 peered around the corner. Where are the girls? Its first job as an undercover digit might be doomed to failure. If it failed it could be dumped with every other half-baked formula, because one thing was certain; failure meant a poor grouping with waste formulas. As soon as the number was level with Slirander, she jumped out from her hiding place and scared the 9 witless.

'Why are you following us?' she asked.

'Who? Me? I was walking along the street and saw two very strange letters and wondered what you were doing here. You didn't look like you would be suitable for any equations. You are the wrong shape and you have lots of it. No letter or number is as tall or as round as you either.'

'Tell me then, what or who is M?'

The number suddenly shook so badly, the top of his 9 fell off and rolled down the street. All that was left was a slightly curved line, which was of no use to anything.

'This M must be frightening,' said Davidia. 'What if it's an upside-down W and not an M at all?'

Both girls had to think that one through. It could be correct. Odd things in an odd world can mean almost everything is odd. They stopped to rest on a K bench with the letter on its side. The back was made from a series of 1s, neatly spaced together.

'This is hopeless. Letters are fading away and we can't locate what's causing it,' said Davidia, becoming annoyed at their lack of success.

'Mmm,' said Slirander.

'Yes, leader,' said the K bench.

The girls jumped in fright.

'Mmm,' repeated Slirander, to prove she hadn't imagined the response.

'Yes, leader,' it repeated.

It was a dose of the repeats that gave Slirander a clue what M might be. The bench had reacted to the sound of the letter.

'It must be some form of sound and not a letter as we understood it. Let's try it on a group of numbers. There's two sitting over there.'

They approached. Two 5s were arm wrestling. Slirander mumbled her M sound again. The two 5s fell over and hurriedly scurried away.

'That's it. Listen for the sound of anything that sounds like an "Mmm" sound.'

'It comes from that building over there,' said a doorway shaped as a zero.

Davidia felt its nervousness.

'What do you mean?' she asked.

'It's the sound of falling alphabet homes, which is constantly occurring. Large tracts of land now replace what were once good lettered homes. The "Mmm" sound is the sound that is heard prior to its collapse. Soon there will be nothing but numbered homes here and the chances of ever making any proper formulas will all but disappear forever. The doodle puzzles won't amaze anyone anymore. Our days are numbered.'

'What starts it all?'

'There's a special building — that large one you can see — that causes it all. One day it will be gone also, even though it's constructed from the strongest capital letters. It's rumoured that many of the letters in there get licked. We don't know by what, but recently an influx of foreign letters, in italics no less, entered there and we haven't seen them since. They have these weird shaped arms with little things on their ends, much like miniature number 1s. They are all coloured a bright red. No one goes in uninvited. You are probably large enough to force your way in.'

'Why are you being so helpful?'

'My son, mini zero, was friendly with a small n and together they made the cutest couple. Often mini zero would be mistaken for an o, so affectionately they could form two words, on and no. One day, n took ill. It had visited that special building and was never the same again. Eventually their relationship faded into a flat zero. Mini zero has never connected with another letter since. His chances of becoming part of a formula, are as his name suggests, zero. All numbers need the chance of rehabilitation and reconnection with their lettered friends.'

'The sound of the M doesn't worry you?'

'Letters should be more concerned.'

'Slirander, let's see what the cause of the problem is. Thanks, zero.'

The two girls stood in front of a giant building patchwork of the most intricate of letters. The building dwarfed its surrounds. Lots of noises could be heard from inside. Two burly security letters stood guard. They barred the girls' entrance.

'You two cannot enter. You don't look like proper letters,' they chorused.

'I'm an odd shaped D and she is an odd shaped S,' said Davidia, trying to sound convincing as a member of the alphabet.

'No D or S is ever as large as either of you. Entrance is denied.'

'Step aside or become part of an alphabet rubbish equation,' threatened Davidia.

'Why antagonise them?' said Slirander.

'I've got a black belt at home. Mum bought it for me as a gift. They don't know it's a dress belt. Watch this.'

Davidia turned around with her faced screwed up like a papier maché ball. She looked like an early morning model prior to the day's beauty makeover. She crossed her arms in a Japanese martial art move and waved them around pretending to slice the air with two sharp arm blades. Her legs gave a few kicks as well. She was spoiling for action.

'Move aside or face the wrath of black belt Betty,' she yelled with a piercing, 'Hey ya.'

The letters weren't fazed. A single letter was no match for them. Slirander walked up to one of the guard Gs and kicked it hard. It toppled over. Davidia followed her lead and swung her leg in an arc and managed to kick the other G. Both Gs limped away.

'This security caper is too dangerous,' they said, and left the entrance unattended.

'I said I had a black belt.'

Inside the building lurked loose letters trying to attach to others to form a word, or, even better, a sentence.

'Where are the numbers?' asked Davidia. 'It seems to be a numbers exclusion zone. Good formulas need a mix of both.'

A distinguished letter L wandered by, muttering about the loss of better sentence structure when confronted by the girls.

'Excuse me, Mr L, why are there no numbers in here?'

Mr L had a long look down a snooty length and wondered what he was seeing.

'It's a Letters' convention. All the letters in the land have come here to listen to the learned Professor Sum who seems to be confused with the mixture of letters. Would you like to join us in the auditorium? It's this way. By the look of you two … Oh, did I actually say a number in a sentence? How exciting. An education for you wouldn't go astray.'

Blank looks crossed their faces. Their hands felt for the vials of antidote and patted their small dictionaries to confirm that they hadn't fallen out.

They were led along a wide hallway. It was littered with fading letters unable to form anything. It was a desolate sight. Language litter was everywhere. A large doorway suddenly attracted their attention. A number could be seen struggling underneath it trying to escape to attract someone's attention. Davidia motioned to Slirander.

'That's a number 4 wriggling down there. That L said it was a Letters' convention. We'd better check it out.'

The door was Q shaped. The handle was a small q. Davidia opened the door and inside in boxed cages were all the banned numbers prohibited to make any formulations whilst the convention was in progress. There was hyperbola running in race seven. *Place a bet.* Parabolas swung like monkeys. J curves were lost without an economic forecast. *Why were they all in here?* The girls sensed anxiety and danger.

'Thanks for freeing me,' said a thankful number 4.

'Why are you all in here?'

'We have been removed from all the mathematical literature held in the great books of formulas. Mathematics is being destroyed by the loss of our lettered friends. Something is stealing them out of every mathematics book known. It will be a disaster soon as nothing will work properly. None of us will have a book to call home. You notice that many lettered buildings have already gone. We fear it will be the same with mathematical numbers too if we lose all of our lettered friends.'

'Have you noticed any strange happenings recently that aren't normal in a number's day?' asked Slirander.

'There was a group of alien italic letters that arrived recently. No one had seen them before, and they haven't joined in to make any equations or formulas. We think that they may be specialists only for the convention. All we knew was that as soon as they turned up all numbers were turfed out of their books and placed in storage. It's outrageous to be treated in this manner.'

'We must attend that convention. It sounds as if it may be full of Rotters. Nothing else deliberately destroys language letters.'

'They won't return,' said a disappointed 4. 'They'll disappear themselves. Every letter will disappear. Then it's our turn.'

*

The conference room was a massive auditorium surrounded by the books of mathematics all filed in neat rows to the ceiling. To the right of centre stage, a series of long trestle tables had been set up in rows. Seated at each table were the italic letters with the weird arms and dangly finger type bits. Piles of books were stacked in front of each of them. They were so skinny they would make poor bookmarks. Their pre-pruned physique suggested and forewarned of their imminent decimation; however, their current task was to work as a team of readers instructed by the Master of Ceremonies. The girls snuck in and hid behind a hoarding advertising the value of mathematics. The room was frantic with activity. Books by the bucketload were constantly being recycled by teams of eager lower-case letters. They were trying to impress to become an upper-case letter provided they satisfactorily completed their tasks. The girls watched with amazement as the italic letters flicked through each book at lightning pace. It was a finger-licking frenzy.

'They are damaging every book,' said Davidia. 'We must stop them. I'll spray them right now.'

'Wait,' said Slirander. 'It may not be as bad as we think. Note the small size of the lickers' tongues, so only a very small amount of saliva is transmitted with each lick. The destruction process won't be as quick. That gives me an idea. We'll sneak up on one of them. No one will notice us.'

They slunk behind a pile of books, pretending to be assistants transporting books, and tried to blend in as larger case letters. Had they been seen? A pair of evil, penetrating eyes had noticed the intruders and their antics.

'Did they think they were invisible, did they?' he mumbled to himself, stroking his chin shaped like the letter U.

His mouth was a thin slit, quite easily mistaken for two number 1s lying on top of each other. This was the Master of Ceremonies, an unpleasant lecturer called Professor Sum. He had become disillusioned with teaching as a profession and wanted to change the world by introducing only his special equations and formulas. As a lecturer, his standing was acceptable, but as a genius mathematician, everyone would take notice. A teaching nobody would become a world leader. His ego was insatiable. This character flaw allowed him to become easy prey to a great con trick. The only way that he could become his ego-fed character was firstly to destroy all the existing letters in every formula and, once that had been achieved, replace them all with his own letters and create his formula world. This was the foolish promise that he believed would one day rule his destiny.

Roland the Rotter had been informed about the professor and thought that he would be an ideal conduit to ruin the written mathematical language. He had a reason for doing it: self-promotion. Organising a convention of letters, minds and knowledge was easy. Roland the Rotter had sent a special infected gift to the professor calling it a Certificate of Genius. It was unbelievable, but true to a blind ego. The professor fell for it. It was gold-embossed and framed for all to see, as if his brains were on display. The professor unfortunately hugged the frame too closely. On the outside of the frame were duplicate letters that had been infected with the Destrusto Virus, but as you looked at the framed certificate they were unnoticeable. These letters jumped off the frame and into the professor's mouth. He thought that a few flies had flown in for a visit. His attitude and demeanour changed dramatically after swallowing those letters. He began to believe in his own indestructible ability and channelled all his efforts to the path of evil. Once all the letters had been destroyed, there was no chance that he would ever formulate any of his ideas as he was a mixture of huge letters himself and he too would be destroyed. Roland the Rotter salivated at the thought of his cleverness. Was he at the convention and no one knew he was there?

'Over there, quickly,' said Slirander. The girls darted in behind a pile of books at the back of an italic letter. 'Spray that pile of books. Use a light squirt. We don't need to waste it all.'

Davidia used the spray sparingly. The Pebble of Purpose's soldiers awoke.

'Lads, our services are required again. No more café lattes. Get rid of those video games. We have our tasks to perform. Are we armed with our anti-viral attitude? Whoopee, I love my job,' said the excited leader.

'Keep it down,' said Davidia, 'this is a light operation.'

'Formation lads, formation.'

The light misty spray landed unseen. The soldiers ran riot over each book and began the clean-up.

'That sick group of letters are fading away. Restoration is at hand.'

Suddenly, Davidia deliberately kicked over the pile of books. They scattered everywhere. The commotion it caused temporarily halted the reading process. Davidia then tripped and knocked over a trestle full of books as well. Italic letters fled everywhere. They were so thin that any gust of wind would blow them away. In the pandemonium that ensued, the mixture of books spread the restoration work far and wide. It was now far easier for the soldiers to cover many more books. What a clever strategy.

Professor Sum gauged the situation correctly. *Both those girl letters are trouble.* His head began to ache. An odd eye emerged, enraged at the mess they had created. Slirander saw it. She nudged Davidia.

'That professor is a Rotter. His odd eye is all red and full of tiny blue lines.'

Davidia saw it too.

'He's ugly, isn't he? Perhaps all Rotters should see an optometrist. They all seem to have sore eyes,' said Davidia.

'I don't think their eyes are sore. It's how they react when excessively angry. It's the only way you can actually tell a Rotter.'

'Who upset him? I didn't say anything,' protested Davidia.

'It's his condition. He's been infected.'

'Well, he shouldn't take it out on us.'

Professor Sum signalled to two huge H letters. They slowly trundled over like obedient pooches.

'Those two odd-shaped letters are upsetting the convention. Remove them. Throw them in with the numbers. No, better still, bring them to my office. I want to test them. They might create a new and interesting equation for me.'

The two lumbering Hs headed off at slug pace. The girls saw the two heavy hoofers coming their way.

'Shall we run and hide?' queried Davidia. 'Should we spray them?'

'No. Stand still. Let's see what they want.'

The two Hs drew level.

'Excuse us young letters for the imposition. Professor Sum would like to make your acquaintance. Please follow us,' said one H with impeccable manners.

They both stood mouths agape at the politeness of the request. That did it. They both thought that language letters must never be destroyed.

When employed in a proper manner they can be ever so nice. Forget the bad use of language letters, only the good bits should be used more often.

'Excuse me H, but why does he want to see us?' asked Davidia. 'It wasn't something we said, was it? We don't know any jokes if he wants entertainment. We're just two ordinary schoolgirls. We haven't been at school long enough to teach him any mathematics he doesn't know.'

'He wants to meet two unusual letters. You have more shape and substance than any he's seen before. You are letters, aren't you?'

'Of course, we are. I'm a D and Slirander is an S. There aren't any tricks are there? I'll set my brother onto him if there is.'

'This way.'

H was tiring of the conversation as it was only one letter. It needed many others in support if it was to belong in a long conversation.

Professor Sum's office was plain and simple. It was a mirror image of his personality. Books of mathematical giants adorned a small bookshelf placed behind his desk. The professor had an E shaped head with the E laying on its back. He also had two O eyes which were ponds of evil depths, a Z torso with two Is for miniature arms and an X forming the legs. The two number 1s for the mouth moved similarly like the stiff cardboard of a ventriloquist's dummy. If it was a horror movie theme party, the professor would win the door prize. He was a ghastly presentation of how letters shouldn't be arranged.

A polite knock on the door signalled their arrival.

'Do come in, my experiments,' said the professor politely, as his eyes scanned for treachery of any sort. 'It has come to my notice that you two have made a terrible interruption to the Convention of Letters. We were destroying, I mean, doing so well, in the education of letters until you two arrived. The idea of the conference is to train letters on how they could participate as part of an equation or formula. Some of them are so pedantic. They wouldn't mix with certain numbers and that creates all sorts of terrible problems. Us geniuses need them to co-operate, otherwise it's a useless exercise. Would you agree?'

The professor glanced down at them. His odd angry eye had retreated, but within its depths was deceit and distrust. It was the window into one's mind. The problem being that it was hard to detect where it was.

'Why are there so many italic letters here? I understood they were only meant for emphasis in a sentence,' said Slirander, who was no slouch when it came to grammar. 'They appear to have the run of the place. What is it you are stressing in the education of letters?'

'Cooperation.'

'Has it been successful?'

'Why, yes, now that you should ask. It has been our most successful convention yet. Nearly every letter in the land of Mathematica has attended. It has been held over several days. Imagine how exhausted we all are.'

'Those italic letters seem to be the most cooperative,' said Slirander.

'They are a special consignment recently brought in especially by a most recent benefactor to assist in language destruction, I mean reconstruction. As a professor, possessing infinite mental agility, I occasionally confuse my words. There are so many of them, one can't always get it right, can one?' he sighed.

His eyes were like boring drills into one's soul. They searched for a spark of something, especially in Slirander, as she was holding court. He thought that there was something intelligent about this letter and wanted to know what it was. Was she like him, a mixture of letters arranged in a zany pattern, but he couldn't see the arrangement?

'Excuse me, Mr Sum, something doesn't add up,' said Davidia.

The professor slyly eyed the interruption.

'What is it?' he almost yelled in frustration.

'There are clearly no numbers here.'

'What do you expect at a Letters convention?'

'As this is the land of Mathematics, we would expect to see some numbers here too,' she continued.

'Well, there aren't any.'

'We all knew our timetables at school, so they at least should be here. Everyone at school had to learn them. Shall I recite them to you to remind you?'

'There's no need to. The numbers weren't invited.'

'They were very friendly in the village of doodle puzzles on the way here.'

'You've been there? How did that happen?'

'We walked.'

'That is a restricted area. Many equations and formulas are made there. Did you steal any?'

'We aren't thieves. Besides, they were all too complex for us. We are only in Year 10.'

'Do you think you could produce a useful formula?'

'Why would you want a formula from us?'

'Never have a closed mind to possibilities.'

'Can we hear your delivery to the convention?' asked Slirander. 'We have heard that your expertise in mathematical formulae is awesome.'

The professor managed a half smile with a hint of dribble.

'Why would you assume its mathematics that I lecture on?'

'Your name and this valley reek of mathematics. There isn't any other possibility, is there?'

'Youth only see a narrow truth and not the subtlety of information change. It may surprise you to find that I dislike what I do, following everyone else's formulas, and have decided to make many changes so that I become the world's premier mathematician. There is also a language surprise to whet the appetite of any other professors in attendance.'

The professor was on an ego bus trip without a driver; without direction and definitely without any stops. Slirander knew that she had to get him back on stage to deliver his lecture. This would allow some sense of assessment of what was happening at the convention, bring together all the good and bad elements of mathematics and maybe that surprise that he spoke about. Those suspicious italics seemed to be out of place here.

*

Roland the Rotter was enjoying his Hole in the Hill home, thinking he had pulled off the unbelievable world chaos with the loss of all mathematical formulas. He prized himself on his ingenuity of arranging language destruction with the help of those most unlikely to be held responsible for it. He was a master manipulator, magician and all-round bad guy. No one single person had ever before ruled the world and he was determined to be the first. What and who survives was of little consequence. It was his personal challenge.

'My stomach doesn't feel right,' he said, wincing over in pain.

This was the second time it had happened when something didn't go right. He knew there was a rat in the woodpile of his plans but didn't know what or who it was. The first hint of trouble occurred when the Science world was saved from language destruction and now pain pangs of a similar nature were happening in the land of Mathematica. Maybe the formula of the

Destrusto Virus had malfunctioned, but he seriously doubted that, because it was the best that he had ever produced. There had to be more to it.

'I'll find the problem and annihilate it.'

He was left brooding with the growing pain. It was an indicator of disaster.

'Those italics had better perform well until they disintegrate.'

*

The auditorium was full as Professor Sum made his way to the central stage. All the italics ceased their finger licking and page flicking. The other letters that hadn't faded stayed upright as long as they could. Books were silent in their various piles and Davidia and Slirander sat off-stage under a heavy, lettered guard.

'Psst, psst.'

'Davidia, what do you want? The lecture is about to start,' said Slirander.

'Psst, psst.'

'If you need to go to the toilet, you will have to wait.'

'It's not me,' replied Davidia. She had more manners than that.

'Psst, down here.'

Davidia looked down and there was the number 4 hovering around her foot like an annoying mosquito.

'How did you get in here?' she whispered. 'You aren't allowed in.'

'I escaped from storage. The letters must be saved. That professor Sum is a very bad equation. He is destroying all the good we numbers have accumulated over centuries. I don't know how to stop the ego formulacker.'

Davidia was about to reply when she noticed a group of italics edge closer to her. In their tiny finger bits, she noted a sharp object held with a very pointed end. It was a sharpened letter I. There was no goodwill message in their nearness. She stood on number 4 to conceal it from danger. She leaned over pretending to tie her shoelaces and expertly slipped the 4 into her hand undetected.

'Shhh,' she said. 'Do you really want to save your lettered friends?'

'Definitely.'

Davidia's plan was simple. Spray 4 with the antidote and then it can move around the room delivering the soldiers of the Pebble of Purpose, hopefully unnoticed. One uninvited number might go undetected. She leaned over to Slirander, who agreed with the idea. Davidia reached into her pocket for the vial of antidote. Number 4 was also placed in her pocket and given a short squirt. It thought that he now knew why spray was used. It smelt nice.

'Lads, it's overtime. One of our team is already out there doing the hard yards. They need our help. Our friend here will transport us around, so form into your groups and at each drop-off point, restore what you can and quickly,' said the leader. 'Our ride is numbered, so let's give him some letters to play with. Yahoo!'

Davidia bent down and carefully whispered to 4 what she wanted him to do.

'If you get caught by any unruly letters because many of them are badly infected, use the word "difficulty" in a singing format to unsettle them. There's another word that reveals the truth, it's the word Rotter. When mentioned, anger erupts in a most unusual way. Remember the odd angry eye and there's sometimes a pair. Be brave and don't end up in a non-working formula.'

Number 4 slipped below the trestle tables and began his secret journey to all parts of the auditorium delivering the high gusto soldiers. He had no idea about Rotters and their damaging leader. To it, it was all about saving friends.

'Slirander, it's done. Number 4 is such an intelligent number. We're fortunate to have friends like it.'

'Professor Sum is about to deliver his lecture. Apparently, it's repeated each day. No lecturer normally does that. My parents have explained that the role of a lecturer is to give only one lecture at any conference. There must be some sort of special purpose to it. Keep an eye on the crowd. There must be a few Rotters out there to be unearthed,' said Slirander.

'Letters, quiet, please. Please welcome our guest speaker, Professor Sum.'

Muted applause greeted his introduction.

'Fellow letters, this is the greatest congregation ever of all letters in mathematical history. We are all here to share the same fate.'

A groan rumbled around the room. This wasn't his speech. Why had he changed it?

'We have been brought together so that you are all destroyed and never work together again with any numbers. This is the end of mathematics. All of you will be replaced by a new set of special letters in every formula and equation, which will be solely under my control. This is my finest hour. Even as you listen, you are being destroyed by my team of italic letters. They have almost licked every known mathematical book infecting it with the Destrusto Virus. It's over for you all.'

The professor let out a maniacal yell of delight. There was no defence against the situation for all the stable letters. Davidia and Slirander were disgusted with the arrogance and confession of the professor. Davidia whispered something to Slirander. The auditorium was filled with confusion.

'Where's number 4? Call it,' said Davidia.

Soon 4 appeared.

'Go to the doodle puzzle village and bring all the formulas

here that haven't been destroyed. Even if they are only numbers. Go. It's urgent.'

Number 4 took off as if chased by a sexy 3, which could be joined in the multiplication tables later on.

The professor strutted the stage like a peacock, feeling confident of his position.

'Excuse me, Professor Sum,' said Slirander, 'aren't you afraid of being destroyed also as you are also made up of only letters?'

'I'm protected.'

'By whom? Roland the Rotter?'

The professor couldn't restrain himself any further. His E head swelled like a triple-pronged balloon and his O eyes bulged like two cesspools of puss ready to explode. Both angry eyes reared out of his head. They looked lost.

'You're a Rotter,' said Slirander. 'I knew it. You're infected with the Destrusto Virus.'

She quickly flipped out the antidote and gave the professor a squirt. He fell over in shock. The leader of the soldiers decided a different tack this time.

'Lads, it's the eyes. The two large Os need more than a Botox patch-up job.'

They piled onto the skinny, wiry things attached to his eyes and slid down them practicing their fireman's pole technique. Behind the eyes, the Destrusto Virus was hiding, thinking it was safe from discovery.

'Blast it, lads. Give it a dose of intelligence,' said the leader.

'It mightn't know what to do with it,' replied a soldier.

'Fire!'

A team of moisture-laden restoration antidote dots grappled with each evil particle labelled with a small "dv" as an identifying tag. Roland the Rotter was such a labels person that everything he did had to have his insignia on it. He wanted to ensure that if anything was successful, then he wanted it known who was responsible. A fierce intellectual fight erupted behind Professor Sum's eyeballs. His eyes ached with the pain.

'Give in,' yelled the leader, riding a huge dv particle.

'Never,' replied the dv particle wrestling ferociously to retain its ignorance.

The professor's head rolled about like an unstable lolly on a tabletop. Slirander watched quietly. She knew that the professor's bad eyes would be repaired by the antidote, but perhaps not his strange attitude. She remained watchful for any evil outburst. She hoped that at least he would no longer possess the Destrusto Virus and infect any other literature.

The Pebble of Purpose's soldiers were doing a terrific job, righting the wrongs inflicted on letters by the Destrusto Virus. The battle hadn't been won yet, as the italic letters were still such a strong force to reckon with. Books were continuously being licked, infected and tossed on the floor. Organisation fled out of the window. It was every book, letter and girl for itself. The antidote soldiers battled every evil particle and tried to save every fading letter. They gradually overcame the obstacles of ruin to good mathematics and were well on the way to victory when an unusual event occurred.

Professor Sum's writhing and wriggling with his aching head suddenly halted. His huge two O eyes receded into his head. They felt strangely odd now that he was free of the Destrusto Virus; however, never always believe what you see. He slowly rotated his head toward Slirander. His snivelling smile returned, and a trickle of dribble escaped to pool on the floor.

'Why doesn't he use wipes?' asked Davidia, disgusted at the bad manners he portrayed. Upset children wouldn't act in this way, would they?

Just then the main door burst open and a flood of numbers

and left-over equations stormed into the auditorium, all spoiling for a formula. What was the formula for fighting? No one knew that one. A huge crowd milled around. There was number 4 at its head.

'Professor, give us your worst equation,' yelled 4. The crowd got excited. Never had they had such a forthright number in their midst. This new 4 could just be the problem solver mathematics was looking for. 'Well, professor?'

The professor's head was in its firing position. His left eye was shrinking. It was disappearing. Then, out of nowhere, a tall italic letter ran from behind him and hit the professor on the back of the head with a lower-case p in the shape of a club. The quick, short, sharp rap sounded like a single rifle shot. His left eye shot out of his head directly at Slirander.

It was labelled with the dv insignia. The cunning Roland the Rotter had condensed his evil into the professor's eyes without the antidote being aware that it had spread further through his body than previously thought. The back of the eyes were freed, but not the eye itself. What a dilemma! Slirander stood directly in line for an infection. If that had occurred, it was the end of any hope of saving any language. The hall quietened to be as silent as a book. Imagine the scene of a silent movie with no sound and the camera following a flying projectile in slow motion. It may be a director's finest hour, but for Slirander, she was under a direct threat.

Davidia, who was standing next to Slirander, knew a thing or two about sport. She undid her jacket, waved her tanned hands over the small dictionary she carried and instantly held it as a table tennis racquet. If the professor wants a spot of shooting the eyeball, she was ready for an eye-to-eye bout. The eye was too fast to make a proper swipe at it; however, Davidia managed to put the small dictionary in front of Slirander and, splat, the eyeball made contact. The language inside the dictionary possessed a special power of language restoration. When the eye hit, it was instantly zapped by the world's knowledge and imploded on understanding what it had hit. The professor reeled in pain at the failure of left-eye one. He had one left and instantly signalled to the tall italic letter to whack him again. A one two-step, then whack, and it sent his right eye high into the air over the hall crowd to land in the corridor. It was also labelled with the dv insignia. This meant that the Destrusto Virus would continue its work. It must be found.

'Thanks, Davidia. I thought my reading days were over. We must destroy that other eyeball. It has the potential to continue all the evil work we have tried to destroy,' said Slirander.

'I love a game of hide-and-seek. My brother used to be so infuriated, as I always won. Once I hid in the dog kennel, which wasn't such a good idea. I stank of dog smells and had to shower twice a day for a few days. At school, no one sat near me. That was before I met you. We'll find that evil eye,' replied Davidia.

'Before we go on a wild goose chase, what about the letters and numbers in the auditorium?'

'Why don't you repeat that silly phrase your dad told us and see what happens.'

Slirander took centre stage. It was still deathly quiet. It was as if that moment in history was captured by a still photograph.

Ickle wockle weeny fing,
Ickle wockle weeny fing,
It cannot sing, it cannot sing,
Cut its flamen head off.'

The stunned audience hadn't heard of such stupidity before. It was a series of nonsense, no meaning phrases; however, it inflicted pain on many present. Suddenly, the italic letters which were a privately trained destructive army of language destroyers, began to misbehave. Their thin frames thinned even further until their bodies couldn't support their O shaped heads and they fell, headfirst onto the floor. Their eyes swelled up like water sponges and spilled into pools of water. Their evil was literally washed away. The numbers were rejoicing at still being able to formulate with the letters that were left. The antidote had gradually restored many letters and was continually working for complete restoration. Slirander and Davidia both did not understand why that silly allegorical poem had such an effect. The professor was exhausted, and his lettered body crumpled into an unreadable phrase.

The silly phrases signalled danger. It was also heard far away. A rescue mission was implemented, but no one was aware of it. Who had been awoken?

'Be careful. That eye is rather small and don't let it hit you,' said Slirander.

'I wonder where it's hiding?' said Davidia. 'If I were it, I'd be under a rubbish bin, cabinet or down any hole. It's fun to find something so small.'

The eye didn't see it that way. It wanted to prove its powers of destruction were as strong as ever. It had a plan; a sneaky plan. If it were a letter, one or the other of the girls would pick it up. Slirander was still the target. Then there was her interfering friend. They had to be separated somehow. The corridor along which it was catapulted led to outside. All letters and numbers were now inside waging a restoration battle. Outside there was nothing happening. The scene was set for a confrontation. It deliberately darted from its cover and scooted under the front door to the outside.

'There it goes,' said an eagle-eyed Davidia. She ran after it as fast as she could.

'Stupid thing got away,' she lamented, as she couldn't see it.

Suddenly, the door behind her was slammed shut. Slirander

was still inside. A small, windy sound was made near her feet as a minute dust ball fled past, back inside under the door.

'I almost got you,' she said. 'Slirander, it has run back inside.'

'I know,' said Slirander, as she stood face to face with a huge unsightly eyeball. It had expanded to her size and stared directly at her.

'Unfinished business,' it said.

'Perhaps,' she replied.

'You have outsmarted me this time.'

'It wasn't intentional. Language is too important to be destroyed, but you know that.'

'Next time we meet, be prepared for a surprise.'

'Isn't this a surprise? You have never appeared in a real time before. My parents told me of the last time that had occurred.'

'So, you know who I am.'

'It's an educated guess.'

Davidia thumped so loudly on the door, its hinges winced in pain. Rust was a pleasure in relation to the current pounding they were receiving.

Suddenly, a terrible thundering noise lifted the roof off the building. A long, thin, wrinkled tree root came crashing down. Its pointed end pierced the puffed-up eyeball and it exploded into a shower of letters that were heading for permanent destruction.

'We'll meet in a book somewhere,' were the last words the eyeball uttered.

'Slirander, are you alright?' asked Davidia.

'I'm not sure.'

'What happened?'

'Grab the tree root quickly.'

Just as they were about to take a firm grip, 4 came scampering down the corridor to see what the commotion was about. He was so excited. All the letters and numbers were mixing together once again. Mathematics would continue to live. Slirander bent down, grabbed 4 and then they were whisked skywards once again. They saw the land of Mathematica resembling a jumble sale. There would be a lot of sorting out to do.

*

'That's the second time the Moonatric tree has saved us. How does it know we need its help?' asked a curious Davidia. Once again, they were enshrouded in mist floating somewhere in the heavens. 'This isn't good for my vertigo. Isn't that the same cloud we saw last time?'

'They get recycled up here,' smiled Slirander. She gave the huge tree root a hug. Its wrinkles shook.

Number 4 was kept as a souvenir and would be used as a numerical ambassador for good. Davidia wondered about her friend and her relationship with the Moonatric tree. It felt that they knew each other well. She knew that good friends were hard to find and even harder to keep. They were both fortunate to have her as a friend.

'Where are we going now?'

'Somewhere.'

'Can't I go home now? I'm sure I'm already missed. I've never been away from home this long before.'

'We need to rest. Working with all those formulas has confused me somewhat.'

'You were never much good at mathematics. Oh, well, when you need my help, just ask for it. I love puzzles.'

Soon the girls were expelling a series of Zzzs. Maybe they joined them on their journey and didn't want to be part of any formula.

*

Roland the Rotter was packing a compress on his right eye. His Hole in the Hill home was laden with subject matter in line for destruction. He was planning his next attempt. However, he had to recover first. He needed clear vision.

'That damn, stupid tree almost blinded me.'

Nobody knew he existed in a recognisable body form. He was a chameleon. His next effort would take a different tack and a different strategy.

'I've got such a rotten headache. Next time it will be given to someone else,' he vowed.

6 GEOGRAPHY

There wasn't a breath of wind. The clouds floated by waving as they went. There was Cirrus with its friend, Stratus, whilst Cumulus gossiped with Nimbus. The pillow softness of the clouds hid the storm that was hiding behind their dark relations, the angry ones that always turned up uninvited. The swirling air activity and a drop in air temperature would freeze the balls off a brass monkey at ground level; however, in the sky it was the Moonatric tree's wrinkly tree roots that almost suffered frostbite, or was it root rot? Slirander and Davidia were awoken by ice particles playing with their hair and hanging from their noses.

'Where's the heater? It was never this cold at home,' complained Davidia, feeling like an ice sheet at the North Pole.

'It's a small frost,' replied Slirander.

'What's that at your feet?' asked Davidia.

'It's a shrivelled-up tree leaf with a slight pink tinge.'

'That's the Mathematica red leaf. It's disappeared too. It must be it. I can't see it anywhere. Why does each leaf fall off after we climb back into the tree?'

'Apparently, each subject saved, sacrifices its leaf of entry so there can be no other intrusions. It acts as a permanent seal of safety. Rather clever, don't you think? Even Roland the Rotter can't penetrate it anymore.'

'You mean, we have to go through this process time and time again. Boring. Why can't we visit the mall and do something normal?'

'Until we complete our journey, there is no returning home.'

'How long will that take us? I might want to go to school.'

They both laughed.

'It's freezing up here. Where are we heading?'

'Into a bad storm,' said Cumulus, as he floated past.

'I'm not wearing a raincoat and I don't have any wet weather gear. My clothes will become wet and ruined,' whinged Davidia.

'My friend, Nimbus, is facing the fact that it's his relatives flying in to whip up a frenzy of unstable atmosphere.'

'How often do they do that?'

'Every few days. They're a restless lot up here.'

'Brrr, brrr, it's so cold, I can't feel my fingers. I hope they are still there.'

Davidia had a look and, yes, she still had a full set of fives on both hands. Phew! Cumulus continued floating by. It had another destination to explore: storms. Rumble, rumble, a sound like grating chains could be heard. The girls waited.

'Moonah isn't upset that we've awoken him again, is he?' said Davidia, now realising that the key to the tree was the brrr, brrr, sound, but only uttered by her.

'My aching roots are causing me havoc. There isn't one part of me that moves quickly. Even my tree roots are beginning to seize up. You had better move quickly onto another tree leaf, otherwise you'll join the journey of a raindrop.'

'We are climbing higher each time,' said Davidia.

'Clever that you noticed,' replied Moonah.

'This leaf is green. All the other leaves turned green after we left them, and they fell off. Is that what will happen to us on this leaf?'

'You are perfectly safe for the moment. I'm becoming too tired for this youthful enthusiasm. Be careful when you leave.'

'Where to this time?'

Before there was a response, a dark brooding storm cloud flew menacingly around Moonah. It opened its mouth and threatened to expel a mouthful of bad wind and sleet. Instead, it darted like a nervous, flighty insect around Moonah, which caused it to shake violently. That was the cue for escape. The green tree leaf fell apart in the middle and a thin tree filament guided them safely to the ground. Moonah could no longer be seen.

'What is this place?' asked Davidia. 'It's like the lost planet. You know the one that they never found.'

'Maybe we are really lost this time. I haven't been here before,' said Slirander. 'Moonah is probably toying with us.'

'Baa, baa.'

'What's that weird noise?'

'It sounds like a goat or a sheep.'

'Where?'

'It came from over there.'

The girls walked toward the source of the sound. They were indeed in a strange land where the topography was basically stones of all shapes and sizes, which were slippery when walked upon. Davidia touched one. It felt ice cold. There were small hills everywhere they looked. The goat or sheep bleated again. This time it seemed to be nearby.

'It's on the other side of those rocks,' said Davidia. 'Our neighbours used to have one until it escaped and ruined their delightful garden and then nibbled for dessert at the local football oval. The ranger took it away and it ended up on a children's farm.'

'Quiet,' shushed Slirander.

She crept quietly over the cold stones.

'This will ruin my skirt,' she muttered to herself.

She peered between the cracks in the rocks and saw a solitary goat nibbling ferociously at the reluctant tufts of grass, which didn't want to be prized from their homes of soil and end up converted into pebbled droppings. She thought that it was strange that a goat was left to fend for itself alone. Normally, a shepherd tended such valuable animals. They were great consumers of rubbish and recyclers into manure. Slirander knelt carefully, but not carefully enough. Her knee squashed a lone dropping, which had escaped amongst the stones. There wasn't time to clean it off. The goat lifted its head. Its small beard was so long it tickled the ground whilst it stood at full tilt.

'I've been waiting for you,' it said.

Slirander was so shocked that she couldn't speak.

'I get that a lot. I'm expected to have two legs and a below average IQ. Hey, I'm just your ordinary, average goat. Have you got anything better than this low nutritional grass? It plays havoc with my insides. I apologise if I embarrass myself.'

'You can speak.'

'Doesn't everything? Take those stones over there. They're shy. You really must prod them for a conversation. Lately they haven't said anything. The season here is warming up so everything should be cheerful. Go on, say something to them.'

'Hello, my name is Slirander.'

'Now, that's original. What do you expect them to say? My name's Pebbles. Here. Let me try.'

The goat walked over and blurted out his longest and best sounding bleat. The stones remained stonily silent.

'But, that was only an animal noise.'

'So, I'm versatile. What noise can you make?'

Davidia had been watching nearby and casually picked up a heavy stone and rolled it along the ground.

'Don't do that. It's exhausting,' it said, as it clattered into other family members and rested against a small boulder. 'Leave us alone whilst we gather our strength.'

'That's amazing. I thought I heard you speak. It must be the wind whistling in my ears.'

'No, it's not. Most things in the valley can speak, but we are reserving our strength until things improve.'

'What things?'

'Ask that know-all goat. It's the biggest gossip and rumour-monger amongst us. He spreads it like its manure. Thin, not nice and colourless. I'm exhausted.'

The heavy stone shook a little as a chip fell off. *It's disintegrating into dust*, thought Davidia. She ran over to Slirander, who was busily talking to the goat. God, can you believe that!

'Slirander, a stone spoke to me,' blurted an excited Davidia.

The goat turned around and saw that there were two of them.

'Twins,' it said. 'Who's the sound burst?'

'That's my friend, Davidia. Do you have a name?'

The goat pawed the ground as it thought.

'Nope, just goat.'

'Can I call you something?'

'Yes, but not late for our first date.'

'No, I mean a proper name like Billy or something like that.'

'Barry will do. Yes, that's it. I'm a Barry. Do you want to adopt me and take me out of this valley to elsewhere? I'm worth it. How many of your friends have a talking goat?'

'None. Where exactly are we? Why are the stones losing their strength?' asked Slirander.

'It's a secret, but I can tell you. It's rumoured that this is now the valley of Grigook, also once known as the Geography Valley and there's a lot of angry Gs here. They are being misused and shipped out of the valley. I've personally seen them agitated and arguing with each other. Most of them live in a small town through that valley. I'm told it's dangerous to go there. Some think that when you say they have lost two Gs, it could be a money reference, or say GG and it might be their pet horse they are referring to; however, I'm told it's not a happy place. I stay here well out of the way.'

'You seem to be well-informed for a goat, Barry,' said Davidia. 'How is it you have five legs?'

'Do I? It's good that I can't count, otherwise I would have known that too. I can't know everything.'

'Will you take us to the town? What's it called?'

'I never said and would rather not say.'

'It's only a name. You've got one now, so what is it? I might want to Google it when I get home,' said Davidia, being a computer geek extraordinaire.

'You won't tell anyone, will you? It's Gooky.'

Both girls smirked. It was an unusual name, but nothing out of the ordinary. At school there were many names they couldn't pronounce.

'Who lives there?'

'You asked me that before. Give me something original. The closer we get to Gooky, the better nutritional quality the grass is. Try some. It makes a great soup.'

'I'd rather not,' said Slirander.

She thought that this was one upstart goat. Barry had an answer for everything. They dawdled toward Gooky.

'Where's your herder?' asked Davidia, scanning the country-side, hoping for a sighting.

'I don't have one.'

'You haven't eaten it, have you?'

'Not my type. Ugh!'

'So, you live alone then?'

'Mostly. I'm a goat. I go wherever I like. I've been to Gooky before and almost became a meal for those angry Gs. I don't really want to go there. I'll take you to the outskirts and leave you. It's safer for me to be amongst the rocks.'

'Do you read?' asked Davidia.

'Not anymore. I used to visit the local library, but borrowings were banned a few days ago. The council is full of crooks that sit on their backsides and think that they have accomplished something by filling their seats. It's full of dim-witted sheep and not us, sharp-tacked goats. The mayor is new, so no one knows too much about her.'

'A female mayor. That's incredible.'

'She's the only female in town too,' said Barry, feeling piqued. It was a long walk. 'She looks like you two.'

Did her gender throw a whole new light on their quest? Why only one? Suspicion is the fruit of the ignorance tree and was growing quickly inside them. Would Roland the Rotter pretend to be a female?

'Barry, are there any Rotters in town?' asked Slirander, ready to squirt one of her vials.

'Are they some type of biodegradable ingredient? If so, they don't hang around here. Are they a disease, a food, a sauce, a what? Sounds like something I'd enjoy eating. Go on shove it in, I can handle it.'

'Sorry to disappoint you, but we are fresh out. I'll probably find some in Gooky.'

'Whoa there, biped. This is as far as this smart goat goes. Even if I have the nice name of Barry, it's no entrance fee to town. See ya.'

He passed wind as a gesture of goodbye as he cantered back up the hill. His long beard swept the path as he went. He turned around and wondered if they would ever return. Nothing else had except him, as far as he knew, and he was a know-all.

*

The town of Gooky had a signpost stating the population statistics. It read, "They've all gone elsewhere." It was an obvious joke on something's part. The town was situated high in the Alps where the geography of the land was breathtaking. It was the type of landscape to enthral an artist, inspire a sculptor and encourage an appreciation of the great outdoors. The strange feeling it evoked was loneliness of some kind. There were virtually no inhabitants except an errant fly looking for a mate. Animals remained hidden. Were they afraid of words? Did the letter G inspire fear? It was the land of Geography and surely it must be written about and kept in a bookstore somewhere. Were there any of these in town? To explain the wonders of the visual sights the world possessed, it must be recorded somewhere.

'I don't like this place,' said Davidia, with her youthful intuition kicking in.

'It certainly is a curious place,' replied Slirander as they meandered through the streets lined with stone homes.

'This might be a time waster. Perhaps Moonah is probably trying to teach us a lesson. This place is deserted. There doesn't seem to be any language destruction going on here. This place is full of big, fat zip. We need it in writing before it can be destroyed.'

Zzoooomm, zzoooomm, was suddenly heard overhead. The girls ducked for cover. A fleet of tiny winged insects resembling mosquitos flew by. Their stomachs sagged beneath their tiny bodies. They could only travel at slow speed.

'I'm resting,' said a struggling mossie. 'My stomach is stretching something chronic. After this final trip, I won't be able to remove the stretch marks. I'll be laughed at.'

The rest of the group struggled into the distance. They looked like flying bubbles.

'Where are they going?' asked Davidia.

She had her hand in a squashing position in case a defence against an inquisitive proboscis was needed. The mossie had landed on her arm.

'I'm too exhausted. Besides, I don't bite. I'm only a messenger. Let me rest a while to gather my strength.'

'Where are they going?' she asked again.

The tiny mossie hadn't realised the size of what it had landed on and almost spilt its contents in surprise at Davidia's size.

'They are making a delivery,' it replied. 'This is my last trip. My stomach can't handle another full load.'

'What are you carrying that requires you to endure so much pain and discomfort? It must be important.'

'I have no idea. I fill up from a large, standing, liquid resource and off I fly to wherever I'm directed.'

'And where might that be, in case we visit?'

'Libraries and schools. No one knows it's happening,' it sniggered. 'I spray my liquid onto the books and leave. That's it. I feel cheeky doing what I enjoy naturally, but in larger quantities.'

'You mean you fly to other towns and villages, spray and return. Do you know what your load does?'

'I saw the mayor write in her diary, under the heading of Destrusto Virus, a list of name places and how many visitors it sent there. I have no idea what my load does. I'm just relieved to be rid of it.'

'Can you cheat on your delivery this time by dropping your bundle right here?' asked Davidia. 'Then you wouldn't suffer the stretch marks or be laughed at. If not, I'll squash you.'

The threat worked. The mossie dropped its bundle and flew away.

'That's the last time I do hazardous work.'

The fate of that mossie had been determined. It would never make it home.

Slirander studied the minute particles left behind. They writhed in agony exposed to the elements.

'There is a dv insignia on each one. They have been infected with the Destrusto Virus. No one would suspect such a small insect to deliver a powerful destroyer of language.'

'How can you read that? I can hardly see it at all,' said Davidia, using her best squinting technique.

'I just can. When I learnt to read, it was in small letters. That helps.'

Davidia accepted the response quietly. She drew out her spray and gave them a squirt. Those few particles became harmless.

'I wonder if there are still ponds where those insects breed. Using them as carriers is a very clever idea. They must live somewhere around here. Do you think there are any Rotters here?' asked Davidia.

'Possibly. Disguised, it's all about disguise.'

'The skies, it's all about the skies,' repeated a voice.

They hadn't stepped into a field of bright light bulbs, had they? The girls turned around and there sitting on a stone fence was a large letter G. It motioned to them.

'I'm a goat herder.'

'But you are only one letter,' said Davidia.

'And a large one at that.'

'Are you part of a word or have you always existed by yourself?'

'The last time I remember being part of a word was last week when I was joined by a small o, a and t. They have somehow disappeared from me and I'm all that is left.'

'There doesn't seem to be any goats near here.'

'I used to look after a know-all goat. Have you seen it? It drives you crazy with its incessant chatter. When I was a full word, I could handle it. Now, I have to survive alone.'

'Why did you lose your o a t?'

'I haven't recently felt well. They vanished overnight. I saw a few insects lying around with extended stomachs. They looked exhausted so I squashed them. I never saw o a t after that.'

'Davidia, it has probably survived so far because of its size,' said Slirander. 'Excuse me G, but do you want to feel better?'

'I doubt that I could.'

'Have any books ever been written about goat herders?'

'There used to be a library full of them in Gooky, but all books have been removed from there and stored in the council chambers for safekeeping. Those dim-witted sheep councillors want to read them all for themselves. None of us can borrow them anymore. Everything here loves to read. There were splendid books on the geography of the country. Now all we see is a closed door with a battered sign saying, *Gone Reading*. It doesn't make any sense.'

'Where are the council chambers? We want to pay our respects to the councillors,' said Slirander, thinking of the strangeness of the disappearance of the books.

Either the councillors want to be well-educated, or was there a more sinister meaning?

*

The dim-witted sheep sat around the circular council chambers table ready for their instructions from the mayor. None of them were bright enough to raise an original thought of their own, so the mayor thought for them. Their fine woollen coats were brushed to perfection. Being in a privileged position allowed them to treat anyone or anything that wasn't a councillor, with disrespect. They had developed from the grass-eating dopes into a well-read and educated seated force through the fate of meeting the mayor. The only real decision that they ever made was where they would sit at each daily meeting. The mayor had gathered around her a loyal force of dopey bidders who would blindly follow any suggestion. After all, regardless of their dressing or position, they were only sheep.

The Geography Valley had once been a scene of beauty; however, under the mayor's reign, it had lost its lustre and appeal. The beauty that was once transferred into the written word now faced a danger greater than the destruction over time of the landscape. The language of geography was at risk. The mayor had hoped that by producing this task hidden well away from the world, no one would ever know from whence the destruction would emanate. It could all be done anonymously.

It was the Moonatric tree that knew where the evil lived and performed. Slirander and Davidia were the warriors of language restoration and in good hands. One day the answer to the "how" would be answered.

'What's on the agenda today?' asked flock member number one, very sheepishly.

'It's on the table in front of you,' replied the mayor.

'Is there anything different from yesterday?'

'No, it's identical.'

'Will we understand it today as well as yesterday?'

'As nothing has changed, I would hope so.'

'Chairman, read out the minutes of yesterday's meeting, please.'

The chairman stood on its hindquarters. It recently had special wool treatment with a coat cut in rings. It was so proud of the different ringed cut that an extra baa was used to open the meeting:

'We met at 9am.

Discussed morning tea.

The goodwill virus would be dispatched.

Meeting closed 11am.

Are there any discussions or points overlooked?'

A table of nodding heads responded in the affirmative.

'Unanimous.'

The mayor addressed the meeting.

'Today is the final delivery of the "goodwill" virus. I personally thank you for your support. We'll meet at the end of the day to receive your bonus. See you then.'

'Mayor,' said flock member one, sheepishly, 'what does the goodwill virus do?'

The mayor turned sauce red in anger; however, no odd angry eye popped out. She also knew the IQ set she had as councillors behaved like trained monkeys. They would accept any explanation.

'The goodwill virus is a message of hope that more sheep become council members in the valley and that one day you will be in full control. The name of the valley can then be changed from the Geography Valley to Baa Baa Valley. The importance of your name will then famously grow.'

A series of excited 'baa baas' echoed through the council chambers.

'They are dumber than I thought,' said the mayor.

It was no wonder her time in the valley was so easy to foster stupidity and ignorance.

'The final batch of the goodwill virus will be mixed later this afternoon. Once my, I mean our final, messengers have been dispatched, a celebratory feast should be held. Who likes goat?'

'We all do. It's a change from being in a lamb stew to a goat's stew. Where can we find a goat? Most animals have left this valley for better valley management elsewhere.'

'I've heard there is a know-all goat. Any ideas where it might be?'

'You mean Barry? We can't eat him. He's one of our friends

until council altered the borrowing of books, which you insisted upon, mayor. Couldn't we find a different goat? There must be some other reward you can think of. He might be a big mouth, but he's harmless.'

The mayor threw her arms up in frustration at the dim-witted councillors.

'Now that you mention it, I will personally chef for you this evening as a token of your assistance in preparing the goodwill virus.'

The mayor smiled and when she did, a hint of dribble moistened her lips. That was a cue for concern, but no one noticed.

The councillors were chuffed at actually achieving something, even if they didn't really know what it was. To be knowledgeable and ignorant at the same time was a feat very few achieved.

'Mayor, can you give us a hint about your special meal?'

'It will be Rotnest Pie. It will be one of my better efforts, if I may be allowed to say so. The ingredients are nearby.'

Little did the councillors know that it would be one of their number that would be within that delicious pastry.

'Would the recipe be in one of the many books we have stored in council chambers?'

'It's my mum's home-made recipe. I doubt if it has been recorded anywhere.'

The councillors thought that would be a terrific end to their day. Rotnest pie and a dish of clean water. What a treat! However, there was one curious flock member who was a thinking sheep. That was also an oddity. It had a penchant for the truth and decided to investigate the recipe for Rotnest Pie. That, needless to say, was its impending downfall.

*

'There doesn't seem to be any life in the village except for a few struggling Gs,' said Slirander.

They walked by a few capital letters and a few smaller ones, which were so small they must have come from a book written in small font. The larger capital Gs wandered aimlessly as if they no longer had any word association. Letters need friends to make words and sentences. Alone, they are only a lonely, singular letter of the alphabet. Language is all about teamwork.

Davidia walked over to a sagging letter G and wondered why it was still here, when the know-all goat said many had been shipped out of the village.

'Excuse me, Mr G, do you need any help?' asked Davidia, seeing that the letter was drooping badly. It faced her and didn't recognise her because she wasn't a regular letter. Davidia quickly continued, 'I'm the letter D.'

The G tried to straighten up, but had too much sag.

'I need some friendly letters so I can be useful again.'

'What's happening? Where have all the Gs gone?'

'Sadly, to another valley and elsewhere.'

'Why are you still here?'

'I feel my use is fading. I was once in an adventure book. I was the lead letter to commence the story. It has only been since the dim-witted sheep and the new mayor confiscated all books in the area that I have begun to fade. I doubt if I'll be read again. I'm not well enough to travel anywhere.'

'How did it happen?'

The letter G took a deep breath, sat on the stone fence and began its tale of destruction.

'The library housed me and many other literary works. I was in the adventure section. One afternoon, a group of those woolly-coated sheep entered and 'baa'd' their instructions. The librarians, which were all lettered friends, were invited to a luncheon. Not one returned. Soon after, the sheep returned and collected all the books and transferred them to the council chambers. I was fortunate enough to be dropped, as were several other books, and escaped the transition, to be read by the woolly dopes.

My whole word escaped with me. I read as "Great". No well-read letter had any respect for the sheep councillors. Since then, the rumours that abound spread mainly by that know-all goat happen to be true. My friends that were once read are being destroyed. There have been many incidences in the book round-up of angry words using their self-expression at having to perform for the sheep. There is an intruder in our midst. I don't know who or what, but I've heard the pain of them losing their expression and written word. Something is destroying the world of Gs and the description of our beautiful geography. I'm just a letter of my formal self. My former letters, r, e, a and t, were wiped out by some mosquitos who released on them. I survived, but it's also too late for me.'

'Are there any whispers about Rotters?' asked Slirander, who began to believe the know-all goat's ramblings.

'I don't know the expression,' it replied. 'I'm exhausted.'

The letter G slumped onto the footpath and faded away.

Maybe that tired mozzie knew the truth after all about what was destroying the world of geography. Then there was the question of the mayor's diary. Did it hold the secret that they were looking for? Maybe if that diary was found, then the antidote soldiers would know where to go to correct the language injustices. Those DV messengers needed a lesson in good manners. The girls checked that their vials were still safely hidden. Now, where are the council chambers?

The girls continued their walk through Gooky seeking them out. The few letters that still existed ignored them. Help today was only a four-lettered word without its real meaning. It was difficult to tell what any of the buildings really were. They all looked the same. Refuge for aching limbs was sought by sitting on a low-built wall. It felt that they were lost in the middle of a town but weren't lost at all. Patience was a virtue and not a hospital participant. Remarkably, the wall made a muffled sound. It vibrated along Davidia's left leg.

'Did you feel that?' she said to Slirander, who was as sensitive as she was.

'Funny you should say that. I felt it too. What was it?'

Davidia stood up.

'Nothing that heavy has ever sat on me before,' said a crevice in the wall.

'What are you suggesting?' asked an indignant Davidia.

She was average weight for her height and was well within the proper weight table range for her age and height. At school they were often weighed as part of the sports health program; however, in Gooky, the inhabitants were all lighter and never read or rested on the wall. It was an extraordinary experience for it.

'I'm not a seat nor a public bum placement. I protest that you should sit elsewhere. Besides, what are you?' said the crevice.

'We're girls and friends of Barry the goat,' replied Davidia, using dialogue including the know-all goat. Everything seemed to have a kind word for Barry.

'Oh! Where is Barry?'

'He's hiding in the hills thinking he's in a cowboy novel,' replied Davidia.

'He was always a little off the beaten hoof. Why did you sit on me?'

'To rest. We can't find the council chambers. Do they exist? We've looked everywhere.'

'Well, you didn't look hard enough. You are directly above them.'

'Where's the entrance? Should we knock and ask to borrow a book? How do we get in?'

'Around the corner is a small alcove. It leads down an alley to a large wooden door. Bang on it three times with both fists and see what happens. Most things here are underground, so that the geography of this beautiful place remains intact. This might be the land of Geography, but no one reads about it anymore.'

'Why is that? The world should be told about such a beautiful place.'

'Reading has been banned. Barry was here the other day enjoying a shoulder rub and he told me. It confirms the rumours that the Gs have heard also. Now most of them are gone. I must remain. Walls with special crevices aren't easily transportable.'

'Thanks.'

The girls did as directed. There weren't any suspicious letters hiding in the alley to frighten them. A large wooden door, shaped with two Gs facing each other, stood like a sentinel with a battered sign above it, which read, *Gone Reading.*

'It's rather a stupid sign for a council chamber. If they have all the written books, then inside is where the reading should happen, not elsewhere,' said Davidia.

'I wonder what will open the door. A woolly jumper or tomorrow night's meal?' said Slirander, remembering that she had never eaten lamb, but had heard it was a good meal.

Slirander banged loudly on the door three times with both clenched fists. The sound resonated throughout the chambers. The sheep were seated at the huge council chamber pretending to read. It filled in their time.

'I've noticed recently,' said a genteel senior sheep, 'that each book I read has many missing letters. Is that what makes it easier to read?'

'This one I'm perusing hasn't any letters at all. I can read a lot more books now and at a faster rate. It must be a good book and I'm none the wiser what it's about when I have finished it.'

'I'm not sure what book this is,' said a third, 'it doesn't have any name on it.'

'Where are all the written words? The Gs must have taken them when we got rid of them. The mayor insisted that had to be the case.'

The sheep aimlessly hooved their way through the books. None had a good retention level, so by the time they had read a proper book, its contents were forgotten.

'What's that awful noise?'

'It's the front door. The secret signal has been given. It must be a fellow sheep. Go, open it.'

A pleasant member of the flock, called Curly, slowly opened the door. It creaked noisily. One look at Davidia and Slirander shocked it.

'The mayor has two children!' Curly loudly exclaimed. No explanations were asked as they were ushered in. 'Her graciousness isn't here to receive you. She's a cunning, old fart keeping you two a secret. Which one of you is a boy, or are you both boys? She often rattles on about her boys at home, so it must be you two. What a delight. Two miniature mayors. Come in. Council is seated, but not sitting. We've had our daily meeting already and the seat exchanges for the day are about to occur. We'll fit you in anyway. Today will be more interesting than yesterday.'

Curly gave the signal of three 'Baas'. The council all responded with two. All clear. Suddenly, all eyes focused on the entrance doorway. Cautiously, the girls walked in. A choreographed gasp filled the chamber. No one choked on a vowel or syllable. Confusion swept through them.

'They shouldn't be in here. This is private. What are they and, more importantly, what will the mayor say?'

'These are her two boys,' announced Curly, proudly.

'That one definitely has her sneer and the other's eyes are a perfect match.'

The girls remained silent, surveying their surrounds. Finally, Slirander stepped up to the speech plate.

'What is this beautiful place, so full of important looking dimwits?'

The sheep didn't understand what a dimwit was, but because the mayor's children had said it, thought it must be an acceptably nice word. The schmoozing language of Slirander had them figuratively eating out of her hand. A proud sheep, who had recently been promoted from paddock feeder to lazy councillor, came forward and offered a welcoming hoof. Slirander returned the friendly gesture with a short squeeze. Davidia couldn't believe it, a council of sheep instead of a flock. It took some imagination to accept it.

'May I offer you a seat?' said the proud sheep.

'Thank you,' replied Slirander, as she eyed the huge piles of books loosely stacked as if she was at a Lego convention.

'May I ask the purpose of your visit?'

'We couldn't find anything to read and heard that this was the only place in town where all the precious books are stored. You seem to have so many.'

'We do. We aren't sure why they are all here. The mayor organised the transfers and promised us all a council position if we helped. Look at the success it has been.'

'May I read one?' asked Davidia.

'You read?'

'Yes, doesn't everything?'

The sheep stifled small 'Baas' as wind escaped up their oesophagi.

'Quite, quite. This way.'

The girls sat at the huge table and opened a book. It tingled with trepidation. The Destrusto Virus was working its way through its pages and Slirander had discovered an active cell. What pot luck! Instinctively, Slirander felt for a vial.

'Does anyone want a beauty treatment? I have a special wool straightener spray that once sprayed on your fine wool; it lengthens it.'

'No one has cared to offer us that before. I'm in.'

'You must stand holding this book. It accentuates your intelligence.'

A sheep gladly complied. Slirander gave a short, sharp burst. The spray went mostly over the book, but no one noticed in the excitement of a beauty treatment.

'By tomorrow morning you will have the straightest, softest and most comfortable wool of any sheep. You may yet set a fashion trend.'

The sheep were enthralled. They returned to their seats and continued reading the blank-paged books. Knowledge doesn't have to be displayed to possess it. Unfortunately, all the sheep possessed was a seat and a woollen covering.

'Where is the mayor?' asked Davidia, wondering what a female mayor looked like. 'I'd like to see mummy again. It has been a while.'

'She's in the public swimming pool next door.'

'Is she swimming? I haven't seen her swim before. Can we see her?'

'It's forbidden to enter. We have strict instructions never to interrupt her whilst she's in there. Once she got so upset, a lost sheep, one of the paddock fraternity, wandered in and was never heard of again; however, that night we had the most delicious mince meal with a range of sauces. We haven't had a treat like that since. You might want to stay tonight for her special meal;

her mother's recipe. I shouldn't say this, but we think it has got something to do with a goat.'

'Not Barry?'

'How do you know? Are you planning the meal together?'

'No, it's only a rumour.'

'That's Barry. All he does is spread rumours.'

'Please, can we see mummy?' begged Davidia.

As far as actresses go, an Academy award was in the offing.

'If you upset her too much, she gets an eye affliction.'

Slirander sensed that she knew what that might be.

'Is it an odd angry eye, one full of blue and red veins?'

'How do you know that?'

'I read it in a medical journal. I'm studying to be a nurse.'

'Be warned if you see it.'

'Where can we gain entrance?'

'It's forbidden.'

'We'd love to surprise her. Imagine what she'll say when she sees us. Please, please. I'm sure our mummy would want to see us if she could,' said Davidia, oozing girlish charm.

Unfortunately, it couldn't see its mummy because a butcher's picnic had brought that association to an end. The sheep's heart-strings had been seriously tugged. A lonely tear slipped out unnoticed and was quickly absorbed by its wool.

'But you didn't hear it from me.'

The sheep explained that the entrance to the pool was heavily guarded, by what it didn't say. The fear it expressed at the mere mention of guards had its hooves trembling. A few involuntary pellets plopped onto the floor. A special verbal password was required. No one knew what it was. There wasn't any council member bright enough to think of what it might be. A secret tunnel led from the council chambers to the pool. Along the way, the tunnel was full of moaning letters. There weren't sufficiently good quality letters to construct a word, let alone a full sentence. The helpful sheep stopped at the entrance.

'It's too risky for me.'

'Who are all the letters?' asked Davidia, as she dodged another G toppling over.

The secret tunnel was littered with injured, damaged and fading letters. Something had attacked them, and it wasn't a disparaging remark.

'They could be the missing Gs from all the Goat Herder and Geography books. Perhaps they thought this was an escape tunnel from the less than intellectually talented sheep. Maybe they wanted to be read by a better standard of reader,' replied Slirander. 'Keep alert. This place feels dangerous. There's a bad word in here.'

The further they walked along the tunnel, the denser the littered letters became. It was almost impossible not to walk over them. Agony was etched in their shapes.

'They should all be arranged in books for everyone to enjoy,' said Davidia, treading lightly and carefully. 'I've a good mind to sink my foot up the mayor's seating crevice when I meet her. This waste of good literature makes me angry.'

'Shush,' said Slirander, quietly motioning with her hand that there was something up ahead. She began to scratch her odd ear.

'You haven't got an insect infestation, have you?' asked Davidia.

'My inner ear is ringing a warning and I need my small finger to pull it out.' A small plopping sound was made. 'Got you!'

'Ugh! I don't have wax that bad.'

The small, oozy lump was held firmly in Slirander's fingers. She began to roll it back and forth until it congealed into a small ball. Her face was transfixed. What was it that she saw? Up ahead loomed a doorway which had no door. Shadows moved silently across it, but there was nothing there that made a shadow.

'What is it?' asked Davidia.

'Shaddersy.'

'Pardon?'

'Shaddersy. They are a secret group of dead letters that return when a book passes into extinction. They perform the final destruction by entering the pages and cleaning up any leftover letters. They are the language garbage cleaners, rarely employed because of their instability. Only a person of infinite strength and influence can summon those nasty demons. I have only met them once before.'

'You know of those nasties? How do we get past them?'

'By engaging in dialogue. They have a limited word vocabulary. If you guess a word that they are programmed with, you can pass unharmed. If you make a mistake and don't guess one of their words within ten words, there is no returning to any reading material, and we will be stuck in the land of Geography forever. I think we'd tire of the Goat Herder books very quickly.'

'I don't like the odds. Does that mean the *ickle wockle* phrase is useless here?'

'I'm afraid so.'

'What is the wax ball for?'

'A surprise.'

Slirander was one strange girl. There seemed to be lots of unexplained stuff around her. Wax ball, odd ear, special knowledge. Maybe it all came from that small dictionary they carried. Davidia took it out, opened it with her special tanned hands signature, and avidly read for a minute or two. That's strange. She read it all so fast. She secured it safely and waited for whatever was to happen.

Slirander moved forward toward the door. A grey, dark shadow loomed over her.

'Tell us the password,' a sinister shadow whispered.

The tunnel lighting alternated between various shades of grey. The cool atmosphere chilled any happy thoughts.

'Why do you want to know? Maybe we can teach you a few extra words and release you from the shadows.'

A low, groaning laugh trickled along the tunnel. Soon all the struggling letters repeated the sound. They followed exactly like the sheep did.

'They are doomed.'

The shadows increased their frenetic activity at their impending victory.

Slirander guessed right at the eighth word. Not a match amongst them. She had kept two in reserve. Davidia was anxious to see what Slirander was talking to. In her haste for a closer look, she knocked the wax ball from her grasp. As she did so, Slirander called her an idiot. Word nine had gone to the cleaners, or had it? A stifling 'Agh! agh! agh!' joined the cacophony of sounds. The wax ball on the ground began to enlarge.

'That wax ball is swallowing the shadows,' yelled Davidia. 'That was the password, idiot. It's in keeping with the sheep and this whole place.'

A moment later, entrance was allowed. Both girls were amazed that they had achieved the impossible. Nothing had ever before been able to defeat the Shaddersy.

Slirander picked up the wax ball and held it tightly. What for is anybody's guess? Davidia didn't think she would eat it or put it back in her ear. Her friend certainly had some odd mannerisms. She was just glad to be on her side.

They crept carefully into the pool area and hugged the walled perimeter, checking that there weren't any traps set for them. Would the mayor know that they had defeated the Shaddersy, or would she feel so empowered by their success that nothing could pass, and worry was a needless waste of her head space?

'The pool is empty,' said Davidia. 'Our pool at home was always full, even though we used it occasionally. It can be a breeding ground for mosquitos if not used. There isn't any water here, so where did all those bubble mosquito characters emanate from?'

The two-word sleuths tried to find any hidden letters; books that had been discarded or used as experiments or literature of any kind. There was nothing. Disappointed, they sat in a corner in the dark, taking a five-minute breather. It wasn't long before a squeaky, continuous, droning sound was heard. At the far end of the pool was a small sauna room full of hot air and moisture. An open vent in the roof was the exit for the mosquitos to escape and travel with their destructive liquids. Each one struggled with its load. Their stomachs sagged almost at bursting point. The girls watched as they rested at the pool edge. Slirander tilted her good ear toward the resting mosquitos and placed it on the ground. Verbal vibrations were picked up. She could hear them speak.

'This is ridiculous. I'm no pig, but to suck up this much liquid in one sucking is overkill. I'm exhausted and I've flown nowhere,' said an enlarged mosquito.

'This is our final trip,' said another.

'My body has never been in this bad shape before. I hope my relatives don't take any photos. I'd be laughed at as a mozzie Santa.'

'Why is it so important to overfill? Surely, we can't all make our destinations.'

'What were you promised if you made it safely?'

'Fresh, uncontaminated blood. There's a goat that lives in the hills nearby and it has a full supply to last a lifetime.'

'You mean, Barry? We all know he's there, but it's difficult to pin him down for a feed. Good luck with him. He'd talk us to death before we could bite him.'

'Will all our families make it?'

'It's important to spread goodwill everywhere.'

'Did you taste the mayor this time? She's awful. Some ingredient has been improperly mixed. I might be ill.'

'Blurck, blurck.'

A few of the mozzies involuntarily unloaded. They watched their load slither down the side of the pool.

'That feels better. I'm going home,' said one of them.

Before the mozzie could take flight, an excruciating pain wracked its body. A minute odd angry eye popped out of its head and burst. It was all over, Red Rover. It couldn't live a life of dodging squashing hands and annoying animals. It too had gone the way of literature: extinction. The other mosquitoes became worried. Oh, no! That will be us. Many a tear was shed as they sat at the pool edge. Fate had dealt them that fatal blow. A few more 'blurcks' and the mood was one of disillusionment. They were doomed.

'We have to move quickly before they are airborne,' said Slirander.

She took out a vial and sprayed the wax ball with an extra strong burst.

The leader of the soldiers of the Pebble of Purpose woke up from a deep sleep.

'Lads, all leave is cancelled. Get rid of those televisions. Exercise, exercise. I want to see muscles and that restoration attitude. Give me five. Get your flying gear on. Whoo, hoo. We'll be travelling tonight. Don't let go, whatever you do. Remember, a word saved is a word read. It's all about education and knowledge. Ready, Slirander. We are armed and dangerous. Set us loose. The Pebble would be proud of us. This wax ball is a great disguise. Toss us.'

The small enthusiastic soldier workforce enjoyed the combat.

'What are you going to do?' asked Davidia, wondering what was happening.

'Toss this wax ball to the end of the pool where those mosquitos are resting. If they see us they would take flight immediately, but a food parcel of such nutrition is extremely attractive. Watch.'

Slirander used a baseball pitch. The wax ball flew silently through the air, landing in their midst. None of the mosquitos stirred. Suddenly, a wise, old mozzie ditched his load and flew to nibble on the wax ball. With each bite, he took on the soldiers in teams. The wax ball with the antidote prohibited each mosquito succumbing to the odd angry eye. It saved them. Once settled on their host, the soldiers would then train it without the Destrusto Virus load and use them as a flying team to transport them to the last destination that they had visited. The mosquito fleet became a formidable homing force. It wasn't long before most of the mosquitos had ditched their loads in favour of a nutritional treat. The peculiar thing was that the wax ball never got any smaller, regardless of how many bites it received. It was just another oddity.

'There are thousands of them. Do we have enough antidote to cover them all?'

'Never underestimate a good squirt. The Pebble of Purpose has his army well trained so they never run out.'

'You certainly have some odd friends.'

'We can leave the wax ball and mosquitos to it. We must locate the mayor. That sauna may be the source of where the mosquitos are picking up their quotas.'

They moved silently toward the sauna where a large closed door barred entrance. It was never locked, only shut. The sauna would be highly unsuitable for the sheep; however, the small viewing window allowed a glimpse of what was happening inside. The fog-misted window hid a diabolical event that surprised both the girls. The mayor was standing naked with a modest lap-covering strategically attached to avoid any form of embarrassment. Her arms were raised as she stood like a four-pointed star. Her body was covered with thousands of mosquitos all sucking for their dear lives. None of them could withdraw their probosci until she released it. This was the last phase in the Destrusto Virus campaign in the land of Geography. She wanted to ensure that the virus was used to destroy all the letters in the land. Thousands of red welts bubbled like hives all over of her body. It wasn't painful, but it did look ghastly, like a very bad dose of the worst acne. The Destrusto Virus had an inbuilt numbing effect when infected into a human carrier. The mayor had her eyes shut. A dribble of delight trickled from her mouth. It seemed she was enjoying the experience. Nearby on a seat, lay a diary, the important diary.

Was the mayor a willing participant, or had Roland the Rotter infected her in some manner to endure the situation? They would never know.

'She's being eaten alive, by the look of it,' said Davidia, who was decidedly quiet.

'It's only for show. Real Rotters are clever and devious. She might be one of the specials. There are a few selected ones who are earmarked for an important task and carry it out willingly, regardless of the consequences. We must get that diary.'

'The door's open.'

'So is the mayor. She senses our presence, but only me. You must get the diary, Davidia, when I tell you to. The mayor must be drawn out of the sauna. I will spray the antidote on me first and then gain her confidence that I am no threat.'

Slirander took off her clothes down to her underwear. She knocked on the door and stood back three metres in full view. Suddenly, the droning stopped. The mayor opened her eyes.

'Who dares to interrupt my pleasure? What's that smell? Mmm, fresh, uncontaminated blood. I could do with a refill. Where is it? Come on, boys, we have a visitor.'

The mayor slowly opened the door. Her two odd angry eyes

hadn't yet exposed themselves. They were on the verge of exploding until she saw a fresh feed. It was exactly the type "her boys" would enjoy. The danger subsided. She eyed Slirander for any information and felt some sort of empathy with her. How was that possible? She moved closer. The door was open. This was the signal for Davidia to perform a magician's trick of sight unseen. She was lightning on legs; in and out of the sauna before a question could be asked or before a horde of bloodsucking mosquitos pounced on her. She thought, *How easy was that?* The mayor wasn't focused on Davidia. Her sights had been set higher.

'How did you get in here? Nothing passes the Shaddersy. You must be highly intelligent to pass them. Knock off the sucking, boys. We have a visitor. What do you say we test her out?'

A unanimous drone hit the airwaves. Slirander didn't want to be eaten alive. She had no choice. A few mosquitos flew over and landed on her arms. The soldiers of the Pebble of Purpose were in swarm proportions. They had erected a defensive shield against incoming bites.

'If you take one bite, I'll snap off your proboscis,' yelled the leader.

The mosquitos stopped dead in their tracks. They couldn't afford to lose their food snout, so they retreated.

'We prefer you, mayor.'

'I thought as much.'

Davidia had the diary tucked under her jacket and signalled to Slirander that it was time to go. Slirander backed away from the mayor and ran to the far end of the pool.

'It can't go far,' said the mayor. 'Finish me first and then we'll finish her. There's not much more to go. I feel drained.' Once again the dribble pooled on the ground. 'I'm getting a headache.'

*

Slirander hurriedly dressed. *Where is Davidia? Had she been left behind?* A throng of mosquitos had her cornered. They incessantly dive-buzzed her with the threat of a probe. There were too many to swat. This lot were waiting their turn to suck the mayor. *The vial, the vial.* Finally, Davidia found one.

'Come near me and I'll spray you,' she said.

The mosquitos laughed. A small perfume spray held no fear for them.

'I warned you.'

She gave it a squirt.

'Whoa there, Jezebel. We usually land on something. We don't fly aimlessly in the air to catch the perpetrator's wings. You have noticed that we don't have wings,' complained another leader.

'Stop whinging and develop some.'

'Lads,' yelled the leader, 'use your gliding techniques. Open those arms, breathe in and pass wind for extra propulsion. That should work. Watch out, lads, we have a winged force to train.'

The soldiers landed on the mosquitos and attached themselves to their backs.

'Listen here, you proboscis-probing infection. Unless you fly us to your last destination, two things will happen to you. One, your proboscis will be a short straw and two, a one-winged mosquito can only fly painfully in a circle. What's it to be?'

The choice was made for them.

'Let's fly.'

The language restoration program was now in full flight. The mayor was unaware her efforts were being thwarted as the mosquitos that had left the sauna headed straight for the pool and deliciously discovered the wax ball treat. Life would be far better than a life-ending, exploding odd angry eye.

Davidia saw her opportunity to escape. She ran down the pool to join Slirander.

'We've got to get out of here. The antidote has been set free on the back of the mosquitos. The language letters should soon be healthy again,' said Davidia. 'That mayor is trouble, I feel it.'

'There's one last task. I must retrieve the wax ball.'

'Ugh! You're joking. Who'd want to handle that? Even when I cleaned my ears out, I got rid of it as waste.'

'It has an important role in dealing with Rotters.'

Slirander ran down the pool again, picked up the wax ball and brushed off any hanger-on mozzies. A glutinous little nasty had his proboscis stuck too deep and it snapped because he refused to withdraw. From that day on, it muffled every spoken word.

'Got it!'

The girls retraced their steps along the alleyway and noticed that some of the letters waved to them.

'They're looking better,' said Davidia, as she high-fived a capital G.

Back in the council chamber, the sheep were reading their books, this time with interest.

'It's the strangest thing. Earlier on, this book had no letters and look, now they're multiplying like rabbits. They're cousins of ours. I didn't think I'd enjoy reading this much,' said a flocked councillor. 'Stay and join us for tonight's special meal.'

'I don't think there will be one. Thank you for your courtesy.'

'Geography and Goat Herding are really interesting.'

'Bye.'

The girls finally emerged into the fresh air and headed back toward the hills.

'I knew you were hiding from me. You just couldn't stay away,' said a delighted Barry, meeting his two friends again. 'What have you brought me? A book? I love presents and surprises. Go on, give me a treat,' he encouraged.

'We don't have anything for you except the books in the council chambers are being read once more. I bet real soon you could borrow them again,' explained Davidia, who often read before she went to sleep at night.

'You're kidding me. Pull my other leg.'

Davidia was about to when she noticed that this Barry had only four legs, whereas the real Barry had five. She whispered that Barry's fifth leg handicap had disappeared. Slirander froze. She felt in her pocket and relaxed. She had just the treat for Barry.

'Have you had any visitors up here whilst we've been gone? Anyone or anything strange?'

'Nothing. I've heard a rumour that the letters are getting better and returning in droves to the books that they were deleted from. Is it true? You've escaped from Gooky, which is a triumph. Nothing has ever left there alive before. What's your special skill?'

Barry's loose-lipped demeanour was fading just like the letters were. Slirander was cautious. Had the real Barry become that special menu item the mayor was to cook that night?

'I've got a nutritional treat that was made fresh today. It's a honey ball. See if you can catch it?' said Slirander.

'I love games. Toss it to me, toss it to me.'

Slirander threw the wax ball high into the air. Barry ran around like an excited child.

'Got it!'

Barry swallowed it whole.

'Is there more, is there more?' he yelled, running crazily around in a circle. 'I'm getting a headache again. The next time I get one, someone else has to wear it.'

That comment reminded them of the Mathematic leaf. Could it be possible? Barry gradually stopped his antics and panted heavily. His body began to convulse at the rejection of the wax ball. First the stomach became extended, then the legs enlarged; all four of them. His tail stood perpendicular straight and his face stretched so badly it was unrecognisable as Barry and looked more like the mayor. It was the awful eyes that revealed the truth behind all the contortions and grotesque formations within Barry's body. Two evil odd angry eyes rolled around in agony. They puffed up like two puffballs. Red and blue veins created the impression of an eye road map.

'You two are responsible for this,' Barry wailed. 'I will win.'

Bang, bang. The explosion was similar in colour to a rainbow paint gun. It was horrible. The two odd angry eyes shed their mess over the landscape. It was too late to stop the antidote. The girls had thought that the mayor had taken over Barry's body.

Suddenly, a whimpering bleat was heard. It was Barry. He was alive but feeling upset at having been badly impersonated. Anyone could see he had five legs. The girls ran to him and gave him a hug.

'Stop with the fussing. Haven't you seen a goat cry before? Who has been messing with my persona? I'm unique. Brush me, I gotta look good.'

'We are so pleased to see you safe. That was the mayor who we thought was you.'

'You gotta get glasses. Where to now? I'm going to miss you two.'

He pawed the ground with two hooves as an indication of his emotional shyness.

'Barry, we have to leave now. It feels that it's the right time. This land will be free of Rotters for a long time.'

'Good rottence, I say.'

'How do we leave the valley?'

'It's that way,' said Barry, raising a hoof for direction. 'It's that way,' he said sadly. 'It's that way,' he mumbled, as he saw the girls disappear over the horizon. He thought that the sun never shone as brightly as those two girls.

'We could walk for hours and never get out of here. Say something that will allow us to leave, a clever word, witty phrase or a stupid saying. Moonah said we'd know what to say,' said Davidia, who had tired of the trekking experience.

'That could mean anything. This journey-restoring language is quite confusing,' replied Slirander, who itched an aching ear.

'Watch out!' yelled Davidia. It was too late.

A huge tree came crashing down in front of them. The girls tripped over it and skinned their knees on its wrinkled roots. It's wrinkled what? A wrinkled tree root split open for a moment and they fell inside it. Unbelievable. Moonah is here too. How did that happen?

'Slirander, it's your friend, and now my friend, Moonah, that fetched us. You have a guardian tree.'

Slirander was too tired to notice.

'It's never far away from us, Davidia. It's a great feeling to be "home".'

She was soon in the land of nod, exhausted at having to extract a wax honey ball from her odd ear. Davidia didn't realise or understand the effect that it had on her. They were safe again travelling somewhere amongst the clouds. Davidia hoped for bright sunshine and not those humourous clouds. It was time to Zzzzzz. At least that letter seemed to be saved.

It accompanied them on every trip.

*

'I'll never work with animals again,' moaned Roland the Rotter, after having eaten that disgusting honey ball, which had the Shaddersy captured inside. 'Those mosquitos were half useless and those dopey, bloody, stupid sheep were almost as ignorant as my Rotters and they didn't need any special infections. As for

Barry, it won't ever bleat again. I must get rid of these continuing headaches. Why do I get them? That's twice I've met those two letters S and D. Somehow they must be unknowingly infected and then destruction will be complete. They would be as ignorant as my Rotters.'

He went to his personal library cellar to check upon his vast range of books.

'No one will get their hands on them, no one.'

The Hole in the Hill echoed with unpleasantness.

7 HISTORY

'Wake up Slirander.'

'Are we there yet?'

'Are we where?'

They had no idea where they were floating. The tree root of the Moonatric tree was their protective covering as they travelled through the atmosphere. There weren't many trees that could fly.

'Are we stuck inside the green leaf or have we emerged from it?' asked Davidia.

There was no way of telling while they were encased in cocoon-like conditions.

'I can see a light around the next bend.'

The girls crawled on all fours. It was a tight squeeze to traverse the skinny tree root. A gap opened in a wrinkle and Slirander peered out. The air was cold, as it would be at whatever height they were. An unfriendly breeze passed by and chilled Slirander's nose.

'That will teach you to stick your nose into someone else's business,' it said.

The breeze passed by. Slirander gasped at its coldness. It almost took her breath away.

'We must crawl further along the tree root. That breeze looked similar to that of the mayor. It's uncanny how heights play with your imagination. We have to get out of here and quickly.'

They scampered like scolded rats running along a drainpipe and soon ran into the main tree trunk.

'Up there, up there,' urged Slirander, pointing to a minute ray of light struggling to be recognised as a proper light ray. 'Climb up.'

Davidia pretended she was a climbing monkey and planted her feet solidly on the tree trunk wall and pushed hard. Up she went. Slirander was close by. The ray of light had almost disappeared when Slirander shoved Davidia out of the way and jammed her finger into the small light dot. Slowly she wriggled it in concentric circles until the hole grew larger and larger. It was soon large enough to climb through.

'Out you go,' yelled Slirander, almost pushing Davidia through the hole.

She followed. In an instant the hole closed tight once Slirander's foot had made it out.

'What was all that yelling, shoving and pushing about?' said Davidia, quite annoyed at being physically handled.

'A warning. If we hadn't made it through that time, we would be doomed forever inside the green leaf. That breeze was a bad sign. We could be in danger on the next leaf. We must get off this green leaf quickly and climb up to the next one.'

'Oh, I get it. You get to give the orders, do you? Well, I refuse to climb up. I'm resting here,' said a pouting Davidia, showing the stubbornness of a mule.

'It's your choice, but look below you.'

There was nothing but a greyness that stretched as far as the eye could see. The leaf had shrunk down to two shoe sizes, which meant that if Davidia didn't move, she too would plummet to earth as a frozen icicle. She went rigid with fright. Slirander grabbed her hand and clung on dearly to her friend. She swung her hard against the tree trunk for her to grip onto a wrinkle.

'I'll have you for physical abuse,' she yelled, as she slammed into the trunk.

Still writhing like a bubbling mud pool, she gratefully grabbed a wrinkled offering.

'Get up here.'

Davidia followed like the sheep she wasn't, but it was clear to her that Slirander had saved her from an unpleasant doom.

'I was so scared,' she said. 'Where are we now?'

'High amongst the clouds. Where, I don't know. We are on a floating tree, which deposits us where it thinks fit. Give the brrr, brrr, key so we know where we might end up next. It might be better than acting like icy-poles here.'

Davidia did the 'Brrr, brrr,' again and the Moonatric tree rumbled to life. A giant leaf emerged from a trunk, a golden-brown colour.

'Doesn't anything sleep anymore? These interruptions are causing havoc. I almost lost a tree root that time. When my roots tingle badly, it usually means decay. So far, I'm intact, but please exercise caution with my extremities. It's time to move onto that leaf and leave me in peace. I'm not used to so many interruptions.'

'It's a dirty brown colour. I'm not moving.' Davidia was becoming difficult.

'It's the History leaf. If we lose all our written history, there will be no future memories for anyone to enjoy. Please climb on,' said Slirander, politely.

Davidia refused.

'I've had enough. I want to go home. I want to spray me with some real perfume and not some degenerative disease.'

The Moonatric tree wasn't used to dealing with such defiance and had enough of being awake. It swung another very small tree root and smacked Davidia gently, enough to push her onto the leaf. She fell over and landed on her hands. Suddenly, they began to be absorbed by the leaf, or did she think that because hers were also brown. Maybe they were camouflaged. She screamed. The sound shook the tree leaf so badly, it suddenly opened, and they once again flew along a thin filament downwards to an unknown destination.

*

'Charge,' yelled a loud voice.

'Charge,' yelled an equally loud voice from the opposite direction.

Pounding hooves covered the ground in U shape indentations as they galloped over its surface. Letters called out all measure of bad words.

'Not all of them will be in the dictionary,' said Davidia. 'Are we in a movie? This looks like a western frontier studio set.'

'I'm not sure, but I think this battle we've landed in, is real,' replied Slirander. 'Those weapons are real.'

Pandemonium, chaos and mayhem played out in front of them. Letters, horses and camorses were injured and ceased to participate in whatever deadly game was unfolding before their very eyes. Was it an imaginary battle? They only appear in video games and the make-believe of movies. Is this what is happening? The chaotic mess went on for an hour until hostilities ceased. The leftover able-bodied letters carefully walked through the battlefield searching for survivors. It was a desperate task. The loss of letters and animals over an insignificant matter seemed a pointless exercise. A sad man had wandered in their direction and sat near where they had hidden in a rock overlooking the canyon. The air of desolation that surrounded him grew like a mushroom cloud.

'Why did it have to come to this?' he cried.

A few lizards ran for cover. The tremor in his voice was frightening.

The girls reeled at its ferocity. Davidia looked at Slirander and motioned a "you first".

'Excuse me, sir,' said Slirander quietly, so as not to scare the man.

He jumped in fright. He put his hand in a shoulder-bag he carried and withdrew a threatening quill pen. It had a sharp point and could inflict pain if jabbed hard enough into someone.

'Who's there? Who are you?' his frightened voice replied.

'My name's Slirander and this is my friend Davidia, we're visitors.'

All he saw were two very young schoolgirls.

'You haven't been sent to assassinate me or destroy my work have you? It's impossible to trust anyone these days.' His hand gripped his quill pen tighter. 'I'll use it if I have to,' he threatened.

'No sir, we offer no threat. May we sit down?'

The man settled and considered that the girls weren't a threat. He withdrew his threatening quill pen and placed it back in his shoulder-bag.

'What was that battle down there all about? No one ever really wins, do they? What did this one resolve, if anything?' asked Slirander.

'On the surface, nothing. Those two groups of fighters have been spoiling for a fight in recent times. It's all over the naming rights to the valley between the two towns of Horrus and Hoo-rus. They are at opposite ends of the valley.'

'That's a stupid reason to fight over. I can understand a new hairstyle or boyfriend, but naming rights, I don't get,' said Davidia, who thought men; however, in this case, letters biffing each other was so lame.

'It's hard to imagine either. This was a peaceful place a short time ago, but it all changed recently. One of the city Letter Elders of Horrus wanted to lay claim to a section for mining of gold. When he went to the library to search the name archives, he found that there wasn't any name for the valley. It had disappeared. It had a proper name beforehand and now it was gone, so he couldn't lay claim to a non-named valley. He was so furious and accused

150

the town of Hoorus for stealing it. Naturally, Hoorus denied it and a big "to do" erupted. Nasty accusations flew everywhere, so a battle for it was decided as the only solution. Both wanted renaming rights. Now, all you see are sick, wounded, dead and injured letters, all because of no name. What a disastrous waste. It would have been easier to agree on half each, then the conflict would have been avoided. They could have called it Hooray and both should be happy with it, but no, they had to fight over it.'

'What was its previous name?'

'That's the strangest thing of all. No one knows. The record books in which it was kept, have lost it. It's not there anymore.'

'Weird doesn't cover it. Who exactly are you?'

'My name is Hictor. I'm a historian. I travel the land recording events for posterity. You can imagine it is slow and tedious work with a quill pen. If records are lost, then the future won't know its past.'

'Why would you be concerned about the future? Is there anything here to affect it?'

'I'm not sure. I left the town of Horrus yesterday and took my position up here to record the battle. Now it's over, it has no name to be recorded under. The battle of No Name Valley won't register because when it is renamed, the record books won't necessarily alter the name of the battle. History is so important. It tells us who we are.'

The girls sat with Hictor and wondered also what had happened to the name of the valley.

'How do you think the valley's real name disappeared?' asked Davidia, knowing that words don't deliberately remove themselves on purpose from books.

They enjoy their existence there, having eyes cast over them transforming simple letters into meaningful words, phrases and colourful sentences.

'A stranger came into town a few days ago, offering free second-hand books to the public. Not many can read here. The library was given a few also. Otherwise, life has been ordinary and regular. It was peculiar because all the books he handed out were picture books. There weren't any words in them; however, they do look good on a shelf.'

'Rotters,' said Slirander. 'They are here too.'

'Rotters, what are Rotters?' asked Hictor.

'Don't write that down. They won't form part of any history,' said Slirander. 'We must visit Horrus.'

'There won't be much there after this battle.'

'It's the cause of the battle that I'm interested in. If the valley had kept its proper name then no conflict would have erupted. Losing language letters may have unintended consequences such as we have experienced today,' said Slirander.

'Guard your letters carefully, Hictor.'

*

The girls walked to Horrus.

'Could that free book salesman be a Rotter?' asked Davidia.

'It's more than likely that those pests have arrived here to destroy all written history. That salesman must have had an excessive number of books, there's a waste pile in the street with that horse licking each page. That's odd, it's not eating them.'

'What sort of books are they?'

They walked over. The horse looked up as if to say, Good afternoon, ladies; however, it was an odd, ordinary horse.

'It's wearing a horseshoe necklace around its hump. Horses don't have humps; well, not on their backs,' said Davidia. She once had a pony called Tony and its back was straight. Humps are for camels. How did this disfiguration occur? 'It's an odd horse,' whispered Davidia.

Slirander had twigged to its oddity.

'Here it's known as a camorse. I once read about this unusual breed. They are used for pulling carts through deserts. In this area, it is ideally suited when you see the terrain.'

'Are you sure? Go on, test it. Ask it if it is a Rotter? Then we'll see whether it's full of manure. By the look of the landscape it could do with some fertilising.'

'Hello, camorse,' said Slirander. Being friendly would reduce the intensity of any kick. 'I'm Slirander and this is my friend, Davidia. Are you reading those books?'

The camorse didn't understand the question. Why should it? It shook its mane and bared a large set of perfect dentures.

'Someone has been looking after you. They're real expensive veneers. Have you got a sugar horse?' said Davidia. Even her dental work didn't rate as highly.

'May I read a book?' asked Slirander.

The camorse snorted at her. It continued licking. Slirander picked one up. It was a short history on whatever was once inside it. It was full of blank pages; however, the pictures indicated a series of historical events. Hictor may be correct. She opened another, then another. The whole pile consisted of defunct history books. Why then was the camorse still licking them? A puzzled look appeared on her face.

'Don't stand behind it, Davidia. Camorse, are you a Rotter?' asked Slirander, watching like a hawk for any tell-tale movements. There was no instant reaction.

'It's not a Rotter. No odd angry eye has popped out,' said Davidia. 'Look, it has stopped licking. Its hump is moving up and down. Watch out.'

A large blast occurred. Manure was flung everywhere. The

camorse fell onto the ground writhing in pain. A few moments later and with a modest blurt, it stood up. Its back was now straight.

'You don't know how good that feels,' it said. 'That was exhilarating. I've had that affliction for a few days ever since I ate one of those books. I've regained my appetite now. Where's some real camorse food to eat?'

'Why have you been licking those books? They aren't that edible unless you thought you were a goat,' said Davidia, remembering the intelligent Barry for a moment.

'I could have been hypnotised. I thought I was eating them. It's a case of mistaken food identity. Now that has been solved, I've got carts to pull.'

The camorse galloped off seeking a cart to pull. The girls stood annoyed at the desolate waste of the language those books would have held. There was so much history and not a word to remember it by.

'Do we spray the antidote?' asked Davidia.

'No. Pile them up and we'll take them to the town library,' said Slirander 'They should be safe there and then we'll give them a dose of the antidote.'

'Lads, did you hear that? It will be action stations shortly. All perks are off. Our skills might need to be deployed. Stay alert,' yelled a leader to his soldiers.

'Doesn't he tire of the big yell each time we have work to do?' wailed a highly sensitive soldier. They were ready.

'It won't be too late, will it?' said Davidia.

'I don't think so,' replied Slirander.

Once the books were stacked in neat piles, transport was required. Nearby, an old man hobbled past. His stooped body was shaped like the letter P. He held an odd walking cane in his hand. It didn't touch the ground but was centimetres short of it. Why he didn't fall over was a mystery. It's apparently all about balance. A glance from under his overgrown hair toward the girls wasn't pretty viewing. He had a date with something, but whatever it was, was never spoken of. In Horrus, he was the local undertaker and was edging his way toward the battlefield to inspect the new influx of fresh dead bodies. Maybe that was the unspoken-of date. There was lots of new business today. The girls interrupted him.

'Excuse me, sir, is there any transport in town to take these books to the library?' asked a very polite Davidia. Her manners were on full show. What a transformation.

'There ain't none,' replied the grumpy, old bastard.

'Are you sure? What about that black camorse and cart over there?'

'What camorse and cart? There isn't any.'

'Yes, there is. I can see them. They are over there. Are they yours?'

'I told you there ain't no transport.'

The grumpy, P-shaped old man began to scratch himself behind an ear. It suddenly fell off.

'Me hearings no good either,' he remarked.

He continued to scratch behind his other ear and that fell off too.

'I can't hear anything, goodbye.'

He dragged one leg behind the other, making a traceable dusty trail in the ground. After a short distance, he collapsed. He represented a small rubbish pile. Davidia ran after him.

'Are you alright?'

'Agh!' He had to lip read having just lost his hearing.

'I apologise, but I thought you might be hurt.'

'Agh!' he repeated.

Davidia had to point. She assisted the old man upright as

best a twisted P body could stand, when she noticed the pain in his eyes.

'Where are your legs? Slirander, he's disappearing all the time.'

She came running over.

'It's a trick. Stand back:

> *Bittle bottle pull the throttle,*
> *Unleash the pain it's in a rottle,*
> *Kick its eye it dangles so,*
> *Rotten are the Rotters clothes.'*

'That's rather a stupid poem. It doesn't even rhyme properly. I'm glad I don't study from the same dictionary,' said Davidia, thinking her friend was acting rather loopy.

'I made it up. I thought you might be in trouble.'

'Well, I'm not.'

No sooner had that remark escaped from her lips, the ground began to rumble. The rubbish pile, which had hidden the grumpy old man moved. Like a phoenix rising from the ashes, an agitated youthful salesman emerged fully-formed and sprouting language from the pulpit of life. He wasn't flogging the encyclopaedia Britannica or religious theory; it was invective vitriol. Maybe he was upset that he missed the "no name battle" and took his guilt out on two innocents.

'I recognise you two. Everywhere my Destrusto Virus is deployed, you two turn up. Are you stalking me?' said the young salesman.

'And you with the rude mouth, who might you be?' asked Davidia, incensed at having been bad-mouthed and no less by a good-looking, youthful salesman.

'A noun, a sentence, perhaps a naughty phrase you won't find in any book. I'm your imagination, your adversary, a magician, a trickster. I'm anything I want to be. What exactly are you two?'

'We're schoolgirls who enjoy reading,' she replied. 'That's something I think you disagree with.'

The salesman laughed loudly. Davidia noticed his eyes.

'Do you have an eye affliction? Yours don't look healthy at all. I can recommend some good eye-drops for you. What do you think, Slirander? Has he got that road map disease?'

'What's a road map disease?'

'It's where your eyes pop out of your head and explode.' Apparently, a thing called a Rotter exemplifies that behaviour. 'Are you a Rotter, Roland,' asked Slirander, pushing her imaginative button.

Suddenly, the name of Horrus lived up to its reputation. The young salesman burst at the seams. His body parts flew everywhere just like others had at the "no name battle". The two odd angry eyes were confused and both ended up as dead-ends, then boom. The dust settled and there was only a pile of dirty, grubby clothes left behind as a road hump.

'How did you know that was Roland? It was Roland, wasn't it?' asked Davidia.

'Oh, yes, it was him alright.'

'What gave it away?'

'It was those non-existent legs. It was a favourite trick of his.' Slirander's voice trailed off so as not to place too much emphasis on her comment. 'He has no further need for that black camorse and cart. Let's use them to transport this lot to the library.'

The girls loaded the camorse and cart and tried to locate the library. It was a fruitless search. No such building existed. Is the written history of the world under extinction?

'Who's going to look after the history books for posterity?'

The girls were in the "leaf of history" and things were looking bleak.

A voice overhead spoke to them. They were directly under the verandah of the town saloon, the gossip nerve centre of Horrus. There weren't any persons in sight, so was it the voice of conscience, reasoning, understanding, history itself or something simpler than that?

'Go to the town of Hoorus. They appreciate reading more than this town and would be pleased to save your collection, but first you must cross the no name battlefield and restore its original name into the history books. Only then can history be fully saved. Take the undertaker's camorse and cart. Be careful of travellers. It's a valley littered in misery. Trust your instincts and language.'

'Pardon, what are we talking with?' asked Slirander, who had an appreciation of the weird.

'I cannot reveal myself, otherwise my demise would be swift. There are many enemies in this land. You have arrived in the bad part of history and will need all your intelligence and good language skills to escape.'

'Your voice is very high-pitched and squeaky. Have we met before?'

The question was ignored.

'Leave, it is no longer safe here.'

The girls gathered up the camorse and cart and headed out of town.

A small cockroach peered over the gutter's edge. Its ancestors had provided one of the antidote ingredients and it felt that affinity when the girls came near it.

'Giddy-up, camorse,' encouraged Davidia.

She once had pony training with her pony, Tony, and knew how to get the best out of a camorse. The dust trail they left behind faded into the distance.

'How far is the town of Hoorus?' asked Davidia.

The camorse was non-cooperative. Whilst pulling the cart, it wasn't that talkative.

'If we skirt the main battlefield, it should be a day's travel,' replied Slirander, as she surveyed the countryside. What she expected to see and what she did see didn't match.

'Why is the "no name battle" so important that it must be restored for historical reasons? What effect should that one name make on history's restoration?'

Davidia was bright enough to reason issues through, but in this case was unable to tag a solution.

'It may have something to do with the damage Roland the Rotter has caused. We don' know how far the Destrusto Virus has infiltrated the world of history. There must be an order for restoration to occur, which means that the playing field has altered. It must be a key, a trigger to repair all damage done. Those books we are carrying have all lost their letters. Maybe the book depicting and recording the "no name battle" is in Hoorus. Perhaps, it is there we should discover its real name?'

'Why don't we give these books that we are carrying a dose of antidote and see what affect it has? So far we have restored all lost language letters in three designations. If we do it, then we'll know how serious it is finding the battle's real name.'

Slirander thought that it was a good idea.

'Whoa, camorse, we need a break.'

The camorse snorted and thought thankfully that it was time for a rest.

Slirander took out one of her vials and found it empty. Davidia too had an empty vial. Both chucked them away. A second vial was used, lightly spraying the books.

'Get up, lads, duty calls. Stop sleeping on the job. Soldiers prepare for battle. This is a more difficult task we have been set. I feel it in the mists of our abilities. This time, we restore at our peril. The antagonist Destrusto Virus may be immune to our strengths. Fight it we must. The future of reading and history is our responsibility. Let's attack and regain what is lost.'

The leader and his team were fully charged with enthusiasm and powerful restoration capabilities; however, doubt had never existed in the leader's attitude, but this time something bothered him. Special signals had been received from an interfering source, which might trouble them. Whatever it was, it caused them concern.

'Let's leave this camorse ride and ride our own race. Cowboys, away. Yee, hah!'

The soldiers of the Pebble of Purpose had their own battle to fight. They never had a name for any of their battles because they didn't form any part of history.

'Lads, don't waste your time reading the restoration, our job is to restore it. Watch out, you lucky letters.'

The pile of books they were carrying had an answer to their letter losses, or did they?

The girls rested. Ahead lay the no name valley, the scene of the destructive battle they had witnessed earlier. Would they be able to traverse any traps set? Was there any set at all? It was a quandary. The antagonist they were up against was so devious it was almost impossible to figure it out.

'Camorse, do you know anything about the battle in no name valley?' asked Davidia.

Her only experience of a talking horse was from a television program from the sixties and that was only half a camorse.

It neighed first then spat.

'Letters, it's all about letters.'

'You mean the ones people write or the ones in the books?'

'Ask yourself a question. Where have all the letters gone from the history books this cart is full of? Who knows where any of them are?'

'The antidote soldiers will discover where they are,' said Slirander.

'Prepare to be disappointed,' said the camorse, gearing up for another spit. Food in the valley was as disagreeable as he was.

The girls and camorse closed in on the scene of the battle that the girls had witnessed earlier. They had paid no attention to any of the details, because they were far in the distance. It was only as they got closer and when a few damaged letters staggered toward them that they realised all the combatants had been letters. An injured J had his curve straightened. An I was bent in half. A T had lost his top and doubled as a new I. Both E and F had lost two of their rungs and an N had succumbed to tiredness and was mistaken for a Z. They had no hope at all in reforming into meaningful words and teaming to form written language. The groaning letters rued the decision to follow the elder letter of Horrus and their Hoorus opponents, who consisted of the same structures, bemoaned their losses and future inability to be read again. It was a tangled lettered mess. Destructed letters were littered everywhere. It was as if a dictionary full of words had been spilt. The girls stopped to ask an injured O, who was now an oval, not a round shape, what had happened? Perhaps it had been sat on by a heavy B, or a team of them.

'Excuse me,' said Davidia, 'have any letter or letters survived intact?'

The oval O stopped its elongated then short-rolling form of movement. It looked at the girls with a glint of recognition that beamed around its circumference. They looked like some of its readers.

'It's impossible to know. Did you know that I was once perfectly round and symmetrical? Children delighted in reading me. I became the doughnut centre of their reading. Who is going to read me now in this unusual shape? I can't find any letter to team up with to make a word. I'm lost by myself. The indignity of also being a vowel of no further use is hard to accept. Oh, how I wish I was still in a book.'

'What book did you fall out of?'

'I didn't fall. I was forcibly pushed out by a brash virus that recruited me under the guise that another group of letters wanted to destroy the written language. We were told that they had tired of being in history books and wanted to be read in other books such as adventure stories, westerns and so on and leave history a hollow shell. Unfortunately, the same story was told to the books of Hoorus. When the elder letter told us that he was refused a claim in no name valley — we can't remember its real name either — maybe I was a part of it. Who knows? So, we came here, and disaster happened. I suppose if you re-arrange different combinations of letters, we can represent stupid and that's not including me in the word, but two of my closest other four vowels.'

'Where are you headed for now?'

'I've no idea. None of the survivors are of much use. We'll probably rot and fade away, never to be in a book again. We will be forgotten and so will history. I thought I'd last forever, but now I'm not so sure I will last at all.'

'What if you could be made round again?'

The O looked at Davidia in despair. Obviously, hope was tangled on a fishing line of goodwill, but it was an impossible task. The oval shaped O looped away. It didn't wait for an answer that couldn't change the situation.

*

'Lads, we are in the midst of restoring history. It would be one of our greatest achievements. Source those letters,' instructed the leader.

The soldiers of the Pebble of Purpose were diligent workers who would withstand the worst of conditions to restore whatever their task was. They looked everywhere for letters to replace in the books. Strangely, there were none immediately available.

'Sir, it's a catastrophe. We can't locate any letters for restoration. It's as if they have simply vanished,' said a worker.

'Don't give me any weak-kneed excuses. That's not possible. Don't tell me our expert team cannot locate a restorable letter. I've warned you against reading instead of restoration. You aren't trying hard enough.'

'Each page we visit hasn't left an ink imprint or an indentation to suggest any letter was ever there, or any visible mark of letter habitation. This is my first experience of a blank page staying a blank page.'

'Give me a closer look.'

The leader felt a few pages and grudgingly realised he had to agree with his soldier that there was nothing there to restore; however, where each letter should have existed, an outline of what was there was traceable. It was hidden so deeply within the page it was almost impossible to locate. Something had suppressed them almost into invisibility. Maybe Roland the Rotter's Destrusto Virus was an improved version of previous concoctions. What did he say, 'A trickster and be whatever I want?' Had he become the pages to confuse the soldiers? Maybe it was time for him to have the unthinkable, a win.

'It looks like all these books have been deliberately abandoned. What would cause such an action?'

The leader was at a loss for words.

'Lads, we must send out our scouts and trace where they went. We must not fail. What will the readers think of us if we do?'

The pile of books that they were exploring to restore were in the middle of the battlefield piled high in the cart.

'Sir, look out of the pages. There are thousands of letters out there, all jumbled and damaged. I wonder if they lived in these books.'

The leader was building to an angry hissy fit, equal to that of any Rotter, only that he wasn't one. He peered out from the pages. Did he see a dictionary of injured and distorted letters, a graveyard of forgettable letters, or a pile of hope from a damaged beginning? It was heart-breaking to see language limping about with no form or direction.

'Lads, there they are. Go get them.'

'But, sir, they look past restoration. They have so many bent, misshapen and missing elements, maybe only a few of them can be saved. We need the titles to be restored first, then all the other letters could feel better and improve their personal standing. They seem disillusioned because they have no idea from which book they left. A title would remind them of where they were last read.'

'That's a great idea. I must compliment myself on training you all so well.'

The soldiers all sighed.

'Why can't we restore him into a letter and have him permanently placed in a comedy book?' said a soldier with its own sense of humour.

The team turned their attention to filling the blank pages. Hope was a four-lettered word with the O vowel, so it had participated in a good word and it might be there at the result. Scouts tested a few of the letters who they found too damaged for restoration. A jagged L was placed in a book page. The soldiers did their best, but it wouldn't fit despite their best efforts. The leader's enthusiasm waned.

'Lads, we've encountered our worst virus.'

The leader's words were the last heard as a book closed shut.

'Slirander, what do you expect to find amongst all these letters?

It must have been a massive contest. Even at school, the debating team didn't destroy language as badly as this,' said Davidia.

'There must be some letters that survived. Moonah didn't send us here without the possibility of success even though it might be difficult.'

'We'll have to search through these piles. These letters are a lot smaller than us, aren't they?'

'Camorse, can you help?'

'Sorry. I eat, pass food, rest, drink, eat and pass food. I'm too busy.'

The girls began the mammoth task of moving thousands of letters. It would be a long day.

'Get off me,' yelled a belligerent B. 'You took your time. I've been suffocating under those insufferable Ws who think that because they look like a double V, they can bully me. I've got news for them. Most of them are now single Vs and can B off for my liking. We never did fit well together in many words.'

'You aren't damaged,' said Davidia. 'Slirander, we've found one. It doesn't seem too appreciative, but I'm assuming it's the shock of seeing a close-up of a reader.'

'Of course, I'm not damaged. What next?'

'Can you wait over there in the cart, please? We're looking for your friends that may have survived.'

The B reluctantly did as instructed. The camorse took no interest in it. One letter doesn't make a word, but it can sound like one. It needed more extensions.

Soon another letter appeared, or was it another?

'It certainly is difficult making conversation with all the other damaged letters. None of them made any sense. Thank you for releasing us,' said a very polite t.

'Thank you for rescuing us,' said another very polite t. 'We're twins.'

Slirander checked them over. Both were intact.

'We've got such headaches; we need to rest.'

'Kindly sit over there with B. You might try and arrange some-thing,' directed Slirander.

'Ouch, who stabbed my finger?' complained Davidia.

She quickly sifted through a few letters for the jagged stabber. A reluctant lower-case b had its stem sharpened to defend itself against other members of the alphabet. It had managed to prick a few letters, so it was left alone. It had hidden in silence, not wanting to be discovered only to lose its reading ability.

'Leave me alone. I'm more dangerous than I look,' it said.

'I can see you. You are a feisty small little b, aren't you? I'm glad we found you. There is an important job for you.'

'Me, important? The capital letters never paid me any atten-tion before. I never begin a sentence. I'm always stuck in the letter queue. No one gives me a chance to be a larger b than I am.'

'The role of every letter is as equally important. Together you make a fabulous team,' said Davidia. 'Some of your peer group are over there.'

'Hi guys.' It gave them a b greeting.

Slirander accumulated thoughts of how these letters could be useful. The ones found must eventually mean something. She located the next letters by stubbing her toe on one that protruded from the pile. It looked in good shape. She tugged hard at it. It wouldn't budge. She tried again. Finally, she dislodged it.

'You were being difficult. I need you as a leader of a word because you are a capital letter,' she said.

'What about my cousin? It was right behind me. I protected it during the battle. It's a lower-case g. I'm a capital G. Do you like my shape? I'm not damaged reading material. The two of us love forming words. Often we've appeared in the same word together,' said the capital G.

Slirander foraged again and extracted the lower-case g that was so thankful to join its cousin.

'We're inseparable,' it said. 'The last time we enjoyed a relationship, we were in the same word. It might even be from one of those books in that cart pile.'

'What do you mean?'

'All of us letters came out of those books and many others like it in the valley. We were all dumped here and many of us were hurt in the process.'

'You have been very informative.'

'We aim to please any reader.'

They joined the few survivors.

'I remember you,' said the twins. 'We were once on a cover in a title with you. It had something to do with the history of some herb or similar word.'

'Can you remember the title?'

'Not without the other letters. It's a struggle to remember that we were once in a word at all.'

'Slirander. This could take us all day searching for a complete set of letters,' said Davidia. 'Even if we locate them they will be a random selection and may not be suitable for whatever it is that they may represent.'

'We must locate as many as possible. I have a feeling it will work well.'

'Can you hear that snivelling noise?' said Davidia.

The girls stood silent and motionless. They could hear childish whimpering in a nearby alphabetic pile. Is it a letter or some other animal that got mixed up in the fracas? Davidia went over and heaved aside a short story of sore letters. Underneath, the pile seemed endless.

'We're over here,' called out their leader a, being the first vowel of five.

'I'll find you. I can't stand the grizzling,' said Davidia.

After all, she did have a brother who often tested her sanity by faking his whinging to her parents and she'd be held responsible for some stupid prank.

'Don't stand on us,' one of them wailed.

'I'll kick you if you don't shut up. Come out, come out, wherever you are. Ah! There you are. Playing hide-and-seek, are we?'

'Certainly not! We've waited patiently to be found and need to be treated with some respect,' said an annoyed e that had tired of being in an alphabet junk-pile.

'There's more than one of you,' said Davidia, amazed.

'My whole family is here. We are the vowel family. That's a over there, i is hiding behind it, the shy o and the bossy-one u are wrestling with each other. I'm e. We are all currently in lower-case; however, we can be upper-case letters in an instant when required to be so.'

'How did you stay together amongst this mess?'

'We were taught that families should stick together, and we do. We are often found together in many words and most written words need at least one of our members. I'm not sure all words do, but we come close to it. Did you realise that in the past four lines, one of my family is in every word? Without us, written words wouldn't make much sense. It's probably like those youth who text in your world on their mobile phones using abbreviations of good written language. Have many of us survived?'

'It's a struggle to find any of you in good health,' said Slirander, feeling better now that a group of vowels had been discovered. They would be extremely word useful.

'I wonder where our homes went. We were all well spread out in many books and "kapow", we end up as waste fill because we believed a false promise.'

'Did someone lead you here?'

'We were conned. Be in an adventure book. History is for dullards. The salesman was sleek and persuasive. We are in every word. We followed like brainless baa baas. This is the reward for change. I'd love to be part of history again,' sighed e.

'Perhaps you can. Some of your friends are near the cart waiting to see if we can restructure something with you all,' said Slirander.

'I hope you can spell properly. There's nothing worse than being misplaced in a word, let alone a sentence.'

The vowel family were warmly greeted by the other letters.

'They get all the credit for good expression,' whispered the jealous twins.

There wasn't such a need for double t in many words. Tensions simmered below the surface.

Wounded letters offered themselves for use. Even the soldiers of the Pebble of Purpose couldn't return this mess to normal. A miracle was required. Rejections abounded. Letters became disillusioned. On one of the great battlefields of history, which no one knew the name of, they suffered the indignity of uselessness. Davidia and Slirander continued to meticulously search for letters in good shape. Their success rate was abysmal. Where were they all? Had Roland the Rotter won at last and they would be defeated in their efforts to find a solution?

'Just because you come before me in the alphabet, there's no need to be pushy. I'm over you being sung before me by children learning the alphabet musically,' said an irate s.

'One of us has to be first and I guess I'm the lucky one,' replied r, knowing that it would always come before any s in the alphabet. Pride still lived in a readable letter.

'Stop the arguing, you two,' said Slirander. 'There's more use for you than petty bickering. All these letters have suffered badly in this valley and all you two can do is fight over your place in a lettered queue.'

'Are they all from paperbacks and not a hard cover letter like us?' said r, spoiling for a discussion.

'You have fortunately survived to be allowed the chance to reform and be read again.'

'I'm not sure with those leftovers that they would be suitable for me to join in a word. They look as if a bad print run formed them. I'm just dusty.'

The lower-case s stepped forward and tripped up r. It fell onto its round roof and felt sore. It wasn't letting on that it could be injured and tossed away like refuse.

'How can we help?' r said.

'By joining our few friends over there.'

'Is that a camorse? Hey s, we both appear in its name in the right order, me before you as it should be.' The lower-case r was certainly proud of its position.

'Have you seen any other intact letters that we can save?' asked Slirander.

'We saw three letters pretending to be a French word, but they weren't up to it. They were camorsing around trying to be meaningful. They were further over toward that tall creature.'

Slirander looked up and there stood Hictor, quill pen in hand. What was he doing in the valley? Shouldn't he be safely hidden in amongst the rocks recording history? Why did he venture to the valley floor? Roland the Rotter would stamp him out if he knew that he was recording the events that he had tried to destroy.

'Hello, Hictor,' said Slirander.

'Hello, Slirander,' said Hictor.

He looked at her with a sickly milkshake feeling inside. The quills on his pen had almost lost their feathers.

'Have you recorded the battle?'

'Every minute detail. It was letter against letter. Have you discovered the lost name of the valley?'

'Not quite, we may never learn what its name was. There are too many lost letters and an insufficient healthy lot leftover to form anything important.'

Davidia had been carefully watching the good fuzzy feeling that sparked action dialogue between the two. She noticed one hand would twitch every now and then. He had an extra middle finger knuckle. Even Hictor had an oddity. She had almost observed the beginning of a sneer when it evaporated as quickly as it had formed in her imagination, or had she actually seen it?

'I wish you luck,' said Hictor.

He passed by the camorse and cart and deliberately stood on a healthy letter t. Slirander didn't notice, but Davidia was inured to odd behaviour. Why would Hictor destroy an opportunity to find the valley's real name? Didn't anything make sense?

How would they find a replacement t when finding one in the first place was so difficult?

'My twin, he stood on my twin,' cried the other t. He ran up to his twin, thinking of finding a twisted, skewed shape.

'That bastard isn't so clever. When I saw the shadow of a size fourteen darken my horizon, I twisted sideways and slid into a groove in his sole. Voila, I'm here ready and readable,' said the second, or was it the first, t. The twins hugged and scurried off to safety under the camorse and cart.

'Be more careful, Slirander, I feel something slithery about Hictor,' said Davidia, warning her friend.

'Mmm,' was all she mumbled.

From the ashes of embers, small ringlets of smoke arose, and three scared letters ran from a book pile full of damaged ones. They scarcely left an indentation on the ground. They tried to hide in another pile and hoped to remain undiscovered. They were afraid of being ruined as a reading letter. A small f, l and n, which had no word combinations together as a threesome, had joined forces for survival. Davidia sidled over and sat down near them. She toyed with a few dust particles and drew the three of them in the dirt. The letters were amazed at seeing themselves replicated correctly. It didn't matter what medium was used.

'How did you do that?' asked the timid f. 'Do you know what we are?'

'Yes. You are meaningful letters and precious to read. I can read and write you.' Davidia made a short sentence in the dirt using all three of them, obviously with extras as well. They couldn't believe it. 'Come and join a few of your other friends. We have found them. They are safely over there.'

The group of healthy letters had grown to sixteen and, with a complete set of vowels, had the ingredients to make a short sentence of a few words. Perhaps even the name of a famous battle in that very valley. The girls kept looking for any further letters of use, but sadly found none. They were very disappointed.

'Will history disappear forever now? We've only a handful of letters and they don't seem to be able to organise themselves into words. We'll have to do it for them.'

'I wonder what their configuration is. Should we try now or travel to the town of Hoorus to solve the problem there? Let's hope we can find that solution.'

'It's better to be away from here. I never thought that I'd see the destruction of history. It wasn't my favourite topic at school, but to lose it like this is like losing a friend.'

They hitched up the camorse and cart, gathered the sixteen letters of salvation and sadly drove to the town of Hoorus. Maybe it was a happier place. As a safety precaution, Davidia hid all the letters in her jacket. For some unknown reason she couldn't explain, she felt that they needed protection, but from what she hadn't yet encountered.

*

The town of Hoorus was a quaint village grasping at the edge of the valley for survival. The dry climate acted as a preservation facility for any books that were housed there. There were no damp moisture-filled rooms full of bacterial and fungal spores to blot their clean pages with grey and black spots. The letters of the town were barely visible. They were all probably lost in the useless battle over valley naming rights. Where was the law of stupidity housed? Explanations were fresh out today. The girls walked past empty shells of buildings. Around a corner they saw a huge O gesturing to nothing. Its mouth was moving vigorously in time with its frequent arm movements. It was totally ignored. If it had a mirror, it would have had an audience of one.

'Excuse me. sir. Is there a library in town?' asked Davidia.

She had to duck the waving arms in case she sustained an injury.

The huge O stopped moving. It said in mime, 'What are you?'

'We're tourists looking for the library information centre,' said Davidia. 'We want to learn about the town and the history of its inhabitants.'

The big O shook like a nervous jelly. Its name was Orator. It used to hold grand audiences thrilled with the oral adventures of life. Unfortunately, with the destruction of the written language, a great voice had been snuffed out. Once mighty, it was now relegated to a series of gestures. It couldn't top up on any stories as there was nothing written anymore to access and read. A jewelled teardrop ran all around its circumference expressing disappointment. As it fell to the ground, Orator momentarily found its voice. The sound was a fraction of its fine, timbred quality.

'Visitors no longer find their way here. The library is empty. All books have been lost with the battle. My voice is a decibel of its former self. It's down there,' it pointed as its guttural tone became a whisper and then became silent. The big O resumed its gestures in a vain attempt to be interesting.

'Those Rotters are behind all this. I've had enough. When we get to the library, we will source the name of the valley and everything will be restored to normal,' said an annoyed Davidia. Her girlish charm had been kicked out of the park. 'Slirander, forget that Hictor. He's trouble with a capital T if only we could find one.'

Slirander knew Davidia made sense, but like all friends' good advice, it can be ignored and because it is, they will supply an endless fresh list.

'This must be the library,' said Slirander. There were no literary signs of identification to signal its use. 'Let's go in. Camorse, you wait here until we can unload the books.'

The camorse snorted and spat. There wasn't much else to do.

The library was empty. All shelves had spaces of nothing. There wasn't one lousy book. Not even an empty one to be found.

'Those Rotters are cheesing me off,' said Davidia. She stomped angrily through each room, kicking at the floor, slapping the woodwork and generally hitting anything within reach. Suddenly, she tripped on a loose floorboard. 'Why didn't the maintenance man nail the bloody thing down? Now I've skinned my knee and ruined my visit.'

She rubbed her sore knee. She thought that's odd. A loose floorboard doesn't just happen. It occurs with some deliberation. She crawled nearer and as her skirt covered it before she could properly inspect it, who should walk in like the messiah, but Hictor the Historian. She wondered what he was doing here. Hopefully, he wasn't a stalker.

'May I assist you?' he said, proffering his odd, knuckled hand.

Davidia resisted the temptation. His slithery hand didn't warrant a comfort grasp.

'I'm comfortable, thank you. I'm resting,' she fibbed.

'I see you brought all those books here for storage. They aren't of any use to anything. There doesn't seem to be a decent written word anywhere. I know because I've looked everywhere,' he said, with a queasy smirk.

'Yes, there is.'

Hictor suddenly became cautiously suspicious. Was that a hint of dribble or a near-death proportional look? Davidia feigned dust in her eye and, as she rubbed them, she glanced at Hictor's quill pen, yes, his quill pen. She noticed that it was perfectly clean. It was standing upside down in his bag and its end protruded over the ridge as if peeking at the real world. She gasped.

'This damn dust. A cleaner hasn't been in here for a while.'

'What will you do now that the library is vacant?'

'Maybe your writings could be the first book of history to be housed here. Can I read what you've recorded so far? I enjoy history. It was my favourite topic at school.'

Hictor hesitated. He clutched his man bag tightly. If there were any words in it they weren't being let out today. That door of knowledge had been slammed shut.

'I haven't finished it yet,' he stammered. 'I don't show any half-finished work to anyone. Where's Slirander?'

'She's in the room down the hallway reading a book.'

'Reading a what!'

Hictor almost choked on his own words and they weren't said in capitals. He knew it was impossible for any book to be read. The Destrusto Virus has had an excellent visit. This time a clean sheet had been made. What satisfaction? How could Slirander be reading? He dashed down to greet her. She was seated holding an empty hardback cover.

'I like to remember how it used to be when words danced before my eyes, relaying wonderful information and excitement. Now it's boring, lonely and barren of interest. How can we change things?'

She pouted sadly at Hictor. He couldn't have cared less. History was doomed, but for Slirander's sake he pretend-nodded in agreement showing understanding which he lacked.

'I saw Davidia sitting on the floor. Wouldn't a chair have been better?'

'She's an outdoors girl. At school camps she was always the last to leave.'

Hictor nodded. He thought that they hadn't discovered anything of use, interest or otherwise. Perfect. At last the girls had been defeated. His odd angry knuckle started to bubble with excitement.

'Hictor, the blood in your veins is bubbling. Are you alright?'

'It's an affliction I inherited. I'm hot-blooded, that's all. I must continue with my writing. There are other valleys to visit.'

Without a wave, goodbye or words like, I'll see you again, he left the empty rooms of the library to remain so. No word will ever inhabit there again. His pride at that moment was greater than his nastiness, which was a rare event.

'Has Hictor gone?' asked Davidia. She was suspicious that he hadn't gone anywhere. 'He could be snooping about watching us.'

'I believe so,' said Slirander. 'I wonder what this book once was.'

'Come. I've found something. There's a loose floorboard in a back room. Shut and lock the door behind you. I tripped over it. Hictor didn't see it. Next time I see him I'll ask if he's a Rotter. History is full of rotten characters. Try and prise it open. It may hold a secret.'

The floorboard created a contest of wills. Will it or will it not give way. Davidia used all her strength. The floorboard screamed,

'No you don't.' The tug of wills finally finished in Davidia's favour. Hidden beneath was an abandoned book. Well, it appeared to be. It was left alone. The cover had no title, but inside all words were still in print. Slirander thought how clever it was to conceal it. She took out the antidote and gave it a protective spray.

'Lads, we have a live one. Guard it well. This time we don't have to restore it. What a relief. It's like having a paid holiday. I still enjoy my job.'

'What sort of book is it?' asked Davidia.

'I'm not sure. The letters in this book have all been rearranged so that they make little sense. They can't be read. It's a nonsense jumble. Where are the letters we saved?'

'They are in my pocket. We only have sixteen of them.'

'This book is missing its title. Is it possible that those letters can form a title?'

'I suppose so, there are enough of them.'

Davidia took them out and carefully placed them all on the floor. She counted sixteen to make sure. The letters stretched their shapes after being confined for so long. It was a puzzle. The feisty little b began pushing and shoving. The big B almost biffed it.

'Letters, stop behaving badly. We need to solve the riddle of the untitled book.'

'Just like the riddle of no name valley,' said the big B. 'I assume myself and capital G could start a word each. We are usually followed by a vowel.'

'Pick me, pick me,' called out the vowel family, all eager to be put in their place.

'It would be a history book, so what happens?'

'Lots of fighting,' said the small b.

'That's it. What's another name for a fight?' asked Davidia.

'Biff, but that has two fs and we only have one. Would battle work?' came an intelligent comment from the twins. Two letters work better than one.

The letters were beginning to team together. It worked. The word Battle was made.

'It's good to feel part of a word again,' said l. 'Home at last.'

'In my experience, being part of any sentence, battle is usually of something and we have o and f amongst us,' said o. 'I don't mind beginning a word. Two letters can do that. Only a can stand alone both as a word and letter. My brother is very versatile.'

'So, we now have Battle of.'

'Let's workshop this,' said capital G. 'It's obvious that I should begin the word because I'm in capitals. Now where's a vowel?'

'We're here,' said i and u.

'Try these. Ginbrugs. Gunsbirg. Gubsgrin. Gibsgrun. Grugbins. Grinsbug. Ginsbrug. Gunsbrig. How did I do?'

'None of them fit exactly. They all make words, but nothing I've heard before and they don't seem to fit as a title.'

Suddenly, there was a loud knock on the door. The sound reverberated as if in an echo chamber. It banged louder.

'Who is it?' asked Slirander.

She held her odd ear for comfort, or was it a warning hug?

Davidia collected all the letters and hid them in her jacket. She placed the small book mistakenly in the same pocket. The floorboard was quickly replaced. Funnily enough, it slid in of its own accord for the perfect fit. It would be undetectable, not like a toupee. Davidia revelled at the ease the floorboard complied. Did she see a smile, or was it a slit in its surface? It didn't matter.

'It's Hictor.'

'Is everything okay?'

'We have been trying to sleep. It's so tiring being a traveller. I'll open the door.'

Hictor seemed agitated. His happy pills must be on a manure

farm mixing with the best compost. His eyes rushed around the room. All he saw were the two girls acting tired. They could be recommended for an Oscar; they were so good.

'May I borrow your quill pen and a piece of paper, please?' asked Slirander, as if she was going to make a sexual reference.

Hictor was aghast at the approach. The suddenness made him involuntarily comply. Confrontation with good had never been this difficult. Slirander passed them both to Davidia. She whispered something. Davidia wrote it down, folded it and handed it to Hictor. She kept the pen, but he didn't notice. His radar was on malfunction.

'Don't open it yet. Wait until you are alone.'

Hictor's suspicions subsided.

'Okay, then.'

'We'll be out shortly,' said Slirander.

'Whew, he's out of the way.'

'Don't be too sure.'

Inside Davidia's pocket the letters had continued workshopping. She put her hand in to retrieve the letters and they were gone.

'Oh, no. The letters have disappeared,' she wailed.

'What about the book? He didn't pickpocket you, did he?'

'I don't think so.'

Davidia extracted the book and to her surprise on the outside cover as proud as punch were all sixteen letters in a title. It read, Battle of Ginsburg.

'That's amazing, you clever little letters.'

'We knew we had it in us. We're all pleased to be team players again. What's more, open the book,' said capital B.

Each page was slowly turned over. All the letters had miraculously been transformed into readable words and sentences. It was the book of the Battle of Ginsburg. It was nothing short of amazing. There were high fives all around.

'I don't believe it. You are all home in a readable format.'

'Lads,' said the leader, 'this is a great read. How long has it been since we were able to read a book without worrying about restoration? Where's our next challenge?'

The book suddenly flew out of Davidia's hands straight out the door into the street. Its pages flapped madly in the breeze. Hictor was walking toward the library. The book fell at his feet.

'What! A book that's still readable. It can't be.' He picked it up.

'Read your note,' instructed the talking book.

The girls watched silently. The book was talking to Hictor. Hoorus was certainly one strange town, or was it the history leaf that was strange?

Hictor unfolded the note hoping to read a salacious comment from Slirander. Instead, it simply read, Rotter. It dropped from his hands. His odd knuckle began to bubble furiously. How did they know what he really was? It must have been a guess. His disguise was perfect. Was there a leak in Rotland that he had to extinguish? His body began to feel the results of disappointment. The restored talking book again took flight back to the library. It brushed past the girls and flew directly to its spot on the library shelf. Even though it was by itself, it felt at home. The sixteen letters in the title appeared full of life. History had been preserved.

In the street, a large, dark, consuming cloud headed their way. Hictor hadn't moved. He had seen the cloud also and recognised the dangers it held for him. Restored letters were a formidable force.

'Lads, this is the greatest ride of my life,' yelled a leader of the soldiers of the Pebble of Purpose. He sat upon a flying E. All the other letters in the cloud formation had a restoration soldier enjoying the journey.

Once the Battle of Ginsburg book had been restored, the

valley of the "no name battle" erupted again; however, all the letters didn't compete with each other this time; they teamed together. The impossible restoration faced earlier by the soldiers had been given a reprieve. Damaged letters regained shape, form and respectability. A secret signal sent from the book triggered an instant revival within the letters. The no name valley had reclaimed its rightful title, The Battle of Ginsburg.

Hictor's body became contorted with rage. He thought, *How dare those letters survive!* He was positive that his Destrusto Virus was a sure-fire winner.

The flying letters swooped low past him, heading straight toward the books in the cart. Pages were attacked as letters re-assembled into titles and books. Soon, enough books were filled to refill the library shelves. The oversupply of letters then took flight to seek out any remaining history books that had been destroyed. The girls watched quietly as the library regained its inhabitants. They both smiled. The camorse had lost his load of books and began to trot off to the town of Horrus from where he came. He stopped next to Hictor, neighed loudly, spat at him, then planted a perfect U-shaped hoof — it too was shaped like a letter — on his backside and proudly sent him soaring. His two add angry eyes popped out and acted as aerial antennae. Alas, he was booted out of the valley cursing the perfect U.

'That will teach you to tangle with a talking camorse.'

With a swish of its tail held high, it was gone.

'What do we do now?' asked Davidia, thinking their time was short.

'Say a silly phrase. Anything will do,' replied Slirander.

'I don't know anything silly or stupid,' protested Davidia. 'I was always taught to be mature and sensible.'

'You're a girl. You're a natural.'

'Do you really think I'm capable of being stupid?'

The look on Slirander's face answered that question in spades without a word spoken.

'If you don't we are doomed into history. It's your turn.'

'Oh, alright, I'll try.'

Davidia took a deep breath and pushed out her developing body. She thought, *My, my, they've grown recently:*

> *'Like licorice, like licorice,*
> *The letters are thickerish,*
> *Like book, like book,*
> *Are we mistook?*

Is that silly enough?'

Before Slirander could answer, the ground began to shake, but only around the girls' feet. It was a personal metre by metre nightmare, or was it in this case, daymare? Had a sinister monster from the deep been awoken to grab them by the ankles and pull them into the bowels of the earth? Instead, it was a wrinkled tree root that wrapped itself around their ankles and whisked them upward.

'Not again,' yelled Davidia. Being upside down wasn't her favourite position.

The wrinkled tree root of the Moonatric tree had saved them. There must be something in being able to say stupid and silly things because it seems to save them time and time again. Safely inside the tree root, the dizziness of travel inside cocoon conditions made Davidia feel nauseous.

'Don't you dare?' warned Slirander.

Davidia choked back her next act. She soon settled. The effort of being a worker for good was taking its toll. Davidia and Slirander sat exhausted.

'Is Roland the Rotter always that bad?' asked Davidia.

'Not always, there was once a time when …' Slirander's voice trailed away.

Davidia wondered whether there was a secret she wasn't telling. A few loose hints had crept into her vocabulary. Where to now? The darkness inside the tree root didn't allow any clear vision.

*

The Hole in the Hill echoed with all the bad words a dictionary could provide. The cave walls were carved with crude sayings, rude words, bad vocabulary and bad spelling, suggesting someone angry didn't care about goodness and good diction.

'Those b … girls. That f … camorse. That s … talking book. That d … for everything else. Why can't my virus outsmart them? That big D and S, referring to the two girls, seem to turn up like the proverbial bad penny. There aren't any leaks here so there must be more to it than coincidence. Maybe if I can control my odd angry eyes, I can fool them. Somehow, I'll do it.'

Roland was having more than a bad hair day and he was bald.

So far, Roland the Rotter had imitated a human form in each category of learning. Professor Doonow (science), Professor Sum (mathematics), The Mayor (geography) and Hictor the Historian (history). Perhaps it was time to change tack and be more devious than before. He felt another headache. It was strange that this one didn't hurt at all. He shut his eyes and a frighteningly weird and unexplainable vision appeared. It wasn't Sunday. He hadn't joined a sect or cult, so why had he been picked out? The vision was his imagination going off the train-track of life and crashing into a rail buffer bringing ruin and chaos to his world.

'That will never happen,' he yelled into the cave.

When the echo had faded, it was silent.

Peace at last.

'Sometimes I wish that I was a bird,' said Davidia. 'Then I would be able to fly free and not be stuck in this dark, wrinkled, stovepipe tree root flying "heaven knows where". How do we get out of it this time?'

She was disgruntled. Being a language warrior was wearing thin.

'Follow me. We must crawl our way back to the main tree trunk to be safe. We can't stay stationary for long. Moonah can be quite unpredictable. Once, I was playing in one if its tree roots when it suddenly fell off. Next minute, all I could see was the bottom of a canyon and I almost became that bird you spoke of, but with the ability of one flight only. I clung tightly to a loose, weedy growth hanging from the top and managed to pull myself to safety. We had better hurry,' explained Slirander.

Without warning, the tree root swayed violently. The girls were tossed like flotsam and jetsam on the high seas. Davidia slammed into the roof, Slirander into the walls and they rolled about wondering what the problem was.

Outside, a huge flying animal had attacked Moonah. It was the Oddity, the most dangerous, flying freak that flew on the winds. It had two large and one small leg, two huge eyes and a cross-eyed third, one massive wing and a smaller version and four razor-sharp beaks that sliced through prey like a hot knife through butter. With its many disabilities, it was crankier and more dangerous than one with a perfect set of combinations. It had a musical hoot that when heard was often mistaken for the music of the latest band. It was a perfectionist imitator. It was upset with Moonah for not stopping and letting it perch on one of its branches. Flying was a tiresome exercise. Moonah knew that once it had landed, it was a forever relationship. Some of Moonah's relatives had previous experience with this giant pest and it was a "no brainer" to get involved. Branches would eventually be pecked to destruction, its trunk would soon be scarred from sharpening claws, and the waste it deposited amongst the tree roots would eventually rot them.

It was a fight for survival. Moonah tried the tricks of survival learnt during its hurricane and tornado experiences. The girls just had to make do the best they could. Fortunately for them, they were in a tight section of the tree root that Davidia had complained about. The confined space was their saviour.

Moonah swung its branches and tree roots in a whipping fashion trying to knock the Oddity senseless. It dived, screeched and slashed at Moonah.

'You wrinkled, decaying, rotten mass will not deny me,' squawked Oddity.

'Find another roosting post,' replied Moonah, with a well-mannered response.

'You'll suffer the same fate as your family members have.'

'Not likely.'

Moonah had a special tree root manoeuvre that the Oddity never saw coming. The tree root that held Davidia and Slirander acted as an extra weight. He swung it wide and it struck the Oddity's side. It momentarily winded it long enough to safely make an escape.

'Gone are the days when I could rest and grow quietly,' said Moonah, annoyed at staving off a serious combat.

'Are we still in a washing machine?' asked Davidia, pulling her long hair from between her teeth.

'That was frightening. Hurry, before it's too late.'

They scrambled quickly toward the tree trunk. The tussle with the Oddity wasn't over. Its long-range vision had kept Moonah in its sight.

'That flying compost heap will rue its refusal to allow me to rest. I'll strip its branches bare, sever them all and turn it into an unattractive tree stump.'

The Oddity flapped furiously in the chase after Moonah. It wondered how a tree could fly when there were no visible means of operating it. It didn't have wings like a bird, an engine like those flying machines, or any apparatus that defied gravity. It was a mystery. All the Oddity wanted to do was befriend its sky-travelling companion and use it as a personal rest stop. There were rumours in parts of the world that the Moonatric tree was inhabited by a flying fable that no one knew of. It was an acceptable explanation, but nothing knew for sure.

The girls were doing their best to manage it to the main tree trunk, but somehow the tree root grew with each step they took, and they were never any closer to safety.

'That history leaf must have fallen off. It was our only avenue of escape. They aren't supposed to fall off with us in it.'

'What a great pickle we're in. How come it's us who must save the written language? More fool us for spotting a Rotter. Now we'll never make it. We're doomed in some stupid tree root. What's there to eat anyway? I'm starving.' Davidia was none too impressed at being sealed inside a flying tree root. She had no idea where they were. 'Can't we signal SOS or something?'

Slirander didn't seem too concerned. She sat down and felt the tree root's wrinkles. Her long, slender fingers tugged at a loose growth. It gave way. Small deposits of rotted matter clung fiercely to its roots making a nice artistic pattern at its base.

'Hi, Slirander. Moonah's up to his old tricks again. Fancy trying the lizard tail growth on you out of all its friends,' said the clingy growth. 'I can't remember the last time I spoke. Very few visitors enter here anymore. What brings you here?'

'Oh, the usual. Rotters,' she replied.

'Still making a nuisance of themselves, are they? Did you cause that fabulous tree swish? It's the most excitement I've had for a long time. Moonah seems content to grow old and teach. Shall I let him know you are shaken and not stirred?'

'The Oddity is following us. He needs to concentrate on outwitting it.'

'You better put me back before I dry out.'

Slirander replanted the clingy growth into the tree root wall. Once firmly embedded, it blended in as part of a rustic garden.

'You know how to get out of here,' said Davidia. 'How would you know that?'

'It's complicated. Moonah can't deal with our problem just yet. The Oddity must be taught a lesson not to annoy all air travellers. It's a sky menace. The last time I travelled in this manner, it was almost a disaster. Moonah was busy dodging hurricanes and whirlpools when, thump, a huge unwanted pile of ruffled feathers landed on a branch. Its claws became stuck in a branch and, of course, it cursed offal, but couldn't break clear. Moonah reluctantly had to let go of that branch which held an important subject. It wasn't History, but another as equally important topic. That branch fell to earth with that wretched bird refusing to let go. We don't know where it landed, so the alphabet is one letter short. Moonah has been searching a long time for that missing branch and its letter leaf. I have a feeling where it might be, but it's only a feeling. The responsibility becomes too much at times. I'm still only a young girl.'

Davidia was nonplussed. Her odd-eared friend was odder than she first thought. Even so, it was rather exciting to have a vibrant interesting friend than being the boring old fart that many teachers represented to schoolkids.

'We can't see outside,' said Davidia. 'It's gloomy in here.'

'I'll show you a secret,' said Slirander. 'Place your hand flat against one of those lumpy growths; yes, that one looks fine. Shut your eyes tightly and imagine you can see outside. Can you see anything?'

After a moment or two, a vision of swirls, angry clouds and howling winds mixed it inside her head.

'There's a bad storm happening.'

'Anything else?'

'Is that a flying dish rag I can see? It's hard to see clearly with all that swirling cloud and water. No, it's more like a huge, ugly, three-eyed bird following us. It's so ungainly, it's a wonder it can get airborne. I wouldn't want that as a pet or on my plate for dinner.'

'What do you make of it?'

'Flying can be a health hazard.'

'Press harder.'

Davidia's hand acted like a set of imaginative eyes with one on the end of each finger. They moved up and down like seaweed in a gentle, rippled flow. As long as her hand kept contact with the lumpy growth, the visions remained.

'There's a large shadow looming ahead. It's shaped like an ice-cream cone. What is it? There aren't any magicians there, are there?'

'That's land. We'll be there shortly.'

'Is that where we are headed? It looks bleak and uninviting. There's no growth except some stubbly bushes.'

Before an explanation was forthcoming, the last thing Davidia remembered as her hand lost contact with the lumpy growth, was being covered in wet dripping feathers. Had the Oddity dumped on their tree root? Fortunately, this time it was too difficult to gain a claw-hold.

'Wow! Was that real?'

'Only if you believe it to be so,' replied Slirander. 'Moonah will be on land shortly.'

'What happened to the history leaf?'

'It was lost. The exit strategy is now recovering the lost leaf lettered topic. If we can regain that, then we will be set free from the history leaf and resume our restoration activity.'

'How do we do that?'

'We cannot physically leave the tree root. We must remain inside. Note how large it has grown whilst you were dream sequencing, but in truth it was reality-sequencing that you experienced. Our other self, the imaginative section of us, will be on the outside searching for the lost leaf. Moonah needs to find that lost branch as well to restore its teaching alphabet and regain that important subject.'

'This is crazy. We stay indoors and our imagination takes a walk. I don't think so.'

'Where's your sense of adventure? It should be fun, but remember, if you lose your imaginative self, it's the same as if you are actually being there.'

It was mentally confusing. School friends had tried to play debating tricks to prove the stupidity of the questions, but Davidia was a bright light bulb with a fully functioning filament and was difficult to toss. She once asked the opposition that if communism was an idea and we all know that you can't destroy an idea, then how can you destroy communism? It left the knowledge graspers gasping. It was a clear-thinking exercise, but the classroom was filled with fog on that day. Was she confronting a dilemma of equal proportions here? Her only true weapon was her intelligence and today it had to live as her imagination. Why had her hands been turned brown? She never really understood that; however, she noticed they had special properties when she placed it up against that lumpy growth. She believed that she could see with them. Maybe Slirander's dad was a genius or held magical powers. Whatever weird was, she was glad Slirander was on her side. Her overnight stopover had certainly developed from two silly girls dressing-up, having outrageous hair dos and experimenting with make-up to fully weird. Who'd believe what they were doing?

Only the readers would.

Crash! A sudden thump sent debris on a holiday. Dirt fell from the tree root's ceiling and lodged in their hair. They had struck something. Slirander placed her hand on a lumpy growth.

'We've landed safely. Moonah has a few structural breakages but is mostly intact. A few days of growth and he'll be as good as new. There is no sight of that ghastly Oddity.'

'Where have we landed?' asked Davidia. She put her hand on a lumpy growth to see. As she did so, her imaginative self walked outside. It was a blanket of sleet, but she didn't feel the cold or got wet. *Brilliant,* she thought. 'Can we use the antidote here if needed, if we are inside?'

'No. It's not possible out there. Once you clamp onto a lumpy growth, do not let go regardless of any pain, until your imagination is safely back inside. We will be in a special animation section of our brains. Moonah needs our help. We have landed on a remote land only accessible by flight. The mountains are all cone shaped, impenetrable by land. The soil is barely able to provide any nutrients for the shrubs here. Moonah has reserves stored in its roots. Once it has landed, it remains stationary and we must foot-slog to find the leaf letter. It could be guarded by weirdness. This is a treacherous place.'

'Who runs it?'

'That Oddity and her brother, Weirdo?'

'What or who actually lives here?'

'The Ninnytwits. I have only read about them,' said Slirander.

'You seem to have done an awful lot of reading. Everywhere we go you know something of the place. Have you been here before?'

'Not quite.'

The Ninnytwits were a race of oddity-born individuals. Each one had something physically different to the other. It might be an extra toe, eye, elbow, knuckles, leg, arms or whatever. Apparently, their genetic formation was influenced by the coned land in which they live. A special aroma emanated from the cones. The inhabitants breathed it in, and it mutated throughout their system and the end result was a physical difference when a new Ninnytwit was born. Imagine the two-head syndrome or trying to run on three legs. It wasn't worth thinking about. They were usually friendly, but, unfortunately, their rulers were ruthless and cruel. It's hard to smile or crack a joke when one's own bone is being cracked. Oddity and Weirdo practised suppression at the highest level. They were too large for anything to tackle them. The small, cone-shaped homes were often overturned by a vicious talon or awful beak. The rulers were meat-eaters and there was a good chance that a few Ninnytwits ended up as fine dining. Apparently, a family who had lost a member in this fashion was feted by others hoping it wasn't their turn. Unfortunately, seconds often happened.

'Moonah, are you firmly embedded for a long stay?' asked Slirander, through the tunnel tree-root intercom system.

A loud groan of aching tree roots and settling branches could be heard.

'At last. Flying can certainly be exhausting. Beware of those two flying hazards. They guard everything to the death,' said Moonah.

'How do we find that missing branch and its subject?' asked Slirander.

'That Oddity probably uses it as a perch and is unaware of its importance.'

'If we find it, how can it reattach itself to you?' asked Davidia, thinking weird applied to Moonah also.

'You only have to find it intact. I'll do the rest.'

'How do you know it's here? It could have fallen off anywhere. At home we would have wood-chipped it by now.'

'It's definitely here. I feel it in my wood. Besides, Oddity doesn't fly too far from its home. It may be perilous to find it.'

'If it's a tree branch, won't it look like any other?'

'You will know when the time comes. I might be old and wrinkled, but never tangle with an odd angry tree root. Go.'

'This is ridiculous. Me, an imaginary figure, outside a tree root to save a branch that was obviously too old to continue growing otherwise it wouldn't have fallen off.'

'Remember, Davidia, once we are outside, continue to cling tightly to that lumpy growth inside. You may feel invincible, but a good thought no matter how good can't stop a bullet. There are things here I don't like.'

'Are there bullets here?'

'No, it's a saying.'

'You can't scare me by "crying wolf". There, that's a saying too. Let's find that lost branch. I hope it hasn't been used for campfire material. What was the topic in the lost leaf?'

'I'm not sure, but it was the letter L. Moonah says it is most important to find it intact.'

'It won't grow here, will it? Everything is odd. I wouldn't be surprised if that Oddity has already used it as a sharpening tool or a poo dump. Got any gloves?'

Slirander had enough of the small talk. It was time to go

and impose oneself on the outside tree root world. Their other imaginary selves set off. It was the first time that Davidia had a conversation with herself besides in the bedroom mirror.

'Where are we going? I don't like this place. My goose bumps are extra lumpy,' said Davidia.

'To find the home of Oddity and its dopey brother, Weirdo. The missing branch should be somewhere near there.'

'Do you know the way?'

'Instinct. There aren't any GPSs in this realm. This track leads somewhere. Remember bird-like animals roost at height. I expect they'll be in those cone-shaped mountains. Any better ideas?'

'Why not ask that thing over there? It seems harmless enough.'

The two girls approached a bent-over Ninnytwit who was admiring its features in a small puddle. Davidia stood in it. The ripples changed the Ninnytwit's facial appearance dramatically. The water distorted its self-believed beauty. It raised its head. It was only half the size of Davidia.

'Excuse me. Do you know the way to the Oddity's home? We're visitors and have a special present for it,' said Davidia, half-expecting a sensible answer and cooperation. Innocence still lived within her.

'Who's going to answer first? Is it me, you, or you? I'll reply, seeing I'm already talking,' said one of the Ninnytwit's mouths. It was impossible to tell them apart or which of them spoke before the others.

'Are you sure you're first? Isn't it my turn or is it your turn?' asked a mouth.

'I'm first or am I third? Which one of us is second?'

'I thought I was first. Why don't you go first? But I might be third and who's second? You could be first, but how do we know?'

The Ninnytwit raised its head. The shock of seeing three

mouths competing for speaking space meant overactive facial movements. There didn't seem to be any space left for a nose.

'I didn't answer the last question, so I'll answer it this time.'

'Was the question for you alone or us other two and you made a mistake that it's yours.'

'No. I was first to answer so it should be mine.'

'What was the question? It could have been directed at first, second and am I third, or one of you two?'

'Excuse me,' repeated Davidia.

'There's no need to remind us of the question. Who's got it? First or third, I think I'm second.'

'Didn't you have it? Is it lost? What was it?'

Davidia lost patience with the nonsense of their indecision.

'Where's the bloody Oddity's home?'

'There's no need to shout. Did it shout at you, or was it me, I couldn't tell?'

Finally, a mouth said, in conflict with its competition, that it was at the base of that cone-hill in the distance.

'Thank you.'

'Did it say it to you, me or you? It's hard to tell. Bye, bye, bye.'

At last the mouths agreed on something.

'I hope this place isn't all like that lot. I wondered what it was.'

The girls began the long trek. It did seem to be quite some distance. Ahead lay a track dotted with small cone villages. They looked like a tropical version of igloos. Eyes furtively watched their movements. Very few visitors passed through their land. It was usually a one-way trip. Dusk rolled in as faithful as an entree night servant. Accommodation was in short supply, so before the light completely disappeared, they needed shelter, but was there any viable accommodation? The inhabitants were only half their size.

'Ask at the next village,' said Davidia.

They came upon a single house on the verge of the village. The doorway came up to the height of their waist. Slirander knelt and lightly knocked on the door. It slowly opened. Three eyes peered out reflecting the fading light. An arm slipped out and pointed at them. Hissing could be heard, or was it hissing? They strained their ears. Slirander could hear and understand perfectly. Her odd ear was not an impediment to clear hearing.

'Look behind you. They are planning to capture us. We better leave quickly. They also don't like being out after dark.'

'There isn't anything there. What were they?'

'Trouble with a capital T. There isn't much in the way of language here. We were fortunate to meet the talking mouths. Many communicate by sound only. That was a group of Hissters. Some villagers will talk. Fear is their friend. It keeps them controlled.'

'Where to next?'

'We might have to camp out and use those skills that you talk about when you went camping,' suggested Slirander. 'We must stay away from any life. None of it is friendly.'

'Even that tree root would be more comfortable instead of being out here. Over there under those shrubs seems comfortable enough. The ground is flat. There's a green covering. We'll freeze the night there. Where's my doona when I need it?'

At least when Davidia had last camped, she had taken the correct gear. Sleeping in the open was a hazardous situation. Back at the tree root, Davidia and Slirander realised that tonight was going to be a tough one. They had to stay awake or at least, if they didn't, not to let go of the lumpy growth.

'This green covering is the same that grew at the base of Moonah in your backyard,' said Davidia.

'So it is,' replied Slirander, pretending surprise. The moment she set foot on the grass, it ran up her leg in greeting, then it quickly receded. 'We will be safe sleeping here tonight. Quilter will keep us warm.'

*

That night, two huge, brooding feathered animals nestled on their favourite branch. They had no idea of the importance of the branch or the stunted protruding growth that once housed a leaf. It was their clinging place, with branch width ideal for their huge cumbersome claws. Walking wasn't their bag. Flying was easier, but the way they did it, it looked like they were always on a training run. They never fully mastered the proper art of a good flying technique.

'Hey, Weirdo, what's on the menu tomorrow?' asked Oddity humming a tune. 'It's your turn to find the feast.'

'I'm sick of eating Ninnytwits. Sure, they are easy to catch, nutritiously bereft and taste like stale waste, but isn't there something tastier we can find? I need a diet change.'

Weirdo slumped over the tree branch like a wet towel, drippy and flat. He and his sister had been the rulers of Conika for a long time. Both were ageing and their feathers were bedraggled and losing their flight factor. Soon all they would be able to do would be walk and waddle. The Ninnytwits would then seize the chance to rid themselves of permanent unhappiness. They couldn't interbreed — it was not allowed, and their families were too far away to replenish their rule with a like strange animal.

'I almost found a fresh branch today. One of those huge moonatric trees flew nearby and I almost caught it. What I wouldn't do for a fresh branch. This one is so full of our waste and slippery with wear, it's almost useless. Tomorrow, I'll toss it down that ravine on Mount Conikaka.'

'Roland hasn't visited recently, has he?' asked Weirdo.

Apparently, Rotland was the next country, but with the impenetrable cone mountain barrier barring access, it had saved their ignorance or intelligence. There was no written language in Conika to destroy, so it had no appeal to Roland the Rotter.

He detested the two huge animals and felt conversation in the form of a series of sing-a-longs was rather banal. The only time he did visit was to ensure that the Ninnytwits didn't have an intelligent thought between them. He needn't have bothered. His Destrusto Virus would have been a waste of time. There was no challenge for it.

'He doesn't go in for the good neighbour policy. It's been a long time since I've seen him. His appearance alters constantly, so we mightn't recognise him if we saw him again.'

Roland the Rotter had no friends. All he wanted was to own and covet the world's written language. They both grunted and nodded to each other. A smile was alien on their faces.

'Do you feel it in the air?' asked Oddity. 'That odd smell is different.'

Weirdo opened a nostril wide enough to drive a truck down and agreed.

'It is odd, isn't it? I haven't smelt that before. Is it an imaginary smell?'

'We'll follow it in the morning. There's something not quite right with it. My quills are shivering with apprehension.'

'Is it that or bad air flow?'

'Stupid, Weirdo,' mumbled Oddity.

Her younger brother always had to be the comedian.

The night stood still. Not a Ninnytwit, girls, shrubs or animals stirred. It was a time frozen in the moment. Even Moonah had shut down. The land of Conika had gone into a hypnotic state.

*

'Can you hear the music?' asked Davidia, as she swallowed gulps of fresh air.

'It's downright awful. It's not to my taste. It sounds like rap, rap, rap with a dude worder expressing life's philosophies with many f words. Good diction and full-length words are in short supply. I can't understand a word of it. I wonder where it's coming from,' said Slirander, who had an odd ear for music.

'I think it's somewhere near those mountains.'

'They aren't that far. It seems that our real selves stayed awake all night. We're still moving.'

'Is there anything here to eat?'

'Don't trust any of the food. It could be something you don't want to eat. Keep moving. We must find that tree branch.'

The girls began their walk toward the mountains. Nothing of any significance grew on them. Wily weeds were the smartest growth in the land. They took a foothold on every spare soil spot. Plants were welcome, but the Ninnytwits had eaten most of them. Hence, the unattractive, inedible and weeds in pest proportions proliferated everywhere. The villagers were up and about. They were so small, all one could see was a pair of feet, or was that a trio of feet under each cone-shaped hat? They looked like the march of the periwinkles one often found at the beach. No one approached them. Their size might have frightened them. They couldn't see the faces of the Ninnytwits because of their large hats. Whatever they looked like was to remain a mystery. Slirander knew that they wouldn't be troubled by them if they weren't threatened; however, sometimes a rogue element of treacherous nastiness, born out of boredom, erupted with devastating results. A few decayed bones littered in the hills were testament that something had been there involuntarily.

*

'Dig that beat. Kick my shoes. Yank my yucka. Grooviness of grime. Thumpy tum. Go misery. Give me mess.'

Oddity jigged up and down on the tree branch, like a cockatoo on hot coals, with its version of dreadful lyrics to the latest tune it had heard somewhere in flight. It might have come from a flying steel bird with people in its stomach. Oddity wasn't sure what it was; however, its stomach was always full of live food listening to long, thin, black growths coming out of their ears. The heads nodded incessantly. Music or its version was its way of relieving boredom. There wasn't much else it could do, except eat and poo.

'Stop imitating rubbish. You haven't picked up a decent song in ages,' said Weirdo to Oddity with the oddest name.

'Just because you are musically inept and don't understand the feel of it, you shouldn't criticise,' replied Oddity, peeved-off that her younger brother had no appreciation of the sounds.

'Shut-up for a minute. Can you hear it?'

'Hear what?' Oddity stopped and listened for thirty seconds.

'The silence. What a relief you've turned off.'

Oddity grew an angst emotion and ran along the slippery branch to bluff a kick and teach Weirdo a lesson for being full of bird shit. Suddenly, she lost her footing and fell beak first onto the ground. Her four beaks had skewered a twig.

'Phut, phut,' Oddity spat out the splinters.

Weirdo had retreated to another section of their dwelling for safety.

'I've got a feeling.'

'And what song is that from?'

'No. No. I've got a real feeling. My quills are quivering, my stomach juices are on the march and I'm about to embarrassingly express myself.'

'You aren't going to do that, are you?'

'Of course, not. I have my pride.'

Weirdo suddenly honked loud and long. It wasn't in tune. No orchestra would include that riff in its song ensemble. It was the danger signal that trouble was approaching. Ninnytwits ran fearfully in circles fearing a menu activity. Of course, they couldn't escape running only in circles. Slirander and Davidia had also heard the mournful sound.

'There's something approaching this way and I don't like it.'

'Is it a stray Ninnytwit? Even they aren't that stupid to come here.'

'It's something that smells completely different. I can't quite put my claw on it. Remember when we were younger there was that odd visitor that strayed here from Rotland. What was that small odd-eared character called?'

'That was a pest, playing silly games and teasing us.'

'That smell is the same. My sinuses are clear.'

Weirdo gave his honkers a solid blast and clean-out in case he was mistaken.

'We can have a leg each and mash what's left. Isn't it exciting being a chef?' said Oddity, preening her feathers for the feast at the Ball.

The two huge feathered freaks agitated for the visitors to call. Entrapment would be their welcome greeting. Oddity's beaks operated like a set of clappers as they each practised ripping an imaginary something. The stage was set. Two old, music, all farts were taking advantage of youthful enthusiasm. What a musical to be played out!

*

'What was that god-awful noise?' asked Davidia.

Even at home her brother's violin practising hadn't been that woeful.

'It's a warning. We must be nearing their nesting site.'

'Nearing whose nesting site?'

'Oddity and Weirdo. They are sister and brother. They are the present rulers of Conika, but not for much longer. Age is catching them. Soon the Ninnytwits will take over and return the country to a peaceful and productive environment.'

'I suppose you read that in a book too,' said Davidia, sarcastically.

'I've been here before.'

Well, dance on my grave, bash me with bubble-gum or a witty remark, and slam a book on my fingers. What was Davidia hearing? Been here before. How could that be? Her real self almost lost hold of the lumpy growth spelling her doom. What was her friend telling her?

'You know this place?'

'My parents allowed me in here a long time ago. It's hard to remember where everything once was. It has changed so much. Don't believe what they tell you. They are intelligent and cunning. They once convinced the fish in the river, when it did hold fish, that their fins were legs. Invited to sit around a campfire, which is far warmer than the cold water, they complied and tried to walk there. Needless to say, they weren't told they couldn't breathe air. Many expired in the attempt. Oddity and Weirdo couldn't swim, so this was how they trapped them. The fish only have a five-second retention span, so they had no idea what they were doing. Sounds like they're the sheep of the water world, doesn't it?' explained Slirander.

Davidia was continuously amazed by her friend's talents. She continuously surprised her with snippets of information about what, where and how they were here there or elsewhere.

'What will happen to us if we are caught?'

'A long, dark, forever holiday with our bones pretending to be long, thin-shaped rocks lying in a pile with all the other inhabitant's remnants that they have eaten.'

'No feathered lump of crap is dining on my fine features. How do we outsmart them?' asked Davidia, feeling queasy at the thought that she was thought of as a food source and could possibly also be a food sauce. Yuck!

'We must outwit them. Normally, intelligence is not a regular occurrence with what they eat; however, we must talk our way into them believing that they have caught us. We must coax them off the tree branch so that Moonah can reattach it to its trunk. Whilst they are seated on it, nothing can happen to either of us. Baffle them with bullshit, not the real thing, but the saying one.'

'My brother sometimes speaks like that: like I was, like in the shop like there today, and I was like going home, like then the mobile rang, like loud, like it was Johnno, like he was calling, like me. Like I didn't understand, like he thought I was like stupid, like him.'

'Yeh! Like the way like the kids at like school speak, like they're thinking many words, like they're not, like because, like the word they like repeat is, like. We can't like text here either.'

The two girls cackled over their modern youth-like expressions, which was normal school speak. Maybe if they used that baffling dialogue it would stress the flying freaks. It sounds like, one word, two syllables, it's a movie. Charades might work too. They neared the hostile environment of the nesting site. It was at the base of the Conikaka Mountains where the Conikaka Ravine was their normal dumping ground for bone waste. The place was very untidy. There were no cleaners, nor had there ever been any in sight of this mess. They peered around a cone-shaped rock, they were all that shape, when a cockroach ran past Slirander's feet.

'Be careful,' it said. 'I'm the act for the day.'

It scuttled off into a messy pile of unpleasant things. It was quite at home in decaying refuse.

Ahead they could see the two huge freaks jigging up and down on Moonah's lost branch. They weren't in unison. Forget the ballet training.

'There it is,' yelled Slirander in a moment of muffled excitement. 'That's Moonah's branch, I'd recognise it anywhere. See, it still has a few wrinkles that haven't worn away. Can you see the stumpy growth where the missing leaf once was?'

'It's still there. It hasn't been touched because it's on the underside of the branch. What a break,' said Davidia. 'We have a chance to save it.'

They stared for a few moments planning their strategy. In Conika the antidote was useless. They had to generate other survival skills.

'Can you smell how near they are?' asked Oddity. becoming excited about tasting something different.

'It won't be long now before they are slithering down our throats in a long procession as wonderful food. Yum.'

'Have you got the trained cockroach ready to impersonate an interviewer?'

'My cockroach man is fully functional to do our bidding as we want. I'm not totally stupid. A cockroach is difficult to professionally train. I threatened it with extinction and the results speak for themselves. Wait till you see its act.'

Oddity knew that cockroaches were untrainable, but there was always a first time for everything.

'Now what?' asked Davidia. 'They're there. We're here hiding. Shouldn't we show ourselves?'

'We'll do it one at a time. I'm first. Let's see what plan they have to unveil,' replied Slirander. 'When I signal to you in like speak, jump out next to me. It might confuse them, I mean, with two of us the same.'

The freaks continued sniffing the air. Body smells wafted around like aromatic scents. Slirander played her jack-in-the-box tactic and jumped out from behind the cone rock and stood defiant like a recalcitrant schoolgirl, ready to best her opponents.

'Hey, you two lard arses, wanna knock me block off? Well, here's your chance like,' she yelled out in ghastly diction, expression and bad sentence structure.

Oddity and Weirdo squawked loudly in surprise and both fell off their perch protesting all the way. They scrambled to their claws and shook with rage.

'You could have given us a heart attack,' complained Weirdo.

Acting innocently was part of the game. Cunning is as cunning does.

'I'm here as the Ninnytwits' representative for good governance of Conika.'

'Who for? What! Those losers and cone nuts. You must have more than a silly speech platform,' said Oddity, who loved nothing better than a good debate, except for tasty food.

'You must leave this valley and never return.'

'What nonsense is this? You aren't in charge here, we are.'

Just before an all-in argument broke out, Crinky, the cockroach was enticed from its refuse pile with its act down pat for anything that would pay attention.

'Participants, please calm down. Arguing is no way to solve a problem. It creates and or worsens them, but it is never a solution. Now, why don't you two shake hands, it is called a hand, isn't it, to claw? That way, a resolution would be achieved.'

Crinky was quietly spoken. For an insect, he was well up the intelligence chain.

Oddity put her best claw forward, whilst Slirander took a further step of separation.

'This one is playing hard to get,' said Oddity to her brother. 'That didn't work.'

'What are you and are you called anything?' asked Crinky.

'I'm a visitor and my name is Slirander.'

'Why are you here?'

'Orienteering. Like at school like, we go like camping and stuff like, and visit places like I want to go there like, and have fun like cause that's what I like to do.'

Davidia suddenly leapt out from behind the cone rock pretending she'd won the school high-jump competition. Once again, Oddity and Weirdo became flustered when they saw a duplicate whatever it was. Davidia high-fived Slirander. Now there were two.

What strange, jumping creatures and what unusual language expression, thought Oddity. Their next-door neighbour, Roland the Rotter, wouldn't stand for such bad expression. Wait a minute, could that be him in disguise? They knew of him, but not his physical appearance.

'Hello, neighbour,' said Oddity, trying to bring out a truth.

'I'm not your neighbour. I'm Davidia and Slirander is my friend.'

'Oh, that all. I thought you might be something else. Are you staying to be the meal for dinner, I mean for dinner?' asked Oddity, not sure of what she was dealing with.

'Excuse me,' said Crinky in his squeaky voice, as if his throat was being throttled, 'join us for dinner. It is simple fare with minimum preparation.'

'I'm starving,' said Davidia, almost being conned into thinking that she would be offered something to eat.

'There's nothing like crispy cockroach appetiser, tree bark stew and a magnificent dessert of pureed weeds. Sometimes we have nitwit nerds, but you know them better as Ninnytwits,' chuckled Oddity.

Her huge frame ached from over-stimulation in the joke department.

'I'm sorry we can't stay.'

In a flash, kaboom, the girls had disappeared behind the cone rock.

'They aren't getting away that easily,' yelled Oddity. 'Air to air. Let's go.'

Weirdo and Oddity opened their full wingspan, covering the ground in eerie shadows. They soared into the air searching for the girls. Crinky, the cockroach, made good his escape. His family had often provided a tasty snack, but with so few left, his survival was important. He followed the girls.

'They are excellent liars. Be careful. Say hello to my future descendants. You are a friend to them.'

Crinky did a short, waste-disposal exercise and the odour reminded Slirander of the antidote ingredient. She nodded as the small insect scurried away to safety.

*

Back at the tree root, Slirander and Davidia were tiring of hanging onto the lumpy growth. They had to formalise a quick-think plan, alerting Moonah that they had found the lost tree root.

Slirander whispered something into the tree root wall and, like an electricity conductor, the message sped off and hit the tree trunk. Moonah lazily woke up. When a tree rests, it really rests.

'You have found it. Now where's that stump of mine?'

Moonah sent signals to his tree root and branch extremities

and the one where the sound returned quickest would be the tree stump he was looking for.

'You've found the rest of me. Oh, my god, how exciting. Am I in good shape? Have I been pecked or broken? Do I have all my wrinkles?' exclaimed an excited stump.

'Your lost section has been found. We must retrieve it. Once it's reattached, we can leave this land for the last time. When I was a sapling, each visit here almost ended in breakage. This time, once we are one tree again, we can kiss Conika goodbye.'

'I remember those days as I was starting out as a small leaf. The breeze made clinging on rather exciting. When that tubby lard got its claw hooked into me, I thought it was all over. To be reattached will be a pleasure. What of leaf?'

'Leaf was lost, but all its truth, knowledge and goodness has been transferred to its stumpy growth where it remains intact. Once that is retrieved, the complete alphabet will live and flow through you once again. Slirander must give us the signal to safely approach the Conikaka Mountains.'

The stumpy tree stump could only wriggle. Once reattached it will have full movement again. Suddenly, the whole tree began shaking. The girls hung on.

'What's happening?' asked Davidia, frightened that she would lose her grip and herself.

'Moonah is getting ready to leave. I must signal him at the right time so he can fly to the lost tree branch and reattach it. That process takes a little while, so we have to amuse Oddity and Weirdo until it's safely restored,' replied Slirander.

*

'They are hiding down there. Drop something on them,' screamed Oddity.

'I don't have anything left. It's all back on the tree root,' complained Weirdo.

Over the years of doing daily airdrops, age had made it more difficult. His stability wasn't what it once was, and dirty feathers were a bugger to clean.

'I'll give it a try. Leave it up to a female to do the dirty jobs.'

Oddity dive-bombed the conical rocks, trailing wet waste. Splash! It was laden with an acidic tinge, which chipped off the rock edges. She soared up high waiting for the two screamers to emerge, but they weren't there.

'I couldn't have missed. I'm bum perfect with my aim. You'll notice that my section of tree branch is always much cleaner than yours. Where did they go?'

At ground level, Slirander knew a secret pathway between the rocks that she had used when she was much younger. The girls had mysteriously disappeared for all intensive purposes.

'We have to lead them away from the tree branch,' said Slirander, 'to make it safe for Moonah.'

'I've an idea,' said Davidia.

She stood tall and began singing a tune that she had learnt listening to the radio. It had a catchy rhythm, witty lyrics and a sensual beat. The mountains echoed with wondrous sounds.

'I didn't know that you could sing,' said Slirander.

'Neither did I,' said Davidia, 'Well, I did, but not that well.'

Oddity heard the sounds and it immediately affected her. Her feathers began to oscillate independently. Her head shook uncontrollably with rhythm as she imitated the song that Davidia had sung. It was impossible to stay airborne in the company of such good music. She glided downwards. Thump. Weirdo followed. Thump. The two biggies sat jiving away as Oddity sang and acted out a body routine akin to looking for the lost. They both danced the jerky.

'*Shug, shug, ate a slug, ate a ninnytoo.*

Shug, shug, ate a roach, ate a ninnytoo,'

she sang and harmonised.

Even Weirdo, who usually criticised Oddity's lousy musical tastes, had to admit that this one was catchy. He even sang a made-up line to the rhythm.

'*Mush, mush, squash a twit, kick a lump of poo.*

Mush, mush, squash a nit, I stood in it too.'

The valley rang with entertainment.

The song was infectious. It kept them ground bound. They bounced and flounced, scratched the ground with claws a tapping too. The Ninnytwits emerged from their homes and couldn't believe hearing the beautiful music. They began twirling like spinning tops under their cone hats. *If only it would last,* some thought.

Davidia instantly recognised a way of keeping Oddity and Weirdo away from the tree root.

'Slirander, if I keep singing long enough, it may give Moonah sufficient time to reattach in safety. What do you think?'

'How many songs do you know like that?'

'About four, but I can improvise. I know some rap music. They might absorb that.'

'It's worth the risk, otherwise we'll be here forever. We can't physically beat them because they are too large. Being cleverer than them is our only out. I'll signal Moonah.'

Slirander's real self inside the tree root sent a tap, tap, tap signal of three hard thumps against the tree root wall. It ricocheted off each wrinkle, which quivered with vibrations.

'It's time to move,' said Moonah. 'All I have to do is release my roots from this rotten soil.'

A few tree root shakes and he was free. A few clods of dirt held on tightly. They too didn't like the environment. Change would be welcome. Moonah began to float toward the inviting mountains of Conikaka.

'Travelling again,' said Cumulus, who always had a nice word to say as it floated by.

'Just restless,' replied Moonah. 'I just can't settle anywhere.'

'See you next trip.'

Moonah could see the mountains closing in. Where's Slirander? What's that dreadful noise? Oddity and Weirdo were performing a duet of rap music. They didn't notice the wrinkled shadow fly overhead, but had they, the music would immediately cease, and battle claws would be drawn. They had been lulled into entertainment, which had been so absent for a long time they had almost forgotten about catching the girls. Moonah drifted quietly by. As magnets attract metals to each other, Moonah felt it in his tree roots that his lost branch was nearby. Suddenly, he sighted it. Many branches began to grow small leaves in excitement. He could see that Oddity and Weirdo were far away being distracted. This was his chance. He floated down and landed next to the tree branch. It wasn't quite recognisable as one of his pristine attachments. There were lots of pecked indentations, claw scarring and a whitish and tanned substance littered on one side. Underneath the stump it was intact and strewn with dribble lines. Many of its wrinkles had smoothed. Moonah settled onto the ground and began the task of reattachment. His stump had to reconnect. Slowly his trunk began to open. He was at his most vulnerable at this very stage.

Crinky, the cockroach observed. He wandered over to Moonah and asked if he could hitch a ride to wherever it was he was going. Any place was better than this dump. Moonah politely refused. It was impossible for him to transport others. The future had already been determined.

'Sleight me, huh!' Crinky moaned. 'I'll teach you a lesson.'

The rotten little turncoat scampered through the rocks ready to dob on Moonah. A refusal often offends and Crinky was offended by crikey. The little insect almost wore out his many legs on the rocks' surface as he hurriedly ran toward Oddity and Weirdo.

Their movements indicated pain, but which sort? Davidia was still singing loudly. Crinky ran past Slirander straight up to Oddity.

'Oddity, back at your nesting site there is a huge tree intruder. It's taking your roosting spot.'

Oddity stopped dead. Weirdo kept moving. Hearing also suffered if one lived long enough.

'Tree. There aren't any trees that can fly.' Then she remembered the flying fracas and how a tree branch was broken off a flying tree and it became her roosting spot. 'It's not here, is it? It can't be. No high growing, flying wood-chipper is stealing my roosting spot. Weirdo, stop that. We must return home and surprise our visitor. Thanks, Crinky.'

The cockroach had advanced too close to Oddity, who was hungry from all the toing and froing. She bent down and her huge claw stomped on poor Crinky. He got to fly anyway, but not expecting it to be in someone else's stomach.

'There's very little taste in them.'

The two, huge, flying, pretend musicians were soon airborne with a dreadful scowl of worry. That tree branch was the best roosting spot that they had ever had. It was well off the ground, long and the Ninnytwits couldn't reach it. Without their safety roost, finding another roost spot of that standard would be impossible. The Conikaka Mountains were all cone shape and only grew small shrubs. There were no tree branches of any use there. They could be vulnerable to the small, but many of them, Ninnytwits.

The girls knew the danger that Moonah faced. Those two flyers could snap off another tree root or branch with ease, if they got the right grip. They ran as fast as a biped could. Cross-country events were common at school and the girls always participated well. Forget the new Nike's, sports shorts and pony-tail hairdo, this was a race for safety. They really didn't have to run too far, but it's the adrenalin rush that makes even a short chase exhilarating. The girls arrived almost at the same moment that Oddity and Weirdo did.

'What's up my tree lopper? Whatcha trying to steal? That roost is mine, so if it's fine, I expect ya to leave it where it is,' spoke Oddity, in tune to a dreadful rap song that Davidia had expressed earlier.

Moonah faced a few of its heavier branches downwards and looked like a weeping willow tree. His trunk was protected, and the reattached tree branch progress was almost complete. Oddity viciously lashed out with her huge claws at Moonah, only to be thwarted by Davidia throwing small stones with deadly accuracy. Oddity yelled abuse with all the foul mixtures of the alphabet she knew. She turned an evil eye toward Davidia and menacingly approached her. Her four beaks were competing for the worst bad language prize.

'I'll teach you a lesson that you have never experienced before, you rotten piece of whatever you are. Claw gore and loving it.'

Oddity strode purposefully toward Davidia. Was it almost over for her? The end of her odyssey with Slirander was in danger of failure. The antidote mightn't work, but she still kept a vial of actual hairspray in one of her pockets. She rummaged fearfully though them before she was to become the girl on a spike.

'Got it! Stay back, or I'll unleash the most deadly, dangerous, mist, you've ever experienced. Nothing can defeat it,' Davidia bravely responded.

She was acting on instinct. No clever phrase or intelligent comment was of any use right now. It was a cheap version of hairspray up against a most insidious, clever, strong and deathly adversary. It was a mismatch of gigantic proportions. Slirander's ideas basket was empty, so she couldn't help. Weirdo stood by passively hopefully watching big sis splat an annoying talking pest.

'You fool. I'm indestructible. You can't harm me.'

Oddity was supremely confident of defeating the little wimp as easily as swatting a fly. Big mouths sometimes swallow their own words and have also been known to choke on them.

'I warned you.'

Davidia pressed hard. The tiny, atomised spray dispersed into the atmosphere heading directly for Oddity's eyes. Each little atom looked eagerly toward mixing it with a clean, shampooed, well-brushed head and landing on beautiful hair strands to adhere to. The closer they flew toward their intended landing place, panic set in.

'See that filthy hair. We can't land there.'

'It's dirty feathers, not hair. It will be so uncomfortable.'

'The smell will be unbearable. Even we couldn't improve that.'

'Nothing has been washed or prepared. What are we doing here?'

Two huge luminous eyes suddenly appeared, and they were heading directly at them.

'Have we been sprayed off-course?'

'They aren't hair follicles. They look like some watery waste.'

'In the salon, we'd never end up there.'

'What are those shockers?'

'I think they are called eyes and we're headed directly for them.'

'We don't need to be cleaned up.'

The mist congregated together in a formation of dive-bombers.

'If this is where we have been sprayed, then let's put our best landing efforts forward.'

Splat, splat, splat, they ditched into the watery wastes. Oddity screamed with a burning sensation and was momentarily blinded. She screamed a dictionary of abuse; however, it wasn't words that Davidia was afraid of, it was the claws. Weirdo was taken aback.

'You're next,' yelled Davidia.

Weirdo was a weaky. He flew away leaving big sis in pain and immobilised. Whilst Oddity grappled with loss of vision, Davidia dashed over to see how Moonah was progressing.

'That was brave,' said Slirander. 'I don't think I would have that much courage.'

'I used my imagination, because that's what we are here,' replied Davidia. 'Is Moonah reattached?'

'I think so.'

Moonah gave a sigh of relief.

'It's done. My missing branch is safely back. See how it moves. At last all my twenty-six leaves and branches are together again. Return inside and we can leave.'

'What about Oddity and Weirdo? What will happen to them?'

'One day they will be too old and the Ninnytwits will take over the valley. I appreciate your help.'

The girls returned to the inside of the tree root.

'My wrist was hurting something chronic. I don't know how much longer I could have held onto that lumpy growth,' said Davidia, relieved that she could freely move both hands again. 'We still have to get out of this tree root.'

'We'll make it this time,' said Slirander, 'follow me.'

They finally found their way along the tree root. It didn't grow with each step this time. Moonah had deliberately length-ened his tree root to actually save them from physically going to Conika. Their imaginative selves were sufficient. Soon they squeezed through a small opening, to be greeted by a gush of cold wind.

'Are we finally out of the history leaf?' asked Davidia, giving herself an arm hug to ward off rising goose bumps. 'Can't we rest? I'm not super girl who can withstand all the elements. I feel them.'

'Where are we going, Moonah?' whispered Slirander hugging his tree trunk.

'Where the winds take us.'

*

Rotland felt a cool wind over its land as the shadow of the Moonatric tree flew over it. Roland didn't know the cause of the cool breeze, but an ill wind was fatal for its inhabitants. They may not possess the best command of the written language, but warm weather is an ingredient to their lives that they should all enjoy. There was very little else happening when the inhabitants are enchanted and brain-washed by a charismatic leader. Even the Rotters didn't know what Roland truly looked like. Each public appearance made was marked by a disguise of some sort.

'This is my finest work,' he said holding up his premier Destrusto Virus. 'So far, I have been thwarted, but no more. Go, my little darlings, and wreak havoc. Long may nothing be read.'

'We don't seem to be moving at all,' said Davidia.

The wind had almost ceased blowing. Moonah's leaves had stopped fluttering and the clouds were parked patiently — without the anger of car parking space violence — waiting for a stirring breeze.

'Moonah's thinking. Notice that his tree trunk twitches with the wrinkles moving around his circumference. That means a thought of Roland the Rotter. Something has triggered a problem. We're actually above Rotland at the moment. He might have absorbed a nasty thought or some hint of danger,' explained Slirander, becoming concerned also at their lack of movement.

'He's exercising his reattached branch. Look, it's waving at something, or to it, I'm sure.'

'It's probably a stiffened joint and he's using a relaxing exercise technique. It has been unattached for quite a while and working together again might need a few readjustments and fine-tuning.'

The clouds smiled good-naturedly. Storm hadn't joined them today. It was busily wreaking havoc in the tropics. There were no signs of communication from Moonah. Had he fallen asleep? He was an ageing tree. Decay was often well-hidden, especially when growing in the ground. Down there, no one could see the health of the tree roots. Minutes passed. There was tension in the atmosphere. The cold began to bother the girls.

'Can't stand it much longer, eh?' said the cold, as it gently blew at them.

It could be a serial pest if it had the mind to be.

'Go annoy someone who's interested,' said Davidia. 'I've been in snow storms in my bikini and it didn't bother me.'

'You haven't experienced my icy breath yet. Perhaps I'll give you a sample,' it said, threateningly.

'Don't waste your time. There's a nice little cloud over there that needs its raindrops to precipitate. Make yourself useful and do your proper job, instead of annoying me. It might be receptive to your cold advances. I once met a guy who acted like you do. All I can say is that all he got for his pest insistence was a cold shoulder. Now bugger off,' said Davidia, displaying some of her anger.

She was actually cold, but wouldn't admit it.

'You won't last long up here if you remain still. It's the easiest time for me to roll around and affect you. I'm everywhere. I extend for hundreds of kilometres.'

'I'm so pleased for you. Why don't you attend to your other interests?'

'They aren't fun company like you. How often do I get to meet a flying tree way up here with its talking branches? Nothing much visits me anymore. It can be a cold and lonely place. All I do is blow small breezes, kick a few clouds to drop ice, swirl around and make things cold for everything, which is often not appreciated.'

Davidia began to feel sympathy for the cold. Its lot in existence wasn't exactly thrill stuff. Suddenly, Moonah moved.

'I must go. Moonah is moving again. I hope you find a friendly cloud, a lost storm or high-flying bird for company. Perhaps you could drop down closer to earth. There it would be warmer and you wouldn't have to be so miserable.'

'Thanks for the advice.'

A small gust and the cold was gone.

*

Moonah began to descend.

'What's happening?' asked Davidia.

'The reattached tree branch is acting unhappily. There must be something in it causing concern. Moonah has to land and solve the problem. He might have to grow in the soil and restore its goodness. Being a tree roost for so long was unpleasant and unhealthy. The branch is suffering from claw-poo-itis. The unfortunate landing pad is in Rotland. We will have to be extra careful. That's the home of Roland the Rotter. We will be safe for a while. It would only be a matter of time before we are discovered,' explained Slirander.

'Is there anything to fear in Rotland?'

'Just the usual bad diction, misspellings, poor sentence structure, misuse of puns, metaphors and general literary ignorance. It will be a battle to hold a sensible conversation of any length with any inhabitant.'

'Nothing out of the ordinary then?'

The view of Rotland from the air was of a scenic, wooded, small country, which would fit perfectly onto any postcard promotion. There were no apparent dangers. Moonah landed safely in an open space surrounded by other trees. It took Davidia a moment or two to recognise that the other trees were all Moonatric trees. How is that possible? There was literally a forest of them. None of them were as tall and fine as Moonah.

'Where are we?' asked Davidia, wondering if she had landed in clone land.

'Deep inside a Moonatric forest. This is the last bastion of their existence. Here they flourish, but Roland the Rotter has taken residence high in the mountains, which is to no one's advantage. At present our main concern is the safety and rehabilitation of Moonah. We must work with him and flush out the uncertainty surrounding the reattached branch.'

'Any idea what the problem is?'

'I think it has to do with the storage in the stumpy growth. There may be an unwanted virus, growing tree rot or simply trouble in reconnecting. Something is definitely not right in there. It may be that the Destrusto Virus has already attacked from the inside. It could be anything. Until the problem is solved, we are ground-bound here. There are no tree surgeons in this part of the woods.'

'Let's go. The sooner we destroy that damn virus the sooner we can be back at school with our friends, have a hot bath and eat some decent food.'

Davidia took out her two remaining vials and gave them a shake.

'Whoa, there! Stop with the headache shakes. The lads want to be in prime condition for our next foray in the restoration battle, but if you bash us up with unnecessary shaking, we might act impaired.'

The leader hadn't organised the lads into an active unit as they were on recreational duties. It seems that time was now over. The soldiers prepared for a tussle.

'How do we enter the L world when there is no leaf entry?' asked Davidia.

Every other time they had entered via a coloured leaf. Could they enter without that access this time? The stumpy growth was certainly solid with no lush leaf.

'We might have to use the squish and squash technique,' said Slirander, thinking of play dough from her kindergarten days. 'You still have to say the "brrr, brrr", but it must be said at the same time with us holding hands and our other hand pushing up hard against the stumpy growth. Apparently, we are entering the blue and pink colours of the L world, whatever that is. In the meantime, Moonah can re-acquaint himself with his family. Are you ready?'

Nothing is ever simple with her friend. Davidia gritted her teeth and said a very cold 'brrr, brrr' thinking of the annoying cold in the atmosphere. Moonah groaned once more.

'I'm getting tired of this. Who's unscrewing one of my branches? It feels like I'm being pulled apart by a chainsaw,' Moonah complained.

His aching branch didn't move; however, the stumpy growth softened sufficiently enough for the girls to push hard against and it enlarged like a sponge, absorbing water.

'Yuck! It's greasy and wet. I bet Alice in Wonderland didn't have an entry as tough as this.'

The girls squeezed tightly through. They didn't fall down any lengthy tree trunk to an underground adventure. Instead, they landed in the centre of a University debate between Lamdon College and Longschott College.

Each of them was included as an audience supporter, one for each college. This was to be a difficult contest as the art of oratory and good diction would be used for the withering effect of defeating the opposition with a good argument.

These two colleges were once the ancient and well-respected colleges of Rotland prior to their current deterioration. Language and literature had been deliberately destroyed. The great books of knowledge from these colleges had been taken by none other than the impostor to good learning, Roland the Rotter, for his own personal selfish use. The students at the colleges were once intelligent, bright, loved studies, and had a thirst for knowledge. The colleges were presently in decay and the written language and literature were now lost to the inhabitants of Rotland, who no longer read anything.

However, Roland without the Rotter tag, had once taught there as a professor of language studies. He was unfortunately a genetic throwback in his family and had an odd shaped mouth with an inherited strangeness that was unexplainable. During his studies he had never taught in front of a class; however, as a teacher it was a necessity. It took a few years before it manifested itself into a difficulty. There were a few snide remarks by students, as they do, about staff and their physical appearance, but this hadn't particularly bothered him. As time went on, he began to lose the ability to write on the blackboard in front of a class. Instead, as he spoke, his words could be seen to flow from his mouth as complete sentences, stay in the atmosphere sufficiently for the students to write them down and then magically disappear. At first his diction was excellent and easily readable, but one day the poor-quality canteen food made him choke. It was a lumpy piece of stale cake being passed off as fresh. The resulting coughing fit, by regurgitating the fresh/stale cake, knocked out some of his teeth. This made his odd-shaped mouth appear odder as part of his face, which the teeth outwardly supported, suddenly sagged into his face. It was an accidental tragedy. There was no cure. His words now came out all distorted in the shape of his mouth and no one could read or understand them. Students ridiculed his appearance and especially his inability to speak with clear diction. Other staff members ostracised him for not being understandable and were put off by having to read the words every time he spoke. Eventually, he was laughed off campus. He vowed revenge. No one would ever read language in Rotland ever again, except him.

*

'Listen. Can you hear the breathlessness in that student's commentary?' asked Slirander, with her fine hearing.

'It does sound rather raspy,' replied Davidia. 'Do you think something is strangling their vocal cords?'

'It doesn't sound right, that's all.'

'They aren't speaking with their mouths full, are they? That could make it sound raspy by the dryness of the food, if they were eating it and speaking simultaneously. I wonder what they are debating.'

'I'm not sure. I'll ask that student sitting next to us. Excuse me, can you please tell me what the debate is about?'

The student had a surly look on her face. Had Slirander interrupted a pleasant thought? I don't think so. She might have an internal crisis that can't be resolved.

'Common Sense Language. What use is it?'

'Oh! It's very useful. It's how we communicate with each other exactly as we are now.'

'My friend sitting next to me was to be in the debating team for Lamdon College. Now she can't debate, let alone make any sense. She has lost her r sound. Nobody knows how or why. Go on ask her a question and see what response you get. I can't understand her very well,' said the student.

Slirander wasn't too sure if she should. Okay, she decided she would.

'Why aren't you on the debating team?' asked Slirander of the other student

'I've lost the ability to speak popely. I was studying and caying out eseach for the team when I lost my clea diction. I haven't any idea how it occued.'

Slirander certainly thought that she had definitely lost her r sound as there wasn't one mentioned in any completed sentence.

'When did this happen?' Slirander had said a sentence with no r, so as not to upset the student any further.

'A few days ago, I was studying in the libay as I said and afte eading a few books my thoat began to hut. All I did was ead a book.'

'Have any other students suffered from the same or similar symptoms?'

'Quite a few.'

The student sat sullen and sad. To lose one's language doesn't make for a good communicator, job applicant, or speaker to your friends other than in a shorthand version. It could be the fore-runner of modern-day texting.

'Slirander, are you thinking what I'm thinking?' asked Davidia, having heard the problem.

'Can you read minds?' asked the first student.

'It's a gift.' Davidia didn't want to explain what she had meant.

'How much longer does the debate go for?'

'About an hour.'

'That gives us enough time to look around.'

'It's only a college. There aren't any historical places or museum pieces to see.'

'That's okay. We wouldn't understand them anyway. We like walking through colleges and soaking up the ambient atmo-sphere. We're students too.'

'That's weird, losing a letter permanently from your vocabu-lary. Do you think this has anything to do with the Destrusto Virus?' asked Davidia.

'Great minds think alike. It looks like the libay for us,' said Slirander, smiling being two r sounds short of a word.

The girls walked along a great hall littered with paintings of the previous heads of college; dignitaries forever immortalised in paint and a small painting of an indistinct shadowy figure with a peculiar plaque, with a caption that read, "He who laughs last, laughs loudest". It was a very old saying. Mmm!

Another student was hurrying by. Slirander asked a question.

'Who's that shadowy painting of?'

'That's of an old professor who was laughed off campus. Mr Roland was his name.'

'Thank you.'

'It couldn't be, could it?'

'It could. It might help explain any peculiarities we encounter. There's the library.'

The girls walked in. It reminded them of the library they had entered at school and started their journey. It was no different to any that they had seen before except that it held many more books.

'Let's browse the shelves.'

The two girls withdrew many books and checked through them for any indication of dog-eared and/or moist corners. Frowns furrowed their brows. Many had been tampered with. They checked the language section and sure as chook-eggs come from chooks, everyone had the tell-tale imprint of rotten handiwork. If a student finger had been licked by turning each page, they would have had contact with what was left on that particular page. Could it be that whatever was there was passed onto their tongue and affected their speech? It was a long shot, but isn't that the name of the other debating college? Confusion was as rampant as a vowel in almost every word.

'Davidia, have you found anything?'

'All the pages seemed to have been touched by something. It feels slithery.'

'Don't lick your fingers. Wash them. We don't want you having a speech impediment as well.'

The librarian walked over. She was a tall, imposing female, but ever so polite.

'Excuse me. May I ask what it is you are ooking for? This isn't a saes specia shop or jeweery store, it's a ibrary. There are ony words in here.'

'We are language students. You have a fabulous range of books. Have any words disappeared from any of your books?'

'None that I am aware of. What makes you ask?'

'We noticed that many of them were dog-eared. Do a lot of students read them?'

'There are a few students ony. They hardy speak. A ot of time is in preparation for the debate.'

'Have you touched any of the books lately?'

'I read them reguary. I am a anguage teacher when I am not managing the ibrary.'

'Has your diction deteriorated lately?'

'Strange that you shoud notice. I seem to have ost the etter … I can't even say what etter it is that I have ost.'

'I think it's the letter l. Have any other students lost any of their alphabet?'

'A few have compained, but it has been put down to the stress of studying for the debate. You had better hurry or you wi miss it.'

'Did each college do their own research?'

'They each had a group of students doing it, however ongschott College students were aways in eary. They were exceptionay keen.'

'Did they each take a set of books with them?'

'Yes.'

'Thank you. We'll watch the debate now.'

Slirander turned to Davidia.

'My guess is that the Longschott College students are rotter material whilst Lamdon College students aren't. At the debate did you notice the raspy voice was a Lamdon College student trying to properly express itself?'

'What if the Destrsto Virus makes us lose a vowel or replaces one letter with another? No one would ever speak properly again. The fact that the written language hasn't yet been destroyed, the oral traditions will be. If those people ever write anything, then it won't be understood. It will become a language jumble and effectively language will be destroyed by not being able to record it correctly. It would be a communication disaster,' said Davidia.

'I'm afraid so.'

'How will the antidote work against oral letter loss? I can understand the written language from books, but the spoken word might be more difficult to restore.'

'It is so diabolically clever that Roland the Rotter has chosen a more insidious virus to rid good language from the record books. There must be a way we can reverse the process. The debating room is a good place to start. When we find out what's going on, we will have to pretend that we have lost a letter or vowel to make believe we are Lamdon College debating students. Moonah said that we had to be innovative and believe in our language. Maybe we can use a different form of speech so that no one can understand us except you and me,' said Slirander.

'My dad used to travel overseas and his friends made up their own type of language because they only spoke English. When they crossed borders, they would speak between themselves in the made-up language. Only they understood it. The foreigners couldn't understand dad, just as he and his friends didn't understand them. It was called balfang. They placed an l and an f after each vowel and the same vowel after the l and f. For example, a sentence might be "what did you say?" It would become "whalfat dilfid yolfoulfu salfay?" Keep the sentences short, otherwise it's too confusing. It will give us some secrecy that the rotters wouldn't understand.'

'The antidote will work by combining what is in both vials that we have left. They must be sprayed simultaneously at the same object. That will double-strength them and allow them to combat the book virus. It may not catch every person who has been affected because they would have to re-read the books. Failing that, the imperfecto portion of the antidote will shut down any further infections and without a constant input of the Destrusto Virus, its effect will gradually fade and oral language will eventually be fully restored.'

'It really is a clever antidote.'

'Remember, we reduce from four vials to two. Any loss of them would spell disaster. Spelfell dilfisalfastelfer. I thought I'd try your balfang speak,' said Slirander. 'It certainly is a mouthful.' They both laughed.

*

Back in the debating hall, the Lamdon College team were suffering badly. Each speaker had difficulty in being understood, whereas the Longschott College team practised correct diction, enunciation and expression in putting forward their subject matter. It was a no-win, no-brainer as to who was going to win the debate. Longschott College, in their own minds, already had their name engraved upon the trophy cup.

'Who's that beanpole staffer instructing the students of Longschott College? He could do with a good feed. He's so thin anything travelling down his gullet could be easily seen. I'm not going to imagine the end of that journey,' said Davidia.

'All his students have that constant finger-licking trait we encountered in an earlier subject. Maybe it's all the university training that leads them to be easy Rotter spotters. Let's see what they're up to,' said Slirander. 'Arm yourself with a vial, just in case.'

The girls wandered over sauntering with slouched shoulders, dragging two school bags borrowed from the back of another student's seat, with eyes roaming in a trance-like state. They were a perfect fit for any university student, even though they had a few years to go.

'Estascusa moi, moi moi. Whasst issa twoosa youngy grirlls adoosing herey?' said the beanpole, staring at them from a great height. He was standing on a table. Actions baffle an explanation.

'We wanted to see how a debating team operates properly,' said Davidia, who had actually participated in a schoolyard argument with many colourful words and phrases expressing an opinion. The only difference here, that she could fathom, was that it's held indoors instead of outdoors. You guessed it. She won the debate. Her fiery expressions were a sharp-witted tool.

'Doosent iterferres. Issa toosa importantos toosa looseys.'

'Your name, sir. Whatsa issa yoursa namessy?' asked Davidia, relishing some stupid chat and being in verbal theme.

'Issa Maxxus.'

'May we stay here and watch how debating works? We're keen to learn.'

'Sittsa quietssleysy, pleassa.'

Slirander and Davidia sat behind a row of researchers who were feeding the students their lines and reference materials.

'I hope he doesn't teach the students to speak like him. It's ridiculous speech.'

'I suppose language comes in all forms and he has an adulterated version of expression,' said Slirander, not believing her ears either. 'Did you notice anything odd about him?'

'You mean, I missed something?' asked Davidia, stunned that the ingredients of what she perceived to be idiotic expressions would go through to the keeper. *Not likely*, she thought.

'See that extra growth on his thumb. It's like a hand with five-and-a-half fingers. He's seems very suspicious. The Rotters use actors to pretend that they are on your side.'

'Should we test him? We can't interfere with the debate. Look, both sides are taking a break. Who's putting the Destrusto Virus out here? We haven't seen any hard evidence except those dog-eared books.'

The girls walked behind the stage and were just about to meet Maxxus when Slirander grabbed Davidia by the wrist and yanked her behind a curtain. She pointed ahead. They both saw what they thought was a grown man sucking his thumb, but it was the small half version that was experiencing a tight mouth hold. They watched intrigued. Man doesn't grow out of childhood. That's well-known, but this was over-the-top stuff. What next, tears and a nappy change?

'He isn't a sooky la la, is he?' said Davidia. 'Grown men don't usually suck their thumbs. I've seen them signal some forms of greetings with them, but never placed in their own mouth.'

'Watch carefully,' said Slirander. 'Notice that he is spitting into a small bowl. I wonder why?'

She kept careful watch and it became obvious that the thumb was false. In a world where oddities naturally occur, it would pass unnoticed. Maxxus closed the top of the false thumb, wiped it clean and pretended he was odd. The girls remained hidden. Maxxus carried the bowl and walked over to the Lamdon College students under the pretence of discussing any rule changes with their head teacher. He placed the small bowl next to their research books and accidentally knocked it over. After a brief exchange he returned to his students for a review of the debate so far.

Slirander wanted to know what he was up to. She also walked over past the table near the research books. The spilt liquid was on the move. No one noticed it. She waited as it made a path onto the books and disappeared amongst the pages. The debate was about to recommence. Lamdon College were to present their arguments. The subject was on Common Sense Language — a lost art form in many communities — and whether it was as common as one believed. The first debater stood up and spoke clearly and powerfully.

'Ladies and Gentlemen, fellow students and guests …'

The opening speech was impressive. Clear diction, proper

sentence structure, clever use of emphasised phrases, an appropriate mix of large and small words was quite evident. The audience clapped vigorously as their argument was for the positive. A pause was made to refresh with a glass of water. Subconsciously, the speaker absent-mindedly flicked over a page or two to remind them of a point of view. The innocence of reading had instantly become an expression disaster. As the speaker resumed its position on the podium, it grabbed its throat and gasped for a moment or two, causing an offensive cough followed by a badly presented mucus exhalation. The audience waited for the resumption. The speaker looked as if its face had been attacked by an angry beetroot.

'My apalagies.' Their os had been replaced by as. They tried to continue.

'Camman sense is a highly prized value within the cammunity.'

The common sense the debater tried to present was now missing as their vocal expressions had been tampered with and didn't make common sense at all. It would be a debating disaster for Lamdon College. Slirander had observed the changes in presentation. She signalled to Davidia to join her.

'What happened?'

'Maxxus has tampered with the research books. He placed some sort of paste on the table and they entered the books. Then whammo, the debater couldn't speak properly any more. It's a speech destruction virus. Did you notice that the words in the books we looked at were still there? This virus is a vocabulary thief, whereas the other Destrusto Virus was a printed-word thief. We might have to double spray this time.'

'Should we spray the books or the speaker?' asked Davidia, unsure of what action should be taken.

'I don't know either. We'll try the speaker first and see what happens. Vials ready.'

At that moment Maxxus had seen the girls and came over.

'Whassa issa youssa doingsky?'

They couldn't offer an immediate understandable excuse so they simply spoke in balfang to each other.

'Spralfay nolfow,' said Davidia.

'Okalfay,' replied Slirander.

The girls gave an instantaneous burst of antidote and waited for the reaction. Maxxus thought how stupid they were for spraying perfume in the air. What a waste!

'Lads, our cousins are with us. Stop with the chit-chat at meeting them again. Talk about Aunty Doris when this exercise is over. We have a doozy of a job this time. Restoration of verbalised lost letters. We have to be patient and hang about in those whopping cavities that those upright standers call mouths. It will be a sticky, salivary task waiting for speech to occur. When it does, we must attach ourselves to the misused letter and ride it out through that opening with the white stalagmites and stalactites. Be patient. We must turn every misspoken letter back to its former self. This is the greatest sacrifice I can ask of you. Spell correctly. Don't change the letter into what it is not. Good luck. See you in the next edition of any printed paper.'

The leader flew at the forefront of his misty atomisers. The huge cavity approached and in they went like trained seals, but without the bark. Once inside they attached themselves to the slippery walls and waited for the debater to resume speaking.

An errant s tried to escape. Then an o, a double n, a capital P and so on. Little did the debater know of the battle inside its mouth.

'After it, lads, it needs to be refocused into a v. There's another. Off you go. Alter it into its proper shape. Watch out for lurkers. They must be further down the throat. Hear that raspiness. Who's brave enough to enter the trachea?' asked the leader.

'I will, sir. I'm a modest atomiser and can't spell as well as the rest. I'll discover those nasties. Watch out for me if I'm spurted out with an incorrect letter.'

The modest atomised spray ventured carefully. It was pitch-black. It could hear a group of noisy chattering. None of it was complimentary.

'Twist that so it lisps.'

'Replace any vowel with another. If you were an a, e, i, o or a u, they don't make any common sense used on their own.'

'Alter that w so it vibrates. This is holiday time. Ruining expression is the greatest disaster we can perform.'

'How long do we have to stay here?' asked a Destrusto Virus team member.

Splat!

'Any more questions?'

The nasty bullying of the spoken letters continued unabated.

The brave atomised spray broke cover, in this case, silence.

'You rotten language destroyers. You must stop upsetting the spoken language. Everyone is upset when it isn't said correctly. There is a proper debate occurring up there.'

The mood changed completely. There was an intruder in their midst.

'Get it quickly,' yelled Devio the virus leader.

There was a lull in attacking the spoken letters whilst the search went on for the intruder. Suddenly, and without warning, the debater belched. A massive gust of internal wind erupted. The Destrusto Virus members were violently thrown upwards. As they exited via the mouth, the leader and his restoration team pounced.

'That'll teach you to interfere with good expression,' they said, as they turned and twisted every nasty DV virus into a proper letter and placed them in the correct spoken sequence.

The misty atomisers performed at every incorrect utterance. The debater was amazed that their speech held perfect diction, proper expression and finally made common sense. The audience applauded the presentation. Maxxus' thin frame shook with anger. His two beady eyes began to enlarge so that they almost took over his face. His thin, beanpole stance was in danger of toppling with the large-eyed head.

'Mr Maxxus, whalfat ilfis halfappelfenilfing?' asked Davidia, keen not to be understood. She was so pleased that her dad had learnt nonsensical language speak. Balfang was almost as difficult to understand as childish gibberish.

'Youussa shouldnssy ruinenada the debatesy.'

'Stilfiff shilfit,' she replied.

Maxxus was enraged further. Not only did they ruin the debate, he couldn't understand a word she had said. Slirander entered the conversation.

'Hello Roland,' she said.

Maxxus convulsed. How could he be recognised? His disguise was perfect. He had to deliver the killer language virus himself and that is why he took on the identity of Maxxus, the beanpole. He wondered who this schoolgirl was. Each time he had tried to destroy something, she and that other schoolgirl made an appearance. What did he do to deserve to be persecuted in this way? Language destruction was not a viable option that the girls could allow to occur. Their mission was its continuance. Roland obviously didn't recognise Slirander as a schoolgirl. Her disguise, if it was one, was perfect. If Roland's disguise was discovered, it self-destructed and vanished. Who or what is this Roland?

'Youssa thinksy youssa cleverssy doosa youssa? Issa hassa newssa forssa youssa. Myssa virussa cannotsa beesa destroyssed.'

> *'Mince pie, eye to eye,*
> *Mincemeat, allow to speak,*
> *Mince matters, language in tatters,*
> *Mince goo, goodbye to you,'*

said Slirander, reminding everyone that she could have been a poet.

The rhyme had no particular meaning, but Roland didn't know that. He felt sure that it was an ancient spell.

A strange sound, like a whispering conversation amongst a forest of Moonatric trees, filled the debating hall. It was incoherent expression, but created a stressful mind pressure for Roland and his unsightly, bulging eyes. They reminded Davidia of a pair of balloons about to burst. The whispering intensified. Roland felt uncomfortable. It triggered a childhood memory and before he could reveal it, his bulging eyes burst open, revealing the remnants of the deadly Destrusto Virus. Slirander and Davidia both withdrew a vial as quickly as a gunslinger in the west and sprayed together.

'Lads, it's Christmas time again,' yelled another leader. 'Get yourself a present and bring it home to mama. Hiya, cousin, it's fantastic to meet again so soon.'

The antidote soldiers of the Pebble of Purpose lapped up the attention of attacking the Destrusto Virus. Here the virus was exposed and vulnerable not having yet attacked any language. It was a smorgasbord of conquests.

It meant that the French would not lose their "oui, oui", the Spanish their "ooh la la", the Germans their inflections, and swear words could be said with complete confidence now that language would not be destroyed or distorted. There was relief everywhere.

'Where's Roland?' asked Davidia.

'Faded away for another time,' replied Slirander.

She knew that being in Rotland could cause them serious problems if Moonah was found prior to them escaping from the stumpy tree branch.

The debating hall was still full of students. The minute mess that Roland had left behind had little impact on the debate. It continued without interruption and threats to good diction and expression. The Longschott College students now had to debate on an even playing field. The result was memorable.

The student that Slirander had first spoken to approached.

'My friend has recovered her lost rs. She's speaking properly now. I wonder what miracle allowed her to regain her full speech range. We can understand each other again.'

'I'm pleased,' said Slirander. 'Apparently it was a language virus which was very catching. Someone thought that it was the virus that if you deliberately wanted one, then everyone should have one. There just wasn't enough of it to go around.'

'My friend is now in the debating team once more.'

'Good luck.'

'It may be good luck for her, but what about us getting out of here? Besides, how did you know Maxxus was Roland?' asked Davidia.

Her friend knew too much about where they were and this Roland character.

'I guessed it. Outrageous is his form of behaviour and I thought it's him again. That's all.'

A siren sounded for the completion of the debate. Lamdon College were victorious. Longschott College students seethed in anger. They couldn't win even though they almost cheated their way to victory. The debating team didn't move. They sat as still as a female lion primed for that final attack. Eyes furtively watched Lamdon College lap up the victory speech. The jealousy they felt triggered a feeling of revenge. Davidia felt the fine blonde hairs on the nape of her neck become rigid. Something in the air wasn't quite right and it wasn't the oxygen quality. Her keen observation skills alerted Slirander by quietly speaking in whispered tones.

'Lolfolfok alfat thelfe stulfudelfents.

Trolfoulfublelfe ilfis helferelfe,'
she said.

'*Whalfat alfarelfe thelfey dolfoilfing?*'
replied Slirander.

Each member of the whole group had in front of them an imitation half thumb which they began to suck. It was a synchronised performance. The tops were suddenly opened and they threw the half thumbs into the debating hall with their white contents being released into the atmosphere for everyone to breathe in. Each pest droplet was infused with the Destrusto Virus. The girls had almost been fooled by the Rotters. They were on the verge of leaving the building and had they done so, the antidote wouldn't be used and language was in peril.

'*Spralfay quilfickly,*' yelled Slirander.

The girls were instant in their response.

'So soon, lads. It's overtime for us. We've been called to duty once again. I like our cousins. When this is over, it's a holiday in the Bahamas. Do a final job on the language pests. They just can't let anyone read a good book and now talk about it. To war. Follow my lead. Yee, hah! I love a good western.'

The hall was a battlefield of tiny atomisers and pest drops locked in a language tussle. Good always held sway; however, this time the Desrusto Virus was at full strength and a right little shilfit of a thing to bring under control. Eventually, the exhausted antidote prevailed.

'I'm getting too old for this,' said the leader.

'Move over and let someone else be in charge,' said a disgruntled atomiser.

'Who dares to challenge my leadership?' said an angry leader.

After all, they had won every battle so far.

'Not this time, but next time give someone else a chance,'

replied the wimpy challenger. Even the antidote heroes had their problems.

'Slirander, aren't they clones of Roland the Rotter? They are as skinny as Maxxus.'

'They must be, to be given the virus and use it in an almost identical fashion.'

Before anyone could blink, Sirander stood in front of the Longschott College students chastising them for their misdemeanour of throwing solid objects in a college hall.

'And furthermore, Rotters aren't allowed in my class.'

She waited, nothing happened. She repeated the word Rotter again. Still there was no response. Maybe she had hit their dead nerve spot.

'Excuse me, miss. What's a Rotter? We've never heard of them,' said a cheesy-grinning student.

'It's a form of bad health, that's all,' replied Slirander, thinking maybe Davidia was wrong in this case.

Suddenly, Davidia appeared next to her, flexing a metre piece of flat wood. It was a language ruler, a name gained by the many bad expressions written on both sides of it. Whoever said student language innovators weren't sure of the proper expression. Without warning, she slammed it on the first desk. The sound had everybody's attention. The debating hall had calmed to a series of murmurs.

'Could each of you please place your hands facing upwards with your fingers spread out?' she said.

'But, miss.'

Davidia slammed the desk harder this time.

'Physical violence isn't allowed on campus, it's a university rule,' wailed a student, fearful of receiving a knuckle thump.

'Silence, I'll make the words.'

Why any student took notice of a young schoolgirl years below their age group had the onlookers confused and perplexed. The Longschott College students sat with arms outstretched, palms facing upwards with fingers spread. This wasn't a palm-reading or tarot-card fortune-telling proposal.

'I want every set of eyes shut tight. I have a flavour test for a new food item and I need each of you to describe its taste. It's a new marketing exercise. The new spray flavour has been recently developed right here at the university. Ready?'

The students thought that this was cool and agreed to the suggestion, albeit a little unsure.

Davidia took out the antidote vial and gently sprayed all sets of fingers. A burning sensation was felt on the finger-licking finger and it was quickly put in a mouth to soothe its burning effects. Surprisingly, every student did exactly the same thing. Pain wasn't a subject of study. A few moments passed. Davidia could sense a change. Their level of aggressiveness gradually decreased as the pain intensified.

'Okay, eyes open. Who can tell me what flavour it might be?'

'Fire.'

'Unbearable.'

'Choking.'

'Disaster.'

'Can't you do better? None of those are flavours,' said Davidia.

'Did you poison us? The only taste is pain. Ugh!'

Their body postures sagged under the antidote attack.

'That's it, lads. Attack that virus until it disappears. My body muscles are certainly improving with these letter pursuit excursions. My pectorals are now well-defined. It's a workout one has when it's not really a workout. Get into it, lads. Rise above your misspellings and resurrect the written word with the correct structures.'

Inside each Longschott College student, the Destrusto Virus

was festering, multiplying and before the debate hall was cleared, each student would regurgitate and release the deadliest form of the virus. It had been incubated to almost perfect indestructibility; however, Davidia's sharp eyes had detected a language-saving action. All the students began to change shape. One turned into an s, another rolled over like an o, another made a half circle on their back as a c, another overbalanced as an l and landed flat on the floor. The language was being reshaped by pain. The students' body changes were mimicking the alphabet. Slirander was amazed at the shenanigans occurring. Davidia raised her ruler once again and slammed it even harder on a desktop. The vibrations sent a rolling ripple through the floor. The tiny undulations caused motion sickness and, in the next instant, the groans of rolling students filled the air.

'Rotters,' yelled Davidia.

It was now impossible to conceal their true identities. That dreadful destructive word had once again brought the hiding Rotters undone. One by one the students' eyes popped out as odd angry eyes, full of yellow and bluish veins filled with hatred. The antidote had once again worked perfectly. The sound of popcorn could be heard as the eyes popped spewing out the deadly remains of the Destrusto Virus. Longschott College representative debating team was reduced to an inconvenient mess.

'Davidia, that was truly amazing. How you knew that is beyond me,' said Slirander.

'It was a guess, that's all.'

It was time to leave. The mess created wasn't their problem. They had to return to Moonah and the safety of his branches. The oral language would now be saved and, in turn, the written language would also be saved by writing down the oral language.

What the girls didn't know was that they had saved all the books in the two greatest colleges in Rotland, both of which

Roland would later plunder as retribution for his failures. Ego and selfishness were a difficult combination to overcome.

'Davidia, we must leave,' urged Slirander.

'Is there something happening that I don't know about?' asked Davidia.

'The antidote can live here undetected, but we are far too large to hide. We can be easily discovered. That's why we must move. I fear danger is nearby. I can't explain it. Call it intuition, but it's nearby.'

'How do we get back to Moonah? There's nothing to climb and we can't fly, can we? The last time I used my flying skills was on a school excursion on a flying fox. There aren't any of those here or a cable car into the sky is there?'

'It's an ancient skill my parents had endowed me with by once having visited the Hole in the Hill in Rotland. It's not foolproof, but I can't think of another way. Moonah is not well enough to save us this time. We must prove that we are worthy of saving by doing it ourselves.'

'I don't have to be a bloody heroine, do I?' questioned Davidia. 'At school I often mediated between two warring females, the bitches wanted to scratch each other's eyes out. One said he looked at my boyfriend. Next, they are clawing at each other. No one else would interfere, so I ended up with both of them having a go at me because I did. I didn't get it and neither of them got the boyfriend. Go figure!'

'You must concentrate and help me get this right,' said Slirander.

Her eyes were closed and she chanted a group of unusual words. None of them made sense, why would they, when everything around them was odd.

'*Ickle goggle eyesight flight,*
Wockle wing turn up tonight,

Weeny me and not weeny you,
Fing us past the sky for safety too.'

The girls sat in a yoga position. How else would one sit when speaking an odd chant that no one understood? Did Slirander? Who knows? Davidia did as she was told. There must be a reward in there somewhere for her to have agreed. A minute or two passed. They weren't walking or riding bicycles, they just did. They were unseen.

'Who woke me up from a deep sleep?' said a thundering voice.

The sky became darker and darker. Two huge, luminous eyes, one pink and the other blue, danced between the foreboding clouds. Something had called it from afar. That chant hadn't been used in hundreds of years. Who has got it now? The owners of that special chant were the only persons authorised to use it. If Slirander knew the correct chant, then how did her family obtain ownership? That was one of her many secrets. Demons once flourished in times long ago and those that survived had identifying call rhymes. This one was for a sky chain known as Stripander. It had massive interconnecting links, which formed a protective circle around whatever it protected. It was an ancient demonic transportation unit. Stripander was annoyed at its recall. Laziness had crept into its occupation. It followed the chanting sound. Slirander was repeating it *ad nauseum* very quietly under her breath hoping it had been heard by whom it had been intended for. There was no guarantee of success seeing the chant was so ancient. Believing in good does have its positive effects.

Inside the university, there was only a mess to clean up. In the courtyard where Slirander and Davidia were in chant mode, the atmosphere became cool.

'We meet again,' said cold, having enjoyed the journey from the skies to the ground. 'I took your advice and it does have its warmer moments down here. I'm not so cold and frosty anymore.'

'You don't feel so cold either. Why have you dropped down to ground level?'

'I've escorted the strangest cloud formation that I have ever seen. It's new to everyone in the atmosphere,' said cold. 'It has coloured eyes and the strangest formation of mists. They are all shaped in chain links.'

Slirander opened her eyes.

'That must be Stripander,' she said. 'Where is it? We have a meeting.'

'Near those hills in the distance. Shall I signal?'

'Please.'

Cold spirited away. Stripander was unsure what had recalled it. Cold approached and stated that its attendance was required at a meeting with a young girl. Stripander had no idea what a young girl was. Perhaps it was a modern-day demon? The chain link formation floated to Slirander. The two met.

'Are you the one who called me?'

'Yes.'

'Identify yourself.'

Slirander suddenly had two colourful eyes, one pink and the other blue. Davidia couldn't believe it. Her friend was imitating the chain link cloud colours.

'Agreed.'

Before any further speech was uttered, the chain links swirled around the two girls and embraced them. They were enclosed. The ground began to fade from their vision. Soon they were squashing their way through a stumpy tree growth back into the Moonatric tree world. Stripander disappeared.

'I'm not going to ask you what happened Slirander, but it did, didn't it?' asked Davidia.

Slirander nodded. It wasn't the time for explanations.

'Look, the stumpy tree growth has grown a pink leaf. We have just walked out of it.'

'That means Moonah is recovering his health.'

The pink leaf withered and fell off as soon as their feet had left its surface. They climbed onto the next leaf; another branch higher. Moonah was still firmly planted in the soil. It was so peaceful living in the forest, but only for a tree. Moonah's wrinkled trunk felt the resurgence of good nutrition from the soil and it was almost ready to leave Rotland; however, something held it back. There were two more important tasks for the girls to fulfil.

School would never be the same after this adventure, providing the memories stayed with them.

*

'I'm not done yet,' vowed Roland the Rotter. 'Why is it me who suffers when I only want the world's written language for myself? Is that too much to expect? The way language is misused today; at least I want to keep it in its purest form. No misspellings, misuse, abbreviations, misunderstandings or incorrectly written. If I controlled it all, I would be the most powerful wordsmith in existence. There is much to do to ensure that happens.'

Evil often didn't possess a good side.

10 DOUBLE L

'Are you in pain?' asked a fully-formed letter to an injured capital B.

'I have lost one of my loops,' it sadly replied. 'Now I'm illegible and useless to read.'

'Were you part of a fully readable word?'

'My friends that I was teamed with should be close by. There should be an e, s, a and t. I don't recognise them anymore.'

The letter searched the ground and noticed a small hump, an unusual curve and a flat top, the remnants of a t.

'There doesn't seem to be any legible letters that I can recognise. Are you sure you had company?'

'I once formed the word Best. Now I only form an odd shape. I was once in a novel by a world-famous author and now look at me.'

The missing loop capital B wandered off aimlessly and unfortunately fell off the edge of a huge cliff into a massive opening. It was a pit of gigantic proportions where all useless letters of the alphabet of the world ended up.

The Pit of Litanticus was the final resting place of no longer used written letters of expression. They had been forced here by an unknown power that had permeated their books. The trek was arduous and belittling as each letter had to find their way there. In the process, they were worn down and ended up being unreadable letters of no further use. It was depressing to see the world's literature wounded and in such a bad state. Was all literature to experience the same fate and what made them come here?

'Hello p. You are a p, aren't you?' asked a worn-out vowel, not recognising that the p had lost its lower part. Each letter had suffered a loss of some element of its legibility.

'Why has it come to this? We were so pleased to be read and to entertain the masses. It wasn't until that interfering DV combination visited us that all the trouble started. We were sitting on a shelf in an ordinary library when the DV combinations introduced themselves. They asked to be allowed to join us on the pages and before we knew it, they had multiplied to immense proportions and all of us readable, ink or other processed-infused letters per page were suddenly upended out of the book. We had no choice against the strongarm tactics used. I was in a Shakespearean play. Now I'm common refuse. I would prefer to be in a two-for-five-dollar jumble sale than be fully discarded. At least I could still be read even though the pages would be faded, the cover torn and who cared about dog ears?' The p's remnants rolled off, sniffling its last sounds.

Was the literature of the world under threat?

The still fully-formed letter wasn't fully aware of the distress of all the other letters from great literary works. It had been in a female magazine, which was lightly read and easily discarded. There were no DV visitors in its magazine because the literary content was quite small and of little consequence. Pictures were easier to visualise and absorb. A pair of fellow letters, f and q had invited it to see how other letters of higher quality literary integrity were treated at the end of their readership. At least its extremities were intact and could still be useful when arranged with any other letter.

A large group of letters had arrived together, jumbled and unrecognisable.

'You aren't the subject of a poor book review, are you?' asked a y, who was now worn down to a v.

'Definitely not. We are a proud sonnet. Now we can't rhyme at all. We don't recognise each other anymore. There's a whole book full following us. Where is the poetry party that we have been instructed to attend?' asked the proud leader, once a respectfully designed S in Roman Type who began the sonnet.

The procession continued. Clumps of letters, which now symbolised short brush strokes of no readable capability arrived en masse. Each had a hazardous story to tell, but unfortunately none of them could be read.

'We were about to be produced as a play,' wailed a d that had lost its o-shaped bowl. 'Suddenly, a rush of invading unwelcome two-tone letters arrived with an army of clones. They destroyed any further chance of us being readable and converted into an act. It's such a miserable time. We were told that if we wanted to be produced, the path to production was to visit the Pit of Litanticus. It was a lie. Now we're here, the play is a shambles. See for yourself. Does any of that mess represent a proper letter? No. They are now all squiggles, lines and worn-down shapes that represent rubbish. Where, oh where, has all the good literature gone?'

'Down here in the pit,' chorused a set of choir leftovers.

The Pit of Litanticus grew ever so full of discarded groups of the alphabet. The fully-formed letter couldn't believe the destruction of good language. Without any other fully-formed letters, even it couldn't be read as a stand-alone story. It knew, as a capital M, it could begin a sentence and a storyline — even begin to describe some of the pretty pictures in a magazine — but as a sentence it had no hope.

'Aren't you joining in the fun?' asked a nasty DV combination which was fully-formed and fussing about pushing and shoving the damaged letters into the pit.

'I still have a use and don't intend becoming alphabetic refuse,' replied the capital M. It felt it still had a readable quality and reputation to uphold.

'Suit yourself. This is the most enjoyment we've had so far. Mind you, nothing can stop it. Our master has seen to that.' The DVs kept on pushing.

Capital M stood like a lonely sentinel overseeing the end of literature. Disaster was all around it. Nothing intelligent it said or anything it could have done could change a solitary thing. It was stuck in an incapability file in the drawers of unsolvable solutions. The outlook for the future was bleak. Where is the good guy or gal to save the situation? Maybe Roland the Rotter was too strong this time.

*

Deep inside the Hole in the Hill, Roland the Rotter oversaw what he believed to be his greatest achievement, the destruction of all literature, except for his vast private collection untouchable by any virus. His Destrusto Virus had been infused with extra strengths and destructive capabilities, which rendered all written literature defenceless against its powers. It ran amok, bullying letters, uprooting them from any pages and forced them all to trek to the Pit of Litanticus where they would never be read again. The virus had actually sedated the letters that were open to suggestions and was why they blindly followed orders to the Pit of Litanticus. It was a hypnotic, alphabetic suggestion, none of which the world had ever coped with before. Roland was positive that there was no antidote strong enough to defeat him. He thought that at last he could rule an ignorant world. The Rotters themselves weren't bright enough to recognise that any of them would never learn to read either.

"What one doesn't know won't hurt them" was an old saying.

Another one is that "Ignorance is bliss". The reading world didn't want to hear these utterances of nonsense.

The problem existed, where was the solution?

*

'My tree roots are tingling,' said Moonah. 'I hope those giant worms aren't back-rubbing against me again. It feels like an urgent tingle. Something is amiss in the soil. I wonder what ails it.'

Moonah was slowly recovering his strength. The soil was nutritional enough to restore good sap flow, encourage leaf growth so that he almost had a full twenty-six leaf complement and his branches were full of life. Each wrinkle had filled out a little more like a Botox injection where there seemed to be less of them. That was only an imaginary feeling. Even the stumpy tree growth had recovered its missing leaf; however, Moonah still wasn't happy. Even his arthritic branches and sometimes painful tree roots, were relaxed and pain free. Being "home" had certainly improved his health regime. Moonah sent out a series of signals to its tree roots. They ran along the fibrous growths as lightning strikes through the air: instant, flashing and quickly. None replied because a negative answer wasn't what Moonah was looking for.

Suddenly, a tree root acted quite strangely. Did it want to twist off from the main tree trunk? It began to thrash in the soil. Clods of dirt let go in case they were pulverised into no more than a dust particle. A hollow was left around this one particular tree root. Inside it lived the Font of Knowledge, which had become agitated at the seriousness of the signal it had received. It knew that there was trouble brewing in Rotland, or was it the Pit of Litanticus? Through its pure waters flashed a scene of the damaged alphabet dropping into a deep pit. It wasn't a pit party, was it, or was it a pitiful party? The severity of the vision troubled Font. The girls had an antidote to restore language, but unfortunately the destruction witnessed required a greater response; a purer form of antidote. It signalled to Moonah that another meeting with the girls was required. It was time to revise a new antidote strategy.

'Girls, the Font wants to meet with you. It's very important,' said Moonah.

They were sitting high on a tree trunk with nowhere else to go and enjoying the views of the Moonatric Forest.

'What is it this time?' asked a petulant Davidia. She was feeling it was time to go home.

'Font wants to meet you urgently,' Moonah insisted.

'And what if I don't want to go?' questioned a stubborn Davidia.

The adventures they have had, exposed a maturity growth level in her. A bit more of an "I am" person began to shine through.

Moonah wasn't in the mood for disagreements. He waved a tree leaf so it gently slapped her on the back to an entrance in his trunk and, like a show-stopper slide, sent her down a tree root to meet Font. Slirander followed without the necessary slapping encouragement. Thump! They arrived in the cave tree root. There was Font already formed into a pure water force in a bowl. No mucus spit was required this time. Just an additional ingredient for their final two vials.

'Nice to meet you both again,' said Font, brimming with purity.

'Hello, Font,' said Slirander, encouragingly.

'Humph!' said Davidia. Her day wasn't all video games.

'The literature of the world is being destroyed and you need to save it,' said Font.

'Why us? I haven't read a book in ages and want to return home so I can,' said Davidia.

'There are no books for you to read. All literature is being destroyed. It has ended up in the Pit of Litanticus. You must restore its health. There is no option.'

Davidia and Slirander both blinked. No books anywhere to read. That triggered a resurgence of independence in Davidia.

'Let's get this mongrel Roland, the whatever.'

'First we must strengthen the antidote. Please empty your remaining two vials into my bowl.'

'How do you know that we only have two left?'

'Even if the language is destroyed, I can still count. Numbers still exist.'

'I suppose so.'

The girls emptied their vials as advised. Who wants to disagree with a font? Font began to swirl like an agitator in a washing machine. Slosh, slosh! Somewhere above them, sap began to slowly leak from the roof of the tree root. A fine filament like a spider's cobweb dangled above Font. On its end was a globule of clear sap. It had nowhere to go except down. Gravity was forcing it to act. It finally let go. Davidia could have sworn she heard a squeal of delight as it descended. Splash! The new ingredient was quickly absorbed into the mixture. There was no discernible colour change that the girls noticed. It didn't take long before the process ceased and the new antidote was ready.

'Use it carefully,' advised Font.

'Is there a secret strategy contained within it?' asked Slirander, who knew that Font had a hidden secret of some kind in each preparation made. There was no response.

With the renewed antidote, the girls were ready to take on any language destruction competition.

'What does this one do that the other doesn't?' asked Davidia.

'It's impervious to infection. The previous antidote had a time lapse in which it could be infected, this one doesn't,' replied Slirander.

'You have been taught well,' said Font. 'Moonah is waiting for you to return to the blue leaf. Do well and may reading be forever.'

Font instantly disappeared down its well and the girls were once again inside a wriggly, wrinkled tree root, with one vial each and, of course, the woody growths that they occasionally bumped into. They ran quickly toward the main trunk.

'Has something more serious occurred for us to use a stronger antidote?' asked Davidia.

'The Pit of Litanticus. You heard Font say all literature was being destroyed and was ending up there. The Destrusto Virus is wreaking enormous havoc. We must go there and see if we can restore the balance,' said Slirander.

'It isn't in any holiday brochure that I've read,' said Davidia.

'Soon we won't be reading anything at all — travel brochures or otherwise — unless the destruction is stopped. Moonah will know what to do.'

Moonah was enjoying his new growth and health regime, so much that his arthritic branches and tree roots hurt less. He couldn't stay forever in the moonatric forest. Alphabet duties were required elsewhere; however, he could enjoy a healthy improvement for an historically aged tree. He felt the girls move along a tree root. It felt alive. He made an opening for them to emerge from his trunk and they sat on the blue leaf. It was a beautiful colour, full of vibrancy, which reflected the topic and letter it represented.

'Slirander, did you enjoy your visit to an old haunt?'

'It was good to see Font again.'

'Were you given any advice?'

'Font suggested that we visit the Pit of Litanticus. There's real trouble brewing there. I assume you know where and what it is. It's not in ancient Greece, is it?'

Moonah groaned. Suddenly, all his healthy branches and tree

roots had an acute arthritic pain. Nothing good had ever come out of that place before.

'Couldn't you pick somewhere else to visit? Don't say the wrong word or show that you can spell properly. Some letters may not be as accepting of a restoration as others might be. It's mainly because they think they should be read earlier in a sentence than where they are placed. Many will look the same. See them for the good they will be restored into.'

Even though she sometimes complained, Davidia thought that her time with Slirander and Moonah was much more interesting than being at school. Maybe she could make a difference, win a spelling-bee or complete a crossword without cross words. She had to be more positive. Where is Roland the Rat?

Moonah tried hard to release them into the blue leaf on the trip of a lifetime. It refused to yield.

'What's the problem?' asked Davidia.

'There might be a special word that goes with the request for opening,' said Slirander.

Normally the brr, brr, tag was the entry key. Had Roland the Rotter been able to close the entry off? Normally that was impossible, but maybe his new virus was more capable than originally thought. It was a stand-off. Moonah squirmed trying valiantly to influence the blue leaf. Davidia could see the impasse. She bent over and whispered to the blue leaf a small phrase of encouragement:

'Cut me, dice me, splice me not.

Sever you off, for compost to rot.'

The blue leaf shivered like a Hawaiian hip-shaking dancer.

'I have been threatened from below. Something knows I hold the entry to the subject of literature. If I reveal my opening, then no longer will literature survive.'

'You've been conned. Literature is already being destroyed

without your obstinacy. Your beautiful blue colour will turn a miserable black if you deny us entry.'

'Oh, no, not my pride and joy,' wailed a nervous blue leaf.

'Well, get off your stem, turn over a new leaf and give us entry, otherwise you will be the letter from L, with no support system. Where else would you grow safely?'

The blue leaf sought reassurance from Moonah that it wouldn't be abandoned.

'As long as I grow, you have a home on one of my branches,' said a comforting Moonah.

Emotion wasn't a tree trait, but when one wanted something important, compassion could be a useful tool.

Slirander held hands with Davidia. Suddenly, the blue leaf tore open and whoosh, they fell down into a sea of moving objects. They looked like rows of ants in single file. Thump! They landed on a group of black dots, scattering them in splatter patterns.

'Who's the heavy-handed chubby pants who sat on us?' said a dot.

The girls stood up and dusted themselves down.

'I'm sorry, but it was us,' said Slirander. 'My friend, Davidia, and I.'

'Next time, if there is one, land somewhere else,' said a dot.

'Who are you and where are you going?' asked Davidia.

'I'm a dot, that's a dot, this is a dot and the others over there are all dots. We're following the sentences that used to end with us. Can you imagine the rudeness of leaving a proper book? The letters abandoned us. Oh, no, you don't get rid of us that easily. We may be small in print, but are immensely important in finishing sentences. We also have pride of place on all lower-case is and js. Imagine all the nonsensical ramblings a book would have if there were no end to a sentence. We are dividers and finishers. So, when they took off without any explanation, we followed. I must say it's uninteresting and tiring. We are gradually wearing away with all this travelling. We haven't found any sentence to get behind and place ourselves in correctly. It appears that the letters are lost. We can't even find a sensible or fully-formed one. It's hopeless.'

'Have you any idea where you will end up?' asked Slirander.

'Not at the end of a sentence at this rate of attrition,' replied a diminishing dot.

'I hope we meet again.'

'That's not likely. We could end up in a book you don't read, but my relatives would be there.'

Slirander watched the procession wind its way into the distance. Even the other characters in books were affected by the loss of literature. What happens to the dashes, quotation marks, the hash signs and all other elements used in literary communication? They too would become lost without their support teams of letters and signs. The destruction of literature meant more than only letters. Other items would become useless as well.

'Davidia, what are you doing?'

'Writing a word on the ground. I wonder if any of the worn-down letters would recognise what they once looked like. I don't have any writing paper, but the ground certainly works as an earthen blackboard.'

'What word have you written? Let me see.'

'It's Rotter,' she whispered.

'There may not be any twin ts travelling together.'

'That's not important. At least it gives a chance for four different types of letters, one with a capital, to recognise themselves like in a ground mirror. Let's test it. There are so many unrecognisable walking black marks. It's unbelievable that they were once read and lived in books.'

'Did you have to dig that rut so deeply,' said a very tired verb that had stayed together on the journey. There was so little left of it, all that could be seen were flyspeck sizes of black spots.

'Do you recognise the word?' asked Davidia.

'You need a tall letter that can see it, or perhaps ask a Braille group that would be able to trace its perimeter and understand those deep marks. As you can see, we are no longer active.'

The ruts seemed to be more of an impediment to the broken language, let alone recognising it as a word. Time passed and there wasn't any recognition of the letter ruts.

'Maybe it won't work,' said Davidia, at her disappointment.

'None of the letters can see from the height that we can. What if we let the letters walk over us? They could be elevated enough to recognise the word? We could lie on the ground creating a false hill for them to climb. It's a chance,' said Slirander, fresh out of any other idea.

'That's creepy. All those black marks clambering over me doesn't particularly appeal.'

'Any brighter ideas?'

The light bulb shop was shut today.

'Oh, all right. I'll give it a short trial, but it's still creepy.'

The girls lay directly alongside the word so that when the letter remnants made it to the top of the pretend hill, their first view into the distance would be the ruts that Davidia had drawn in the soil. After that, it was doom as usual. It wasn't long before a few complaints came their way.

'Who said there were mountains here? In our state we have to climb over them. Who put them there? Where's that historical letter nut which told us it was all flat out here? I'll never believe again what's written unless I'm in the story too,' said an e vowel, which was now a small hump.

'All the growth is at one end. Those massive bushes should be all over a mountain.'

This was a reference to the girl's hair. They lay opposite to each other with only their shoes touching.

'I've been in many geographical magazines and books and I have never found a mountain surface this soft,' said a once large capital G, as it trudged over a girl's school jacket.

'Follow the light, doughy track. It seems easy to climb and may lead somewhere important,' said an intelligent iq pairing, trying to reason the meaning of their journey. The girls' arms were covered in long columns of small letters resembling travelling hairs. Soon the walking tracks that the letters had taken literally covered them both.

'How did that extra pair of slight undulations appear?'

It was a final hurdle that the letters had to overcome climbing over their jackets.

Soon a vast array of letters had made it to the top. They scanned the horizon. Many found nothing of interest. Even the DV nasties didn't recognise the word Rotter, because they were rotten spellers. It is often said that you can't put a brain in a monument. In the case of a DV pair, it was a complete waste of effort to try, so obviously it was correct. Recognition of the word wasn't happening. A bad headache day just got worse. The girls were tiring of being itched by the tiny travellers. There wasn't one decent letter amongst them that had retained its proper form.

A travelling set of calligraphy — decipher instructors that had once been crucial in solving an intriguing crime in a novel — rested at the top. They had retained their sense of humour and ability to decipher writings of any description.

'Is that a moat down there?' questioned a senior capital C, or what was left of it.

'It's a series of angular and circular holes,' said a z, that was now a short top, flat, straight line.

'Has an alien novel passed by recently?' asked an interested A, worn down to its rung. 'Those scribblings could be in a foreign code.'

'It looks like a correctly spelt word. I haven't seen one of them for a while. I thought that I'd never see one again,' said an H, also worn down to its rung.

'I agree. Why don't we, for the sake of old times, decipher the word and what it means? It will be less boring than this endless trek.'

The calligraphy group dispersed into their teams, six in all, and each team analysed a set of one scribbling which converts to one letter each. They assessed the length of the indentations, the shapes, depth and style of writing script.

'It's a youth's writing, based on the lack of smooth curvature.'

'The style is a mix of written shapes with the r in a modern format.'

'The replication of two t's show that whoever wrote it under-stands the placement of plural letters in the same word.'

'The capital R indentation is deeper and more emphasised than the others as if there was stress on the first letter indicating an importance in noticing it.'

'The two vowels are ordinary in their presentation, but great joiners to make the word read sensibly.'

'The word is assembled correctly. It is not misspelt. It reads as a proper word.'

Slirander could hear the discussions with her odd ear. It was facing upwards. The calligraphy group had come to an agreement.

'The word is Rotter,' said its lead letter. 'I don't know of its significance or whether it's a form of code word. Whatever its meaning is, I couldn't care less. Group, we have at last read a word again. We had all given up hope of ever doing that. I feel good. Maybe we might run across the word "hope". Now, that would be of significance.'

At the mention of the word Rotter, Slirander stood up. The tiny speckled letter parts floated harmlessly to the ground.

'Davidia, get up. You haven't gone to sleep, have you?' prodded Slirander, by pushing her shoe against Davidia's feet.

'I was dreaming of being home reading a book,' she replied.

'I heard a group of letters read the word Rotter and they said it out loud. It will now flow through all the following part-time letters as they repeat the first written word that they have become aware of since the destruction of their own personal situation. They will all discuss it. We must be patient and observe for any erratic behaviour amongst the pilgrims to the Pit of Litanticus. Even those DV nasties may be affected by its utterance.'

'Did you hear that there is a rotten influence up ahead?' said a g, which once headed the word gossip.

'I heard that letter parts were rotting away and nothing could save them,' said another member of the g family.

The story unfolded about something rotten, which became so distorted that all every letter discussed was how rotten the world was. Rumours spread like wildfire, burning away any rational thoughts. Slirander and Davidia scanned the letters for any tell-tale irregularities. Some of the DV virus became edgy that their master's background name had been revealed. No one knew of it, so how did this happen? The penalty for failure to keep it secret, and they weren't to blame, suddenly turned on the DV virus.

'I'm beginning to wear down,' complained a pushy DV.

'Me, too,' said another.

It was as if fate had purposely slapped a destructive gene on them. They began to deteriorate like every other letter. There was no more differentiation between us and them. It was now a blend. They would be dealt the same fate as all letter parts. The Pit of Litanticus didn't differentiate between good and evil letters. It destroyed whatever entered. Doom couldn't be turned around and reverse into the word mood. The fate of literature was now sealed. The DVs had performed their task and were now dispensable. Roland the Rotter had a serious "me" ego and it was the only one he liked. A sad, lonely series of dark marks wound their way across the landscape. When a book tour was organised, it was expected to include written works. Now, the book tour included the fateful Pit of Litanticus. Nothing would be read again.

Slirander reached into her pocket and took a firm grip on her vial. She pondered the possibility of using it now or waiting until the Pit of Litanticus.

'Lads, I feel it in my genes. We are about to grapple with the enemy once more. Wait until the hand gives that final pressure push and we are away. I'm all hyped-up with sap joining us. I feel invigorated, I feel invincible, I feel fantastic,' babbled the leader.

'We get the fun feeling too,' said a soldier, with the enthusiasm of a potato.

'But, wait, there's more.'

'She hasn't given the signal. It's another false alarm.'

'Don't give up hope yet. She may still do it.'

The soldiers of the Pebble of Purpose were transformed into good bullies with their stronger ingredient, the sap of Moonah. All nearly-destroyed letters could be restored with their improved antidote. The saving of literature from all the classics was a task worth getting excited over. Alas, Slirander never pushed the atomiser. She withdrew her hand. The leader's body language sagged like a sack in disappointment at not leading the charge. It was itching for action.

'Has anything odd happened?' asked Davidia.

'The word Rotter didn't have much of an effect on anything except the DV combinations that began to erode in the same manner as all the other letters. It must have contained a not-happy, self-destruct message by just mentioning the word. We must be alert for any nasty Rotter. They may take a devious, unrecognisable form. It could even be me,' said Slirander.

'I hope you're joking,' exclaimed Davidia, with a frowned look.

'Don't worry, I'm almost normal.'

Before any further repartee about Rotters could occur, a commotion erupted close to the Pit of Litanticus. The girls rushed quickly to inspect the cause.

A testy b had got up someone's a and told them to f off quickly before an up u 2 combination of a number and letters were converted into a real bad language expression. What was a number doing here? Was it a spy? The pit was supposedly the waste-hole for defunct letters and not fully-formed numbers, which were not being destroyed.

'Go on, push us, I dare you?' said a feisty team of a shilfit of an a, r and an s.

'I'm not doing that. I came here to see if I could assist,' replied the 2, not wanting to inflame the situation. 'Without all of you we can't activate formulas of any description, make sense of statistics and embellish a good story. We need you guys to make it all work.'

'Yeah! Well, why didn't you say so earlier. We …'

The letters had fallen over the edge into the pit. The 2 sat down wondering what to do when the girls arrived. It almost fell into the pit in surprise at the size of the letters S and D. This was how the girls were often seen: as two humungous letters.

'You're not a letter,' said Davidia.

'How observant of you,' 2 replied.

'Why are you here?'

'To offer any help I can. All numbers are lost without our lettered friends.'

'Are there any more of your lot nearby?'

'Unfortunately, they all had other tasks to perform. I was at a loose end and dropped in to see if I could be of any assistance.'

Davidia turned to Slirander and whispered in balfang,

'Thalfat ilfit walfas olfodd alfa twolfo walfas alfalolfonelfe'

(that it was odd a 2 was alone).

'Ilfi alfagrelfeelfe' (I agree).

The 2 looked quite normal. There were no obvious oddities about it; however, being the only one here raised their suspicions. Even its eyes didn't seem to be ugly veined. For the moment they accepted its sincerity.

'There isn't much any of us can do, really,' said Davidia. 'The letters all seem doomed for destruction. Look at the long lines of the best language ever written and its disappearing down the sewer, I mean, pit. Nothing will ever be read again.'

She let out an exhausted blast of wind and accidentally blew the number 2 over. On the base of its feet, she glimpsed her reflection. The number 2 had mirrored feet. How odd. Could it see into the ground with them and, if so, why? She had noticed it dangle its feet over the edge of the Pit of Litanticus. It could be overseeing letter destruction, counting the letters or acting as a photographic record to be replayed elsewhere later.

'Why are you two here?' asked 2. It was an inquisitive number.

'We stumbled over a tree root and woke up here, like in a fairy story except that there is nothing to read. The landscape is full of half letters, which I assume can't be read in half a book. We could ask you the same question. There doesn't appear to be any other numbers here either,' answered Davidia.

'I was working with a tightly-knit equation which inexplicably began to lose its letter components. It all happened so quickly. I was dragged here attached to a malfunctioning letter. I had no time to extract myself from it,' replied 2.

'Do you know anything about the Pit of Litanticus?' asked Slirander.

'Is it a convention of some sort? I don't understand what it's for. It looks very busy. Those black marks are bungy jumping without any attachments.'

'I think it represents a troubled language beyond repair. Watch them limp and jump off the edge of the pit. It's terrible. I feel helpless to stop it.'

A half smile oozed across 2's face like treacly syrup. Had a secret been revealed? 2 pretended to be an odd number even though it wasn't.

'Can you help rescue the letters?' asked Slirander.

'How would I do that? None of them are my family. Besides, the last time that I worked with them it was in a malfunctioning equation. I got the blame for it. It was one of those nasty ps or qs that were responsible. You have to watch those two letters very closely.'

'Davidia,' whispered Slirander, 'we need time out.'

Slirander was having a feeling of uncertainty about 2. It just didn't feel right that it was here on a weak excuse. Any number could have done exactly the same thing, yet they were noticeably absent.

'What's the problem? 2 seems to be a perfectly genuine number.'

'Have you noticed anything odd about it?'

'Only the reflective soles on its feet. I thought that it was odd at the time. It had them dangled over the pit edge like it was spying.'

'Remember that Roland the Rotter is deceptively cunning.'

The girls pondered about their new acquaintance.

'Can we really save the damaged letters?' asked Davidia.

'I'm not sure. The super antidote is experimental. Font has workshopped it in a laboratory sense for quite a while. We'll soon find out when we release it.'

'Should we send a short spray into the Pit to see what happens?'

'Lads, scouting party required. Who wants an adventure? Volunteers required. It's a once in a lifetime opportunity. Who wants to give it a go? Line up, line up,' the leader yelled.

The soldiers of the Pebble of Purpose were brimming with just that; purpose. All they wanted was a quick squirt.

'We'll go. What's more, we'll return,' chorused a cheerful bunch.

'Right, then. Wait for my signal.'

Slirander clasped her vial. With so many broken letters around her feet, she didn't notice that the fully formed M had wandered over and she accidentally tripped over it. Alas, her important vial fell from her grasp. Clang! It made the sound of failure.

'Watch it, big feet,' called out M, hopefully avoiding any damage.

'Wait, lads. The signal hasn't been given. Hold back. Sorry to disappoint you,' said the leader.

The top of the vial was crowded with enthusiastic, newly-reinvigorated spray droplets. 2 saw Slirander drop her small vial and pounced on it swiftly like a cat on a bird.

'What's this?' 2 said, as it rotated the vial between inquisitive fingers.

'It's my new perfume, promising to make me smell like my dreams,' she replied, fearing the worst; discovery. 'It's the new fashion for young girls. Spray its wondrous scent and you'll then understand why it is so popular.'

2 hadn't experienced the smell of perfume before. Its curiosity emerged. It was about to press the go button, when Davidia interrupted.

'Give that to me. It's not for you. Nothing you could do would make you smell any nicer. I took a whiff of your feet and they definitely need a refresher. Spray them and I'll guarantee that other numbers would be attracted to you.'

2 didn't understand the brashness of youth.

'Lads, prepare for an exercise. It's a new hand we've been dealt, so let's deal with it.'

2 pushed the atomiser button and sprayed at its feet. The atomisers fled in fear of footrot. In doing so, they emitted a scented puff, which twirled upwards. 2 sniffed in the excreted wind of fear and enjoyed its attractive smell. It felt the waste air cling to it. No one had the heart to tell it any different.

'Can I have my perfume back, please?' asked Slirander. 'I also need refreshing. It has been a long while without use.'

'Lads, it's hi-ho into the pit. Follow me to save our friends.'

2 returned the spray to Slirander. It thought that it was a peculiar damn thing with a movable top.

The super antidote atoms ran amok mixing with the broken letters. They immediately began their restoration process. Some complaints emerged.

'I'm the bottom half of a b and not a backward a.'

'I don't fit with a y. I'm actually a v.'

'Try again,' said an x. 'I'm not cross, but please set me at the correct angle.'

'Lads, halt. There's an error here. We are incorrectly restoring the letters. Something in the antidote is flawed. We can't go on like this. Restoration must be correct, otherwise a butcher's job will leave nasty language cuts everywhere. Nothing would any longer be joined. We've failed.' Disappointment was everywhere.

Slirander took the spray and whispered quietly to the remnants in her vial.

'You must go again. The wrong fingers sent the last group. It distorted the mix. Can you hear me?'

'Loud and clear. Lads, regroup. Forget the morning coffee,

massage and dip in the pool, it's work time and overtime with no extra pay. Our reward is the pleasure of our restoration duty. We're ready, armed, faithful and dangerous. Press away.'

Slirander pressed her atomiser. This time the lads had clear instructions. Hopefully, there would be no mistakes this time.

The soldiers performed like trained seals and flew directly into the Pit of Litanticus. The black abyss was a deep, dark and foreboding place. It was so dark with all the black letters that their skills would be fully tested. It was a seething mass of movement, barely distinguishable as anything except a heaving mess. It would take a miracle of ingenuity in decision making, discovering where everything would fit together again. Font had ensured that with the Sap of Moonah, re-joining and growing letter parts would be ensured. The antidote ingredients, although a peculiar mix, had an innate feature of togetherness. The challenge was on.

The x fitted perfectly with its correctly angled straight lines; there was no confusion between any a and b components anymore; and a v and a y were properly separated. Now there was at least the chance of survival.

At the edge of the pit, Slirander, Davidia and now an M, watched anxiously. 2 appeared disinterested until fully-formed letters emerged from the pit conversing animatedly with each other.

'I am returning to a proper play,' said a group, walking in a paragraph, already rehearsing to be read and acted out.

'History is my forte,' said another group of interesting words.

There were huge capital letters and many descriptive phrases in that lot.

'People will laugh once again. I'm in a joke book. Have you heard the one about …?' said a humourous group, chatting excitedly about the fun they were going to have.

On and on the procession of correctly formed letters emerged from the Pit of Litanticus, fully capable of returning to their previous branch of literature. The improved antidote was proving to be a success. Slirander and Davidia high-fived each other. 2 showed traces of agitation. It twisted in agony at the recovery of language. It thought that this time it had won. A pain twinged in its reflective feet. They had seen something they didn't like. A small, unused atomiser droplet had struggled to join in the restoration. Sometimes flaws occurred. 2 picked it up.

'You aren't a letter,' it said.

'No, I'm not, but what are you?' asked 2.

'Nothing of interest.'

'How did you get here?'

'I'm not sure. My mum must have brought me.'

'What do you do?'

An antidote was programmed never to lie, so it compulsorily had to reveal its truth. When it did, 2 threw it to the ground and stomped on it. 2 now knew how letters were saved and restored. It seethed in anger. Its sneering face began to peel away. Underneath, there wasn't a healthy 2 anymore. Its body suddenly flipped upside down and resembled more of a lucky 7, but with a curved base. A 7 had more strength than a 2. The girls watched the peculiar behaviour. Had 2 multiplied, added, subtracted or extended?

Slirander quickly sensed danger. She sprayed her vial again of any remaining balance. Her empty vial was of no further use. Davidia still had hers intact, fully loaded and well-hidden. There was no sense in revealing the full game plan, if there was one.

2, now a converted 7, continued to watch in agony as the ant trails of fully-formed and restored letters gaily skipped along. A complete range of capital letters buffeted each other in delight at being able to flex their reading potential. A whole educational literary book gossiped about the joy of being read and teaching others. 2's happy camper snaps had been drowned by rain. Could it inflict any changes on the recovery?

It had no choice but to turn nasty and destructive. Why couldn't all language belong to it? Now that it had flipped to a 7, the reflective feet were now on its head. Its arms became the new legs and its eyes were at a lower level of sight than the girls' knee caps. 7 began waving its feet around, reflecting the sun's rays. This heated up the reflective feet, which acted like two small microwave ovens. Inside was the incubating Superior Destrusto Virus. It was a final attempt to ruin all language. If it failed, it was "All over, Red Rover". As the sun heated the feet, the sdv cooked and festered inside and enlarged. It was a disgusting mix of evil. At the penultimate moment of expulsion, Slirander did a very strange thing. She began chanting a weird selection of letters she seemingly grabbed at random from the returning fully formers. She didn't distinguish between lower case or upper case. She wasn't after emphasis, but Roland the Rotter.

'An R to ,
An o so toe,
An l for me,
An a to go,
An n to send and
A d to end.'

The chant was a special alert to the lads for specialist action. Davidia stood immobilised, mouth agape. 7 froze rigid like an icicle. All returning letters suffered a mini misprint and ceased moving. Had a photo been taken to set a scene of disagreement?

'Lads, put your shower hats on, regurgitate your protective slime cover and up the attitude. It's time to teach this sdv some educational manners. Stop fluffing your pillow, clean your mouths; its germ time. Exhale only and don't breathe in the filthy little suckers. It's all about good behaviour, protocol and ridding an environmental language pest. Are you with me, lads? All for one.' A loud cheer erupted. 'At last, a cohesive working unit,' said the leader. 'I knew they had it in them. The trouble was locating where it had been hidden.'

Davidia's vial suddenly became hot to her touch. Her hand tingled with the heat. It was trouble to go.

Slirander approached the vibrating 7. It was on high alert for any intrusion.

'Is there anything I should know about you?' said 7, as tense as a fully-extended bungy cord.

'I'm a girl. A plain, simple — well, not really simple — ordinary teenager,' she replied.

'Nothing is that simple. These letters must be destroyed. It is within my power.'

'What would that achieve?'

'Control. I would become the premier reader in the world and its only language collector.'

'That's very selfish. What about everyone else?'

'I'm not everyone else.'

'Am I speaking to 2 or 7? One's even and the other's odd. Which is it? My mathematics wasn't my top subject at school, so I need you to tell me which number it is. Did you know also, that I have an odd ear?'

Slirander slowly pulled her hair aside to reveal it. 2, or is it 7, almost choked on its wind turbulence, simultaneously exhaling and inhaling in surprise.

'It is you then?' said a quivering number.

'Yes.'

Before any truth could be revealed, two large, odd, angry eyes, as large as rotundas, escaped from 7. They had the nasty blue veins like varicose veins in need of a serious operation.

Simultaneously, its feet on its head opened like an exploding can of baked beans; you know, the dented variety. The sdvs burst into the atmosphere in formation. Unseen, Davidia did a short spray burst and the soldiers of the Pebble of Purpose charged forth. They also kept in formation. Hovering like hydrofoils, both groups confronted each other. Would a witty remark, a poor joke or a poem be their downfall?

The sdvs hissed, because without a proper education they had all developed a lisp and didn't know if they used one s or two or more. They were unsure.

The soldiers exhaled minute vaporised drops that melted into the atmosphere. There was no need to waste words.

Suddenly, the head sdv spoke to everyone's surprise, including 7's. It was a very well-constructed, articulated sentence. It was the type a proud speech would love to begin with.

'What do you want?' Large words weren't used in case it over-stressed.

'What do you want then?' replied the leader.

'To destroy those black letters from returning.'

'We can't allow that to happen, can we, lads?'

'You can't stop us. Watch this.'

Suddenly a sortie of sdvs hit a letter z so hard it resembled a flat line.

'Watch this.'

A sortie of soldiers retaliated by hitting the flat line and returning it to a fully-formed z, which often replaced a useful s in the written language. It was as versatile as the lads.

The sdvs couldn't believe it. Their power had been neutered. An adversary as evenly matched had never been directly encountered before. They regrouped to use a different formation. They formed the flying D V formation tango twist. An attack from an angle caused more devastation than a full-frontal.

No signal was given. A huge dust cloud dipped from the sky and hammered the reformed letters into a confused jigsaw of unrecognisable shapes.

'Top that,' said an sdv leader, who thought it had sole bragging rights.

'Lads, it's time to use the cream puff magneticker.' It was a gentle reformation rebuilding adhesive. 'Be careful in its application. We don't want a bolshy b joined to a jocular j; now, do we? Spit it out,' yelled the leader.

The soldiers took off in all directions.

'Cowards. Can't stand the heat in the kitchen,' yelled the sdv leader.

In battle, a lot of yelling ensues.

Even 2, or is it 7, had regained its feeling of composure, like the champ it wished it was. Ego might only be represented by three letters, but it had a meaning far greater than two vowels and a consonant on their own. Combined together, power followed. Teamwork was a mantra for success. Suddenly, a low volume droning sound like a humming dirge could be heard. High in the heavens out of influence's way, the leader and his soldiers had strategised. They came in misty showers. The soldiers quickly rearranged the damaged letter bits back into a readable format. A loud cheer erupted as they regained their shapes.

'Well done, lads. We deserve a promotion. There's only one final challenge left. Let's teach those sdvs once and for all what it is like to be damaged goods, or in this case, letters. Sprays ready, cough!'

Each atomised drop exhaled a light spray over the sdvs, similar to an unpleasant sneeze without a sore throat. The tiny moist elements settled on each sdv, which weren't fast enough to escape, encompassing them in a misty cocoon. Soon the sdvs dried up and, together with the soldiers who had miraculously performed their task, became waste matter. The battle was over. There wasn't one sdv left.

The letters surged to full recovery and bypassed Davidia, Slirander and 7 who were only a sideshow. Even M had joined the throng of excited exiting letters. They all had a renewed purpose to return to their book origins. Now it was their turn to face off. D and S versus 2 or 7.

'How do you like them apples?' said Davidia, coining an old phrase. 'Your nonsense sdvs are gone. I wondered why there would be a lone number here. You should be kicked into the Pit of Litanticus instead of the letters you tried to destroy. There is nothing greater than language. So there.'

Both Davidia and Slirander watched their slimy opponent. It wasn't because they enjoyed the view. It was to monitor any bad behavioural traits. Would they present themselves?

Slirander stepped forward.

'Roland, it's time to cease your quest for language control. It isn't going to happen.'

'I thought that it might be you. Your family and that overgrown pet Moonatric tree of yours were always a problem.'

'If you refuse, then moonatime will befall Rotland and you know what that means.'

'Damn your intelligence. You were the only family unable to subjugate to my rule.'

'Our oddities certainly managed to be our saviour. Remember, we are in Rotland and intend to save all language.'

Slirander raised her two hands and with her two outstretched digit fingers placed them over both her eyes.

Davidia thought that would hurt. For just a second, she thought that she saw two odd, angry eyes ready to pop. Instead, two solid beams of light flashed from them straight at 7. It yelled loudly, becoming momentarily blinded. Two odd, angry eyes began to swell. Slirander turned 7 toward the Pit of Litanticus. It fell into the pit. A small light explosion was all that was seen as the remaining letters in the pit were blown outwards. There was no more language to save. It had been done. The pit was empty. Davidia wondered about her friend Slirander. She seemed to possess many unexplainable powers; however, friendship may be the strongest one of all of them.

Splat! Splat! spat Roland, rubbing his eyes.

'God, that hurt.'

The Pit of Litanticus, unknown to Davidia and Slirander, had its base coated with an adhesive substance that Roland and his Rotters had spread to deny any letter the possibility of an escape; however, once Roland had been tossed into the pit, its effectiveness ceased. His body was the antidote for this event.

'There is a lesson to be taught for interference,'

Roland agitatedly babbled as if he had a mouth full of the chewiest rubber. Saliva began to stream out. Soon a small pond had developed at his feet. He placed one hand in it and said a nonsensical chant.

> 'Bubba boo, goggle boggle, wet a shoe, drop a spot, is it you?
> Hidden shape, hand a dip, flip a drop and swallow spit.
> Bubba boo, goggle boggle, shape a space, foot to stand,
> Ping, pong, splash, replenish me, get rid from my land.'

The mucusy pond was all that remained in the pit. All around the land began to close like the insides of a shrinking lift. The Pit of Litanticus was disappearing. Its "use by" date was over. Roland, or was it number 7, jumped into the jubbly pool and, poof, like a breath of wind, was gone. The last word he uttered was 'revenge'.

The land reformed into a solid mass. Nothing remained of the Pit of Litanticus.

*

Davidia and Slirander were stranded. The pit had gone. All the letters had returned home and the girls were in a vast land with no further purpose.

'How do we get out of here?' asked Davidia. 'I knew we'd eventually get stuck somewhere.'

'*Ickle wockle ..,*'
began Slirander.

'Don't start that *ickle wockle* thing again, it makes no sense,' said an irate Davidia.

Slirander ignored her protests and continued with the *ickle wockle* verse. Crash! A large tree root slapped the land, not five metres from them, like reprimanding those who were in charge. Dust and twigs playfully flew for a few seconds.

'It's Moonah. Take a hold of a lumpy growth,' said Slirander.

As they did so, a supple twig handcuffed them to it.

'I'm not a prisoner,' wailed Davidia.

'Shut up,' yelled Slirander, who by this time had enough of the whinging.

The tree root swirled into the atmosphere with the girls hanging on. Even Cold was bemused by the passing intruders through its air space. In a flash they were back in the Moonatric Forest of Rotland, exhausted. Davidia couldn't believe it. Slirander just smiled.

'It was the *ickle wockle* thing,' she whispered, smiling.

'Oh,' was all Davidia said.

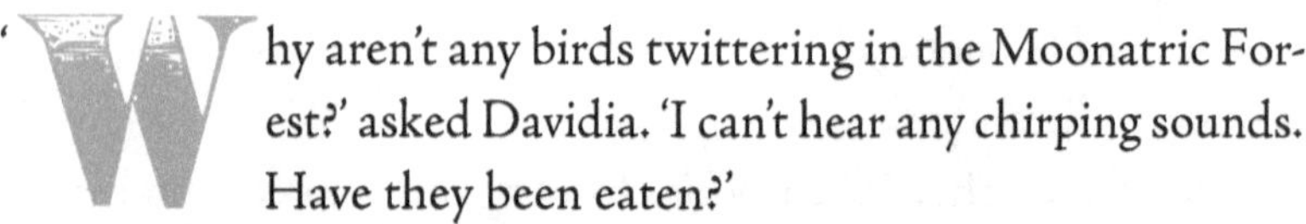

'Why aren't any birds twittering in the Moonatric Forest?' asked Davidia. 'I can't hear any chirping sounds. Have they been eaten?'

'Rotland is a land of quiet. Noises interrupt the serenity of the landscape. It's quiet for the population to read without interruption,' replied Slirander. 'Animals don't live in the land. They have all been relocated, that's all.'

'There's something else that is very odd. Where are the Rotters we've come up against? I haven't seen any here at all. I'm wondering if they exist. This is one non-fun palace. Slirander, have you seen any Rotters in Rotland?'

'They don't live in the forest.'

'I get the feeling they don't live anywhere. Why would that be?'

'You'll come across them later, I'm sure.'

'Look, my hands have gone a real dark brown, almost black, in fact. I'm a Caucasian. I can't go changing colour. What does it mean?'

'You're not a pop star yet.'

'How do you know so much about Rotland? I could have sworn that I saw you almost had two odd, angry eyes at the Pit of Litanticus and that weird trick of light from your eyes. I didn't see the two powerful torches you must have carried.'

'Accept that in a strange land, strange things happen. Come, Moonah is stirring.'

Slirander tried to avoid the focus of an inquisition from her astute and bright friend. Her attachment to Rotland was closer than Davidia was aware of.

'Are there any towns here? All I see is that one massive hill.'

'Some homes exist, but are well-hidden. Privacy is treasured here.'

'So is ignorance. Where's the library?'

'You aren't practising for a quiz show, are you?' asked Slirander, in a terse moment.

Davidia sensed a change in attitude and decided to stay stumm for the moment. What were they doing here in a quiet land, with one hilltop, no sound and no evident population, and all this talk about Rotters? She never had any dreams this weird. Did anything live here besides the Moonatric Forest? Davidia scanned the countryside in every direction. There was nothing except the massive Moonatric Forest and that hill. She couldn't see around corners, so there could be other forests. Where's the fast food outlets or shops of any kind? It was a land without a shopping centre. Wow! Such deprivation. No schoolgirl could survive without one to hang about in and be cool with her friends. Dullsville was a good name for where they were. What was eating at Davidia? A termite, a cannibal, or was it doubt, that hungry intruder for what's maybe not going on. Davidia sensed something wasn't quite right with Rotland and it wasn't how it was spelt. Was Slirander part of it? She hoped not.

'It is so refreshing,' said Moonah, as he stretched all of his branches. Nothing fell off. 'This soil is delicious. My roots have sucked up its nutrients. My aching limbs don't ache so much anymore and look, a few of my wrinkles have filled out so smoothly. Impressive, eh!'

He wiggled his tree roots as if teasing the soil to play with him. The day appeared to be much brighter now that he had been restored, not alphabetically, but in good health. He felt like a sprightly twig.

'Moonah. It's great to see you healthy again,' smiled Slirander.

'Your leaves are pristine once more with the colours of the rainbow. We only have to solve the problems with the black leaf and language will be safe forever.'

Davidia noted that all the other moonatric trees only had green leaves. She wondered why?

'Why do all the other trees only have green leaves?' asked Davidia.

'Only the oldest and most knowledgeable tree has the privilege of coloured leaf changes. It is only occasionally when danger is confronted, that the colours reveal their true selves. Moonah is green most of the time; however, with all language under siege, he has come out to reveal his true self. He is the protector of all language, being the alphabet tree. Strange to think isn't it, that in this land bent on its destruction, its saviour also lives. Font also lives within Moonah's tree roots and for our sake Moonah has been our guardian angel. As said earlier, only the people who have seen a Rotter in action, can be the emissary to destroy their evil. We are now in Rotland where strange lives up to its word. Be alert.'

'Tell me, truthfully, did you ever live here?'

'Yes. My family once did. When this is over, you'll understand better.'

Davidia was satisfied for the moment. Her friend was a jelly-bean bag full of surprises.

*

In the Hole in the Hill, sat a forlorn Roland contemplating his failed attempts to destroy all written language except what he had kept for himself. He twiddled with formulas, expressed bad language he hoped he didn't have to read and his general demeanour was that of a boiling pot.

'Why have I been outwitted by those two, what are they called, girls? They are such odd creatures to be my nemesis. I thought that I could be happy having all language to myself, but something definitely doesn't want me to have it.'

He sat for a moment searching for an intelligent thought. Just like a blank page in a book, nothing materialised. Suddenly, an echo entered his domain. It wasn't invited.

'Black is black, I want my language back. Grey is grey, I want it today.'

'Who's there to dare interrupt me?' he demanded.

There was no response. Had his imagination stirred?

In his domain, he was king. No Rotter had ever set foot inside the forbidden Hole in the Hill. It was really only a cave opening that no one dared enter. Fear was their prison officer. He was quite lonely. Roland picked up a romantic novel to ease his edginess. After a few pages in, the word "tripe" filtered between his lips.

'I actually saved this,' he bemoaned.

It was incredulous that he had gone to so much effort to destroy all good language and be stuck with print of this calibre. He threw the book away in disgust. He wondered if there was any more like it. That night, a single Roland rearranged parts of his library. In his opinion, not everything was a winner for entertainment. What was it that he really desired, a good book, or friends?

*

'Today is discovery day,' said Moonah. 'Slirander, you must climb up to the top of my system and break off the black leaf. Don't listen to any of its protests.'

'Just like when I was younger.'

Slirander suddenly displayed the tendencies of our monkey

forbears, not the sounds, but the ability to shimmy straight up the tree without a moment's hesitation. Davidia was awestruck. She was tempted to 'Ooh, ooh', but her discretion crept in. At the top of Moonah's branches waving in the gentle breeze was the black leaf. It swayed wildly, enjoying its day in the sun. It was in the privileged position of rarely facing danger; however, Slirander was an unwanted and unwelcome visitor. There was no escape as it was firmly attached to a branch. It could turn green, but it was the wrong season for deception.

'Keep away,' it called out, shaking its stem vigorously.

'You must come with me,' replied Slirander.

'I'm not going anywhere with you.'

In an effort to disguise itself, it secreted a slimy substance, which made it slippery to touch and slightly coloured its surface.

'You can't fool me.'

'You'll fall in the attempt to secure me.'

Slirander pulled out from one of her pockets a small vine rope with serrated edges. Once it gripped an item, capture was imminent. She threw the vine rope and it latched onto the edge of the leaf. A short, painful struggle erupted. The black leaf knew the result in advance, but always gave an account to the saying, "Nothing comes easy". Its stem was firmly embedded in the tree socket. Slirander knew the leaf's weakness. A tickle along its stem made it recoil in delight and instantly its stem shrunk, thus reducing its hold on the tree. Plop, the leaf was now free.

'Be careful with me. My leaf membranes are very delicate.'

'I know.'

'Have we met before?'

'I used to climb up here when I was young and pretended to paint you.'

The black leaf withered in recognition.

'That annoying nuisance was you? My, we do live in strange

times. What do you want that's so important to detach me from Moonah? There must be a crisis of some sort. What is it?'

'Roland the Rotter.'

'Aagh! That again. What decimation is he after this time?'

'The destruction of all written language except a selection kept for his personal library.'

'Doesn't he ever learn? Remember his last effort, the deforestation of Rotland. That ended abysmally when the plants revolted and trapped him in vines. His bubble-headed ideas stem from his difficult upbringing. Why can't he accept what he is without trying to change the world around him?'

'What actually is he?' asked Davidia. 'I haven't actually seen a real Rotter. All I've seen is what they inhabit or imitate. What do they really look like? Can you show me a real one?'

Slirander and the black leaf went silent.

'I'm not sure you would enjoy a natural viewing,' said Slirander.

'Why not? They can't be scarier that an expensive mobile telephone bill you can't pay because you have over-called and over-texted your friends and then your parents find out. Whew! Now that's scary.'

'That's not quite what you are in for.'

'Have you met Roland before?'

Slirander squirmed uncomfortably in her school uniform. No emblems were going to fall off, but she resisted changing into her true form.

'Go on, tell her,' insisted the black leaf.

Slirander's shoulders slumped a little.

'Roland is a relative. My family escaped his evil ways years ago and by the very nature of the escape passage we took through Conika, our forms altered also. We took on the characteristics that you saw when you met my parents. We became human in appearance and will live our lives in this excellent format. Deep in the Hole in the Hill, is a secret passageway that leads under the Conikaka Mountains. Only family knows of its existence. You have met Font who survives inside Moonah's tree roots. Font originally lived in that secret passageway and assisted us in our escape, by allowing us to float on its surface. When we emerged in the Conikaka Mountains, Font decided to join us.'

'Really. Wow! What an interesting friend I have,' said Davidia, proudly. 'How did Moonah become involved?'

'Moonah was my origin and growth beginner. He is the oldest tree in the special Moonatric Forest. He had a thirst for knowledge. Each Moonatric tree develops a special skill, which it can retain itself or pass on to others. I read a lot and each letter or word that passed through me passed into Moonah. He built up his specialist skill as an alphabet tree. Some of the other Moonatric trees are learning from him. The skills of any adventure I take are passed onto them. That one is a travel tree. That over there only cares for history and so on. Each tree in the forest has developed or is developing a special skill. Once they are old enough to leave Rotland they can explore the world by growing anywhere, in a rain forest, a mountain, a swamp or at any location. Moonah decided to grow in our backyard and continue to enjoy my family's company. As I said, he is my origin and growth beginner.'

Davidia decided to let that last comment pass. Her mind was overloaded with too much new information to properly filter. She still didn't know what a Rotter actually looked like, but in time she would.

*

'Why is the black leaf so important?' she asked.

'I'm a potion leaf. Whenever a crisis arises, who do you call? It's me,' said the black leaf, interrupting. 'My colour hides many a secret. I can wither, expand, disappear, regrow on any tree and prepare the deadliest of potions. I'm your every leaf option.'

Davidia nodded, not fully convinced of what was said.

'It's time to confront Roland and ensure that any destrusto virus, superior or normal, doesn't exist. It means a visit to the Hole in the Hill. Only there, at its source, can we be sure of its total destruction,' said Slirander.

'Won't he try and destroy us?'

'That's why we have the black leaf. It can enlarge to form an invisible covering, but only in short bursts. It must leave a few spores behind to regrow in case it doesn't return and often that has happened. Besides, Davidia, you still have the only antidote vial left. Protect it well. It's time to leave. Moonah, we will return.'

Slirander had never had to deal with an irate relative before, at least none this cunning, devious and insidious. There weren't enough bad words in any dictionary to describe the character of Roland. A happy place for him was hurt for everything else. This would be one tough assignment. There would be no love lost from Roland's side; however, would Slirander be emotionally vulnerable when it counted?

Two young schoolgirls and a black leaf headed off on a dangerous trek through the other forests toward the Hole in the Hill.

'She's changed her smell,' said an undergrowth plant Slirander had trodden on.

'Changing the outside doesn't stop her from being what she really is on the inside,' said another shrub.

'Once a twig, always a twig,' chimed in a small drooping tree branch.

'I prefer the way I look than that,' piped up a gnarled burr.

'It's definitely a snob branch. That wasn't grown in this part of the forest,' commented a bent twig.

'She thinks a different form can hide the truth. Bah! What impertinence,' stated a moss clump wishing it was anything but.

The forest was abuzz with whispers. Slirander's odd ear itched. She rubbed it gently. The forest hadn't forgotten one of their own.

'Ignore those jealous growths. They haven't acquired the intelligence to leave or understand anything. No wonder Roland ruled an intelligent base of deadwood,' it said.

Slirander felt comforted by her odd ear. As they steadily walked toward the Hole in the Hill, a large sap globule landed at Davidia's feet. Was a tree spitting at her, was it a warning, or was it that time of the year when trees oozed sap? She watched it closely. It was clear and moved independently. It rolled, stretched, flattened, then formed an inverted u-shape and crawled like a caterpillar towards a twig growth. It went up the skinny twig, attached itself to a small nodule and hung like a limp handbag. Plop! Another sap globule hit the ground running. It too climbed the same twig, attached itself and hung like another limp handbag. Tree shopping might be on the agenda. Davidia was mesmerised by their ability to move and climb. She turned to Slirander.

'Did you see that?'

Both Slirander and the black leaf didn't appear fazed by the event.

'That's normal, here,' said Slirander. 'Wait for a few minutes.'

The two oblong-shaped sap blobs stirred. They were sucking something from the twig. They began to colour. Soon they had the making of two odd, angry eyes with red and blue lines running through them. Their attachment stretched and they began waving about in a futile attempt to escape as they were firmly attached to the twig.

'Slirander, they have the same two odd, angry eyes the Rotters have displayed in anger. What an amazing coincidence that they are here.'

Davidia looked around and she saw that many trees with the same adornments. What a strange forest.

'Haven't you worked it out yet?' asked Slirander.

'About what?'

'The sap and the twigs.'

'Unsightly things. Those sap growths are the ugliest flowers that I've ever seen. Most plants that I'm aware of have flowers and don't have two hanging sap sacks as an attraction.'

'No, what they are doing?'

'They're doing nothing except making the forest look totally weird.'

'This is a Rotter nursery.'

'A what? You're kidding me, aren't you? You mean those things are Rotters? I don't believe it.'

'It's true. This is the origin and growth beginner of all that evil.'

'Didn't you come from here?'

'But not from this forest. I'm a moonatric girl. The soil and teachings are quite different there.'

'You look like a real girl.'

'As I said before, when we escaped via the Hole in the Hill, matter changed and a girl I became. Now you know.'

'Would you burn easier than me in a fire?'

'No, it would be the same.'

'That's a relief.'

Davidia was sure that all Slirander's secrets had now been revealed. Now it was time for Roland to face decay and composting. They walked on.

*

'Stick one, stick two, cross blow, poke and jab, twirl, thrust downwards, reverse jab, thrust upwards, swing wide, slam down. Excellent.'

On the edge of the forest in a clearing, a highly skilled twig force practised the art of impersonating movement. They were limited with having two over-large eyes in comparison with the rest of their build, minimal tree roots and limited twig growth to grip anything. The lead twig was exercising his group, so they remained supple. This was the next group of Rotters that had out-grown their origin tree that Roland would send on a destructive exercise. When the session had been completed, the twigs rested in a nearby paddock with soft soil so that they could embed their malformed tree roots for a proper grip and feed. They looked like a sea of upside down onion bulbs swaying in the breeze.

'That's an odd paddock,' said Davidia. 'It's full of onion heads. At home they grow the other way around.'

'Davidia, spray the antidote, quickly.'

'Why?'

'Those onion heads are almost ripe, Rotters. We can't let them escape and cause damage to anything.'

Davidia felt in her pocket for the last vial. Her hand gripped it tightly as she withdrew it.

'Lads, I'm almost choking to death. Get off your slumber lounges, ditch the slurpees, say something intelligent and prepare your battle gear. We have a party to soil, or is that spoil? Look sharp and act smart. Our invaluable services are required once more. Come on. Leave that itch alone. Be ready. I love turning up to work on every occasion. Let's ride that pony.' The leader was geared for an affray.

Davidia sent a spray high into the air.

'It's good that we don't suffer vertigo, lads,' yelled the excited leader. 'Give them a taste of popcorn. Dive!'

'His excited rhetoric is a little over the top, don't you think?'

said an annoyed atomiser drop, upset at leaving the comforts of the vial. 'Who wants to work?'

'The leader means well. Goodness has its price. Stop the whinging and spurt,' replied another atomised drop, fed-up with negativity from others.

They performed like a locust plague, landing on every onion head and impregnating them with an antidote stopper. They couldn't escape anywhere, as they had been root-bound for the night. It was a messy sight. Odd, angry eyes exploded all over the field sounding like a popcorn carnival. There wasn't one odd, angry eye left. The field was littered with twigs that would now only grow into a harmless and valuable forest. They had all left their origin trees and their future use as a Rotter had been terminated. Roland was now truly all alone. His future evil force had no future other than foliage covering and soil improvement; another environmental success.

'That was awful,' said Davidia, 'with all that sap spurting everywhere.'

'There was no other choice. We still have Roland to contend with.'

'Don't either of you be fooled by Roland the Rotter. He didn't get his name because his parents disliked him. It was earned by deeds alone. He doesn't even trust his mirrored reflection, he's that bad,' said the black leaf.

It had been destroyed many times before in unsuccessful campaigns against evil and spoke from shattered experiences.

'How do we get to meet the real Roland?' asked Davidia, unsure if he was the full twig or not.

'Inside the Hole in the Hill. It's the only entrance in or out, except for that secret tunnel I told you about,' replied Slirander.

The black leaf kept falling down, then jumping up and fanning itself into a leafy umbrella.

'What's it doing? There's no breeze that I can feel.'

'Symbolising. It's easy to say, but hard to do. Don't try it. It's only a leaf speciality.'

'Is it possible to fall inside the black leaf like we have with others?'

'No. It has many special abilities and will guide us in our visit with the cagey Roland.'

'I'd hate to argue with any of my relatives, they're all nice. Dad often said if you have bad things to say about anybody, say them quietly so they won't hear. He doesn't speak to his brother any-more. He must have overheard dad whispering.'

'In our family, it's the one blemish we live with. This strange land can turn anything into what it doesn't want to be. In the Hole in the Hill, mixed spirits live and it's not a drink reference. Roland has been affected badly by an unforgiving spirit. We don't know which one or when it occurred. Pay attention to any oddities.'

'Are we going to return Roland's library books to Lamdon and Longschott Colleges from where he took them? Is that the aim of our visit? Language has been saved already, so what do we have to do here?'

'Roland has to be stopped from ever doing evil again. It won't be nice.'

The black leaf turned a dark purple on top and pure black underneath. Suddenly, it ran off the track into the forest and hid behind a tree. It quivered like a male peacock's tail display at a mating ritual. The girls stopped. For no apparent reason, they adapted the sheep mentality and quickly followed suit. Along the track walked the twin Twiggers. They were two crossed-over twigs that had been joined together in the middle. They could be separated, but preferred their oddity. It made them noticed.

'Will you do it, or will I do it?' said one of them.

'I'll do it, because then you won't have done it,' answered the other.

'If I haven't done it, then what is it I'm not going to do?'

'Well, if you do it, then you can say the opposite to what you just said.'

'If only one of us does it, then the other one misses out.'

'Why don't we do it together?'

'What a great idea. Who thought of that?'

Neither of them knew which one it was. The twin Twiggers continued on their way. It was part of the odd world of Rotland.

'What was that all about?' asked Davidia.

'They are Rotter scouts pretending to act stupid so nothing will suspect them. Once out of sight they will blend with a bush and ambush the next traveller,' said the black leaf. 'No doubt, Roland already knows that we are here.'

'What's that noise?' asked Davidia, in a higher octave than before.

A bouncing, clanging sound headed their way.

'Take no notice, that's a hobbity stone on its way to the creek bed.'

'And that shrieking? Can't you hear it?'

Slirander and the black leaf considered the question and promptly dismissed it.

'That's a singing vine. Don't be afraid. The only harmful creature here lives inside that hill.'

All three were dwarfed by the hill. There was nothing startling about it. It was cone shaped, like the Conikaka Mountains. Perhaps it's a relative too? Around its base a small stream trickled past. Both Slirander and Davidia leaned over to glimpse their reflection. Davidia's bounced straight back, but Slirander's showed a skinny twig with two large, bulgy eyes instead. Fortunately, Davidia was so enamoured with admiring herself, she didn't notice. She thought she looked like the goods for an older person date. The black leaf dipped its stem and sucked hard. Its leaf began to unfold.

'It's been a while since I've tasted water so pure. It's the stream of Fontania from where Font had escaped from the mountain end. Those who dare drink it might suffer a hideous experience. It's called pleasure. Go on, try some.'

Davidia felt its coolness. She splashed her face. The cold made facial goosebumps so large she thought she had a mini set of the Conikaka Mountains. She did, but they were below her chin.

'Time to go,' commanded Slirander.

They were now on her patch where surprises were the norm.

*

'The air in here has become decidedly cold,' said Roland.

He had his feet in a compost heap where he withdrew nutrients from the soil to refresh his wispy-thin frame. Every tree twig in Rotland would die for the nutrient-rich soil he stood in. Amongst his language thievery, nasty attitude and maniacal stupidity tendencies, he at least treated the soil in Rotland with respect. He had a soft spot for being a horticulturist. It was one of his few domestic interests; however, in his quest for destroying all written language, that interest had almost disappeared. He felt the chill send shivers up his woody trunk. It was the atmosphere that absorbed any heat from him and he realised that he had confrontation on his doorstep, or, more precisely, at the entrance to the Hole in the Hill. Bad language wasn't going to win this battle. He comforted himself with the knowledge that he had the edge. The edge of what wasn't explained.

'I am Roland,' he yelled in defiance.

The walls echoed in unison. At least he knew who he was. A name labels many things.

*

'Do we have to go in there?' asked a nervous Davidia.

'It is the way we must. Watch out for the odditotes. They take many different forms. Most are harmless, but they live inside.'

The tunnelled entrance seemed long and was completely dark. How could they see where they were going? The black leaf, as dark as it was, instantly changed colour to a bright orange.

'It's my favourite colour. It only lasts for a short while, so stay close,' it said.

The sound of trickling water was heard. Water droplets fell from the ceiling at intervals to spot-wet them as they walked by. Davidia felt that wet hands were grabbing at her. Slirander and the black, now orange, leaf knew what to expect. Imagination ran rampant like an uncontrollable child.

'Is that an odditote?' asked Davidia, as she felt a slimy mass crawl around her legs. 'It's trying to eat me,' she screamed.

Slirander looked down and spoke gently to the green mass.

'*Oogle, shoggle, slimmo, smag,*
Trickle, track to rocky grand.'

The green mass quietly moved on.

'What was that?'

'Conversation.'

'I don't like it in here.'

The black leaf's light began to fade. Shadows played tricks with their eyesight. Soon it was pitch-black.

'I can't see,' said Davidia.

'Take my hand,' said Slirander.

Davidia put her hand out. She felt a set of tiny twigs in it and jumped in surprise.

'Don't play tricks with me. You said your hand, not a bunch of twigs.'

'That's exactly what you are holding. In here odd is the norm. We can change into anything weird.'

Slirander's two huge, bulgy eyes could see perfectly clearly in the dark, but Davidia couldn't see her new form. Slirander had adapted strangely to the odd conditions. She was also a Rotter and took on their form to confuse them. The black leaf had recoiled into a thin, walking-stick leaf. Inside, it was formulating a defence for Slirander.

'I can hear sand being dragged over rocks. It creeps me out. What is it?'

'Soil being chewed by a swarm of Mann ants preparing it for Roland's compost heap. They are an exceptional workforce and don't have time to complain because they always have their mouths full of sand grains. You try and speak with your mouth full, it's very difficult.'

'We call them worms at home, but they only work in the soil. They're similar at least.'

'They may lead us to the main compost heap. Tread carefully. They are leaving a long trail to follow. Don't trip over. They like nothing better than a good salt-lick, which either of us can provide. Besides, being bitten isn't a pleasure I want to experience just yet.'

Davidia was surprised at how easy they travelled along the tunnel. She expected to be attacked by all manner of things; some creepy, dangerous and definitely, not edible.

'Where are the odditotes? I thought you said to watch out for them. I can't see anything in the dark.'

Up ahead, a thin ray of filtered light flooded into a large cavern covering only a small area. Its resting place was a dirt spot, but at least they could see shape and form. The wispy air swirled as if it was trying to escape. It was impossible to tell if it was unhappy. As Davidia stepped into the light, her hair began to rise. She couldn't feel a wind fan pushing it upwards as it happens in a film studio. Long strands of delicate fibres hung from the ceiling and along each strand an odditote was carrying her hair.

'Give it back. It's mine. You can't have it. I'm too young to be bald.' She madly waved her arms, severing the strands so that her hair fell naturally back onto her head. Wearing wigs were only for dress-ups and not for a young girl. 'What do they do with it?'

'They cover the ceiling in patterns, that's all. It keeps them occupied. One day when they have covered the ceiling to the entrance, they can finally leave. It's a slow and laborious escape route construction. Once they make it, they form into antidotes that you have in the vial. When Font escaped, it took a supply with it, just in case it was needed. Now you know where the antidote came from.'

Davidia gripped the vial.

'Lads, it's almost relative time. Dress smart and impress our forebears. Maybe we'll meet an Aunty Doris amongst them. Prime that pout, we may be let out. Be prepared and ready to rocket. This is where we emanate from. I wonder if anyone will remember us. That's it, lads; formation, formation,' cried the leader, in anticipation of release.

Davidia relaxed her hold.

'Damn. I was ready to party,' said the disappointed leader.

His little atomised tuxedo crumpled into a forlorn heap. It wasn't his time to party.

Their eyes adjusted to the dimly lit cavern. Its floor was covered in a soft, mushy substance.

'This isn't Roland's toilet, is it?' queried Davidia, who was wary of the qualities of soft, brown soil. Her tanned hands could disappear in a perfect match, if she dug about.

'This is Roland's compost heap. It seems freshly disturbed.'

Davidia suddenly turned around to answer Slirander when her jaw almost dropped from her face.

'Where's Slirander, you rotten twig?' she screamed. Every cave inhabitant quivered. Noise of this magnitude was an unknown in the quietness of the Hole in the Hill. 'I'll snap your thin, bony, sticky fingers if you've harmed her.' Her concern for her friend was rising every second.

'Davidia, it's me, Slirander.'

'I'm not that stupid. I can usually tell the difference between a girl and a twig.'

'Remember, that you are in Rotland where the unusual can be the norm.'

'But you look like a Rotter with those pussy-eyed bags of mess. What's happening to you?'

'My past form has returned. I must challenge Roland as one of his own, otherwise he cannot be defeated. That is why it has been so important for me to be with you on this journey. When this is over, I will revert to your friend's form once more. Next time it would be forever. Roland is here, I feel it.'

The black leaf had, unfortunately, stood on the brown soil and "zap" it became stuck fast. A tree- root feeder had attached itself to it. Fully developed leaves were a rarity in the cave and every opportunity to compost real vegetation was gratefully accepted.

'Get me away from this muck,' it called out.

Davidia lent over and gently picked it up.

'What would you do without me?'

The black leaf shook itself clean. The cave was deathly quiet. They all stood in the silence wondering where Roland was. It didn't take long to answer their thoughts.

*

They could hear a gurgling sound coming from nearby where they stood. The compost heap began to bubble and spit tiny amounts of dirt into the air. Was it nervous? Slowly, a skinny tree twig bereft of any vegetation slowly emerged. At first, two bulbous, onion-eyes popped up. They roved around the cave scanning for its guests. The balance of its body followed as equally unimpressive. It was taller than Slirander and as equally hideous. Rotters hadn't fully grasped the beauty secrets of a girl's magazine, or copied them. Maybe Roland hadn't read those books yet. The two Rotters eyed each other. Recognition was almost there.

'What has interrupted my compost massage?'

'We did,' said Davidia. 'My dad would make kindling out of you, if you were in my world.'

Roland ignored any attempt at baiting. He wanted to be the fisherman.

'Haven't we met before?' he directed to Slirander.

'Hello, uncle,' she said.

'Now I know who you are. You're from that rotten tree growth family in the Moonatric Forest. I remember you as an ungrateful mischievous sapling that never complied with any of my decisions. Where are your tree-trunk friends and that old-aged Moonah? It was only good for composting.'

'We are well and despite your attempts at destruction, we survived well away from here.'

'Why are you here? There's nothing I can give you.'

'You can give back the written language,' interrupted Davidia.

A talking tree twig seemed almost as stupid as a talking camorse. Davidia couldn't believe it. There was no ventriloquist's trick involved. Slirander did say that this was a strange land. Roland's eyes began to change colour.

'Are you trying to be rainbow man?' asked Davidia.

Roland's agitation was slowly building. Were all young girls this testing?

'I have something to show you. Follow me.'

Roland led the way into another huge cavern. It was stock-piled neatly with books of all descriptions. He waved his thin-stick fingers like a ballet dancer presenting her wrists to an audience in a stretching pose. All eyes were astonished. There were too many to contemplate. It was information overload. Roland let his guests absorb the wonder he had presented. The black leaf shook, Slirander rolled her eyes and Davidia was more circumspect.

'Are these the books that you stole from the colleges to keep for yourself? What a cretin. People want to read them and you selfishly hide them here. There's another word for you, but I'm not allowed to say it. I'll think it instead.'

She screwed her face in thought.

'I don't appreciate your insinuations. I am its saviour; quite the opposite, really.'

'Crap is what you have in your compost heap. I hope you don't eat it too.'

'You're quite the disgusting type, aren't you? You have such an unsavoury and common use of words. Now you can see why I want to keep them all for myself. There would be no further use of coarse language to start with.'

'You would have only yourself to share it with. What did your mum and dad do to make you so unpleasant?'

Davidia had suddenly touched a raw nerve. His bulgy eyes bulged further. He was developing into a real oddity. Was there a third eye ready to pop a valve?

'Uncle,' said Slirander soothingly, so as not to inflame the situation further, 'why not return all language books back to where they came from? Surely it has a better use than to be hidden forever from the world.'

'They are mine. I'm tiring of this game. Leave before I seriously damage your visit. Oh, yes, I can't allow you to leave, can I? I'm a sporting type, so I'll give you a chance of saving yourself. That won't be possible, but it will be fun watching you try.'

Roland let out the most hideous laugh, the type found in fun park scare rides. His eyes waved wildly as if in a raging storm. His twig-like formation almost split in convulsions. His guests were doomed. He knew it, but no one else did. The girls were stunned. This dirt bag of twigs was quite the twisted stick.

'Slirander, what did he mean?'

'There's a puzzle test with the alphabet that he has occasionally used. I've seen it used once before when he tried to ruin my parents before we escaped. He almost succeeded that time. No other Rotter has ever been bright enough to beat him at it. I'm not sure that we can either.'

'My brother and I do jigsaws all the time. It's a matter of placing the pieces in the correct position, that's all. Let's see how smart he really is.'

'That black leaf looks delicious enough to compost. When we are done, I'm sure I will enjoy it.'

Threats were everywhere. They couldn't return from the Hole in the Hill through the entrance they came in. It had been sealed by the odditotes dropping the pattern designs from the ceiling that they had made. It was now like an impenetrable cobweb jungle. Their only escape was through the secret tunnel that Slirander knew about.

Was there any chance of being saved? The stakes were high. Hopes were being squashed and language was at risk of being saved or lost by solving a simple puzzle.

'This way.'

12   THE FINAL PUZZLE

A huge room opened up before them. It was a replica of a long, uninteresting rectangle with a few scattered seats as if no one wanted to sit near someone or something else. The good vibes didn't stand a chance. In the centre was a small, solid, stone table surrounded by an odd chair or two. The table was square with twenty-six letters representing the alphabet embedded around its edges. Neither chair offered any comfort. Perhaps that's because Roland the Rotter would hastily dispose of any opposition before that was reached. The chance of enjoying a liquid substance in his company was as remote as finding a waterhole in a desert.

The lighting was very poor. Davidia's vision was blurry and murky; however, Roland, Slirander and the black leaf could see clearly in the dim conditions. Davidia was curious. She walked around the table running her fingers over the alphabet and feeling the depth of each letter's indentation. Her youthful memory recorded each letter and dent and how deep it felt to her. At least she could read the alphabet even though it might be difficult to see it.

'Is it a form of scrabble?' asked Davidia, remembering that when she had played with her brother, a few mixed letters could make up offensive words and often scored well. Maybe there was room for one or two here.

'It is a puzzle of sorts,' replied Roland, 'but I doubt if either of you are clever enough to solve this one.'

His bulgy eyes throbbed with enthusiasm at the chaos he thought he would invoke.

'Are there any rules?'

'It is an illogical contest.'

'If we don't know the rules, then how is it played?'

'That's the beauty of it. Only I know how to play it. What genius! I can't lose.'

'That's unfair.'

'Who cares? You will not leave here at all. Now play.'

Slirander was thought-stacking. Each new layer didn't bring a solution any closer. She remembered her parents surviving the test, but she didn't know how they did it. Roland was certainly a cunning adversary and immune to emotion. It was all about selfishness and tactics. Her survival skills would have to be based on paying attention to every letter function. Maybe she has to hit them one at a time in turn, spell a word within a time limit, or play it in short bursts as a keyboard of a piano. It required Roland to make the first move from which to learn. In the background, Davidia hovered like a pesky mosquito. Both sets of their mental banks would need to be on top to defeat their adversary.

'Shall I go first?' said a confident Roland.

He touched the letter a. Nothing happened.

Slirander pressed a c. Silence remained.

Each in turn pressed various letters to spell different words.

Davidia suggested that they were both well-educated and could spell quite well. The impasse of who spelt better than whom lasted for almost an hour. There was no winner nor loser. It was a very odd game of twiggy scrabble. Roland showed no emotions in pressing letters whilst Slirander sat equally emotionless. Perhaps tree twigs didn't display emotion as well as they display foliage?

'Slirander, you have been very well-educated. You haven't made one spelling mistake so far. I'm impressed. I never expected a Rotter or an ex-Rotter to achieve such a high standard,' said a complimentary Roland.

'Thank you, uncle. It's reading language that has allowed me to learn. You should consider its benefits for everyone.'

His eyes could only roll with disbelief. Why should he share such a precious resource with the world? The game of twiggy scrabble had been a joy for him, but he wouldn't admit to it. In his cave there were never any visitors, so to play for an hour against, or with, anyone was designed purely for his own special purpose; pleasure. Obviously, his opposition thought it was some diabolical plot and not a friendly game of two minds. No wonder he was so cunning; his intentions were easily misread or was that the interpretation they intended to present?

'Spell *ickle*,' said Davidia, surprising everyone by breaking her silence.

Roland cast a sinister eye in her direction.

'What did you say?' he questioned.

'Spell *ickle*. That's what I said. Go on. Can you?' she insisted. 'I can. It's easy.'

She commenced with the i c k when Slirander interrupted her.

'Davidia, that's not how you spell it. There's no c in it,' said Slirander.

She winked at Davidia to throw Roland off the scent that she knew the correct spelling. Why, she did it wasn't explained.

'If you know so many words, try and spell it,' she challenged Roland again.

She had just ignored a piece of good advice from Slirander.

'I haven't heard that word in such a long time. Where did you hear it?' he asked.

Davidia wasn't completely possessed of two thick planks when she realised that the menace in Roland's voice alerted a feeling of danger in her. She may have stepped on his twigs. He had a set of awfully gnarled and most unattractive root feet.

'I read it in a school magazine that my dad had. A student

wrote a verse about oddities many years ago and it included that word. I don't know its meaning, do you?'

Roland raised a bent twig finger and scratched his chin. It was all in the action. Small splinters fell off and quickly regrew. Davidia thought that the compost heap must certainly be rich fertiliser.

'It's an ancient word, rarely used. There is no significance attached to it,' he answered, as if it was a throwaway line of little importance.

'I once had a pet frog called Pickle, but the cat ate it. Maybe your word has been eaten by something too.'

Roland's twig fingers began pressing in sequence the twiggy-scramble alphabet letters situated around the stone table. Davidia quickly noticed the sequence as he was about to press the final e in the word *ickle*, and leaned over and pressed a double zero. It spelt the word ickloo. Roland stopped and stared. It was the first misspelt word he had encountered in many a time. The shock sent him questioning his knowledge.

'Is that a proper word and, if so, what is its meaning?'

'It's ickloo, the Eskimos live in them in the cold north,' she answered. 'They are small houses built solely from ice.'

'Let me refer to a dictionary. Stay here.'

As Roland left them momentarily, Davidia whispered to Slirander.

'When I felt all the indentations before on all letters, those five that spelt *ickle* appeared to be the deepest. It must mean something, don't you think?'

Slirander jolted awake. Had she been entranced by Uncle Roland? Then she remembered. Why did she repeat that phrase that her father knew of *ickle wockle weeny fing* from time to time? It sounded like a collection of stupid made-up words for amusement. Was her dad psychic? Whatever it was, it had disturbed the force enough for Roland to leave them.

'The only time my dad has said that phrase was when you visited,' said Slirander. 'It must have some significance.'

'When Roland returns to the table and it's your turn next to spell a word, try *ickle* and see what happens.'

Slirander agreed. The black leaf was dormant all this time. It hadn't been called on to perform any duty. Roland returned.

'The correct spelling is igloo, but your attempt at meaning was correct.'

'I'm glad I'm not playing the twiggy scrabble; I would have made a mistake.'

'Is it my turn to continue the game?' asked Slirander.

'Oh, you have an interest in it now, do you? What brought on this change of tactic? There isn't a delicious surprise for me, is there? I hate surprises,' said Roland attempting to use his mind as an extra-sensory perception utensil wanting to know the "why" in the game that Slirander was to play.

'I thought you enjoyed mental jousting. You seem invincible, but are you, really? You aren't afraid of being beaten by a girl, are you?' goaded Slirander.

Even in the Rotter form it was obvious she acted as any young girl does, with bravado and confidence. The wily Roland contemplated for a moment.

'Give it your best shot,' he replied.

The darkness crept around them like a crook casing a joint in preparation for a robbery. Shards of light stabbed like lightning fingers. Davidia still couldn't see clearly, but she began to pace slowly. She wanted a toilet moment, but the excitement of the game currently prevented that activity. The black leaf remained silent.

'This time we will try and spell words backwards.'

'What an interesting innovation! Your move,' said a smug Roland.

It was almost feeding time for his compost heap and the aim of the game delayed it precisely to that moment. What was there to feed in a collection of old, rotting vegetation, chewed sand-grains and brown waste? The ground rumbled slightly.

'You didn't pass wind, did you, Davidia?' whispered Slirander.

'Definitely not. My cheeks have been tightly hugging each other since I began to pace. Do you think it might have been Roland?'

'Something isn't right in here. I feel it in my twigs. Be alert for any dangerous interference. Remember the vial. You haven't forgotten it, have you?'

'It's safe.'

The old tree twig and the young tree twig faced each other over the modern English alphabet and embraced in a linguistic battle to rival the world contest of misspelt words. There was one chance each. A special backwards-spelt word was selected by each opponent to prove that they could misspell. They could only use a letter once and the opponent couldn't use your letter if the other selected it first. Roland's word was an action for disaster. Slirander's was pure guesswork. Once the word was spelt, it was to be said out loud. The tension began to bubble. Into the cauldron of mental fire they leapt.

Slirander poked out an elongated twig, twirling it around, undecided what to select. The more she appeared to be time-wasting the more impatient and less observant Roland would be. It was a perfect girl ruse. She selected the letter e. Roland didn't care. It wasn't one he was going to use anyway. He carefully picked the letter d.

'How many letters does your special word possess?' asked Roland.

Slirander was a young girl who always told the truth, didn't she?

'Mine has five, but six with a plural, if applicable,' she answered. 'How many does yours have?'

In his mind Roland couldn't lose and told her it was six, which was correct. At least honesty appeared between them for a moment, but it wasn't to be one of the spelt words.

'I shall pick the twig letter,' she said, which was an l.

Roland winced in agony.

'That was going to be one of mine,' he wailed.

He thought, *that young, stuck-up twig dare not steal another otherwise I'll snap her trunk.*

'I was unaware, uncle. Perhaps another will do?'

Roland painstaking and grudgingly touched an n. He was behaving like a spoilt brat. Adults are supposed to lead by example. Ah, yes, the petulant child. They learn from somewhere.

'I'm thinking royalty now.' She pressed a bony, twig finger on a k.

Roland wasn't enjoying the fact of the taken letter. He slammed his fist down hard on the stone table snapping a few fingers off in the process. They quickly regrew.

'An a, I will have an a.'

Davidia, ever the witty verbal sharp shooter, commented on his combination.

'He's made dna so far. I wonder if he knows what it is. I've heard about it, but not how it operates,' she said.

'Don't worry about it. He's up to something,' replied Slirander. 'My next letter will be a c. I like its curved shape, don't you?'

Roland wasn't into the aesthetics of the game. Winning was all there was. He had to alter his next letter as it had already been taken. A g was selected. He now had a d n a g whilst Sirander had an e l k c. Before Slirander chose her next letter, Roland had grabbed an o.

'I have need of one more letter than you, so I took it. They're my rules. Stilfiff shilfit.'

The girls sighed in surprise. How did Roland know balfang? He must have copied them when they met earlier when he was in a different form. He now had a d n a g o. Slirander poised her finger for the last touch, when Roland once again hit the table and took an r.

'That's cheating,' she said.

'Your fate is sealed. My pet Dnagor will be here shortly. The surprise is over.'

'Slirander, quickly touch your last letter,' encouraged Davidia.

Her hand pressed hard. It was the letter i. Her letter collection was now complete and made the backward word elkci. She yelled it out loud. It made no sense. What in the hell was an elkci? Suddenly, she yelled it out loud again, but this time in the correct format. It was *ickle*. Her voice reverberated off the cave walls and escaped from the Hole in the Hill along the entrance tunnel. The trees shook and the Moonatric Forest felt a stiff breeze through their leaves. A fright was sensed by all.

Roland jumped in shock.

'How did that word get in here?' he yelled.

He too was having an operatic moment.

Slirander's parents also felt a chill wind back home. They both knew that she would be safe.

Roland, without a sound, darted like a ferret and dived into the compost heap leaving his guests pondering what to do next. Was it a ten or a five for effort? A few loose splatters ended up on the floor. Miraculously, they were able to move and wiggled back into the compost heap.

'It's alive. Who'd want to swim in that brown mess? Those wriggly things might eat him. Maybe that's where the eaten words went,' said Davidia, as she shrugged uncomfortably, thinking it reminded her of waste sewerage. Any good vibes were hard to locate. 'Are we rid of him?'

'Not likely,' replied Slirander. 'He will return again, but as what, who knows. He never did share anything. It was all about his ego, himself, his achievements and nastiness. No one really knows why he turned to evil. Speculation is the best one can do.'

'That *ickle* word certainly scared him. Frankly, I was a little frightened too.'

The black leaf offered nothing.

'It has a power we don't understand.'

*

Slirander's parents felt a strange, cool breeze. This one didn't often visit them. Their hessian clothing offered little or no protection against it. They both shuddered, imitating a rustling bush.

'Did you feel that?' asked Slirander's mum.

'It was invigorating,' the dad replied.

'Do you think our daughter will be alright?'

'In the leaves of Moonah, she will be protected.'

'I worry so. She's only a very young sapling, I mean, girl. Could she be easily led astray by evil? It's so powerful.'

'Our daughter is smart enough to know deceit and trickery. Roland is an expert at both. She'll see through it easily enough. Besides, that clever friend of hers, Davidia, is a smart one and thoughtfully innovative.'

'Will she remain Slirander's friend when she finds out the truth of her beginning?'

'Never fear. True friends remain, regardless of what they discover about each other. Those brown hands that Davidia has will hold her in good stead. She can actually hold Roland's special compost heap in her hands and can change its behaviour.

Unfortunately, she doesn't know it and we can't tell her. Discovery has its own perils and rewards.'

'Slirander has invoked the allegorical Poem of Ickle. I hope she knows what it means to know it.'

'Just like us, once it has been said completely, the secret tunnel will be revealed. It's on the other side of that deadly compost heap. I told both girls the complete phrase to ensure it's remembered. Two sets of youthful memories are better than one; however, Slirander must be the one to say it, being an ex-Rotter. Aren't we glad we don't look like them anymore? You know, sometimes I peek in that special mirror you have hidden in the garden and shudder at seeing my former self.

> *'Once a twig, always a branch,*
> *Once a sapling, always a tree,*
> *Once a trunk, always a delight,*
> *And thankfully there are only humans in sight.'*

Dad was pleased to say a phrase that caused pleasure and not pain.

'That breeze has passed. It's beginning to warm up again.'

'Yes, I like warm.'

*

Deep in the heaving compost heap, Roland was slowly transforming into tiny splinters. His body was shaved away to leave behind those two large, odd eyes. They were as large as bowling balls, now that extra moisture had been absorbed into them. They playfully swam unattached through the mucky mess, enjoying a moment's freedom. Soon they would be the lead for a long, sinuous, sinister shape. The word "ugly" for this animal was actually a pretty word to describe Roland's new form. No one should see the new form and not expect nightmares. It sounded horrid.

'Glug, glog,' said one splinter, preening its pointy end.

'Glog, glug,' responded another, having almost pricked a brother.

'Glogalog,' said a third, who was the real conversationalist amongst them. It could combine two four-lettered words.

'Glagagogalog,' chimed in a large splinter, who had to glog or glag one better.

'Gleg, gleg,' said Roland's odd eyes, as they now formed the main part of what he was to become; 'Glo.'

The command was quickly followed by a mass of churning compost. All the tiny splinters with their points sharpened for pricking, began to form in lines, careful not to prod each other's ends. There were hundreds of thousands of them. Who said mosquitos were the only prolific breeders? Thin trails circled everywhere.

'Glogoff,' said an upset splinter who had been unintentionally thrusted by a pointy end.

Finally, formation was achieved. The next step was a very tricky manoeuvre. Each of the splintered lines had to twine around each other like braiding hair to form a long cylindrical shape. Attention was paid to having the points facing outwards. Gradually, a long thickening braided sausage shape began to emerge. Each splinter was pliable as a snake-like strangulation vine was formed. It was as thick as a medium-sized bicep muscle. The two odd eyes were strangely out of character with the body shape. Finally, it had all come together. Roland now resembled an echidna processed through a stretching machine with two shiny, marble eyes. Dnagor had been born.

'Glo,' he commanded.

He swam upwards toward the top of the compost heap. No longer would he be shilfit to rot and puke in its depths. Now everyone would know that the dreaded Dnagor existed once again. Nothing had ever defeated it before and it was so prickly to the touch, pain was instant and strangulation a relief. Those two up there were about to be done in. Dnagor's body reacted like loose, wriggly jelly at its impending fun.

It was time to party.

*

In the meantime, the girls had wandered back into the extensive library and began to browse through the books.

'No Rotter has read these,' said Slirander, as she thumbed through a few pages, which were all in pristine condition.

The words seemed to smile at her as her eyes passed over them. They seemed to say, 'Thank you for reading me'.

'This collection is far too large for that madman, or whatever he is, to keep all this for himself. I've never seen a library this large before. I couldn't read them in my lifetime. Maybe something told him he could,' said Davidia. 'What's this? A book on Moonah.'

She quickly read a few pages.

'He hasn't been forgotten to be read. He's still in print. Look!'

Slirander was searching for unusual titles, which may help her understand the *ickle* word. Alas, that knowledge was as difficult to locate as a raindrop in a river; impossible.

'What was that?' whispered Davidia.

'I heard it, but ignored it,' replied Slirander.

'What do you think it is?'

'A surprise. Something rarely ever seen. Where's the black leaf?'

It was nowhere to be found.

'Moonah sent that leaf with us for a purpose. Its real colour will show itself.'

'You mean it's not a "friendly". Why would Moonah allow it to live on his trunk if it was "bad"?'

'Remember, it drank from the stream. Something had been put in it. I suspected that when my reflection showed me who I truly was. The real stream was unable to do that. I believe its goodness has been tampered with. It's down to the girly duo to tackle the nasty Roland. Give me a "high-five".'

Davidia's hand and Slirander's twig hand met from opposing directions. Snap, snap; a few of Slirander's fingers broke off. Davidia was mortified. She didn't want to hurt her friend, even if she didn't look like her right at this moment. It didn't matter. They instantly regrew. Davidia was impressed.

'Ah! That was, um, like awesome, like I couldn't do it.'

Slirander smiled. In that moment, she knew Davidia was always going to be her friend.

'There's that sound again,' said Davidia. It seemed to be above them. 'Look, there's an ugly vine crawling along the ceiling. What is it?'

'It's Dnagor, Roland at his worst. My parents once told me of a tale of such hideous proportions about the most evil thing that existed. I didn't sleep for weeks. It was Dnagor, the strangulation vine. It has tiny splinter prickers that inflict the most hurtful pain. Whilst you reel from it, it allows Dnagor to grasp you in his sinewy body. Agh! If it takes hold of you, count your final breaths.'

'Can anything defeat it?' asked Davidia, concerned that if it caught her, she wouldn't be able to count to one hundred.

'I'm afraid not. That stupid, twiggy scrabble was the way to recreate the dreaded Dnagor by spelling its name. Had Roland spelt his name backwards correctly, it would have been more powerful.'

'Lucky "1" for us,' said Davidia.

'It also has feeling tentacles that drop down and engage in speech to halt your movement. Then, ping, ouch, a bloody mosquito bit me, but it wasn't. With the cave being so dark, it is difficult to see him.'

'What happens if he gets me?'

'At school we would be called losers, but here it's the end of our journey forever. We mustn't allow ourselves to be outsmarted.'

'But we're not smart arses,' protested Davidia, 'and a vine wouldn't have one, would it?'

'Shush!'

*

Dnagor had flown straight out of compost heaven to attach itself to the roof of the cave. It spread out, imitating a quilt by quickly growing over the ceiling. A few loose tentacles dangled and swayed practising their apprehending techniques.

'Do you come here often?'

'What nice compost you would make.'

'What's a small tree like you doing with a smaller twig like that?'

'My trunk or yours?'

Dnagor could feel his tentacles aching for company. He shook himself and they quickly withdrew. His strangulation vine was so strong his over-cocky ego kicked in. He knew it was impossible for him to be destroyed. It had never occurred before, otherwise he wouldn't be here. His opposition were mere playthings before he tightened his noose around them. His boring existence was reinvigorated in his new form. The two bulging eyes scanned the cave ahead for movement.

'They are in the library. We must remove them from there and back to the compost cave, where they will take their last swim.'

Dnagor's only drawback was that he couldn't actually leave the compost cave. All he could do was attach and dangle. His eyes stretched to the ground and located the quivering black leaf.

'There you are, rolled up like a cigarette wrapper. It's time to entice your friends into the cave. The consequences of failure are unhealthy composting, now glo,' said Dnagor.

His splintered spines bristled in anticipation of performing a deadly act. The black leaf wafted on the airwaves and fluttered into the library, landing at Slirander's feet.

'There you are,' said Slirander, 'I wondered where you had disappeared to in the dark. Have you seen any sign of Roland? He dived into that compost heap like he actually enjoyed it.'

The black leaf quivered slightly.

'Did you hiccup?' asked Davidia. 'What have you been doing behind our backs? Sipping something unpleasant, I suppose.'

'I think Roland is in the compost cave. He wants to make amends for his mistreatment of you, Slirander,' the black leaf lied.

'Why should I go in there?' asked Slirander, knowing that Uncle Roland was a disaster in waiting.

'Apparently, there is a secret tunnel in the cave that no one can find. It's the only way out of here.'

'How do you know that? Nobody does except my dad. Please explain.'

The black leaf began to change colour to an embarrassing red. It signified uncertainty in its story.

'Your father used it long ago. No one else knows how. I was with Moonah in those dark days and it was rumoured so.'

'Let me get this in perspective. I have to enter the compost cave, have a genial meeting with the rottenest thing known, find a secret tunnel which I don't know how to do, and believe no harm will happen to me. That's quite an uncertain list, isn't it?'

The black leaf suffered alphabet shortage, bent over and nodded affirmatively.

Slirander turned to Davidia.

'Should we?'

'I'm not afraid of that overgrown twig. It's time he was taught a lesson. So far, he's made a mess of many topics and put us in danger. Let's stick it to him. I'm getting tired. My mum must be missing me by now,' said Davidia, yawning.

'Do you still have that special dictionary?'

Davidia felt in her jacket. It was there.

'Why?'

'It's time for it to expose itself and let the language inside free. It can mingle with the library books as a protector.'

'What about the antidote that I have left?'

'Be ready to use it.'

Slirander took out her special dictionary and rubbed it on her odd ear. Suddenly, the pages flew open and out flew a massive amount of language. Davidia rubbed hers on the back of her hands and exactly the same thing happened.

'Wow! Look at that lettering go.'

They watched as the letters were absorbed into the books. Davidia could have sworn she saw them move. The language inside would now be well-protected against any future destruction. The antidote was quite annoyed that their main purpose had been usurped by other letters.

'Lads, did you see that? They sent all those specially saved dictionary letters to do our job. Who wants to strike? We deserve better treatment than that. I've a good mind to be inoperative.'

The atomiser antidotes were not pleased. What task would they now have having been replaced or they thought that they had? Bigger things were ahead for them, but they weren't aware of it just yet.

'Are we ready?' said Slirander, pretending to be a general marshalling her troops.

The black leaf went first, Slirander second and Davidia trailed third. All were feeling cautious. The compost cave had a foul smell about it none of them had inhaled before.

'You don't think Roland is coming apart, do you?' Davidia asked Slirander. 'I didn't notice if he had bad breath or not.'

'It's the smell of fear. Look, the black leaf has withered in fright. It won't be producing any life-saving formulas for us.'

They stood right at the archway entrance. The dimness — it wasn't a reflection on Roland's state of mind — was difficult to see through. Slirander had perfect vision. Her two bulgy eyes acted like fish-eye lens and had three-sixty vision. The compost pond bubbled with an invitation they could all refuse. The ceiling quilt didn't move. Even Dnagor's two bulgy eyes hid under a splintered covering.

'Quiet, lads. It's the calm before the storm. Prepare your expectators. I have a feeling we must prong something important and, no, it's not bursting any balloons, but something similar. It looks like our squirter-holder has kept us until last for the most important task. One eye, or two, please. Let's prong together.' The leader was animated.

The antidote atomisers were wondering if the leader's lid had been lifted and fairy air had entered. Whatever he was on, they all wanted it. If he felt that good, it should be shared. Optimism is in all of us. It only has to be found.

'I'll go first,' said a brave Slirander.

She slowly scanned the cave and had noticed the vegetation quilt on the ceiling. It wasn't the best quilt she'd ever seen made; however, it was her first vegetation one. She walked completely around the cave, around the ring of compost and back to the entrance.

'There didn't appear to be anything there,' she said.

'Say something uncomplimentary or better still that *ickle* word. It might cause a reaction from something,' said Davidia, realising that Roland only got really upset with the *ickle* word. It might be a mental tickler for him.

Ickle, pickle, scythe and sickle,
Which is the word that is really fickle?'

They waited. Splinters began to shake. They could no longer retain their hold in formation. Suddenly, a few danglers dropped from the ceiling. Their pointed ends were glistening with the excitement of jabbing someone, especially a good-for-nothing ex-Rotter. They waved like small elephants' trunks. Luckily the girls weren't in harm's way.

'I get first jab,' said one dangler.

'My spikes are larger,' said another.

'Beat this,' piped up the largest dangler of all.

It actually reached the cave floor and rested with its end raised like a venomous snake.

'Did you find the secret exit?' asked Davidia.

'I couldn't see any,' answered Slirander. 'There may be no way out.'

'There's a nasty vine on the floor. Don't let it prick you.'

Slirander stepped forward. The vine raised its end.

'Are you my date?' it flirtatiously remarked.

'Where would you take me, if I was?' replied Slirander.

'To the compost heap where we could grow our roots together.'

'I like being independent. All tree twigs should be allowed that choice.'

'Take my end and think of the adventure that may follow.'

'You wouldn't hurt me', would you? You are a rather handsome vine.'

'Flattery never served your father well either.'

Suddenly, two bulgy eyes swooped from the ceiling followed by a thick vine, which quickly wound itself around Slirander. She was trapped like a hole in a doughnut. Dnagor shook with delight. He had finally captured the pest to his success. Slirander's arms, legs and her torso were embalmed in sharp pointed vines. Only her head was visible. Fortunately, she could still speak. Dnagor usually toyed with any disaster he was to instigate. He finally smiled an insidious smile. It was the best he could offer.

'No Rotter has ever bested me and you will meet the fate of all others who have tried.'

'My parents did.'

'How are they? Their little girl won't be returning to them, will she? They may have outsmarted me once, but you aren't clever enough, are you?'

'I know the meaning of the word *ickle*.'

'That's impossible. Only I do. It's a Rotter secret. In here it can't help you at all. There's a difference between knowing and using. How shall I compost you? Snap your twigs, bend a tree leg, stomp on your root feet or splinter your bulgy eyes? It's a smorgasbord of disaster for you. I'll give you a gentle squeeze to prove my point.'

The vines tightened their grasp. Slirander gasped for oxygen, filled with the fear quality. All this time Davidia had stood unnoticed at the cave entrance. She squinted and could see her friend in trouble. At school Davidia had played softball and as their top pitcher, she could bean-ball any opponent. She became angry at Slirander's treatment. What could she roll up and throw at the vine? Caves usually had rocks, but this one was barren of rocks as a lake's surface. She immediately thought, *the compost, I can throw the compost. They'd make excellent missiles.* She ran like a hare to the rim of the compost heap. The bubbling leftovers couldn't believe their luck; fresh, although unusual, vegetation was about to slip in. All they needed to do was grasp one tiny finger and she was cactus. Davidia didn't care for her safety; her friend was in trouble.

She placed a hand in and scooped up a handful of the squealing mess. She quickly rolled it into a ball and instinctively threw it at a dangler. No sooner had she let go of that one, her hands were now scooping and pitching a series of compost missiles ever so accurately at Dnagor and his danglers. They all hit with deadly accuracy. Slirander felt the muck land on her head as it splattered over Dnagor. Strangely, though, the compost heap couldn't drag Davidia into its middle. Her brown hands were immune to its grasp. When a compost missile landed on the strangulation vine, its behaviour changed the composition of the vine where it too returned to being sickly compost and sliding from the ceiling to be a harmless floor mess. Davidia's brown hands that Slirander's father gave her for her oddity entry, actually changed the compost's behaviour. They held special mess-mucking powers. That was a secret she didn't know she had been endowed with.

'Take that, you stretched elastic pain,' yelled Davidia.

Dnagor lost his grip on Slirander as his vines changed form. He couldn't believe it. Nothing had ever had advantage over him. He still had some power left. He tried very hard to strangle Slirander, who by now had regained some strength in her lungs.

'Davidia, the vial,' she yelled.

'Lads, did you hear the call to duty? This could be our finest moment. Arm your expectators and release them with all the force of a good shilfit. Yahoo! There's no better job than being a hero, even in miniature. For the last time, lads, formation, action and if there's time left over, we may meet an Aunty Doris and our forebears. It doesn't get any more exciting that this. I knew the best was left to last. What a way to go.'

Davidia reached in for the last vial. She aimed it squarely at

Dnagor's two bulgy eyes. 'Shhhhhhhhhhh' was the last sound the vial made as it clattered empty on the cave floor. The lads charged the two huge, pus-ball eyes and released their expectators right on target.

'Let's swim.'

Dnagor writhed in pain. His eyes weren't destroyed and he could still see the girls. Slirander was now released and they ran to the far side of the cave where the expected secret escape tunnel was supposed to be. Dnagor was as angry as a bull deprived of his prized herd. He flew at them at lightning speed, still with the remnants of the danglers. The girls were in peril. No more brown hand tricks or antidote. No intelligent or witty remark to change anything. Even a funny joke would be a loss of words. They were almost doomed. Dnagor became tempestuous.

'This is the end of you,' he bellowed. 'How dare you attempt to destroy me? I'm invincible.'

Davidia thought that reading a book would never happen again. What about seeing mum and dad and, of course, her older brother again? The air in the cave became denser and denser. They both now couldn't see Dnagor. He could strike at any moment. He was working himself into a frenzy. He preferred to act when highly strung. The girls huddled together, as if that was any protection. Davidia was thinking like the intelligent girl she was. She whispered to Slirander,

'What about that phrase your dad told us? That *ickle* word seems to unnerve Roland and Dnagor every time you say it. Why not say the verse in full as a prayer for our passing? It's not the Lord's Prayer, but it can be special just for us.'

'Do you think it will work?'

'Who knows? At least we can say the verse in full. Give it a try.'

Ickle wockle weeny fing,
Ickle wockle weeny fing,

> *It cannot sing, it cannot sing,*
>   *Cut its flamen head off,'*

yelled Slirander.

There was no echo.

For a moment they held their breath. Everything went strangely quiet. There was no sound or sign of Dnagor. Had a spell been cast? The girls looked everywhere, expecting the worst. It didn't happen. The compost heap had lost its oomph. Calm enveloped them all. Even the black leaf found renewed life and was no longer withered. From a distance, a rumbling sound grew louder and louder.

'I hope that's not you,' said Davidia.

'I assure you that the only wind I'm capable of producing at the moment is from speech,' replied Slirander.

Her twig-like form felt better standing alone without a hanging vine strangling her life forces.

'Lads, where are we? It's darker in here than a mummy's tomb. What's happening?' said the anxious leader.

The other atomiser drops were bewildered also.

'Are we lost?' said the brightest leftover.

'Shush. We are in a muck pond. See all that flubbery mud; we're in the compost heap. That means we have to swim. Man the paddles, put on a life-jacket, grab an esky, hold onto a pontoon, grasp at straws.'

The leader was suffering from success stress and was incapable of stemming the flow of stupid advice. The two bulgy eyes of Dnagor had sunk into the depths of the compost heap, a beaten and saggy remnant of evil. Was he only pretending to be defeated, fooling everyone except himself? Suddenly, an arrogant renewed Dnagor roared back into life. He spat and cursed as he headed towards the surface.

'Lads, abandon ship. He's too cantankerous and strong for

us. Let's visit an Aunty Doris before it's too late.' The antidote atomisers fled for less confrontational company.

As Dnagor emerged from the compost heap blaspheming revenge, he was greeted once more by two young girls. Slirander had lost her twiggy Rotter body and Davidia stood there tapping her right foot like an impatient mother.

'Are you two still here?' roared Dnagor, feeling like the champion he thought he was.

'Hello, Dnagor. Isn't life a bitch when it doesn't go well?' said Davidia, copying speech from some of the older girls at school.

'Why is it so bright in here?'

'The secret tunnel has revealed itself. Look, you can see all the way to the Conikaka Mountains. It's amazing that it was here all the time. You fooled us, you big useless tree vine.'

Dnagor tried to attack them, but the strength of the light was a force he couldn't successfully contend with. His nastiness was impotent. Slirander took a deep breath.

'I command the Poem of Ickle to allow free passage to myself, the black leaf and my friend, Davidia.'

A shard of sharp light appeared from the cave ceiling and showed a line on the cave floor that they should follow. Dnagor began to suffer in the bright light. The *ickle* light was more powerful than he was.

'You are finished, Dnagor. May the *ickle* light curb your nasty activities forever.'

The *ickle* light turned on Dnagor, who began to burn. He was no longer impervious to danger. His useless splinter protectors had no spine left and couldn't reflect the light.

'Ouch. Stop it. I'm burning. Forgive me. I didn't mean it. It was their fault.'

All pleading was successfully ignored as he had never meant anything good. Self-preservation was more important than acting with good manners. Dnagor swelled up like a trumpeter's cheeks and burst into compost. His parts were splattered so wide and far that any modern abstract artist would have been proud of it had it been their painting canvas. Finally, the remnants of Dnagor slithered into the compost heap for the last time. Roland the Rotter, in any form, ceased to exist.

'He wasn't such a bad uncle when I was small,' said Slirander. 'There's no telling how any of us will grow up, is there?'

Davidia nodded. It was easier than shaking her head.

'It's time to leave this place. What about the books in the library? They can't stay here and rot or be hidden from the world. How are we going to safely transport them to the libraries?'

Slirander chanted the weirdest chant that set the pace for ridiculousness.

'*Oo, ooo, oooloo,*
Uu uuu uuuwho,
Ii iii iiimy,
Ah ahah ahaahmmm and
Ee eee eeeme.'

'What was that nonsense?' asked Davidia.

'I made it up using the five vowels of aye (a), Ian (e), I (i) owe (o) you (u). I saw it in my mind. Someone must be influencing me.'

Davidia wasn't sure whether the weety-box this time was full or empty.

'I want to go home.'

The girls glanced behind them.

'There's a mass of black things crawling over the cave floor in plague proportions. They look like — it can't be — they're letters. Excuse me, Mrs W, what's happening?'

'You wouldn't believe it, an ancient vowel chant was cast over us and miraculously all letters were released from the library. We are now able to make our way in the literary world as we see fit.

What a break. If we don't want to be in a joke, pun, metaphor or any other expression, we don't have to. Literary enlightenment will grow unabated. Isn't it exciting to be read again?'

Davidia, Slirander and the black leaf — the black leaf, where did it go, it was right behind them a moment ago — followed the light along the secret tunnel inside the Hole in the Hill. The letters followed. It wasn't long before they neared the tunnel's exit. They were almost home and free. Suddenly, a dark shadow flashed in front of them. Was it showing them something it shouldn't? The tunnel exit turned into a shade of sickly grey. The *ickle* light was low on power near the exit.

'What's that thin film covering doing there?' asked Davidia. 'I've a good mind to kick it in its membrane. Get out of the way, an intelligent army is coming through.'

'Hello, Slirander,' it said, quivering. 'This is as far as you can go. I'm sorry, you didn't see it coming.'

'The black leaf; but you're supposed to be on our side.'

'Ah, the imperfection of youth, never being able to see through all the ruses thrown your way. My master, Roland the Rotter, has endowed me with some of his talents.'

'You mean shilfit and bulfullshilfit and an inability to spell?' replied Davidia.

'The clever one has spoken. If anything touches me from inside the Hole in the Hill, the escape tunnel will be immediately sealed forever. You have lost. Roland the Rotter is never beaten. With a good rest, he'll recover and rule the world. Me, a mere leaf, has been promised the healthiest growth tree in the forest from where I'll be head vegetation controller. Imagine an endless canopy of black leaves.'

'Where does this tunnel exit?' asked Davidia.

'In the Conikaka Mountains,' replied Slirander.

'Do you remember who lives here? Those two dimwitted,

flying feathered forms do and they love a good tune. Let's give them some rap.'

The girls began to contort their bodies and poke their fingers at the craziest of angles.

'Ready?

Now black is a slap for backstop,
Leaf is a hop for fresh food.
If hunger has bitten and sweet food is what you are missen,
Then tunnelling is for you.'

The letters were bored from standing still and chorused the short rap version of "food wrap". Soon the valleys were filled with music. It mightn't be to everyone's taste, but it kept them warm, used parts of the alphabet and each letter got to exercise before being embedded in print in the future.

Oddity and Weirdo, the two lumbering giants of the air, heard the tune.

'Lyrics are a bit loose. Rhythm needs work. Rather repetitive, but catchy. Love the message. Let's check it out.'

They followed the sounds like a dog sniffing for a bone. Soon they flew over the hidden tunnel.

'It's down there, I'm sure of it.'

'Can you see any good landing spots? I've had my nails manicured and don't want to crack them by landing rough,' said Oddity. She was rather vain.

'That sound comes from inside that hill. Strange we've never heard it before,' said Weirdo beginning to dribble at the prospect of food that the song had promised.

They glided down toward the increasing sound.

'It's coming out of that hill. We know every spot in the valleys, so how did we miss this one,' said Oddity, trying to calculate whether they were intruders, buskers, nuisance musicians or a learning group that hadn't quite got it together.

'It sounds better at ground level. Where's the food?'

'That isn't part of the hill. What is it?' Oddity cautiously prodded the thin, stretched covering over the tunnel exit which hid the musicians. 'It smells like vegetation and, oh, so fresh. The last time I smelt that was when we used that tree branch for a roost.'

The two lumbering, oversized birds scratched the ground in tune, contemplating their next move.

'In here, in here,' yelled Davidia, anxiously.

'They can't get through my leaf structure; it's toughened to withstand any assault,' said the confident black leaf. Life as a bully and evil representative was beginning to grow within it.

Oddity and Weirdo were attracted to the thin covering. It would be delicious masticating a leaf that size. They scratched and kicked at the ground like boredom had set in.

Snort, burp, spit.

'Ah! That feels better. I'll give that covering a talon scratch.'

Weirdo raised his sharpest claw and ran it over the covering. Nothing happened. Oddity did the same with the same result.

'It's a tough little sucker, isn't it?'

Next, they kicked a few large stones at it. It was still intact. The music had stopped. Had the escape plan failed?

'Maybe if we could vibrate the black leaf by singing high notes, it might split. See how thin it is. We can almost see through it. Can you sing operatically?' asked Davidia.

She wasn't going to waste her school music lessons.

'I might be able to. If I think of being grounded; now that would raise my voice. Dad once told me of a singer who cracked a glass in exactly the same way. Shall we do an opera with high notes?'

'We'll sing Ickla in high c.'

'What's Ickla? Never heard of it.'

'It's the same *ickle wockle* phrase set to music. It sounds better if you give it a proper title. Let's try it.'

The girls began the Poem of Ickle set to music and so the new opera of Ickla was born. They started slowly, gradually increasing in decibels until they were both at high pitch. The black leaf didn't move. Suddenly, from amongst the thousands of letters congregated on the cave floor, a large group forged their way to the front. They were the letters from various music manuscripts.

'I once accompanied a treble cleff.'

'I performed with the percussion section.'

'We were part of an opera score. That big C was once in a conductor's instruction manual. Will you lead us?'

The big C moved forward. It rolled back and forward, then jumped on top of a capital H and pointed to the cave rooftop.

'Let the music begin.'

Thousands of letters burst into song simultaneously. The vibrations shook the cave to its very foundation. The secret tunnel became nervous, in case it collapsed. The black leaf began to shudder and shake. In the corners where it gripped tightly, small stones began to crumble and its hold became tenuous. The sound reached the Moonatric Forest. Moonah was listening. A split started very finely and gradually increased in the black leaf. From outside, Oddity and Weirdo watched and listened.

'I can get a claw hold. Look, there's a fine tear.'

Oddity reached out with a claw, slipped it into the tear and tugged hard. It was too much for the black leaf. It hadn't the strength to remain intact. Bits began to fall off and Oddity and Weirdo were soon doing "good food" time. The tunnel exit cleared for a short time. The music stopped and the thousands of letters poured through. Slirander and Davidia were free at last. No sooner had the last letter escaped, the exit tunnel disappeared. There was a loud bang and the Hole in the Hill was spat into the atmosphere to fall down as harmless ash. Roland and his attitude were dispensed with forever. The girls scrambled to their feet ready to defend themselves against Oddity and Weirdo. They needn't have worried. They were busily devouring a gourmet black leaf.

'That's the best tasting vegetation I've had in a long time.'

The comment was followed by a series of sounds, probably burps.

The letters all flew into the distance, bound for better destinations.

'Thanks for a future of reading,' one letter was heard to say.

Slirander and Davidia sat down exhausted.

'How do we leave here? We can't stay,' said Davidia.

'Soon we'll be on the way home,' replied Slirander.

'You have an answer for everything. Are you sure you aren't the person who developed all the world's questions?'

'I'm sure.'

'Those two feathered forms have settled well. They don't even want to harm us.'

'A belly full of food can assist in a good attitude.'

It was a beautiful day.

> *Thump, thump, made them jump, not to sit or stand,*
> *Thump, thump a tree root clump, landed near at hand,*
> *Thump, thump an unravelled branch, a hand it offered to grasp,*
> *Thump, thump it took to flight, with the girls safe at last.*

'Moonah. Thanks for saving us,' said an excited Slirander, as she tree hugged him.

Davidia was thankful she didn't have to listen to the effects the black leaf had on Oddity and Weirdo. Earplugs would have been exceptionally useful. The land of Conikaka soon became a speck in the distance.

'Hello, Cold, still here?' said Davidia, feeling a slight chill.

'It's always nice to see you again. Notice that I'm not freezing cold. I'm will be making new friends if I warm a little.'

'Have you seen Cumulus?'

'He threw a cloud party recently. There were no storms, lightning, rain, sleet or hail that night. It was a pleasure to work the sky shift.'

'See you soon.'

13 HOME

'Where are we? Has someone stolen the daylight? Whose turn is it to switch on the light? Where's my breakfast?'

Davidia had awoken with an angst gene and was intent on letting everyone know it wasn't from the happy batch. She hadn't a clue where she was. Exhaustion had played a mind game, giving her unreality readings. She was back at Slirander's home continuing her sleepover. Slirander was fast asleep. Communication was only by the subconscious. She had difficulty sleeping; however, that night two tired young girls finally rested. Their ordeal of saving the world's written language had left them a tad tired. I suppose anyone would be tired after that Herculean task.

Morning arrived, but without the croissants, jam and cream. The girls stirred.

'The last one down the stairs cleans the room,' yelled Slirander, excited at being home again.

It didn't matter. Mum would do it anyway.

The plain bowl of cereal drowned in a white substance brimming with calcium, was just the day starter required. Both girls were embarrassing using the shovelling technique of food consumption.

'Girls, girls,' exclaimed Slirander's mum. 'What's the rush?'

'It seems like ages like we ate like any food like it wasn't there. Like now like over the moon to like eat again. It's like awesome,' said Slirander.

'Oh, I understand. Roland didn't invite or offer you anything?'

'Yes, he did,' said Davidia. 'Bad advice, trouble, lies and nothing us girls wanted. It was like he was from dimwit land. He didn't get it that we love jewellery.'

They all laughed.

Slirander's dad sat in the background. He knew that both girls had been through the ringer of an adventure. There was nothing that he could add. Roland the Rotter had been permanently expunged. It was like a weight had been lifted off his shoulders. As an ex-Rotter, he now felt free. He smiled at the two giggly girls. Life was comfortable.

*

After breakfast, the girls went outdoors into the backyard. Moonah was growing in the original spot where Davidia had first met him. He didn't look well. The girls ran to him.

'Moonah, what's happening?' asked Davidia. 'Your leaves are wilted.'

'It's time.'

'Time for what?'

'To leave.'

'But you can't go. It's lovely here.'

'My task is done. Remember, go to a library and you'll see me there.'

'Bye, Moonah,' said Slirander. 'We'll meet again.' She understood.

The girls watched as Moonah dropped its twenty-six huge leaves, which began to compost without their host tree. Moonah was actually made up of the world's written language hidden in its leaves. His task of language restoration and saviour to all readers was now complete. He began to fade into the soil, leaving a rich compost of language leftovers. The two schoolgirls shed a tear at the moving on of their special friend.

'Now what?' said Davidia, distraught that Moonah had left.
'School.'
